LAMB

THE RENEGADES
BOOK TWO

SYBIL KNIGHT

THE RENEGADES SERIES

LAMB

A DARK NURSERY RHYME RETELLING

SYBIL KNIGHT

Cover Creator: Dahlia Reign LLC
Special edition cover designer: opulent designs
Editing: Kat Pagan, Pagan Proofreading
Formatting: Dahlia Reign LLC

SOCIALS:

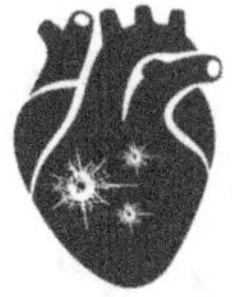

EMAIL: AUTHORSYBILKNIGHT@GMAIL.COM

NEWSLETTER: WWW.SENDFOX.COM/DAHLIAANDSYBIL

FACEBOOK GROUP:
WWW.FACEBOOK.COM/GROUPS/DAHLIAANDSYBILSLITTEDEVILS

INSTAGRAM: WWW.INSTRAGRAM.COM/AUTHOR.SYBIL.KNIGHT

FACEBOOK PAGE: WWW.FACEBOOK.COM/AUTHORSYBILKNIGHT

TIKTOK: WWW.TIKTOK.COM/@QUEENSOFCHAOSBOOKS

AMAZON: HTTPS://WWW.AMAZON.COM/STORES/SYBIL-
KNIGHT/AUTHOR/B09QW5R3MB

DEDICATION

You might have married him.

But I carved your name into his still-beating heart after he cheated on you.

He and I? Yeah, we are not the same.

Yours always,

A

*To all the readers who find **THIS** as romantic as I do.*

TRIGGER WARNING:

Please be advised that the male lead in this book displays sociopathic tendencies. And the relationship portrayed between him and the female love interest should in no way reflect how anyone should be treated.

If you come across someone like this in the real world, the author urges that you run as far and as fast as you can.

But between these pages, in the land of fiction, there's no point in trying. Because he'll be right behind you with a needle in his hand.

That said, the author asks that you heed the following list of potential triggers:

- OVERALL SEXUALLY EXPLICIT AND VIOLENT CONTENT
- FORCED DRUGGING
- DEATH AND MURDER

- PTSD AND TRAUMA
- GRAPHIC INJURIES
- SELF-HARM
- MENTIONS OF DRUG USE/ABUSE AND DISTRIBUTION
- ALCOHOL USE AND ABUSE
- FORCED PROXIMITY AND CONFINEMENT
- FORCED HOSPITALIZATION
- MEDICAL GORE AND TORTURE
- ACTS OF DEGRADATION AND STARVATION
- VOYEURISM
- ASSAULT
- DUBCON
- LIVE BURIAL
- AMPUTATION
- ELECTROCONVULSIVE THERAPY
- LOBOTOMIES (SIDE CHARACTERS)
- ORGAN TRAFFICKING
- STALKING
- INGESTION OF INSECTS
- BLOOD AND KNIFE PLAY
- MENTIONS OF PAST CHILD ABUSE
- FAMILIAL ABUSE BETWEEN ADULTS
- INHUMANE TREATMENT OF MENTAL PATIENTS
- LIGHT BC TAMPERING
- FORCED ORGASMS
- MASKED ASSAILANT
- "HUMAN FLESHLIGHT"
- AND MORE...

BLURB:

She was my brother's fiancée. And my absolute obsession.

There were three things and only three things I knew for sure about the woman sitting across from me at the family dinner table every night for the last week. She was completely off-limits. She was my brother's fiancée. And she was my absolute obsession.

Fact of the matter was, I'd also seen her first. Which meant it was only fair that I crept into her bridal suite the night before the ceremony and took her virginity. She retaliated by slipping into my hotel room and taking something of mine. An appendage. The fifth toe on my left foot. Tucking it away in a box as a sick little keepsake of our short time together.

Blood for blood, or so she claimed.

AND THAT'S WHEN I KNEW THE GIRL WAS IT FOR ME. HER KIND OF CRAZY THE PERFECT ACCOMPANIMENT TO MY OWN... PECULIARITIES.

THE NEWSPAPERS LIKED TO CALL ME *A BUTCHER*. I PREFERRED THE TERM *SURGEON*. AFTER ALL THOSE YEARS IN MEDICAL SCHOOL, I DESERVED IT.

THE TRUTH WAS, I WAS A SAINT COMPARED TO *HER*. BECAUSE MARI DIDN'T JUST KNOW HOW TO CRACK OPEN A RIB CAGE. SHE KNEW HOW TO FISH AROUND WITH A PAIR OF PERFECTLY MANICURED NAILS AND DIG OUT A GUY'S HEART. SOMETHING MY BROTHER FOUND OUT THE HARD WAY.

NOW SHE WAS BACK, LOOKING TO MAKE AMENDS. OR AT LEAST PRETENDING TO. AND I WAS MORE THAN READY TO LEAD MY LITTLE LAMB TO SLAUGHTER...

LAMB IS A DARK SPIN ON THE NURSERY RHYME "MARY HAD A LITTLE LAMB" AND BOOK TWO IN <u>THE RENEGADES SERIES</u>. EACH TITLE IS A STANDALONE IN AN INTERCONNECTED WORLD WHILE EACH STORY IS A RETELLING OF A FAIRY TALE, NURSERY RHYME, FABLE, ETC. THE FOCUS IS DARK ROMANCE SO PLEASE HEED THE TRIGGER WARNINGS AT THE BEGINNING OF EVERY BOOK.

Mary had a little lamb, little lamb, little lamb.
Mary had a little lamb. Its fleece was white as snow.
And everywhere that Mary went. Mary went. Mary
went. And everywhere that Mary went, the lamb was
sure to go.
—Sarah Josepha Hale
"Mary Had A Little Lamb"

"The cure to boredom is curiosity. There is no cure
for curiosity."
—Dorothy Parker

PROLOGUE
ADRIAN

"What the fuck is wrong with you?"

I flicked my glare to my patient's face before continuing with the resection of his abdominal wall. I could answer him, but I didn't see the point. Would you ask what was wrong with a concert hall violinist or those kids who could solve a Rubik's cube without having to peel off all the stickers first?

I didn't think so.

Talent was talent. And I was... talented. Just in a way that wasn't as pretty as others. Which made my particular skill set underappreciated but not any less impressive, despite what some people might tell you. And they would tell you.

I wasn't oblivious to what the rest of the world thought of my work. What words they used to describe me in the various media outlets, even if they didn't know it was me.

Butcher, *bastard*, and who could forget...

"You sick son of a bitch!"

Ah, I was particularly fond of that one. Especially when it was followed up by the sound of their screams.

"Ahhhhhh!"

Hmm, just like that.

My patient let out another high-pitched wail. Collapsing against the metal slab as I tugged the lower portion of his bowel free and deposited it into the collection pan.

I tilted my head and watched the organ slosh around in its juices before finally settling itself at one end of the steel tray like a discarded sausage link someone's mother forgot to grab off the meat counter—and thanks to the obstruction I'd found in the inflamed segment of the fucker's colon, it was about as useful as one too.

Sure, I could have put him under but then I'd miss those screams. The look of horror and panic on his face and the way his body squirmed against the table.

I sighed as I wiped the excess blood from my fifteen blade and set it aside. I guess you could compare me to a butcher, depending on which end of my scalpel you were standing on. A more accurate term would be *brilliant*. It wasn't easy to do what I did. It took a certain level of... finesse.

So, yes, I'd been called a lot of things over the years. But never liar. I wouldn't tolerate being called a liar. I didn't lie. Bent the truth, teased it in a way that it reflected more positively in my direction. Of course. That was just good bedside manner. It wasn't my fault people preferred what they wanted to hear over what I was actually saying.

This won't hurt... much.

You'll feel better in no time.

Who really needs two kidneys? The second one is just excess.

But straight-out lying? That was lazy and unimaginative. Which circled right back to that brilliance I mentioned. I mean, why toss out the whole body when you could just as easily cut away at what was ailing it?

Though I had to admit there was a time when I sank to that level of... mental perversion. The day I rose my hand and swore to do no harm. Just ask the fucker presently strapped to my table. Cursing my name and begging for his life—or maybe he was begging me to end it? It was hard to tell with the blood sputtering from his mouth. I suppose you could say he was gurgling?

I paused to listen to the sound. A wet, bronchial cough. His airway restricted and his lungs probably filling up with fluid.

He wheezed out a breath, and I glanced down at the bright-red dots he'd expectorated all over my white scrubs before three quick taps had me looking up at the glass partition and signaling for whomever was on the other side to come in. The door slammed open, and a large figure contaminated what should have been a sterile workspace.

I couldn't yell at the kid, though. It wouldn't get me anywhere if I did. Donnie was another one of my projects. He and his brother. Patients who became colleagues and then more like family. Blood threw them away while a stranger saw their potential and used it to their advantage. Which was much better than the other option of letting them rot away in whatever hole he'd found them curled up inside.

I was that stranger and it was *this hole*. This facility before I'd turned it into so much more. It was my professional obligation after all.

"G-girl had this with her, b-boss," Donnie grunted, his forced speech a byproduct of the damaged connection between his frontal lobe and the thalamus. There were times when he could control the stuttering; there were also times when he could barely communicate.

Pity I hadn't gotten to him sooner.

Neuromodulation, microscopic limb repair and reanimation—hell, I'd tried shit that looked like it came straight out of a science fiction novel. I'd done it all, and none of it was of any use to the lump of human meat in front of me.

The problem with extensive brain damage was that it was often irreversible. I'd spent years studying the neuropathways, experimenting with tissue regeneration and signal redirection, but the result was always the same. Misfiring connections and sensory delays with little to no improvement in symptoms. The brain was just too complex an organ, and medicine hadn't advanced enough to figure out a way to successfully complete a cerebral transplant that didn't result in personality disruption.

In laymen's terms, Uncle Joe might look like Uncle Joe, but all the intricacies that made him, well, *him* were tied to the discarded organ not the empty cavity that housed it.

"B-bugs says it's for you." Donnie shook the package in my direction. The backyard lobotomy had also affected his ability to read, which had him relying on his brother far more than he should. Trauma-bonding and codependency.

But what did I know?

My gaze caught on the box's nondescript wrapping before sweeping up to the bubbly letters I saw scrawled across the top. I'd recognize it anywhere. A lot had changed, but *her* handwriting hadn't. Neither had the spark I could still feel between us.

My lips curled into a grin as I tugged off my latex gloves and tossed them into the biological waste bin. I was a surgeon, not a monster. Couldn't have those pesky little pathogens creeping their way out of my OR.

Two quick steps found me on the other side of the door, the lock clicking in place and my boots striding down the hallway with the package in my hand and Donnie in tow. My patient could wait. I had more important matters to attend to. Matters that included a certain dark-haired woman who'd been my obsession for the last decade and a half and the contents of the box she'd had her little assistant unknowingly deliver to my doorstep.

Poor girl didn't realize she was part of the deal... or my colleague's vendetta. She also didn't realize how easily her boss would hand her over in exchange for a favor.

"Take that one to the basement. She's Dr. Michaels's problem now," I instructed, watching as Donnie wheeled the prone figure towards the freight elevator, a mop of honey-brown tresses peeking out from the sack over her head.

The metal doors closed behind them and I flipped the little box in the air, listening as the tiny mummified shards rattled around inside, and strolled towards my bedroom for a shower. My steps much lighter with the knowledge my little lost lamb finally found her way home to me.

Took her long enough...

PART ONE

Chicago Tribune

OFFICIALS SAY CRIME IS ON THE RISE

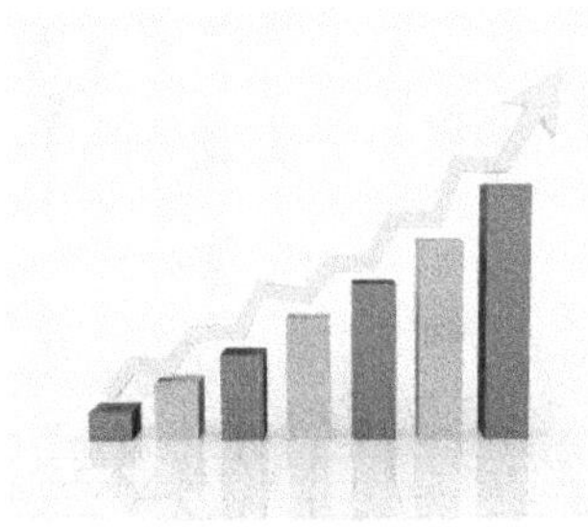

As the cost of prescriptions goes up so does their street value, sources say.

Chicago is grappling with a significant public health issue: the illegal use of prescription drugs. This crisis is fueled by the proliferation of opioids and is exacerbated by the increasing presence of a new illicit substance with properties similar to ketamine and MDMA. Despite recent efforts to combat this epidemic, the situation remains dire, especially amongst the younger demographic more inclined to indulge in recreational drug use.

Overdose deaths in Cook County reached a record high with over 50 fatalities, the majority of which involved this new compound that is said to combine the euphoric feeling of MDMA with the sedative nature of ketamine. While opioids such a fentanyl continue to be the leading cause of unnatural deaths in the county, surpassing homicides and suicides, this new designer drug is becoming an increasing concern. And is projected to only get worse.

WHO IS BEHIND THE SUDDEN SURGE OF ILLEGAL PHARMACEUTICALS?

A concerning development is the detection of this compound in the illicit drug supply. Last year, Chicago reported over 160 suspected cases and 12 confirmed overdoses linked to the ketamine/MDMA combo with naloxone—the standard overdose reversal drug—proving ineffective. This highlights the evolving nature of the drug crisis and the challenges in treating overdoses with no clear-cut solution in sight. Hospitals remain on high alert for cases of accidental overdoses, and health care professionals advise parents to be on the lookout for potential symptoms and warning signs. Some of which include: nausea, abnormal heart rate, poor body temperature regulation, seizures, fever, unconsciousness, lapses in memory or lost time, and poor coordination and judgment. If you witness or suspect someone you know may be a victim of an accidental overdose, you should escort them to the closest medical facility for immediate care or contact emergencies services.

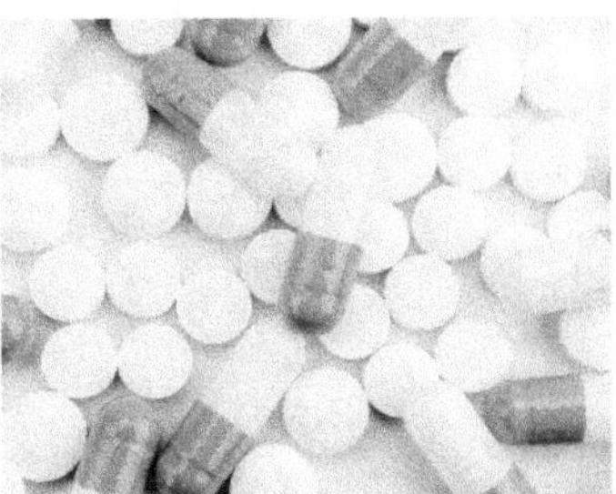

Medicine cabinets are the new gold mines for drug dealers.

1

ADRIAN

FOURTEEN YEARS, THREE-HUNDRED AND TWENTY-FOUR DAYS, AND SIX HOURS PRIOR— BUT REALLY, WHO'S COUNTING?

The first time I saw her, it was nothing more than a hair flip. A blur of dark locks brushing by me. Bouncing and swaying across her back, the motion drawing my gaze downward so that I couldn't help but stare at the checkered pattern that accentuated the curve of her perfect ass.

I shouldn't have looked. Textbooks were my focus. Not miniskirts. Proving that the bastard blood that ran through my veins wasn't worth less because I was pushed out of a cunt a few shades darker than the one that gave life to my half-brother. Not proving that the fucker was right.

Tate Edward Prescott III. A name that sounded as pretentious as the man behind it. My big brother was born with a stick up his ass and a silver spoon shoved into his mouth. He knew it and took every opportunity to make sure I wouldn't forget that my mother was the help *or* that his had owned the keys to the kingdom.

Made me smarter, though. I had to work for everything that was handed to me. Orchestrate and manipulate. Never let my guard down. Move the pieces across the board so that they benefited me. While he could stand there like the incompetent prick that he was. Hoping there were enough pawns between him and whatever new challenge was tossed his way.

But mine was the long game. I was a patient man. I could wait. And watch. And commiserate. Until it was the perfect time to strike.

Then check-fucking-mate, big brother. Check-fucking-mate.

Everything was going according to plan too. Following the path I'd carefully laid out. Everything until her. The girl with the hair darker than my cold, dead heart. And eyes that I couldn't see but could definitely feel. Glancing my way before pretending like I didn't exist, just like all the rest of them. And for the first time in my life, it irritated me to feel unseen. To blend in so well I didn't stand out.

She would see me. I'd make sure of that. Even if I *wasn't* sure why I suddenly gave a fuck.

I rolled up the sleeves on my white dress shirt. Clean, crisp, without a speck of dirt. Because appearances were everything. At least that's what Prescott liked to remind me—I refused to give that old fat fuck the benefit of being called my father. Which he probably appreciated.

What he didn't appreciate, or tolerate, was the way I spit his name like a curse. Earned more than a few backhands before I realized it was in my best interests to keep my disdain for the man to myself.

I stalked forward, watching as the dark-haired girl pushed her way through the library doors, the sway of her wide hips begging me to follow her. My black leather Velascas sprung off the concrete steps without me realizing I was moving. Hypnotized by the floral scent that clung to the air long after she'd turned the corner down the first stack of books. Expensive shoes did more than just look nice. They were quiet. Another lesson I'd learned over the years. Which meant she couldn't hear me but I could see all of her.

I didn't believe in love at first sight. I didn't believe in anything I couldn't study and dissect... Quickly dismissing the increased heart rate, dilation of pupils, and elevated body temperature as simple physiological reactions. Attraction. To one of the few women to catch my eye in a long time.

I watched her bend over to scoot the little stepstool forward before climbing on top and reaching for a book on the highest shelf. Her gaze swept in my direction, almost as if she could feel me standing there. Of course she couldn't. I made certain I remained hidden. When she stepped down again, the same book cradled in her palm like it was the most precious thing in the world, one side of her mouth tipped up into a smirk as she brushed away a sheen of dust that seemed to dance around her before disappearing again.

But it wasn't until the light from a nearby window

illuminated her face that I realized how truly fucked I was. Because this girl had my heart stuttering in my chest. An indiscernible cardiac event that had no other explanation besides the curious creature in front of me.

I continued to watch her, waiting for the rhythm of my pounding chest to even out and normalize. It took longer than I cared to admit. Then I blinked my eyes and she was gone. Almost like she'd never been there in the first place. Like I had dreamed up the whole thing during some sort of delusional state.

Of course I hadn't.

The name staring back at me on the screen in the registrar's office a few hours later told me the girl was as real as the sweat trickling down my face after breaking in through the unlocked window in the janitor's closet.

Marisela Cruz, a transfer student. The daughter of some diplomat or politician or something. Not that it mattered what her old man did, just that her family was out of my league. And yet, that didn't make her any less mine.

In fact, a sick part of me liked the idea of someone so above me being forced to look up at me when I finally got her on her knees...

2

ADRIAN

Marisela.

Her name had a certain taste to it. A mixture of something sweet and savory. Mouthwatering. Almost as if it clung to my tongue without ever having spoken it aloud.

I couldn't explain it. I honestly didn't care to either. I enjoyed the irrationality in my overly rational world. It helped me focus on something other than the stench of burning flesh, the sting of the leather popper as it broke through the first layer of epidermis tissue.

The scars had healed over a long time ago. I cracked them open again to remind myself where I'd come from. In a place where no one could recognize me.

The black plague doctor mask I'd hand-stitched from the tanned leather of my half-brother's favorite race-horse—after the poor beast lost and the fucker shot him during one of his fits—assured that my identity remained a mystery, while the cash I shoved into

Mistress Sadi's heavy palm kept her mouth clenched tighter than her pussy lips. She didn't fuck her clients. Just beat the shit out of them and had 'em thanking her for it too.

And I did thank her, even if I didn't get off on the pain.

I needed it to breathe. Otherwise I felt like I was living underwater. The colors duller, the air thicker, the sounds muffled. Except whenever I was given a chance to cut into a cadaver. Then the curiosity enlivened me. More than the crack of Mistress Sadi's nine tails.

The flashing of the lights told me our session was over, the time passing much quicker than it usually did with my mind so focused on being somewhere else. With someone else.

She released my arms from the black trident cross, which assured my safety just as much as hers—you were much more likely to injure a moving target—and stepped back. We had an understanding, she and I. I wasn't into being dominated. I didn't like the degradation or masochism.

I needed the reminder. The feel of broken flesh. The dampness of blood seeping through my white dress shirt as I buttoned the sleeves and set my cufflinks into place. I needed my perfectly composed exterior shattered so that I could build it up again. So I had a reason to hide the monster I tucked away behind a tailored suit and a pair of perfectly polished shoes. The abomination my old man claimed me to be since birth.

Self-fulfilling prophecy and all that.

And Mistress Sadi was a professional. Not my girlfriend. It wasn't her job to question why. Only to control the environment. That was something we shared in common. The need for control.

Her tall, thigh-high boots clicked against the tile flooring. The effect intentional. She wanted her clients to hear her coming. She wanted to build the anticipation of the first blow, and the next and the next. Once again, the theatrics were wasted on me. Because I wasn't interested in what she looked like, just what she could do.

I watched as her red hair swished across her back as she disappeared behind the velvet curtain. Currency was always exchanged upfront, another concession that assured minimal interaction afterwards. It wasn't anyone's business why I did what I did. And the only aftercare I wanted was the solitude of an empty lab.

I wouldn't see her again until next month, when I would need another reminder and she would require another payment.

I swiped up the bottle of water I was obligated to down before leaving the premises and paused mid-chug. I didn't feel that lightness I was used to experiencing immediately following a session. There was no release of endorphins, the epinephrine and cortisol still flooding my brain and keeping my muscles tight.

The reason was obvious. It was her. The girl with the dark hair. I couldn't relax when my mind was so obsessed with knowing everything about her. So I did the only thing that made sense. I tugged my leather mask back over my face, shoving my arms through the sleeves of my black trench coat before fastening the buttons into place. And went in search of the little schoolgirl with too much time on her hands and not enough cock in her mouth.

Even as the crude thought entered my mind, some part of me shuddered. Because it felt as wrong as it did right.

3

ADRIAN

The skin of my back burned as I leaned against the large tree overlooking Marisela's bedroom window. The air was thick, my cock thicker. I could feel it throbbing as I did my best to keep the sensitive flesh from grating against my zipper. It was lust, for sure. Pumping through my veins. The testosterone building. Clouding my logic and making this kind of risk-taking seem reasonable.

I wasn't an adrenaline junkie. But suddenly nothing seemed better than slipping in through that window and taking this girl in her sleep.

Something about her told me she was a fighter too. The type to kick and scream and claw at my back. Open old wounds and create some new ones of her own.

I needed a release. I needed it more than I needed to eat, sleep, and breathe. And it was like she knew it. Like she knew I was watching her. Like she wanted me to watch her. As she approached the window and tugged the pretty pink curtains back. And then she was staring down at me as I took in a deep breath and slipped a palm past the waistband of my pants.

She couldn't see me. Not like I could see her. I was a shadow in the blackness of her yard while she was illuminated like an angel above me, her long, dark hair cascading over her shoulders and her plump red lips pursed into a smirk. I didn't know what she was smiling at, but I didn't like that it wasn't me.

The longer she watched, or at least appeared to watch, the harder my dick became. It was reckless. To stroke myself in plain view for anyone looking to creep up behind me. One palm flat against the bark, the other pumping like my life depended on it.

Yep, it was reckless and I didn't give a shit.

When she licked her bottom lip, I imagined her licking me instead. And when she perched her ass on the windowsill, the slight breeze blowing her hair back out of her face, I pictured that same ass bent over my desk. Two globes bouncing in rhythm with my panicked thrusts. My imagination was so fucking vivid I could almost feel her. Taste her. Until I then felt myself teetering dangerously close to the precipice of coming.

My hand stilled. I yanked it free and readjusted my zipper. Ejaculation meant losing control. And I wasn't ready to do that yet.

Maybe I was a masochist after all. My balls sure as fuck thought so. But control was the only weapon I had in my arsenal, and I refused to give that up to anyone. Myself included.

I lifted my mask, just long enough to shove a finger

into my mouth. The salty taste of my own precum a poor substitute for what I really wanted. That first taste of virgin pussy.

I sucked on the tip for a moment, imagining the light shade of pink smeared across my white bedsheets when I found her hymen intact and took that first deep thrust to rupture the thin membrane that had my name written across like an open invitation.

Property of the bastard son of Tate Prescott. It had a certain ring to it.

Was she a virgin? Who the fuck knew? That tidbit of information sure as shit wasn't in her school file but I liked to think she was. I liked to think I'd be the first man to taste her. Fuck her. Bring her to her knees.

I groaned at the thought, dropping my hand from my mouth and shoving my mask back over my chin. My gaze was drawn upward, and I watched as Marisela tilted her head, almost as if she could hear me. Once again, she couldn't. But I enjoyed the thought that she could. And that she liked it. She liked the idea of me defiling her. Of turning daddy's little princess into my own personal whore. A fuck toy for all the fucked-up things I wanted to do to her.

Maybe not today. But someday soon. It was a promise as much as it was a threat.

4

MARISELA

I was used to being watched. Gawked at. Whispered about. I might not have been the son my father wanted, but he found a way to turn me into the asset he needed. Children were loved, but assets? Those were protected. Until they reached profitability, and then you had to cash in before depreciation forced you to cut your losses.

See? You could have a nice set of tits and a sensible business acumen. But who was I to argue with a man who still believed female castration was a very real solution for teenage promiscuity? Though I was pretty certain a GPS tracking device with a flashing red light wouldn't help Papa or his associates find the clit.

How unfortunate for their wives. And Mama.

Truth was I didn't know what it was like not to feel the weight of everyone's eyes on me. But something about tonight was different. A chill traveled up my spine that had nothing to do with the night air and everything to do with the man I could feel watching me.

I didn't know who he was. Hell, I didn't even know if he was a *he*. I could only assume. What I did know was that he was down there. Somewhere. Looking up at me. Watching my every move like I fascinated him.

That was the difference. Whoever it was wanted to shatter my ivory tower, not keep me locked inside it.

Could it all be in my head? A fantasy dreamed up by a girl with too much time on her hands and not a vibrator in sight?

Sure. Pent-up sexual frustration could drive even the most respectable of us mad. And I never claimed to be respectable.

Picturing the look on my father's face if I tried to slip a certain *phallic-shaped* package past his security had a smile tipping up one side of my lips. Hernando Alonzo Cruz would never allow his daughter the impropriety of owning a vibrator. But there wasn't shit he could do about her fingers. Taking those away would only decrease her market value and ruin his chances of furthering his political career.

So it was just me and the shadow man. Playing a game of chicken to see who would be the first to cave.

It wouldn't be me. I'd mastered this game over the years, daring my father's men to cross the line between bodyguard and mixed bodily fluids. But, unfortunately for me and luckily for them, no one had taken the bait. So I remained painfully untouched. A pretty package waiting to be unwrapped by whatever sleazy predator was deemed wealthy enough to be named my husband.

I could feel it. The moment my little Peeping Tom slunk back into the shadows and disappeared. The air was somehow both warmer and cooler at the same time as I slammed my window shut and pulled the curtains into place.

The boredom was the worst part. Brief moments of exhilaration followed up by long stretches of stifling boredom. My father wasn't the only one who wished I'd been born with a little more between my legs. Having a cock might have significantly lowered your brain cell count but it also gave you the luxury of blissful ignorance. Not knowing or caring how the world worked because shit was always in your favor.

Had to admit it sounded like a nice way to do things.

I plopped down on my bed, stretching my arms above my head while allowing my lower body to dangle off the mattress, and stared at the underside of the canopy. It was odd, how much contempt I could direct towards an inanimate object. More specifically, its color.

Pink. Like the cheeks I was forced to pinch to that perfect hue. Like the curtains that shielded me from the outside world. Like the rose-tinted glasses everyone seemed to wear when all I wanted to see was red... like the *red*-hot rage burning through my veins.

I traced a thin line across the left side of my face from temple to jaw with a pink-tipped finger. Over and over again until I was digging deep enough to draw blood. And as soon as I felt that warm droplet trickle towards my eye, forcing me to blink out of my trance, I pushed up from the bed and stalked towards my walk-in wardrobe. With one thought on my mind.

Getting the fuck out of this pretty *pink* prison.

5

ADRIAN

The first time I heard her voice, the sound was breathier than I expected. Deeper too. Marisela was not delicate and soft-spoken, like the floral wallpaper and all the lace-trimmed pillows inside her bedroom would lead you to believe.

Though that could have something to do with the fact she was currently dangling from her windowsill, her palms bearing the brunt of her weight as she attempted to push off the side of the house before landing on a bed of flowers with a few choice adjectives tossed out into the night sky. It was hard to appear demure with a mouth like that—the dirt covering her ass and the leaves clinging to her hair didn't help either.

But I didn't like my women demure. Where was the fun in that? Who wants to play with a toy that's already been broken?

I tucked myself closer to the side of the house, the stone exterior cold against my heated skin, my eyes glued to my target as she brushed off her pants and glanced around. Likely looking for the guards that were supposed to be walking the property line in thirty-minute intervals. Her old man was a paranoid fuck, which meant he probably had a reason to be.

She wouldn't find them. Her father's men.

They'd been… incapacitated for the time being. A hefty dose of ketamine worked wonders in a pinch. It was one of the reasons understanding chemistry and the way the body reacted to different components was so important. Too much of this additive or too little of this solvent could mean the difference between knocking someone out and killing them. Both had their uses, depending on the circumstance. And right now, two dead bodyguards were more of a headache than their organs were worth. Which meant they'd wake up feeling like they were tossed into a gutter and stomped on. But at least they'd wake up.

Realizing she wasn't about to be dragged back into Daddy's office and thrown over his knee—though mine wasn't out of the question just yet—Marisela crept towards the stone wall surrounding her family estate, grabbing the ledge and scaling over the top much quicker than I had cleared it a few minutes ago myself. Except I was trying to get in and this little wandering lamb was itching to get out.

I counted to ten in my head before following her, being sure to keep a few paces between us. It was easier said than done when every neuron in my brain was firing off and screaming at me to reach out and touch her.

When she turned the corner, slipping behind some

abandoned warehouse, I quickened my steps, rushing to catch up with her only to stop short when I found myself staring at a brick wall in an empty alleyway.

I glanced from side to side. *Where the fuck had she gone?*

There was no other way in or out. And this wall was much too high for a girl her size to scale without a leg up.

"Who we looking for?" a soft voice whispered next to my ear as I pivoted in place to find a pair of wide green eyes staring back at me.

6

He really did try. I'd give him that. His steps nearly soundless as he did his best to maintain a conservative distance between us. Even went as far as to control his breathing so I couldn't hear him huffing when he rushed around the corner to follow me.

Unfortunately for my shadow man, it was his scent that carried in the breeze and gave him away. Cool and minty. Maybe his aftershave? With a hint of smoke and leather that could be attributed to the stupid mask he was hiding behind.

I rolled my eyes, even though he couldn't see it. How anyone thought they could blend in dressed like something out of one of those black-and-white horror movies my *abuelo* liked to watch was beyond me.

Then again, I wasn't interested in what he was wearing or why. Not when I was more focused on the fact this fucker was stalking me.

I was able to get the slip on Mr. Tall-Dark-and-Creepy with a move as generic as dunking under the dumpster and popping up on the other side. I inched closer on the tips of my shoes, mindful not to kick at the stray gravel rocks separating us. Dropped my lips to where I thought his ear should be and whispered, "Who we looking for?"

I stepped back just in time to see the way my voice sent a chill down his spine and had him quaking in his— I flicked my eyes to his feet—nine-hundred-dollar Oxfords. Imported leather. Italian, judging by the distinct sheen. My stalker had expensive tastes. Lucky me.

"A little lamb that seems to have strayed from its flock." I couldn't see him grin but I could hear it. Almost like the slight curve of his lips somehow softened his tone.

"This lamb of yours, you sure it isn't just a wolf in sheep's clothing?" I lifted a challenging brow, waiting for my retort to stick the landing while my fingers danced towards the pocket knife I'd tucked into the back of my pants, my glare plummeting when my hand came up empty.

"Looking for this?"

I peered up to find him pinching the familiar bright-red hilt between his thumb and index finger. And swiped out a hand to grab it at the same time he lifted his arm, dangling the knife just out of my reach.

"Ut-uh, finders keepers, princess," he hummed before slipping the little blade—*my blade*—into his coat pocket.

It took me a minute too long to realize he was talking about more than my knife, though, as he lunged forward and quickly pressed me up against the bite of the cold brick wall.

What was that saying? Something like if you went looking for trouble, eventually it'd find you...

This was my version of that. Except there wasn't the terror you'd expect to come along with it. Instead, there was a thrill that traveled to the apex of my thighs and settled there. I'd wanted this after all. Been dangling my virginity on a string hoping some poor fucker would be tempted enough to take a bite. Put the big black spot on my reputation that would offer me my freedom.

What I didn't expect was it to happen in a back alley in the part of town where *little girls shouldn't go walking alone*, as Papa would tell me. Especially without their pocket knives, as *I* would tell *him*.

But I guess beggars couldn't be choosers.

I just needed this guy to rough me up a bit first, to make it look believable. Which meant I had to find a way to get under his skin. Shouldn't be hard to do, seeing as he had no problem peering into strangers' windows in the middle of the night.

I mean, that was how most sexual deviants got their start, wasn't it?

7

ADRIAN

She was testing my restraint, and something about that both annoyed and infatuated me. I lifted a brow without meaning to, the gesture causing a slight shift in my mask—it was the only reason I knew I was doing it in the first place. Until my glare dropped to the red streak raising the skin on the left side of her face.

I reached out a hand, rubbing my thumb over the line of blood that had caked and dried on her cheek. Fresh. Maybe thirty minutes old. A fact that then led me to question who the fuck else was with her in that room of hers. Because that mark sure as fuck wasn't there before she yanked her curtains closed.

"Who?" I barked out the word, unable to articulate more than that as the irritation seeping into my voice threatened to spill over. "Who've you been sneaking around with, princess?"

I watched the way her pupils dilated for a second. A mix of fear and arousal before she shut her emotions down and glared back at me with a fire that shot straight to my cock, which was already in no mood to be teased.

Her lips curled into a grin as she brushed a hand along the waistband of my pants. Baiting me. Little did she know my mouth was already firmly wrapped around that hook, my willpower dangling on a string, my better sense just waiting to be filleted wide open.

"Wouldn't you like to know?" she hummed.

"I want a name, Marisela," I grunted.

"And I'll give you one. After you give me yours."

I pushed off the wall, attempting to walk away before I did something *she* regretted and *I* felt a tad less apathetic about later. I didn't get more than a step when Marisela was tugging me back by a belt loop. Truth was, I wasn't trying all that hard to leave, and we both knew it. My palms slammed down on the brick, inches above her head. So I was forced to look down at her while she dared to stare up at me.

She craned her neck to one side, her hand inching dangerously close to the bottom of my mask. Before she could make contact, I snatched her arm midair, closing my thumb and forefinger around her tiny wrist. A quick jerk to the left and I could break it. But that shit wasn't my thing. At least not in the bedroom. The surgical table was a whole different story. In the pursuit of science or whatever else you wanted to call it.

"Careful, little lamb." I lowered my face to her ear, breathing in the scent of her floral perfume. Something exotic. Something I couldn't quite place. Which was new. "Out here, no one can hear you scream."

I could feel her grin, the minute shift of her zygomaticus major pulling tight when her lip curled, before I felt something else entirely. A sharp, searing pain in my lower abdomen, followed by a wave of adrenaline and a comforting warmth.

"I'm counting on it," she whispered as my eyes dropped to the glint of her pocket knife, the clean edge now splashed red beneath the ominous glow of the streetlamp.

8

MARISELA

I shouldn't have enjoyed it as much as I did. I'd always known I had a thing for violence. Liked watching my own blood rise to the surface and pool over. But I'd never actually stabbed anyone before. Thought about it, sure. Fantasized about what it would feel like to jump one of my father's men, hold a gun to their head, and fuck them till I decided to blow their brains out.

But who hasn't?

Fantasies were very different from the reality of it. The blood warmer than I imagined it being. And the thrill... Well, that was goddamn intoxicating. Arousing in a way I didn't think possible. Part of me wanted to twist the blade, plunge my arm inside the gaping wound and feel around for a bit. While another part of me wanted to see what it was like to make this fucker snap, force him to wrap his hand around my throat and squeeze until we both saw stars.

Except my shadow man appeared to be just as fucked up as I was. His erect cock digging into my stomach as he leaned forward and groaned against my ear. The sound more pleasured than pained before he lifted his mask to just under his nose and sank his teeth into my shoulder. I heard the distant clank of metal hitting asphalt, telling me I'd dropped my knife, but I had no recollection of actually letting it go, as my arms closed around the back of his head and tugged him closer. His breath hot and minty against my skin and his neck muscles tight and rippling under my touch.

I wanted to see his face as much as I didn't want to know who he was. There was just something so erotic about the idea of getting fucked by some stranger. About parting ways and never having to see him again.

I didn't care that my back was scraping against the wall. Didn't give a shit about the friction burns on my thighs as he ground himself against the tight material of my pants. While the fact he was ruining my clothes as he continued to bleed out from his abdomen was more of a turn-on than anything else.

I reached a hand between us, slipped it into his pants, and listened to the deep moan he made in his throat as I brushed a palm across the blood pooling on his right side and used it to ease the movements of my back-and-forth motions. Drawing out long, red strokes from base to tip. Exploring the smooth skin. Pressing my thumb against the little slit at the top before gripping the end like a joystick.

I didn't know what the fuck I was doing. Didn't much care either. The satisfaction I felt each time he met one of

my strokes with a drive of his hips was all the encourage-
ment I needed. My orgasm teetering on the horizon as I
released my grip and yanked him closer, practically
forcing this stranger to fuck me through the several
layers of clothing that still separated us.

9

ADRIAN

Anyone else would have seen the blood seeping out of their gut as a bad thing. Me? I'd been fucking entranced. Staring down and watching my black shirt turn an almost purple color. The fabric tacky against my skin, the wound warm to the touch with that slight metallic scent that tainted the air.

I was the kind of guy who liked my steaks rare and my cadavers fresh. But I wasn't numb to the pain. I felt it. Felt every delicious twinge. More than that, I liked it. I liked the push and pull of the blade as it penetrated my skin. Enjoyed the gleam in her eye. The sheer joy she seemed to experience the moment she believed she outsmarted me.

I knew I'd left myself open to her. Vulnerable. I just didn't care.

Not when I had her squirming beneath me, grinding herself against my thigh like the little whore she was pretending to be.

I had to pay attention to the blood loss. I knew that. I couldn't fall out in some alley in the middle of the city and allow just anyone to find me. But I couldn't bring myself to leave her either. Especially when she started probing at the open gash, using her fingers to separate the layers of epidermis before dipping them inside to use my own blood as lubricant for my cock.

I groaned, and even I could hear how animalistic it sounded.

A few quick strokes left me rock-hard and dying to plunge into any one of her holes. At this point, it didn't matter which. Her mouth, her ass, that virgin pussy. I didn't care. Not as long as she kept making those high-pitched whimpers in the back of her throat.

I watched in awe through the slits in my mask as Marisela slowly crouched in front of me, balancing herself on her haunches as she eyed my cock. Which was now level with her face. Bouncing and throbbing while she stared at it like it was the most fascinating thing she'd seen in her life before peeking out her tongue and taking a tentative lick. Tasting both me and my blood.

I leaned forward to brace myself on the wall behind her to keep from crumbling to my knees when she then sucked the tip between her hollowed cheeks. Her actions as bold as they were curious. And I knew my assumption had been right.

My little lamb was aching to be touched. To be defiled. And I was the man to do it. Just not right now. Not like this.

I wanted to take my time with her. To bring her to that edge and leave her there. Panting, twitching, cursing my name. I wanted to ruin her for any man who even thought about coming after me.

An image that gave me pause and sent a fresh wave of rage rushing through me as I tugged Marisela to her feet, shoved her back against the closest surface, and dropped to my knees. Then I reached out a hand, feeling around the asphalt until my fingers were curling around the hilt of her little pocket knife, and grinned.

10

I'd let my hormones get the best of me. Not that it was the first time. I'd inherited this impulsive streak from my mother. Or so my father liked to remind me every chance he got. He also liked to remind me what happened to *impulsive women*. Told me all about the procedure his surgeon friend performed on Mama the last time she tried to run away.

She was never the same after that. Almost like she'd had the life drained out of her, her eyes vacant and unseeing and her expressions stiff and emotionless. She was compliant, sure. But her spark was gone. She didn't sing or dance anymore. She barely looked up whenever someone entered a room. She was nothing more than a bag of organs and bones packaged up in a pretty flesh suit. Alive but no longer living.

And I refused to follow in her footsteps despite the loveless marriage that was hanging over me.

Climbing out that window was foolish. Seeking

comfort in this man, fucking idiotic. Especially as I watched him wrap his heavy hand around my pocketknife and drag it up towards my navel. Pressing the tip close enough for me to feel the pressure but not enough for it to pierce skin.

I held my breath, waiting for the sting that was sure to come. But didn't. Then I watched as he pivoted the blade back into the handle, tucked it into the inner lining of his coat pocket, and pushed to his full height to tower over me again.

I didn't need to see past the mask to know that he was grinning. I could just tell by the way he held himself. His head slightly cocked to one side and his posture relaxed as he rocked back on the heels of those same stupidly expensive shoes.

"If you want it back, you'll have to come find me, little lamb."

"And if I don't care enough to go looking?" I narrowed my glare in his direction while crossing my arms over my chest. "I have a dozen of those in my nightstand."

This seemed to give him pause. But only for a moment. "What else do you have in that nightstand, Marisela?" he asked, reminding me he somehow knew my name and I still didn't know his.

"Pepper spray and brass knuckles," I hissed, and my shadow man let out an amused laugh.

He thought I was joking. I wasn't. If someone crept into my bedroom in the middle of the night, thinking they'd do to me what they did to my mother, they were in for one hell of a surprise. In the form of burning tear ducts and bruised egos.

I'd sooner jump out the window head-first than let some quack scramble my frontal lobe with a brain pick.

"Fair enough." He shrugged. "But you know what they say about curiosity?"

I rolled my eyes. "It killed the—"

Before I could get the words out, my shadow man was *tsking* his tongue. The sound amplified by the emptiness of the alleyway. "*It's the cure for boredom. And some-*thing tells me you are exceptionally bored, Marisela."

11

ADRIAN

I couldn't help but slip in the quote from the book I'd spotted my little lamb checking out of the university library the other day. Was it smart? Would Marisela even recognize it?

Who knows?

I guess some part of me wanted her to know it didn't matter where she was or where she tried to run off to. Either way, I'd find her.

But there was more to it than that. I needed to know that she felt the same pull. The one that made her both the most interesting and dangerous person I'd ever met. Because I didn't think there was anything I wouldn't do for this girl. And I barely knew her.

Hell, I'd let her stab me, while enjoying the fire I saw staring back at me from her eyes as she did it. She didn't hesitate. Didn't appear to feel the slightest bit of guilt. And it was fucking intoxicating. Her afterglow better than any orgasm I'd ever experienced. Her natural inquisitiveness nearly as deep-seated as my own.

I saw the way she eyed the break in flesh, the layers of muscle tissue underneath. Like she was two seconds away from coming from just the thrill. It was a peculiarity I understood. And there was so much more I wanted to show her. Even if it meant strapping myself to a slab and handing her the scalpel myself.

The clearing of a throat had me looking up just in time to widen my stance as Tate tried to shoulder-check his way past me. I'd been so lost in my head I hadn't heard his approach. A mistake I wouldn't make again. The fucker was like a poison looking to seep under your skin the moment he thought you were distracted enough to choke it down.

He paused in his tracks, his eyes flicking to my abdomen—to where my palm was clutching my side—before shooting back up again. "What the fuck happened to you?" he asked, and not because he cared. But because he was a nosey little shit, who liked to tuck information away until he found the most opportune moment to dangle it over your head.

I guess I wasn't much different when it came to that. Except my motives were strategic, whereas my big brother's were cruel.

"None of your fucking business," I grunted in reply, not bothering to offer him a glance as I continued down the hallway towards my room. Which was nothing more than a refurbished storage closet inside an estate that boasted over thirty guest bedrooms. Then again, I should have been grateful Prescott didn't force me to sleep in the stables with the rest of the livestock that were one broken leg away from the slaughterhouse.

I didn't have to look back to know Tate was following me. I'd piqued his interest. That was on me. Though I didn't know what he was doing down here anyway. Probably creeping on one of the maids. Or worse, forcing himself on one of their daughters. I could only hope Justine remembered to lock her door. Her girls weren't even legal. Though I'm not sure if being of age really made that shit better. It just felt like it should.

By the time I stepped into my bedroom, Tate was pushing his way inside after me. His eyes sparkling with the sadistic streak he tried to hide behind that clean-cut image of his. My gaze swept up to where his blonde hair was already thinning at the top and I couldn't hold back my grin. He might have had the cookie-cutter features that made him a Prescott. But I'd take my thick black hair and darker complexion over being a pale, bald prick with a small *prick* any day.

"Get the fuck out," I snarled in his direction, as I pulled my little medical kit from the top shelf and went in search of the sterile needle I kept for situations like this. Though I wasn't usually the one who needed suturing. *That was a change.*

"Of the room in the house I own?" Tate hummed. "No, I don't think I will."

I did my best to ignore him. Reminding myself to be patient. The fucker's time would come, and when it did, I would enjoy the way his smugness would so quickly devolve into panic and terror. His laughter into shrieks of agony...

He stepped around the small space while I leaned back in my chair. Took a breath, contracted my abdominal muscles, and braced for the first stick. I didn't bother with an anesthetic. The pain kept me from standing up and wrapping my palms around his throat.

I wasn't sure what he was looking for. I didn't have anything of value. Not here. All the cash I'd managed to squirrel away was safely deposited in offshore accounts with no ties to my name unless computer hacking was in your repertoire. It wasn't in Tate's. While anything that held any sort of sentiment to me had been stolen or destroyed before I was old enough to outsmart him. The fucker had almost two decades on me. Which meant I learned from a young age just how twisted my big brother could be.

"This was where it happened, you know."

"Where what happened?" I couldn't tell you why I responded. Other than it was an unconscious reaction as I tied off the fourth stitch. *Marisela got me good.* A little deeper and she would have punctured my small intestine.

"Where I fucked your mother for the first time." He grinned.

I knew what he was doing. Asshole was goading me.

He pivoted on a heel, his hands tucked into his pockets with a confidence he hadn't earned and sure as fuck didn't deserve. "Funny enough, a difference of a few months and you very well could have been calling me *daddy* instead of brother. Then again, the moment I found out some whore was carrying my bastard, I would have thrown her ass down the stairs. Lucky for you,

Father always did have a soft spot for..." Tate glanced over at me like I was a pile of horse shit he accidentally carried in on his riding boots. "...your kind."

Yeah, I was *lucky*. And right now, so was he. Lucky I didn't cut out his fucking tongue and make him choke on it. I might not have known my mother, but that didn't mean I didn't feel some sort of loyalty towards the woman. At times.

"She squealed like a pig the night you were born. Could hear it three floors up." He removed a hand from his pocket and gestured towards the ceiling. Dropping it at the same time he smirked down at me again. "Father refused to let her go to a hospital. Even after your big-ass head got lodged in that tight, cock-strangling pussy the old man was nice enough to pass around to me... and all his friends. No wonder he insisted on a paternity test. Fetus could have belonged to anyone, really."

I fisted the needle in my hand until I was dripping blood onto the table in front of me. Pushing up from my chair and crossing the room without even realizing my legs were moving.

The rage had cortisol and adrenaline flooding my brain, my body acting without processing or storing the details. And the next thing I remembered, I was standing over Tate. My fist bloodied to the bone and his nose and jaw offset in a way that meant that aristocratic profile he was so keen on possessing would never be the same.

Oops...

12

MARISELA

"*Something tells me you are exceptionally bored, Marisela.*"

The words had been playing in my head since last night. I didn't know if it had been intentional or not, but they reminded me of a quote from a book I'd checked out of the university library the other day. He'd rephrased it, sure. But the message was the same.

Which also meant my shadow man had been watching me for far longer than I'd realized. And not just in the shadows.

Was that his way of letting me know? Or was I reading too much into it? I couldn't be sure.

My eyes flicked to my right, a puff of air parting my lips on an exaggerated sigh. Mama was drooling again. Her head dipping forward and her once-beautiful, long black hair now knotted and unkempt as it floated around in her soup bowl.

I loved my mother, felt a heaviness in my heart as I watched her deteriorate. But I was also mad at her.

I resented her for choosing a man like my father to spend her life with. Because that's what it was. A choice. She was intelligent, well-spoken, with the kind of looks that had men gawking at her wherever she went... at a time... But love made you dumb. That was what she'd whisper into my ear when she didn't think I was awake at night.

"¿Que es esto del amor que nos hace ser muy estupidos, nena?"

Or I guess it was more of a question she was asking herself. What about love makes us so stupid?

I wish I knew the answer, Mama. It was just another reason I needed to stop obsessing over some lunatic with a mask kink, who seemed to enjoy being stabbed as much as I liked stabbing him.

The slamming of my father's fist against the table had me glancing up from the fork I was twirling around on my plate and into a pair of deadened eyes. The hatred that crackled in the air was the unspoken type. Who needed words when looks said it all?

He hated me because I looked like her. And I hated him because he was a narcissistic asshole who should have been put down a long time ago.

Porque familia es todo, Mari. Family is everything. At least we liked to pretend it was. Hence these family dinners every night, spent in insufferable silence while Mama was propped up in her chair like a posable doll, then quickly stowed away in her glass case when my father was done playing with her.

"Marisela," he hissed my name from across the table,

"Yes, *Papá*?" I hummed in reply, intentionally thickening my accent the more he tried to hide his.

It was a newer habit, his way of erasing who we were while he did his best to blend in with his rich white friends. We weren't even allowed to speak Spanish in the house anymore, not that I had anyone to speak it with. My father surrounded himself with the type of men he was trying to emulate.

Women-hating pigs.

He lifted a threatening brow, and I slumped in my seat as I begrudgingly corrected myself. "Yes, Father?"

"I have someone I'd like you to meet," he grunted in a way that told me I wouldn't *like* it one bit. But it wasn't a request. It was an order. I didn't have an option. At least not right now.

I nodded once and resumed swirling my fork around my plate. The rest of dinner consisted of Mama mumbling to herself every now and then, and my father ignoring her until he was done eating. Then he quickly pushed up from the table and slammed his chair back in place, not even bothering to glance over his shoulder at us as he slinked away to his office and closed the door.

But family was everything, right?

13

ADRIAN

No matter how good it felt, I shouldn't have snapped. Not over something we both knew was a lie.

My mother might have been dumb. Enough to actually believe Prescott when he told her he was ditching his wife to raise their bastard. And sure, she had her flaws, like leaving her child in the hands of her rapist, but she wasn't what my half-brother made her out to be.

She wasn't some whore. She was some *kid*. A nineteen-year-old girl trying to do her job and not piss off the man in charge of her paycheck. Even if that meant keeping her mouth shut after his leering turned to inappropriate touching. That touching to full-on rape, that rape to an unexpected pregnancy that threatened to ruin the old man's picture-perfect gene pool.

At least that's what I'd been told by the wet nurse whose care I'd been entrusted to before the afterbirth was even fully wiped from my skin. Couldn't say Miss

Louise liked having someone else's brat attached to her tit 24/7. But at least the woman never beat me. Though that could have been more out of self-preservation than anything else.

Daddy Dearest had no problem raising the rod—*but god forbid someone else do it and ruin all his fun.*

What became of my mother after that night was nothing more than rumors and fucked-up ghost stories whispered between staff when they didn't think I was listening. Until I'd narrowed it down to two possibilities.

Enough cash was shoved down my mother's throat to have her packing up her things and never looking back. Or enough dirt was shoveled over her body to ensure no one would ever find her if they cared enough to try digging her up in whatever hole he'd paid his henchman to drop her into. Neither option was all that comforting. Though there were some days when I preferred one over the other.

Today was one of them. Because, kid or not, if I found a way out of this place, I wasn't certain I'd ever chance coming back either.

Sure, Prescott might have spared my life, but that didn't mean he gave a shit about me. Or about anyone other than the person he saw staring back at him in the mirror. He didn't have a soft spot. He had an ego. A deep-seated affinity for himself, which kept him from killing me. Because it would be like killing some part of him.

That wasn't to say he didn't beat me to a pulp whenever he felt the urge. Sheer stubbornness alone had kept me from aspirating on the contents of my stomach numerous times over the years.

I could only hope it did the same right now. Seeing as age seemed to only exacerbate the fucker's thirst for blood. *My bastard blood in particular.*

The first strike of the leather riding crop was more jarring than anything else, the little spikes at the end breaking the skin and sending a chill down my spine. Prescott had the device specially ordered for me shortly after my fifth birthday when he insisted that "if I was going to act like an animal, he would treat me like one." Apparently, proper children didn't speak unless they were spoken to, and I was plagued by a curiosity that had me asking far too many questions out of turn.

Other than the moisture I felt dripping down my back, I was numb to the second blow. And the third. The fourth. The fifth. So detached I didn't notice his arm had stopped moving until I heard the wheeze of his strangled breaths as he tried to suck in a lungful of air. He was tiring himself out much quicker these days.

Then again, it had been years since my last lashing—because I'd mastered being unseen and it was harder to hit a target you couldn't find—and it was clear the old fuck was out of practice.

It took several long minutes before he'd regulated himself enough to step forward, a slight tremor to his hand as I glanced over a shoulder and watched him reach for his cane. A part of me had been hoping he kept going till cardiogenic shock left him sprawled out on the oriental rug he loved so much. His eyes glued to the ceiling as I feigned chest compressions that never made it deeper than the half inch mark, his O2 count dropping as I sucked more air out of his lungs than I was putting in.

Okay, that was a lie. All of me had been hoping. But I liked to at least pretend to have some sort of empathy for the man whose favorite pastimes included preying on teenage girls and beating on children.

He gestured for his goons to drop my arms, and I rubbed at the stiff tendons in my wrists before grabbing my shirt off the chair and striding towards the door. Funny enough, Prescott wasn't into pillow talk any more than I was.

I was two steps away from freedom when he called after me. "I want you in that operating room tomorrow. If there's a single bone out of place when John's done with him, I'll give them the go ahead to use your face as a live donor."

They could try. If they were stupid enough to transplant an allograft without first testing for an immunological reaction. Just because we shared some DNA, it didn't mean Tate's body wouldn't reject the implant. But that wasn't my problem. Not yet. I had a few years left before I was required to take the oath. And even then, I wasn't all that keen on keeping my word.

I dipped my chin in acknowledgement, chewing on the smart-ass remarks I had dancing around in my head as I slipped through the door and left a trail of blood from my father's office to the comforting silence of my bedroom.

I could have killed them years ago. Slipped a little arsenic into their food and watched their heads hit the dinner table with a synchronized thud. But the truth was, I didn't want my father and half-brother dead. I wanted them to witness what I was going to become under their noses and know there was nothing they could do to stop it. I wanted them to suffer. And that took time and more cash than I had on hand right now.

It also took a shit-ton of fucking patience.

14

MARISELA

I clicked my bedroom door closed, even as everything inside me screamed to slam it, and glared at the pink-on-pink that stared back at me. Until a bright-red package on the center of my bed caught my eye.

It wasn't there when I was summoned for dinner, and I sure as shit didn't leave it there myself. Which meant someone had been in my room. And I had a good idea as to who that someone might be.

I should have put on a hazmat suit and tossed the little box back out the window it likely came from—there was no other way in or out of here. If there was one, I would have found it a long time ago. But I was the first to admit that both curiosity *and* boredom had me closing the distance and swiping it up instead.

The paper was thick, *expensive*, the tape cut with precision rather than torn as I peeled back the first layer to examine the white box underneath. I could only hope that if it was a bomb, it would take my father out with me. Otherwise I had no doubt he'd use my *untimely demise* to press whatever bullshit agenda he had in the works right now.

I could already see my face plastered across every news outlet, the poster child of using fear to make rich men *even richer*.

I removed the lid and pushed the tissue paper aside, and before I realized what I was doing, my fingertip was tracing along the hand-stitching of the red leather mask, a much more feminine version of the one the shadow man in the alley was wearing.

If this was his way of asking me to be his girlfriend, he should have picked something a bit shinier... and sharper. Like the pocket knife he'd failed to return.

I glanced back towards the window again, even knowing he wasn't there because some part of me could just sense that he wasn't, and lifted the mask from the box. A little notecard fluttered out with it before settling face-up on my pink comforter.

An address and a time. Nothing else. Apparently I was surrounded by people who didn't know what a question mark was or how to properly use one in a sentence. Demands were second nature, much more convenient for the types of men not used to hearing the word *no*.

One side of my mouth tipped up into a grin as I pressed the mask to my face, inhaling the scent of the polish until I was feeling lightheaded and giggly.

Good thing I was used to making those types of men regret forcing me to say *yes*.

15

ADRIAN

I glanced down at a pair of bloodied gloves—which funny enough *didn't* belong to me this time—before sweeping my glare over what remained of Tate's nasal cavity. Red, yellow, and a hint of black. Severe fracturing of the connective tissue and a deviated septum, though that last part could have had as much to do with the repeated blows my knuckles landed on his face as it did with all that coke he liked to snort. The clumps of dark blood vessels blistering to the surface agreed with me, so did the little perforations in the lining of his mucosa.

I continued my visual examination until a suctioning sound had me looking up into the face of my mentor. Thick brimmed glasses perched on top of a long protruding nose, accompanied by a tuft of facial hair that may as well have been whiskers. I couldn't see John's mustache beneath his surgical mask but I could picture it. Oddly thin and bushy at the same time. Just like I could picture the smirk I knew he was wearing along with it.

Where I enjoyed dissecting the human body and discovering all the secrets each layer told me, this fucker got off on it. You could see his cock dancing in his light-blue scrubs, bouncing around with the weight of his overfilled balls whenever he stepped away from the table to reach for another piece of gauze. The guy had no shame. What he did have was a weird aversion to underwear.

I should be disturbed. At the very least, a little uncomfortable. But the truth was, I knew enough about the way the brain worked to also know that there wasn't much you could do when it came to ignoring a natural stimulus. And this shit was his.

I mean, he really, really liked his patients immobile. Corpse-like.

I'd be concerned about the welfare of all those stiffs in the morgue next door if I wasn't so sure he liked his bodies warm. Wet. My eyes drifted back to the layers of peeled flesh in front of us. And sticky. John liked his patients warm, wet, and sticky. I liked mine conscious, so they could feel everything I did to them.

Take that how ever you want.

He shot out an arm in a grabby motion before barking his next order. "Suction."

No matter how much I wanted to tell him he could suction that shit with his lips for all I cared, I kept my expression neutral as I skimmed the plastic tubing over the opening of the incision and listened to the gurgling noise it made as it vacuumed up the pooling blood.

Though it would have been much better if Tate was the one gurgling instead of having his pretty fucking face pieced back together with cadaver bone—probably less-than-ethically sourced from that same morgue I *wasn't* concerned about.

But only the best for big brother.

John's methods might have been... unconventional. Definitely immoral. But I had to admit the guy did decent work. Maybe that was what happened when you enjoyed what you did. And, like I said, Dr. John Rath really *enjoyed* what he did.

Despite all the swelling and discoloring of the skin, which was no worse than any other cosmetic procedure he'd undergone in the past, my half-brother looked almost human again. Ironic, considering Tate was as much a monster as I was. Just a different type. Not so ironic when you remembered that most monsters came wrapped up in pretty packaging.

A few weeks and no one would remember I'd beaten him to a pulp. I'd remember though. I dreamed about that shit. About the feel of cartilage crumbling under the force of my fist, the way he squealed like the pig he claimed my mother to be...

Thirty minutes later, Tate was stitched closed, bandaged up, and rolling out. Heading to his private recovery suite to sit pampered and privileged until our father deemed him ready to see the light of day again.

I ripped off my gloves and tossed them into the red bin before making my way towards the industrial sink. The squeaking of a pair of designer loafers on the linoleum tiles told me John was following me. His mask gone and the bulge in his pants still waving around like a stray cord on a flagpole.

You didn't have to be discrete when you *thought* you owned everyone. John didn't own me, though. I was just on loan from my father.

"Your old man thinks it's time you come work for me. Keep your hands busy so they stop getting dirty." The fucker talked at me, not to me. John never bothered to look at me when he spoke. Because you never looked a dog in the eye—I was guessing for fear it might bite you. And that's what I was to my father and his associates. A dog to be leashed, biding my time till I was able to chew myself free.

I lifted a brow, even though he'd yet to make eye contact. "At the hospital?" It shouldn't have been a question but it was. This surgical "spa" as John liked to call it was only one of many buildings with his name on it. And that was the shit I knew about.

He finally turned his head to peer up at me as a sick grin tipped up one side of his face. The other side was dead from all the Botox he used. Just another reminder that a doctor should never become his own patient. Those skills didn't translate well when you were looking in a mirror.

"No, not at the hospital," he replied in that mocking tone of his.

16

MARISELA

This wasn't what I was expecting when I looked up the address on the little love note my shadow man left in my bedroom and the results turned up with the name of an underground sex club—that obviously wasn't so underground if Google could find it.

Unless they meant more literally.

I descended two sets of stairs before I was led to an open lounge area that, despite the obvious difference of dress code, could have been one of the fancy cigar bars my father liked to hang around whenever he wanted to talk shop. The words "Original Sin" scrawled across the large plaque on the wall in shiny gold lettering, accompanied by their logo. A little apple with a bite taken out of it—*Steve Jobs would have a field day with that one.*

I continued to eye the rest of the interior. All the high-end furnishes, crystal chandeliers, and expensive artwork. Dark, hand-carved woods and black-on-black accents that made the room feel both intimate and expansive at the same time.

The music wasn't at all what I expected either, more soothing and melodic than the thumping base of a nightclub. The air smelled somehow both masculine and feminine, a hint of lilac and spice, without all the body odor that came with crowded bars and poor ventilation.

My eyes flicked from face to face—some masked, some not—as I was guided towards a long hall with doors flanking each side. Metallic numbers passed me in a blur of gold as the girl in the leather riding pants and a matching crop top escorted me to the farthest one.

All I had was that card. Nothing else. But she seemed to be expecting me, which told me my mystery man was less of a mystery within these walls.

She turned around, her blonde hair pulled back high on her head and hanging down her back in a straight line. It toppled over her shoulders when she craned her neck to the side. But it was the little silver heart that sat just above her collarbone that caught my eye for no other reason than it looked more like a piece of jewelry you'd buy for your pet and not a gift for your girlfriend.

She followed my line of sight and grinned before laying a gentle palm on my shoulder. "If at any time you feel uncomfortable, there's a red button on the wall. Press it and someone will escort you to a recovery room."

I nodded once, because I honestly didn't know what any of that meant, while my ego wouldn't allow me to ask. Then I watched her make her way back down the hallway, her hips swaying with each step she took in her impossibly-high heels before defiance had me pivoting towards the door again and shoving it open.

Red lighting danced across more black furnishings. A couple antique-looking sofas with the high backs, a dark circular coffee table that added a hint of modern to the rest of the aesthetic, a tray with a bottle of champagne, and a chaise lounge off to one side, closest to the wall. Once again, not exactly what I was expecting.

I didn't risk my neck or my ankles climbing out of my bedroom window just to find myself closed inside an emo kid's wet dream with some Poe-wannabe spitting sonnets in my direction.

I was two seconds from turning around and going in search of my own version of fun when the door crept open again and a familiar figure stepped inside. As tall and brooding as I remember him being with the black plague doctor mask on his face that matched the red one I decided to oblige him by wearing. That and I didn't want to risk being recognized. It was one thing to sneak around my father's back, another entirely to have it make the papers.

He took two steps forward, and I took two in the opposite direction. Not because I was afraid. But because if that night in the alley taught me anything, it was that I liked the way it felt to be backed into a corner and forced to fight my way out.

My shadow man continued to walk me backward, and just when I thought he was going to pin me against the wall, he stopped. Popped the cork from the bottle of champagne and poured me a glass.

"You look parched, Marisela," he hummed.

"I look horny, *pendejo*," I replied, listening as a low chuckle rumbled his chest.

"Is that why you think I brought you here? To fuck you?"

"No, I think you brought me to a sex club so that we could braid each other's hair and exchange bedtime stories."

Another laugh had me stomping towards the door. He stepped in front of it, blocking my path. "These rooms aren't just about sex, little lamb. They're about intimacy, trust, exploring the kind of desires you didn't even know you had. But if you really want to leave, all you have to do is press that button." He gestured to his left before pointing behind me. "Otherwise, go sit your pretty ass on that sofa like the good girl I know you're dying to be."

I didn't want to be a *good girl*. I wanted to do all the *bad things* his filthy words promised me. But I didn't want to leave either. It was that irritating point where what I wanted very much conflicted with my natural stubborn streak. And I didn't like the way that made me feel. To want to give in as much as I didn't.

"What's it gonna be, Marisela?" he urged, a hint of cockiness belying the smirk I was certain he was hiding under all that leather.

"You have five minutes to come up with one good reason I should stay." I walked back towards the sofa, lowering myself down on the middle cushion while glaring at him with a leg crossed over a knee.

"No, I have five minutes to show you why you'll never want to leave."

17

ADRIAN

She was annoyed with me. More than that, she was attracted *to me*. Despite never seeing my face. Not knowing my true identity. And despite how easily she'd ignored me that day she brushed by without ever bothering to look back.

She thought I'd brought her here to fuck her. And her nonexistent panties—I could tell she wasn't wearing any the moment she'd crossed that ankle over that knee in defiance—were all twisted up over the fact I hadn't made good on whatever fantasies she had playing around in that head of hers. Not that I hadn't thought about it myself. That was the ultimate end game. To have her sprawled out in one of these rooms, a mess of sweat and cum as she cried out my name loud enough for the rest of the members to hear her.

Then again, she didn't know my name. And it was better for both of us if we kept it that way.

Sure, this little game of cat and mouse was a nice

distraction. Better, less costly, and more gratifying than my sessions with Mistress Sadi—who refused to cause any long-term physical damage. Believe me, I'd asked. But that's all it was. A distraction. A stress-reliever. Maybe a bit of an obsession. Definitely an *addiction*. The kind that sneaked up on you before you even realized the needle was embedded in your arm.

But then you gave in to the thrill, the high of doing something you knew you shouldn't be doing. And that's what this was for Marisela and me. The lure of the forbidden.

I watched her finish her champagne, the pursing of her mouth and the constricting of her throat muscles as she swallowed, and pictured her swallowing something else. More like choking on it. Her eyes watering and her mascara running. But I wasn't picky as long as she was on her knees looking up at me. Her cheeks puffed and her lips swollen.

But I also meant what I said. Being in this room was about more than sex. It was about trust. The kind of trust I wanted to build between us before I returned her knife and let her use it on me again. I had to give Miss Stab-Happy a stern lesson when it came to anatomy *before* she landed herself in an orange jumpsuit—or worse, in a padded cell at Briarwood.

That place wasn't just a literal madhouse. It was one lobotomy short of being overrun by a mob of patients whose deadened senses gave them the physicality of a bunch of angry gorillas, while their lack of a functioning frontal lobe gave them no reason not to use it against the guys in white coats who kept them captive. The old sanitorium was also one *citation* short of having its doors closed for good.

Not that I gave a shit. I was no saint when it came to what I liked to do with a scalpel whenever my attending wasn't watching. There was no progress without experimentation. No experimentation without curiosity. Which brought me right back to my little lamb and all the "experimenting" I wanted to do with her. And *to* her.

Marisela slammed her glass down on the table, and I took that as my cue to show her the real reason I brought her here. I had about another fifteen minutes before the MDMA I'd slipped into her drink took effect, which meant it would hit her at the same time I planned to bring her first orgasm to the surface.

Was it a dick move to drug her? Probably.

The club would also have a field day if they found out. It was against the rules and the waivers we all signed upon entry. But it wasn't like she was unwilling. She'd already admitted to wanting to fuck me. Or should I say wanting me to fuck her? And that trust I was talking about? It didn't need to go both ways. Unless she was trusting me to know what was best for her, and what was best for her was the feel of my mouth on her pussy at the same time that first rush of adrenaline hit her system.

"Your five minutes are up, shadow man," she spit in my direction.

I quirked an eyebrow at the odd nickname, even if she couldn't see me do it, and crossed the room, shoving her back in her seat the moment she tried to stand. "And your fifteen just started."

"Fiftee—"

Before the question could fully form in her mouth, I was tugging her ass to the edge of the cushion, dropping to my knees, and positioning myself between her thighs. If Marisela was as observant as she thought she was, she would have noticed the alterations I'd made to this mask just for her. The beak no longer pointed but rounded *for her pleasure* and the bottom arched and hollowed out for that same reason.

I had unrestricted access to her pussy in this tiny skirt she was wearing, and she had nothing separating her from the feel of my mouth. The lap of my tongue. The heat of my breath. The wet-on-wet sensation that would have her digging her heels into my back and tugging me forward.

18

ADRIAN

The first time I tasted her, that first flick of my tongue over a pair of swollen pussy lips, it was... otherworldly. *Transcendent.* Like the first time I'd run a clean stainless steel scalpel over a bare chest cavity. The first time I'd felt the push and pull of flesh beneath my hand. The first time I'd heard the cracking of a live rib cage. Nothing could compare... until now.

Until I was buried nose-deep in Marisela's bodily fluids, her nails clawing at the leather of the sofa. Her head tipped back and her knees clenched around my head in a vise grip. She was tangy but not bitter. A little salty, but not over-seasoned. Just enough to leave you wanting more. So that each bite, nibble and suck wasn't nearly enough to sate that hunger deep inside.

If I wasn't careful, I was gonna come before she did. And it'd be a pity to stain these pants. For Marisela, it might just be worth it, though. Because I finally understood the depths of my fixation on this woman. It was primal, a need too great for me to ignore. I wanted her. Every part of her. To own her. Consume her. To mark her as mine even if that meant losing a part of myself to her along the way.

This need overshadowed everything else I thought I wanted in this life. It didn't matter how fully I dissected the brain, how much I understood its inner workings. The chemical reactions that induced lust and promoted the human connection so that we were driven to procreate. Because this feeling, this urge, was so much better than the nothingness I was used to. It was even better than the pain... the rage... that inherent need I had to destroy...

There was only one motivator greater than revenge. One stimulant more rousing than the feel of your enemies' blood on your hands. And it was pleasure.

I stared up at her from where my face was still buried between her thighs, on my knees for the first time since my father stopped having the strength to bring me to them. Watching and listening and savoring. Marisela didn't whimper. She didn't hold back. She leaned into all the sensations she was experiencing. Arching her spine and shifting her hips until I was exactly where she wanted me. Like she was the one in control. And as much as some part of me wanted to argue with her, some deeper part was too transfixed. Under whatever spell this woman—*this girl*—had over me.

But I had to keep her on that edge, building higher and higher without actually jumping over, teetering on the precipice until the moment was right. The moment when her neocortex was flooded with serotonin, dopamine, and norepinephrine and her senses were overcome by warmth. That moment when she couldn't tell where her pleasure began and where it ended, because it just felt like a continuous wave washing over her body and taking her deeper and deeper into its depths.

The timer on my watch beeped twice, counting down the last few seconds before the drugs should fully saturate Marisela's system, and I took that as my cue to stop holding back. To stop all the taunting and teasing and coaxing. And finally grab her orgasm by the tail and tug it forward.

I wrenched her thighs apart, baring down with the weight of my forearms as I exposed her pussy to the stale air of the room that offered a slight chill when the AC finally kicked on. *Right on schedule.* This place was temperature controlled, of course, but MDMA affected the body's ability to self-regulate, making it easy to over-heat and dehydrate if you weren't careful.

Lucky for Marisela, she was in good hands. Gentle hands. Experienced hands. The kind of hands that could hook her up to an IV before she left if she needed it. And as wet as she was right now, she might just *need it.*

But she wasn't just wet. She was relaxed too, her limbs melting against the sofa as I tugged the lower portion of her body to the end of the seat—all her squirming had her migrating higher and higher on the backrest—and lifted it to meet my mouth. I lapped around her opening before pulling back again and slowly inserted the blunted nose of my mask inside her. Just the tip. A respectable size that would ensure that little membrane of skin remained intact for me, while also giving her some added pressure to help intensify her orgasm.

She tensed but she didn't fight me. Her sensitivity heightened and her heartbeat erratic—I could feel her pulse beating through her cunt—as I slowly pumped in and out. My tongue stretching as far as it could reach and my fingers working their magic on her clit. She was trembling, groaning... So lost to all the stimuli bombarding her nerve endings she was a puddle of weightless limbs in my arms.

I didn't need the drugs to make her feel this way. I needed them to fuel the addiction. To reprogram her mind and body to crave me as much as I craved her. So that the chemicals in her brain associated this level of therapeutically-induced euphoria with everything I did to her. Forcing her to have no choice but to seek it out. Seek *me* out when I was done with her.

I was more than a little aware it was like having a cheat code for the female anatomy. Then again, knowledge gave you power. The kind of power to outmaneuver your opponent. To think two steps ahead before they'd even taken to the board. And it wasn't my fault I was studious.

Three more thrusts of my mask and twists of my thumb had Marisela letting out a guttural sound. High-pitched and breathy. Then she fell back against the sofa cushions, in a fit of giggles that had me grinning along with her.

Like I said, *euphoria*.

19

MARISELA

I woke up in my room. Alone. My head pounding and my mouth dry. I opened my eyes and immediately closed them again. The dim light seemed brighter somehow. Biting too. Like it could burn me through my eyelids. My stomach was churning and I could feel the thin layer of sweat that had dried on my skin.

The fucker drugged me. I knew it the moment I took the first swig of the champagne and that familiar bitter taste danced across my tongue.

Molly. I knew her well. I liked her too.

Pot made me hungry, coke just made me paranoid, but Molly? She made me feel everything and nothing all at once. Couldn't sneak a vibrator past my father's men, but a couple of tabs in my pocket and they were none the wiser.

I should have been annoyed. *I was annoyed.* Not because my shadow man had dosed me but because he thought he could do it without me knowing. Because he thought he had a hand up in this little game we had going on between us. Because he didn't realize the only reason I was running was because I wanted to. Because I liked someone chasing me.

You didn't grow up in the home I did, with a man like my father, without knowing how to keep one foot inside the box they put you in and one dangling out. I could be whoever they wanted me to be, while never being that at all. It was a delicate balance I had to constantly maintain or risk everyone finding out the truth.

I was smarter than them. I *could* outsmart them. And I had. More than once. They were all just too dumb to realize it.

Just like my shadow man.

I stretched my arms above my head, groaning at the tightness in my limbs. I was used to this feeling. The chills and the blurry vision. The tension in my jaw that had my teeth clenching and the pounding in my chest. What I wasn't used to was the slight bruising I spotted at the crook of my elbow when I finally pried my lashes open again. Yellow and purple with a miniscule red dot in the center. A needle prick.

I didn't mind popping the occasional pill or even snorting some powder up my nose, but my veins were off limits. I wasn't a junkie, and I couldn't afford to look like one either.

I remembered his mask dipping between my thighs, the feel of his tongue on my pussy, the heat of his breath and the weight of his heavy palms spreading me deliciously wide. What I didn't remember was what happened after that. Or how he was able to slip a needle into my arm without me realizing it.

Then again, I was flying high after the multiple orgasms. They were unlike anything I'd ever done to myself before. Thigh-clenching, earth-shattering, mind-numbing. That must have been it. He tongue-fucked me into a coma.

I had to admit my head wasn't throbbing all that much either, a dull ache—just like the one between my legs—but not the usual axe-through-the-brain I was used to feeling after a long night of indulging in all the things I shouldn't.

It was nothing a few glasses of water wouldn't fix. So I peeled off last night's clothes, tossing them in the back of my closet and not the hamper, and threw on a pair of pink pajamas with long sleeves to hide the bruises before slinking my way downstairs. Past my father's closed office door and into the kitchen. By the time I opened the fridge, grabbed a bottle of water, and shut it again, my father was staring at me from the other side.

All the blood whooshing through my ears meant I didn't even hear him approach. He must have heard me, though. He must have been waiting for me too. It was the only time he ever sought me out. Beratements and birthdays were all this man knew about being a parent. And today wasn't my birthday. Not that he ever wanted to celebrate.

No, that little tic mark on the calendar wasn't about me. It was about him. Every year came with another reminder that I was one year closer to having to pay off the debt I owed him for coming home from the hospital in a pink hat, instead of the blue one he was expecting.

I was pretty sure that's why he insisted on surrounding me in it. All the pink. So I would come to hate the color as much as he did. The type of conditioning I learned about in that psychology class I took last semester. The one with the dog and the bell. My father was Pavlov and I was his obedient pet... until I sharpened my teeth enough to bite off his hand.

Another thing I had learned in that class? Back an animal into a corner, and its survival instincts would kick in. And right now, my hackles were rising to the surface, my pupils dilated by more than the leftover drugs in my system. The body sensed danger long before the brain did.

My father cleared his throat and I waited for him to address me before speaking. I was too tired and too dehydrated to provoke his temper.

"Dinner will be served at five o'clock sharp tonight, Mari," he grunted.

Two hours earlier than usual. But that wasn't what gave me pause. What had my heart plunging into my stomach and stirring up the waves of nausea that had already settled there. It was the way he smirked at me. The smallest break in his cold exterior that tipped up his mouth so that he appeared more disturbing than cordial.

"Don't be late," he added, his tone dryer than the back of my throat. "I have a surprise for you."

I have a surprise for you. The most terrifying words to ever leave my father's mouth, especially when his idea of a surprise was always more horror story than Hallmark.

20

His fork tapped against his dinner plate, and I watched as he shoved another piece of meat into his mouth. The juices splashing over his lips and dripping onto his chin before he used his free hand to grab the cloth napkin and dab at his cheek.

My eyes honed in on the sunken, sagging skin covered in little spots that spoke to too many hours spent on the golf course and swollen, shaky knuckles that told me he couldn't properly clutch a club anymore. Hinting at the fact he probably did more drinking than anything else when he was there.

Then there was the way his jaw clenched as he chewed, the little hairs on his face sticking out like an electrified porcupine. It was nauseating. His teeth more yellow than white while his bushy eyebrows looked like two fat hairy caterpillars were ready to crawl off his face at any moment.

I was an observer. It was second nature. A survival

instinct I'd developed at a young age when being *seen and not heard* wasn't just a suggestion. It was an expectation. So I lived in my head, spent so much time there I hardly realized anyone else was around. Until they caught me staring.

Like right now. Our dinner guest cleared his throat, and I smiled and quickly returned my attention to the bland chunk of steak in front of me. I never understood the correlation between tasteless food and rich people. As if they had an aversion to every seasoning other than salt and pepper.

My father was one of those people now. Which meant I was forced to adopt the palate of someone who looked like they belonged in a nursing home, rather than sitting across from a girl who was a quarter of his age for god only knows what reason. The same man who was currently gawking at me like he wished it was me he was gnawing on instead.

I might have looked away but he sure as hell didn't. Nor did he seem to care who noticed.

He dropped his fork onto the table with a clank, his focus locked on me and my father's focus locked on him. Assessing the stranger assessing me. "So, *Mary*, tell me," the man sneered. "How are your studies going?"

"My daughter is at the top—" my father started to answer for me, only to be cut off by a wave of that same trembling, condescending hand.

"I didn't ask you, Henry. I asked *her*." The man's penetrating glare flicked across the table before landing on me again. And I had to stifle my laughter. For two reasons.

My father hated being called Henry. More than that, though, he hated to be talked over and corrected. This stranger had done both.

I straightened my spine, meeting the wrinkly old bastard at eye level even as he tried to puff out his chest and rise higher in his seat. "Besides the incompetence of my classmates, they are going just fine." I lifted a shoulder into a half shrug. "Then again, it isn't difficult to maintain your marks when everyone else is below the curve. So maybe I should be grateful they've made things so easy for me."

I could feel the heat of my father's wrath boring into the side of my head. I didn't bother acknowledging it as I awaited the shitstorm I could feel headed my way.

The man's lip curled into a snarl, his nostrils flaring and the veins in his neck pulsing in a way that suggested if an aneurism didn't get him, a heart attack might. Then he slapped a heavy palm on the table and bellowed out a laugh. The sound so unsettling and manic I jumped in my chair before I could stop myself.

"She's perfect." He continued chuckling as he set his napkin on his plate and shoved it aside. "Tate never did like the quiet ones. No, the boy needs a challenge. Someone who will..." The man paused, as if considering his words for a moment. "...keep things interesting. In the bedroom. If you know what I mean." He turned and cocked an eyebrow at my father, who was still shooting daggers at me.

"Of course. If only we could all be so lucky," my father grunted, his leg dancing under the table as he tried to calm his tone enough to address me without yelling. I could feel the subtle knocking three chairs down. "Mari, this is Mr. Prescott. He wanted to meet you in person before we discussed the details of your betrothal to his son."

I forced down the bile quickly rising in my throat and plastered on another smile. Why? Because all my sass seemed to get me was a wedding band weighing down my finger. And I didn't even want to consider what *other things* my future husband *liked in the bedroom*. Though I was pretty certain consent wasn't one of them.

"It's a pleasure to meet you, Mr. Prescott," I croaked out.

"Please, call me *Tate*." He grinned. And there was that look again. The one that stressed his choice of daughter-in-law was as much for *him* as it was for *his boy*. Who, judging by the age of the man in front of me, wasn't much of a boy at all but closer to a creep in his thirties. "Unless you find it uncomfortable, dear. I can only imagine what it must feel like to yell out for the son and have the father come running."

I didn't reply, offering another tight smile instead as I excused myself from the dining table and rushed back up the stairs to my room.

I knew this day was coming. I'd been prepared for it long before I had any concept of what getting engaged to a stranger meant. But that didn't make the realization any easier to digest than that piece of flavorless meat my father had just tried to force me to swallow. It didn't make me any more willing to choke it down either.

21

ADRIAN

I positioned myself in the chair in the corner, the darkest thing to enter the sea of pastel that made up this room, and waited. I saw the irony in me being here. In seeking her out when the plan had been to turn things around. I just didn't care to acknowledge it.

I didn't need to.

It was much easier to accept your fate than to fight against it. And my fate was linked to this girl. She was a speeding train that sent everything I thought I knew veering off course. And this was me... adapting. Clearing out another path before we both went up in flames. Which wasn't out of the question just yet.

I knew who her father was. I'd looked him up after I'd found her name in the registrar's office. I also knew what sorts of things he had his hands in and why he was so protective of her. Marisela was his safety net, a bargaining chip he dangled in front of his political backers. *Do this for me, and I'll let you do whatever you want to her.*

We shared that in common. She and I. Loose morals and shit fathers.

I felt closer to her somehow because of it. In an odd way, it took hiding myself to feel more seen than I ever had before. Because she shared my darkness. She was attracted to it, and I was attracted to the way she looked at me without ever having to see me.

And that was exactly why I was here. Sitting in the blackness of her bedroom. Risking one of her father's men busting in and finding me.

It wasn't long before I heard the familiar sound of her footsteps padding up the stairs. Turning down the hall and heading this way. I recognized the rhythm, how she walked and held herself. The creaking of the floorboards and the twisting of the knob.

This wasn't the first time I was in this room. It was just the first time I was letting her catch me.

The door cracked open, and Marisela slipped inside without bothering to switch on the light. Not that it mattered, because as soon as she went to turn around, I'd closed the distance. Crept up behind her. One hand clamped over her mouth, the other locked around her waist, pulling her back against me.

I couldn't help but breathe her in. That floral scent triggering the memory of her sprawled out beneath me less than a few hours ago.

I felt her spine stiffen, the huff of air against my skin as she sucked in on a gasp, and then the sharp sting of teeth sinking into the meat of my palm through thick leather at the same time a grin spread across my face. My little wandering lamb forgot how much I liked a bit of broken flesh. She also didn't seem to realize how much *more* I liked it when she was the one doing the breaking.

I leaned forward, lowering the mouthpiece of my mask to just under her ear and whispered, "If I let you go, do you promise not to scream?"

She nodded once, but I could feel her smirking beneath my gloved hand. She wasn't even trying to hide it.

I stepped back. Crossing my arms over my chest, as she spun around and quickly flicked on the light.

"Surprise—" I grunted the word, because before I'd finished speaking, Marisela had landed a shoed foot between my legs. A direct hit to my balls that left me stumbling as she shoved me back against that same chair I just vacated in the corner. It was still warm.

She was *warmer* as she leveled a palm on each of the armrests, lowered her head to mine, and hissed, "I fucking hate surprises."

"Dually noted," I sputtered out as I waited for the searing, white-hot pain spreading across my thighs and lower abdomen to dissipate.

Maybe she knew her anatomy better than I thought?

Marisela eyed me for a minute, indecision pursing her lips, before she pushed back and crossed the room again. She was all twisted up about something and it had to do with more than the masked stranger she found hiding out in her bedroom.

"What's wrong?" I didn't mind when she was angry. I liked it. I liked coaxing out all the negative emotions she wanted to keep bottled up. I liked her raw and uninhibited. What I didn't like was the worry creasing her brow.

"What are you my therapist now?" she countered.

"You want to play doctor, Marisela?" I leaned back in the chair and steepled my hands. "Because I am more than qualified."

She stared at me for another long moment. Studied me. "You mean that literally, don't you?"

I shrugged, not bothering to answer. Because, for some reason, it *did* bother me to lie to her.

"Do I know you?" she tried again. "Who are you?"

"I'm whomever you want me to be," I replied.

"Can you be me?" Her voice cracked in a way that had me cracking along with it. "Because I'd really like to not be me right now."

I pushed up from the chair and took the two long strides that had us standing toe to toe again. Cupping her jaw and forcing her to look up at me. I recognized the desperation I saw there. The brokenness that wouldn't break. Swirling in the depths of her waterless eyes. Even as she refused to cry. Because crying left you vulnerable.

"No, I can't be you. No one can be you, little lamb. But I can make you forget who you are for a bit. So I can forget who I am too."

"And who are you?" she repeated.

"Yours. I'm yours, Marisela. That's all that matters," I told her, right before I switched off the light again. Pulling my mask off my head and tossing it aside. Her knees buckled the first time I kissed her, and we toppled onto the bed as she tugged me forward. Her hands clawing at my back just like I knew they would.

If she could feel the fresh gashes under my shirt, it didn't seem to stop her, just entice her to leave some more of her own.

22

ADRIAN

I didn't know what it was. It certainly *wasn't* for a lack of willingness. From me or from the girl squirming beneath me. But I couldn't bring myself to fuck her. Maybe it was the delayed gratification I was looking for. The knowledge of how much better it would be, the longer I put it off. Maybe some part of me knew crossing that line would either end this obsession or increase it tenfold. Or maybe I was just too young and stupid to know what was good for me. Because this girl, she was better than good. She was fan-fucking-tastic.

She was also the best worst thing to ever happen to either of us.

I grabbed her wrists in one hand, stretching them high above her head as I slowly trailed my mouth from the skin just under her ear, down the curve of her neck and over the rise and fall of two perfectly-pert nipples. Closing my teeth around one through the fabric of her dress and tugging. Just enough to induce a mix of pleasure and pain. Then I continued gliding my hot breath over her torso, her lower abdomen, stopping at the apex of her thighs. Dropping my grip on her arms to yank her legs apart.

I didn't have to even touch her to know how wet she was for me. The spot darkening her underwear—the one I could smell more than I could see—was all the confirmation I needed. It was also a barrier I didn't want. I gripped the thin material at the sides, wrenched it down and tossed it aside until the only thing separating me from the best pussy I've ever tasted was the air between us. Air that carried her scent straight to my nostrils and had me feeling feral.

I reached a hand into my pocket, fishing around until I found the two tabs I'd shoved in there when I'd decided Marisela was the distraction I wanted to lose myself in for the next few hours. I placed both on my tongue, pausing so that the saliva had a moment to start breaking down the outer composition, and then I lowered my head and took my first lick.

Tonight we were both gonna be jumping down that sensory rabbit hole.

I could feel her stiffen beneath my grip, likely startled by the tingling sensation that accompanied my tongue this time around. But a couple more quick flicks had her head falling back and her muscles relaxing.

And I had to admit, a few minutes in and mine were doing the same. *A few minutes in* and my movements became more sloppy and less refined. More need-driven and less controlled. A few minutes in and all the external stimuli seeped inside, like an extension of myself and her. And nothing and everything.

This wasn't my first time experimenting with the drug. I wasn't an avid user either. It was just the best way to understand the effects it had on the body. Better than any medical journal or outsourced accounting. I was both doctor and patient until I was ready to have someone else strapped to my table.

That chill returned to the base of my spine, running up and down and spreading out so that I was somehow hot and cold, fizzy and smooth, as I forgot who I was for a moment. Like I promised I would.

It didn't matter how futile this game was, how close I was to losing everything and far I was from the goal line. Instead, calmness and excitement smothered what was left of my common sense as I buried my tongue and nose as far into her pussy as it could go without cutting her open. I didn't want to taste her. I wanted to devour her. I wanted her inside me as much as I wanted to be inside her. A thought that was both exhilarating and dangerous for a man who knew how to use a scalpel and had plenty of practice dissecting a body.

Neither stopped me from pushing up on my knees, tugging Marisela's legs up with me as I tongue-fucked her cunt. My cock thrusting against the side of her mattress hard enough to shift the entire bedframe closer and closer to the wall. I was grunting and she was groaning and I had no doubt the entire world could hear us. I didn't care either. That was what this drug did to you. Made it so that you could see, feel, hear and taste everything. Smell everything. And all of it was so jumbled up you couldn't differentiate between which was which.

She gripped the sheets and it felt like she was gripping me too. Like she was running a palm up and down the length of me. Like I was sinking deep into her cunt as she locked herself around me. Like I was so deep I was poking out the other side, curling back in and going around again. And then she was coming and I was coming too. On her. With her. Inside her. None of those, yet somehow all of them.

She pulled my face up from between her legs. Forcing me to crawl over her body. I didn't remember climbing onto the bed but here I was, my knees digging into the mattress as my limbs melted into a pile of pink sheets before the chill of a blade bit into my fingertips. Familiar and forgiving. And I realized I was cutting into live flesh. Separating the layers and staring at the subcutaneous tissue underneath.

It was dark, too dark to see the figure in front of me. But I could *feel* the red. The yellow. And the white of two eyes staring back at me.

I just didn't know whose they were anymore.

PART TWO

Chicago Tribune

THE BUTCHER: WHO IS HE REALLY?

Police activity spotted on the 2700 block of West Taylor Street in East Garfield Park.

A human arm was found on the 2700 block of West Taylor Street in the East Garfield Park neighborhood. The Cook County Medical Examiner's office confirmed the remains were indeed human. An autopsy was conducted, but the results were pending at the time of the discovery. It has yet to be concluded if the victim is reported to be male or female. This incident marked the fourth time this month that human remains were discovered in Chicago, following the earlier discovery of skeletal remains in Arlington Heights and unknown traces of blood in Orland Park.

WILL LAW ENFORCEMENT FIND HIM BEFORE IT'S TOO LATE?

The discovery of dismembered body parts and the potential existence of a serial killer, dubbed "The Butcher" by local news outlets, underscore significant challenges in public safety and law enforcement. Such cases often involve complex investigations, especially when the remains are dismembered or disposed of in public spaces—complicating efforts to identify victims and apprehend perpetrators, sources say.

Residents are calling for increased resources. The city's history with notorious figures like John Wayne Gacy and the unresolved cases of the Chicago Strangler contribute to a climate of fear and mistrust among the public. As investigations into these disturbing discoveries continue, the city of Chicago faces the dual challenge of solving these heinous crimes and restoring public confidence in its ability to protect its citizens.

Victims have yet to be identified as families are left wondering if their loved ones are missing or dead.

COMPLETE CHICAGOLAND FORECAST ON PAGE 16

23

ADRIAN

THE NEXT MORNING...

My head was pounding, thrumming against my temples like a jackhammer trying to crack through skull instead of concrete. A dull pain radiating down my jaw and up through my sinus cavity. My arms stiff and in desperate need of electrolytes. But I could move them. Enough to apply pressure just under my eyes, using the nasalis muscle to ease some of the tension on my face, before I cracked my neck from side to side.

I took a deep breath and immediately shot up in bed at the distinct odor of copper. Blood. Dried and tacky against my skin. My fingertips. Drip marks down my wrists. Hours old. Then I glanced to my left and spotted the little blade, its mirror image imprinted on my sheets. An outline of dark red and brown against a bleach-white backdrop. Accompanied by the kind of splattering that suggested it had landed there wet.

I needed to think. To remember how I got here. And figure out whose blood was quite literally on my hands. But everything was a blur. Until another familiar scent made its way to my nostrils. My shirt smelled like her. Her bodily fluids mixed with her perfume. Marisela. I could still taste her on my tongue too. Salty and addictive.

I'd scaled the side of the estate and climbed into her window again. Sat in her room and waited. She'd been upset over something. And wanted to forget. And I'd wanted to be the one to help her do it.

There wasn't anything I wouldn't do for that girl...

I remembered placing the tab on my tongue—I had to increase the dose to account for our combined body weights. And even though it wasn't an exact science with all the variables that came with skin-to-skin absorption, one tab shouldn't have been enough to leave me feeling so disoriented. Unless I'd cooked up a bad batch.

I knew I hadn't. I was too good at what I did.

I pushed up from the mattress, stained with blood that I was certain wasn't my own, and followed the trail that led to my bedroom door. Down the long hall and out the back entrance. Where it stopped abruptly. Likely absorbed into the grass and washed away by the rain I could still feel thickening the air.

This place was a giant crime scene with a bright-red arrow pointing in my direction. But that wasn't the worst part. No, the worst part was I didn't remember doing it. Who it was or how the fuck I got home. Which made covering my tracks that much harder, especially when the white spot on my black pants suggested I'd left a decent amount of DNA behind.

I couldn't panic, though. Panicking was what got most killers caught.

So I shoved down the memory of Marisela clawing at my back, refusing to even consider the implications, and got to work.

I might have fucked up. That didn't mean I had to be a fuckup. I could fix this. I *had* to fix this.

24

ADRIAN

I lowered my face to the ocular lens and stared at the glass slide with the help of a microscope, adjusting the magnification until I found what I was looking for and hoping against. Or should I say what I *didn't* find?

The lack of a Y-chromosome amongst the cell staining told me exactly what I was dreading. Female. Whoever this blood belonged to, they were genetically female.

I tried to shake away the terror gnawing at my insides. The insecurities I hadn't felt since I was old enough to stare at myself in the mirror.

The fact I'd been with a woman didn't mean anything. Statistically, women made up half the population.

Not so statistically, some darker part of me knew the sample could only belong to one person. And she wasn't answering any of the text messages I'd been sending her from the burner phone I purchased this morning. In cash, just to be safe. The last thing I needed was my number popping up in some murder vic's call log.

I also knew she wasn't that. Marisela wasn't just *some* anything. She meant more to me than I realized until the thought of not having her became a very real possibility.

I wouldn't have killed her for no reason. I wasn't bloodthirsty. Just enthusiastic. More experimental than anything else. And half out of my mind on drugs. Which meant things could have gotten out of hand...

I'd wanted to feel inside her. To consume her. But not in any way that would have me pulling a knife and actually cutting into her skin. At least I didn't think so.

I glanced back down at my phone. Tugging off my gloves and scrolling through the only messages in my log.

ME:

> Good morning, princess. Just checking in.

I couldn't bring myself to use her pet name. Both out of self-preservation and shame.

ME:

> I need you to respond, Marisela.
> Right now.

ME:

> This isn't a game. How are you feeling?

ME:

> Are you there? A simple Y or N will suffice.

ME:

> Send me a goddamn emoji for all I care. But send me something, Marisela.

I'd lost my cool with that last one. But it was too late now. There was no taking it back. And I honestly didn't want to. If she was fucking with me, it was long past the point of being fun. Or *funny*. Considering the extra time I'd spent to measure the sample's telomeres did more to heighten my anxiety than dispel it.

This blood didn't just belong to a female. It belonged to a *young* female. An adult female, forty or under. Likely under.

I swiped the glass slide from the stage clips and tossed it across the room. Watching it shatter as soon as it hit the tile floor. There wasn't much else it could tell me without running a DNA test. And I didn't have the time or patience for that.

No, I needed to know what happened last night. Which meant I was breaking the first rule of not getting caught. Returning to the scene of the crime.

25

ADRIAN

I stood back from the sidewalk. A crowd of spectators already flocking around the bright-yellow crime tape that separated the outside world from whatever was happening inside the towering gates of the Cruz family mansion. Except I knew what was happening, while the hordes of plain-clothed officers were still trying to figure it out.

What I didn't see was a body bag. Nothing on a stretcher. No medical examiner either. Which was a good sign. I guess. It told me that I wasn't completely incompetent when it came to cleaning up after myself. Though it still didn't answer the question lingering in the back of my mind.

Where the fuck was Marisela?

Because she wasn't standing next to her father as he shouted orders at the highest ranking official on the scene. And I refused to accept the fact that I would have hurt her, knowingly or not.

I ground a palm against my twitching orbital muscle, dropping my hand to my neck and popping the collar of my long black trench coat, and stepped away from the chaos. I needed to get out of here before I was spotted and someone started asking questions.

I could feel everyone's eyes on me even as I knew no one was looking. It was paranoia. Another side effect of the drugs still in my system. Drugs that weren't metabolizing as quickly as they should have, and I'd yet to figure out why that was either.

By the time I'd made it back to my room, John was waiting for me. His hands clasped behind his back as he eyed the sparse space like it held anything of interest to him. It didn't. It was just his way of feeling superior. Because he had more than I had and I didn't even have this, seeing as everything I owned belonged to my father. And Tate.

"There you are," John grumbled as he pivoted on his heel to face me.

"Here I am," I parroted as I shrugged out of my jacket, shaking out the wrinkles in the fabric as I set it gingerly on the hook to my left. I might not have had much to my name, but at least I took care of it. Unlike the fucker in front of me who liked to toss aside the gadgets in his collection every time something newer and shinier came along.

John raised a challenging brow, meant to caution me, before he took another step forward. "Grab your bag and a change of scrubs. You have twenty minutes to meet me in the car."

I didn't bother arguing with him. I didn't see the

point. We both knew I had as much of a choice as any dog on a leash when its owner came calling.

"Where are we going?" I asked as I prepped my med kit, including a number of sedatives and narcotics I'd formulated myself. I ran my fingers over each of the vials. Any one of which could leave the man in front of me foaming at the mouth within seconds.

I glanced up from my kit and found John staring at me. He'd been doing that more frequently now. Dissecting me with his eyes, when he'd barely ever acknowledge me before. Though I couldn't figure out if he was more intrigued or disgusted.

He paused a moment, his predatory glare dancing over my face like he was looking for something before he answered, "Briarwood. There's a patient I'd like you to meet."

26

ADRIAN

My shoes sent several rocks tumbling forward as I dug my feet into the gravel walkway and peered up at the sign that read: *Welcome to Briarwood Sanitorium.*

Despite what the metal placard was trying to imply, there was nothing really welcoming about the barred windows or the crumbling angel statues that adorned each of the cornices along the roof. The distant screams I could hear in the background or the manic laughter that harmonized it.

But I had to admit more than a little bout of morbid curiosity had me moving closer again as I followed John past the large wooden double doors and down the first long corridor, our footsteps echoing in time with each other. Like a sinister dance. The swish of my bag so much louder in the quiet of the white-on-white hall while the buzzing of the halogen bulbs spoke to the old wiring hidden behind the freshly painted walls. A few updates meant to cover up all the ugliness that happened underneath.

It worked, for most people. Not for me. I enjoyed the ugliness. Even more when I had to dig around to find it.

John led me down another long hall, taking a quick left before pushing inside a door to his right. An observation room with a large window fitted with a two-way mirror, a couple of chairs, and an old-fashioned rotary phone. Nothing else.

I looked to John, whose focus was hinged on the other side of the glass, before setting my bag on the counter in front of us. Widening my stance as I crossed my arms over my chest and followed his line of sight to see what had him so entranced his dress slacks were already tenting at the zipper.

There was a girl spread out on the metal table, a thin hospital gown barely covering her tits as a team of doctors and nurses swarmed her like vultures on a carcass. Attaching electrodes and uncrossing wires before stepping back again. I couldn't hear past the glass that separated us but I could imagine the sound of all the machines, the biting odor of a sterile workspace, and the feel of a pair of latex gloves on my hands.

The girl remained perfectly still, her forehead strapped down to the platform beneath her. Her jaw distended by the cotton bite block and her arms stretched out at her sides. Until the first jolt of electricity sent her muscles dancing against her restraints. The lights flickered and the window rattled in its frame as the attending physician cranked the ECT machine to the next setting, and the nurse repositioned the electrodes against the girl's temples.

Twenty minutes later, she was carried out of the room and another patient took her place. Rinse and repeat as the bulge in John's pants grew as wide as the menacing grin that was spreading across his lips.

We didn't have that in common. I might have been a killer but even I had standards. I also didn't get off on watching a bunch of teenagers piss themselves.

27

ADRIAN

I looked up from the clipboard in my hands, to the kid in front of me, and back down again at the initials scrawled across the top. KM. No other identifiers. No billing information or social security number. Which told me no one was worried about the coding.

His intake paperwork claimed he was in his early teens but he presented younger than his stated age with white-blonde hair that had been shaved down to his scalp. Pale blue eyes and a slight, malnourished frame. Other than the smirk he was wearing like armor, there was nothing remarkable about this patient. At least from what I could see.

Clearly, John saw differently. Otherwise, he wouldn't have dragged me all the way out here. He wanted something. From me or the kid. Maybe both.

I tilted my head and watched my patient for a few more minutes, never saying a word as he smacked his chewing gum, blowing a bubble as wide as it would go before popping it and starting over. I was sure he was analyzing me as much as I was analyzing him.

"What's your name?" I decided to start simple. I didn't need the answer. I just needed to see where it would take me.

"You tell me, Doc." He grinned. Then again, he never stopped grinning. Not since I walked in here. When I didn't take the bait, he huffed out a breath. It was no fun when the game was one-sided and it was obvious this kid wanted to play. "You can call me Kaz."

I nodded once before making a little note on a blank page of the chart. I didn't have to write it down. It was just a way to keep my hands busy and my attention on something other than the patient who was thirsting for it.

He inched forward, trying to read over the lip of the folder before I tugged it closer to my chest and landed him with a smirk of my own.

"Come on, Doc," he whined. "Just give me a little peek. You'll find I'm good at keeping secrets."

"Yeah? What kind of secrets?" I questioned, even though I knew I shouldn't. But I had to admit I was curious. Because I knew how to keep secrets too. For very different reasons.

"Why don't you drop your pants and find out?" He lifted a challenging brow and suddenly he looked much older for his age. Trauma did that to you. Though I had to wonder if it was trauma at all. Could just as easily be for shock value.

"No thanks," I replied as I made another scribble across the blank page. More nonsense. Because whether or not this kid was serious, I wasn't writing that shit down.

He craned his head and narrowed his eyes at me. "Why not?"

"Because I'm not a perve." I shrugged, and he laughed.

"Yeah, I've heard that before. But guess what, Doc? Everyone is a good suck away from becoming one." He followed my line of sight as my eyes flicked to his legs before I could stop myself. "You'd be surprised what I can do in this chair..."

"Yeah, everything but hang yourself, right?" It was the one thing of interest I did find when I was flipping through his file. A failed suicide attempt. Not all that long ago either.

"Give me enough time and I'll figure that out too," he grunted, tugging back on his wheels before pivoting himself out of the room. I'd pissed him off.

Guess my new friend didn't want to play anymore.

28

"So?" John prompted the moment I walked back into the room with the blonde kid's chart tucked under my arm.

I still wasn't sure what he wanted from me. More than that, I wasn't sure if I *wanted* to give it to him. "Anti-social tendencies, oppositional defiance of authority figures, possibly histrionic. But I'm not a psy—"

John cut me off with a sharp *thwack* to the back of the head, hard enough to have my ears ringing. Something my father used to do to me whenever I got an answer wrong on my homework. I quickly learned it was better to just accept the blow than to try to dodge it. But I never lost count. Waiting for the day when I would match their numbers at a rate of two to one.

"If I wanted more of that psychology bullshit, I would have called in one of the useless pricks from the third floor. Did you see his legs?"

I ground the teeth in my jaw as I did my best to

temper my anger. "The result of a severe spinal injury to the L-4," I recited the findings I'd seen in the kid's chart. But there was nothing noteworthy about that. The damage was usually irreversible and crippling.

"Congenital analgesia," John clarified, and suddenly my interest was piqued again.

"Insensitivity to pain," I muttered more to myself, as my mentor's eyes lit up like a pedophile playing Santa on Christmas.

"He's the perfect patient. No need for anesthetics, none of the obtundation that comes with pain management. We can crack him open and see the effects of nerve manipulation in real time." John didn't even seem to be speaking to me anymore. His grin wide and his hands moving enthusiastically in the air as he paced the room. Almost like he could already picture the kid on his table.

"You think we can help him walk again?" It seemed unlikely, but the implications were fascinating. To be able to work without an anesthetic meant you could adjust your incision, keep the spine open and manipulate the connections without having to wait for the proper healing periods between.

"I don't give a fuck if that brat's in a diaper for the rest of his life," John hissed. "We just need to keep him breathing and speaking." I could see the wheels turning in the fucker's head. Motivated by lust or greed? I didn't know which.

"Parental consent?" I pressed, watching John's teeth clench, much like mine had moments ago. *Good, because I was just as irritated with him as he was with me.*

"What about it?"

"Do we have to worry about obtaining it?"

"He's a ward of the state. You should know that," John snapped. *I didn't know that* because it wasn't in the file—intentional I was sure. "Abandoned by his whore mother and communist father."

"And what if the kid doesn't agree to lie still?" I asked, though something told me I *did* know the answer to that one.

"He doesn't have a choice. It's your job to make sure he understands that."

29

ADRIAN

he wind was howling behind me, twisting and curling and hissing at the night sky as the branches seemed to reach out from all sides. Trying to wrap around and grab at my arms. Which seemed heavier than usual. Because they were heavier than usual, weighed down by the figure currently pressed against my chest. A girl.

She was small and thin. And she smelled and tasted like flowers and copper with long black hair covering her face and deadened limbs that swung with each step I took forward. Like the arms of a clock counting down the time I had left.

Tick. Tick. Tick.

I had to hurry. I didn't know why, but it was important. The reason ebbing and swaying at the back of my mind so quickly I couldn't grasp it. It was there, though. I could feel it. I could feel everything and nothing.

I was moving through the woods. Somewhere close to home. I could feel that too. No, I was running. Running but standing still as the ground clawed and swatted at my boots.

Those seemed just as heavy as my arms, caked with mud and grass instead of a girl, as I glided one foot in front of the other.

I stopped short when I found myself behind the old well at the back of Prescott Estates. Though I didn't remember the path I took to get me there. Here. To this spot. Rain was beating against the crumbling stonework, which was cracking with age, cold droplets dripping off my nose and through the thin fabric of my unbuttoned shirt. My chest heaved as I tried to focus on what I was doing and why I was doing it.

And why I was in such a hurry.

I hadn't been to this spot in years. Since I was little and Tate used to tell me stories about the ghost that haunted these woods and this well and would climb up its walls and grab you if you weren't careful. But I didn't believe in ghosts anymore. I didn't need to. Mankind was much more terrifying.

It didn't take me more than a few seconds to shove the metal grate aside with one hand before depositing the figure I was holding into the depths of the giant hole in the earth. I watched her fall, that same black hair whipping around her face before revealing two bright-green eyes. Eyes I recognized. Eyes I remembered staring back at me when I ran a blade across her carotid artery. Eyes I watched the life drain out of at the same time her blood coated my hands.

Marisela's eyes.

Panic had me reaching out an arm, leaning down as far as gravity would let me without toppling after her. One palm gripping the lip of the well, the other swatting at air... and vegetation... before clenching a handful of sheets.

I shot up in bed, throwing on a pair of shoes and shoving my arms through my trench coat before rushing down the hall and out the back entrance. Following the path I'd seen in my dream. Nightmare. Memory? Whatever the fuck it was. Only this time, I couldn't hear the wind past the beating of my own heart in my chest and nothing clawed at me except from my own conscience.

As soon as I wrapped my fingers around the grate and tossed it aside, I could smell it. The odor of decomposition that wafted up from the depths of the well. It was faint. Barely discernible unless you knew what you were looking for. Bacteria breaking down the tissue on a cellular level. Hydrogen sulfide and methyl mercaptan. Similar to the stench of rotten eggs and wet cabbage if you were to leave it out in the sun for too long.

I twisted around, leaning my back against the side of the well as I sank into the mud. Because all of a sudden, everything was painfully clear as my mind tried to weave through the distortion of the chemicals in my brain and wrap itself around the truth.

There was a body floating in that water. I'd been the one to put it there. And I knew who it belonged to. Even if I didn't want to accept it. Because I was pretty certain I loved this woman... almost as certain as I was that I'd killed her.

30

MARISELA

I didn't think he'd actually do it...

Not until I saw all the blood. So much blood. Seeping into the sheets and dripping onto the floor. Covering my feet and his hands. He stared back at me over a shoulder, his mask firmly in place but I didn't need to see his face to know what he was looking for. My approval. He was trying to read me. Figure out if I was disgusted or appeased. If I was gonna scream and go running or if we were about to skip off towards our own version of a happily ever after.

It was no minor ask. Having someone kill for you. But my shadow man never hesitated. Not when he'd followed me out into the hall, my father's men within shouting distance. Not when I'd used the spare key I made to unlock my mother's bedroom door. Not when we crept up to the side of the bed or even when we'd found her eyes wide open and staring back at us.

She'd been so still, lifeless but breathing. The same way she'd been since the night my father had her dragged out of the house kicking and cursing. And spitting. I'd never seen my mother spit before that night. Now all she could do was drool.

She hadn't bothered to fight us off. She'd barely made a sound as he ran the razor-sharp blade across the largest vein in her throat and we watched her bleed out in front of us. Almost like she'd been expecting it. Some lost part of her wanting and waiting for it.

It was the humane thing to do when you saw someone you loved suffering. I also couldn't leave her behind... *with him.* I could only imagine what my father would do to her when he found out what I was planning. We'd taken that option from him.

And now that it was done, we could run away together. It seemed like a brilliant idea when you were both drugged out of your mind. Less brilliant when you were sober. But we had a few hours before that would happen.

I nodded once, and my shadow man tucked the blade back into his waistband as he leaned forward and pressed a hand to my mother's throat and again to her wrist. We had to make sure she was dead if any of this was going to work.

I also didn't have long before the extra Molly I'd slipped him wore off, and I couldn't chance him changing his mind. Or me losing my nerve. I could already feel that warm sensation slipping away while my shadow man could barely stand upright. It was clear only one of us was a chronic user. It was the same one of us who knew shit about disposing of a body. Which meant I had no choice but to leave my mother lying here.

I knew it was selfish. Everything about tonight was. Because asking this stranger to slit my mother's throat wasn't just about putting her out of her misery. It was about ensuring no one could use her against me.

She would have understood, though. If she were in her right mind enough for me to explain it, she would have understood. At least, I hoped she would...

31

MARISELA

I narrowed my glare at the figure in front of me. I couldn't see him through the blindfold that covered most of my face and eyes. Couldn't curse his name through the bite guard that was shoved into my mouth the first time I'd tried to scream out for help. But I could feel him. Looming over me. His shadow blocking the light that was so bright it pierced the thick fabric and heated my skin.

He didn't speak as he poked at me with the tip of his bony finger. Grazing a hand over my rib cage, circling along the middle of my torso, and stopping just under my breast line. Tentative and curious. *Creepy.*

I waited for him to touch me again. Instead, he pulled his hand back. I felt the brush of his sleeve retracting as I took a deep, irritated breath through my nose. Everything smelled so clean. So sterile. Like bleach and alcohol and... bubblegum. The fruity pink kind.

I could hear him chewing. Blowing and popping and

gnawing. Followed by the sound of whining wheels on polished tile before it was just me and the blinding light again. Sprawled out on a stiff table with nothing but a thin piece of fabric separating me from the cool air that was being pumped into the room on a continuous basis. No different from a piece of meat they were afraid of spoiling.

But this place wasn't just my icebox; it was my new prison. Not as pretty but just as suffocating. If I was lucky, all they'd do was slice me open. Then again, something told me these guys were more interested in the holes that were already there and less interested in creating their own.

My arms were numb and warm, my feet cold and tingling as I tried to fight whatever drugs were in my system. The ones that were trying to lull me under and keep me quiet and compliant. I was too mad to sleep, though. I was also too stubborn to give in.

I wanted to be awake for everything they planned to do to me. I wanted to feel it. Remember it. Use it to fuel the rage that was directed more inward than anything else right now. At myself.

Because this was my fault. I never should have trusted him to get me out of there. My stalker might have jumped at the chance to kill for me. But it came with a price and that price came with friends. And those friends had more in mind for me than a prenup and a white dress. I could only imagine what that more was. Though I knew it was nothing good if it required drugging me up and stripping me down.

I'd fucked up. I knew that now. And the worst part

was admitting to myself that maybe my father was right all those times he insisted that the devil I knew was better than the devil I didn't. One might have kept me in a cage but the other made sure to clip my wings so I fell faster into the hellfire. And right now, I was both freezing and burning up.

32
MARISELA

"Good Morning, Miss Cruz! How are you feeling today?" A man with dark—nearly black—eyes and a shaved head pushed through the large metal door that separated me from whatever was on the other side of these padded walls. All four of them. Gray with yellow stuffing and the occasional blood splatter peeking out from the seams.

He was the first doctor I'd seen since I was transferred from the icebox and deposited into this giant used tampon, his way-too-chipper voice and the dramatic swish of his white jacket telling me he must have been dipping into his patients' meds on the regular.

Part of me was appalled by the idea. Another part was hoping he'd share because my fucking head was killing me.

"Like someone who got run over by a four-by-four and woke up in a nuthouse," I grunted in reply. I'd figured that last bit out as soon as the blindfold was removed and I found myself under lock and key. Bars on the windows and not a shoelace in sight.

The man *tsked* his tongue while clicking a bright-red pen against his clipboard. "Now, now, we don't use that kind of language around these parts, Miss Cruz. It's insulting to all the good work we do here at Briarwood," he corrected, and I could only imagine what that *good work* entailed.

I shivered at the thought. At the memory of what they'd done to my mother. At the memory of what I'd done to her myself...

The asshole flicked his pen against my forehead, three quick taps that had me gnashing my teeth and glaring in his direction. I might not have liked the taste of rare meat but not enough to keep me from biting.

His mouth twisted into a snarl and his voice dropped an octave as he squinted his eyes at me. "Don't make me put you in a collar, Marisela. I promise you it's not as nice as it sounds." Then, like nothing happened, his smile was back. "Your father bragged about your impeccable manners. Let's not make a liar out of him or a *fool* out of you."

"My father?" I shouldn't have sounded so shocked. This was exactly the kind of thing he would do.

"Yes, Hernando spoke very highly of you over the phone. He failed to mention how pretty you were, though."

I could feel the weight of the fucker's gaze skimming me from chest to clit. Like he could see through the fabric of this flimsy hospital gown. Truth was he probably could. It wasn't very doctorly of him, though.

Then again, I wasn't above fucking my way out of here. The guy was an asshole but it was amazing what you could do when you felt trapped. He wasn't bad looking either. A strong jaw, those dark eyes, muscular arms that hinted at the tattoos he was trying to hide under the sleeves he would tug at every now and then like he was worried someone might realize the kinky shit he was into when he wasn't peddling pills.

I was one quick breath away from offering to suck his dick, after he got me out of here because I was smart enough to know to make the fucker pay upfront, when he pivoted on his squeaky shoes and slammed the door behind him. He was still there, though. Lurking in the hallway. I could see his shadow through the little glass window between us.

"Be careful who you play games with here, little girl," he whispered through the door. "They might just play back."

Then he walked away, his footsteps continuing to squeak down the hall until all I heard was silence again. Silence and the occasional scream.

33
MARISELA

I stared out the window as the little white dots ran circles around another slightly larger dot. The grass overgrown and wooden crosses looming along the side of the hill, an ominous mixture of the past and current residents. Neither more likely to escape this hellhole than the other.

I huffed out an annoyed breath and started all over again. *One... two... three...*

Counting was the only thing I had to occupy my mind. Twenty white dots and over a hundred crosses—it was hard to tell the exact number with all the foliage in the way—and more than half were bent, broken, or missing.

The breeze that rattled the cracked glass was nice, though. Especially compared to the stale air of the room. Other than the ants outside and the weird visit from the creeper in the lab coat, I hadn't seen a single soul. And the lack of human interaction was on the verge of giving me a reason to actually belong here with the rest of these nutcases.

Four... five... six...

I made it to seventy-seven crooked crosses before the sound of the door cracking open again had me spinning around and staring at... an empty hallway. Until I dropped my glare and spotted the chair. I recognized the whining of the wheels. He must have been the one groping me up in the icebox when I first woke up here.

The boy eyed me for a moment before reaching into his pocket and flicking his wrist in my direction. A red rubber ball hit the padded wall to my left with a soft *thud*, quickly falling to the floor and rolling towards my socks—the grippy kind that everyone joked about.

I bent down and picked it up, not bothering to adjust my gown as it bunched at the front and revealed what little you couldn't see beneath the threadbare fabric. Then I looked from the ball back to the boy taking up most of the doorframe with his arms crossed over his chest and a single blonde eyebrow raised.

"Cut it in half and tuck the pieces behind your ears," he said as he tossed a packet of bubblegum my way.

I caught the pink packaging midair. "Why?"

He shrugged a single shoulder. "Or don't. Whether or not your brain gets scrambled really ain't my problem, princess."

The nickname gave me pause. I didn't like the thing it did to my pulse or how my body instantly reacted to the thought of my shadow man. Or maybe he was never *mine* at all. Not if he was working with my father...

But I had more important things to worry about. Like

the fact my door was wide open now. I rushed forward, only to have it slammed in my face before the lock clicked over the front.

I pounded on the metal with my fists, my knuckles bloodied by the time I gave up and yelled out, "What the fuck am I supposed to cut it with?"

"You got teeth, don't you?" the boy yelled back a few seconds later. Which told me his room wasn't far. *That*, or more than one of these fuckers was watching me.

34

MARISELA

I looked to the left, then quickly turned my head to the right. Stretching my neck and trying my best to peer over the hunched body in front of me to see if I could wriggle any of my fingers, as each of my wrists was tugged straight and strapped down to a padded armrest. So tight my hands were numb.

The room was cold and windowless—except for a glass partition that took up the entirety of one wall. I couldn't see through it, but I had no doubt someone was there. Probably *multiple* someones, the sort who weren't allowed within five-hundred meters of a school zone. And then went home and touched their wives and kids with the same hands they used to diddle themselves in a playground bathroom.

I didn't know if this was their version of entertainment or foreplay. What I did know was that it was fucked. And so was I if I didn't figure a way out of here.

I searched the room for a knife, a pencil, anything I

could use to cut myself free, before a woman in blue scrubs pinched my jaw, prying my mouth open and shoving a cloth block past my teeth while her counterpart pressed down on my forehead to keep me from squirming. It tasted like moth balls and I had to breathe through my nose to keep from gagging up nothing. Because I couldn't even remember the last time I'd had something to eat.

I stared up into the bright light dangling above me as one more strap was ratcheted in place, so that I had no choice but to close my eyes or sear the image of the circular bulb into my retinas.

Then all the machines began to whirl, buzzing and humming in the silence of the enclosed space. Larger than my little hospital room but much more closed-in with everyone crowding around me. A choreographed dance of prepping syringes, securing electrodes and monitoring my vital signs. I didn't need any of it to know that my heart was beating out of my chest, though.

I could hear it as much as I could feel it. Pounding in my ears and thrumming in my temples.

I'd fought them the whole way here, clawing and biting until one of the orderlies—a bald guy with skin so thick he didn't bleed—had decided it was easier to toss me over a shoulder, the blood rushing to my head and my bare ass on display as I'd watched the hallway disappear behind us. Upside-down.

Now, I was tired and sweaty and my throat was dry from screaming. My nails were cracked and sticky but I couldn't feel them. I couldn't feel anything, thanks to the drugs they were pumping into my veins.

That was a lie. Because I did feel grateful for the little rubber pieces I'd hidden behind my ears with the help of that bubblegum. Especially when the first volt of electricity surged to life. My spine going rigid, my jaw clamping down, and everything else going dark.

35

MARISELA

The next "treatment" was worse than the last. By the third, I was too disassociated to feel much of anything besides the occasional sharp ringing in my ears. A weird humming sound that came with a recurring pins and needles sensation. Like someone was digging around in my brain but only sporadically hit a nerve.

The rubber balls helped absorb some of the shock, but they didn't stop it altogether. Food tasted different. More bland and less tactile. Lumpy and unappealing, no matter what it was. I lost my sense of smell, which didn't help with the food issue. And I couldn't find that part of myself that liked to put up a fight.

She was still there. I could feel her in the back of my mind. Floating around somewhere. I just couldn't reach her.

I shook my head as I glanced down at the gray tray in my lap. I didn't even know if it was actually gray or not.

Everything just *felt* gray. Duller. No matter what color it was. Even the applesauce that had the consistency of a regurgitated fruit cup and the milk that looked more yellow-gray than white-gray.

I twirled a spoon around the bowl, my eyes staring out the window but seeing nothing, and thought about *nothing* when usually I couldn't stop thinking about everything. I'd always been a thinker. Planning and plotting had been like breathing. Second nature.

Now breathing seemed planned, while thinking was like drowning.

I didn't know how much more my brain could take before I wasn't *me* anymore. And that wasn't as terrifying as it should be. Which was terrifying.

"Good Morning, Miss Cruz. How are you feeling today?" a voice called out from the door.

I looked up, slowly. Everything felt slower. Expecting to see the doctor with the dark eyes and the hidden tattoos. Instead of the shorter, much stockier man in front of me. His smile was well-practiced, his tone less playful and more monotone. Or maybe that was me.

"You're not him," I forced the words out, almost like they were bouncing around in my head and it took much more effort to catch them.

"Who?" the man with the off-white *gray* coat asked, his nostril hairs bristling with the loud exhale of his breath.

Was he irritated with me? I didn't remember doing anything to irritate him. I didn't even remember wanting to irritate him.

I reached up a hand and started rubbing at my

temple. I felt like we'd been here before. At the same time, I was almost certain we had never been here before. "My doctor."

"I already told you, Miss Cruz. There are no other attendings like the one you described. Just myself and Dr. Burke."

He told me? When? Had I imagined the other doctor? Was I imagining this one? I didn't know. And I didn't know if I cared to know.

"Okay." I nodded once before refocusing on my tray. Except it wasn't there anymore. My lap was empty, and when I glanced to the window, it was dark outside. Quiet. Because not even the crickets wanted anything to do with this place.

36

MARISELA

"You don't look so hot, princess." The blonde boy was staring at me again, rolling back and forth in his chair while keeping the front wheels suspended. He dropped them to the floor with a *thud* and tossed me two more little red balls. "Might want to start keeping some extra pieces between your fingers and toes."

I watched the rubber balls bounce towards me without making a move to grab them. I wasn't as far gone as I was during those first few weeks, but I still wasn't myself either. More like a version of the girl I once was, suspended in a block of ice. Each day, I would chip away at a few layers and then they'd strap me to that table again and I had to start all over.

"Why do you care?" I asked, though I wouldn't say that I was curious. More confused. I didn't believe in people being helpful out of the goodness of their heart.

Especially in this place. Everyone wanted something. Everyone had an end game. Including me.

The boy shrugged, turning his wheely into a vertical spin. He completed three dizzying rotations before landing his glare on me. "I don't. But he does. And I want to see how this plays out."

"Oh…" It took me a moment to process his words, as another layer of ice melted away. "He who? Who's *he*?" I asked a little too excitedly.

"The new doc," the boy responded, sounding disinterested when I was more *interested* than I'd been in anything in days.

"The one with the tattoos? A big guy with dark eyes?" Maybe he was real. Maybe I wasn't as crazy as I thought I was. And maybe that had always been their plan. To convince me I was losing my mind and belonged here.

The boy grinned in a way that told me he knew exactly who I was talking about and had no intention of admitting it. "Don't know any doc with tattoos and I ain't exactly eye level. Maybe if you describe his package, we could compare notes?"

A smile tugged at my lips and I liked the feel of it. I found comfort in the uncomfortable. Which wasn't what this kid was looking for. He wanted to see disgust. He wanted me to turn away and squirm. He wasn't all that hard to figure out… even though he thought he was.

"Sorry but a lady doesn't kiss and tell," I replied in a dry tone. Sounding more bored than bothered.

"Funny 'cause I don't see a lady," he countered.

I looked across the room, gaging his reaction, then

back down at myself before lifting my hospital gown over my head and giving the kid an eyeful. I had no problem turning the tables when it came to getting someone's attention. "How about now?"

The boy stared at me wide-eyed for a minute before clearing his throat and reapplying his signature smirk. "All right. I'll play. This guy don't look old enough to be a doc if ya asked me. But he seemed to know his shit. More importantly, he seemed to know *you*."

I dropped the hem of my gown, smoothing out a few wrinkles and crossing my arms over my chest. "What makes you say that?"

"He had your name and number in his burner. Was awfully desperate to get a hold of you too, came off real stalkerish." The boy reached into the waistband of his hospital pants. And I watched as he pulled out one of those cheap throwaway cell phones and dangled it in front of me. I shot out an arm to grab it, and he snapped his back. Clutching the device against his chest while *tsking* his tongue at me. "Yeah, I don't think so. This baby's mine. The dumbass didn't even realize I'd clipped it."

"Does this dumbass have a name?" I asked, trying not to seem as desperate as I was starting to feel.

"Show me those tits again and I might just be motivated enough to find out." The boy lifted a challenging blonde brow.

"Find out and I might just be motivated enough to show you my tits again," I threw back at him.

"You drive a hard bargain, princess. But I'll see what I

can do," he yelled over a shoulder, already pivoting down the hallway towards the pediatric wing. He must have also clipped some kind of employee badge, seeing as he came and went as he pleased and I couldn't get past the double doors.

37

ADRIAN

I glanced towards the glass partition, where I knew John was watching me. My guess? It was for more reasons than one. Sure, his bizarre fascination was nothing new, but he also didn't want any of these fuckers seeing his face. That was why I was here. It had nothing to do with my skill set, which was better than his with or without a license.

No, I was closed inside this room—alone, despite my inexperience and without a proper surgical team—because he wanted me taking the heat if something went wrong or if one of the patients didn't respond well to being experimented on.

The kid on the table didn't seem to care too much either way. He was grinning up at me as I assessed his nerve response before flipping him onto his stomach, his blonde hair hidden by a surgical cap and his back littered with numerous scars. Mine were from years of abuse, his were from failed attempts at fixing whatever damage he'd done to land himself in that chair. His skin would heal over time; the darkened epidermis tissue would lighten until the incisions were barely discernible. He had youth to thank for that. What he didn't have was much of a chance of ever walking again.

I had to admit I got a sick thrill from the thought. From the idea of achieving the impossible. I just had to figure out a way to get there...

Today's cut was meant to be more exploratory than anything else. The first look at what I was working with as the kid chatted away like I hadn't just spliced him open.

His heart rate remained steady, his vitals never spiking above their resting values, as I suctioned the excess fluid away from his L-4, the fusion offset and bolted together with screws that could have been from your local hardware store. Kid should have been more than paralyzed; he should have been in agony.

I'd need to chip away at the healing bone, without severing the spinal cord, and either replace the missing disc with a titanium plate—if I could smooth out the edges enough. Or find a way to salvage what was left of his vertebra and resituate the fusion.

Then again, if pain wasn't a factor... there was nothing stopping me from replacing the L-4 and L-5 in their entirety. Hell, I could build the kid a brand-new spine if I could fabricate something that wouldn't hinder his flexibility.

The idea bounced around in my head for a few

moments, more the feasibility than the ethics behind it, before the clattering of metal had me focusing on the incision in front of me. Then the floor, where my patient had sent the sterilized surgical tray flying with a swipe of his hand.

"I'm booored," he whined, his arms swinging along each side of the table as he twisted his neck to eye me over a shoulder. "Aren't ya done poking around yet?"

The real answer was I hadn't even begun to *poke around yet*. But I didn't think the truth would do any of us any good right now. The kid needed an audience as much as he needed to be the center of attention. Which meant today I was both surgeon and circus-goer while my patient slipped into his latest persona. An annoying little shit with the persistence of a squirrel searching for a nut.

"So, you got a name, Doc?" he hummed, his arms now peddling forward like he was working on his front stroke.

"Everyone has a name, kid," I replied as I used a few absorbable sutures to close up my small incision, followed by a couple of staples to secure them in place. I'd barely finished before he was putting all his weight on his shoulders to roll himself over again. It should have been painful, considering I went down to the bone, but the kid didn't even flinch as he narrowed his glare at me.

"Yeah, and what's yours?"

I didn't know what he was after but I sure as shit knew it was something as I analyzed the innocent look on his face, distorted by the hint of a smirk he was trying his hardest to hold back. "The surgeon. I'm just your surgeon," I told him with a shrug of my shoulders.

I discarded my cap, prepared to exit the mini operating room and leave him for one of the orderlies to deal with when the kid called out to me, "Aw, come on, Doc. Don't make me disappoint your *girlfriend*."

He could have been bluffing. Everything in me screamed that he was probably bluffing... yet something had me turning around anyway. "What'd you say?"

This time, he was the one shrugging. I glanced over at the glass partition—I had no idea if John was still there or waiting for me in one of the offices—before looking back at the kid again.

"I don't know what you think you know," I hissed so that only he could hear me, my arm shooting out and fisting his hospital gown. "But you need to forget it."

He leaned forward and whispered back, "Marisela ain't all that forgettable... at least her tits aren't."

I ground my teeth and shoved him aside before I spun towards the door, a little more force in my steps as I tore off my bloodied gloves and stomped down the hall.

I didn't know how this kid knew who Marisela was or what she'd meant to me... I hadn't told a soul. I'd barely acknowledged that shit myself... before it was too late. And now I had her ghost haunting me with the help of a mental patient who hadn't been outside these walls in over a year.

It took two more steps for me to register what that meant.

Maybe she hadn't been the body I'd tossed down that well... Maybe the MDMA was still messing with my head, distorting my memories so I didn't even know what I'd done that night. But more importantly was the realization that... maybe she was here. At Briarwood.

I just needed to find her *without* letting anyone know I was looking for her. After that, I could figure out who the fuck's blood I was really looking at under that microscope.

38

MARISELA

"She's making progress," the fucker with the long nose and wide-brimmed glasses breathed into his desk phone, a bony finger twirling in the air while he talked about me like I wasn't here. Sitting in front of him. Being described like a piece of furniture: soft, compliant, easy to manipulate and maneuver.

They both did it. This guy and his counterpart. Where Dr. Hare was tall and lanky, Dr. Burke was short and wide. Put them together and they looked like the number ten in a skin suit. Their pockets full of pills and their mouths full of bullshit diagnoses.

Were some of the patients here in need of some serious psychiatric help? Absolutely. But that wasn't what these guys were doing. They were playing god while the rest of us were nothing more than ants under a magnifying glass, scrambling around on the dirt. Looking for a place to hide and trying to avoid the heat of their glare.

"A few more weeks and I think she'll be ready for reintroduction." He paused, and then offered whoever was on the other end of the line another sugary-sweet reply. "Of course... Yes, I understand... We appreciate your support. Our research department is nothing without the generosity of benefactors such as yourself, Mr. Cruz."

I'd roll my eyes, if my body could remember how to do it. Right now, breathing seemed too much of an effort though.

I'd been trying my best to appear stunted, to let them think I was withstanding the full-force of their brain fry, but these fuckers had started to catch on, increasing the intensity and frequency of their shock treatments so that the little rubber balls didn't do much to mitigate the effects anymore.

It left me vulnerable to the predatory gaze of every sick fuck who didn't need more than a swipe of a keycard to access my room. It also meant I didn't sleep much at night. Or at all really. As I waited for one of them to take the leering a little too far the next time.

It didn't escape my notice that there weren't many women on this ward. I could only imagine why. Maybe their families recognized a creep when they saw one. Mine certainly didn't. That or they didn't care.

The click of the phone on the receiver had me looking up from my hands in my lap to the condescending smirk that greeted me on the other side of the oversized mahogany desk. "Would you like to go home, Miss Cruz?" Dr. Hare asked.

It was a rhetorical question. A stupid one too. But that wasn't the reason I didn't answer him. It was because it took me so much longer to form words.

"You know," he hummed, not bothering to wait for me to acknowledge him as he steepled his hands, his forehead creasing while he pretended to consider what he was about to say next. "I could be persuaded to expedite the discharge process... *if* I were convinced you're obedient enough to follow the aftercare program I've developed for you."

My brow twitched, the slightest inclination that my curiosity was piqued. It was all I could do. I still didn't trust my voice and my body still didn't feel like mine anymore.

Then he stood from his chair and stepped around his desk, leaning on the edge so that I was eye level with his crotch. "Can you be a good little girl and follow doctor's orders, Marisela?" He grinned, and it took me a moment to realize his double meaning.

He was already unzipping his pants and reaching a hand inside, prepared to expose himself in his closed office, when the door swung open. Dr. Hare quickly tucked himself away again but there was no hiding what he was trying to do from the man in the blue surgical mask.

Dr. Hare reclaimed his seat behind his desk, clearing his throat before glaring in the newcomer's direction. "Can I help you, Ad—"

"John needs a second opinion," the man replied a little too quickly and much louder than necessary.

"I'm with a patient," Dr. Hare barked back.

"I see that."

It was a battle of wills as the two men stared at each other, trying to determine whose unspoken threat held more weight. It didn't take more than a few seconds for the good doctor to curse under his breath, push up from his chair and storm out with the slam of the door.

Then it was just me and the stranger with the dark eyes as his heavy breaths puffed out the fabric of his mask. "Did he touch you?"

I shook my head. At least not in the way he was implying. Because my brain could be scrambled as long as my virtue remained intact. That was what really mattered to everyone who wasn't me.

"Good. Okay..." He chanced a quick look over a shoulder before turning back in my direction. "We need to get you out of here."

I swallowed and focused on forcing out the words in my head. "H-how?"

"I don't know yet." He sighed, and my hope was squashed before it had a chance to take root. He could see it too. At least that was the impression he gave me when he added, "But I'm gonna figure it out. I promise."

Then he dropped the hand that was wrapped around my wrist, almost like he was making sure I was real, and started patting himself down, cursing when he didn't seem to find whatever he was searching for.

"Look at me." He tipped up my chin, and I watched his pupils dilate as his eyes flicked from side to side. "I need you to trust me, okay? I have to leave but I'm coming back for you. Do you understand me?"

I nodded once. Not because I believed him but because I *wanted* to believe him. I wanted something to cling on to. Something to keep the hope from dying out completely. And right now, this guy and his promises were all I had.

39

ADRIAN

Each corner seemed to stare back at me, patients roaming the halls like they were one second away from cracking someone's skull open to find their next meal. Their movements stiff and robotic while the noises they made were like a Romero movie with the sound turned all the way up.

Shit was intentional. Keep the crazies overmedicated and the building understaffed, so there wasn't anyone around competent enough to ask questions.

That was how John liked it. Fucker didn't enjoy the challenge of breaking someone as much as I did. He wanted things easy. Not that I was judging him. It was more of an observation than anything else. A fact of life. Some of us were hunters, while others were more inclined to starve if their meat wasn't chewed for them.

And I wasn't against watching them choke. It was a benefit of natural selection after all. Picking and choosing which traits benefitted the species survival and which should have been eradicated at birth.

I'd yet to determine what category the men I worked with fell into. Though I was leaning towards a mixture of both.

Burke and Hare used Briarwood as their own personal playground, John positioning himself on the other side of the fence, keen enough to look and not touch, which had never been a problem before. It wasn't my business. Until they made it my business. By bringing *her* here.

It didn't take more than a quick glance at Marisela to know that they'd been hooking her up to that archaic electroconvulsive machine the fuckers dug out of the basement. Inducing seizures while interrupting the neuropathways in her brain. It was like pressing the reboot button on your computer over and over again until the damn thing wouldn't turn on anymore.

"Fuck," I cursed under my breath, gripping two fistfuls of hair and tugging until the pain was sharp enough to ground me.

I wanted to drag her out of that office, kicking and screaming or calm and sedated if she refused to go willingly. The couple of vials I had burning a hole in my pocket would have done the trick if Hare tried to stop us. But that would only get us as far as the first hallway of doors. He had her locked up on a secured wing. Away from the more... active patients. Something that was both a relief and an inconvenience. It was also deliberate as fuck. A way for them to keep her under their thumbs and in their sights.

I slammed the car door shut and peered up at the building taking up most of my rearview, as I willed myself to throw the gear stick into drive and pull away. She was just a dot of dark hair in the window, watching me maneuver Tate's old BMW around the circle path until that same dot was nothing more than another memory plaguing my waking hours.

But at least I wasn't imagining it this time. At least she was alive.

Three hours and a fresh change of clothes later, I had a duffle bag slung over a shoulder, several syringes rolled up in a leather carrier, and next semester's tuition taking up most of the suitcase I had swinging by my side. It would have been safer to wire some cash out of one of my offshore accounts. It also would have been smarter to cover my trail. Both were luxuries I didn't have as I grabbed my keys off the hook, only to have my bedroom door flung open and crack me in the face.

Blood trickled down my forehead, wet and sticky, as I tried to clear the haze from my vision without rubbing at my eyes. When I was finally able to look up from where I was sprawled out on my bedroom floor, I found a familiar face glaring down at me. White bandages covering the curve of his nose and the underside of his jaw and a twisted smirk pinching his mouth. A mouth that appeared just as pained as it did satisfied.

"What the fuck do you want, Tate?" I grunted as I rolled over onto my side and used the meat of my palms to push myself upright. Which aggravated the pounding in my temples and increased the blood flow of the wound dripping over my left eye. I knew better than to elevate a fresh head injury but I also wasn't fully conscious yet.

I could hear the sound of his loafers pacing in front of me, his pants swishing with each long stride, back and forth across the small area rug. But I still couldn't see much of anything past the tunnel vision.

"*At first...* I wanted you dead. I wanted to strangle you with my bare hands as you stared up at the same nose you helped piece back together," he hissed, forcing out a huff of hot air before chuckling to himself. "I was going to do it too. Use the spare key I made back when your cunt of a mother still had, well, a *cunt*. Slip in here when you were sleeping and get the job done." He turned and took a sharp step in the opposite direction. "But then, I had all those weeks with nothing but four white walls, a few very attentive nurses, and my thoughts. And suddenly, it occurred to me, baby brother."

"Yeah, and what's that? The fact that I'd have you knocked on your ass before you made it two steps through the door," I grunted, trying to stand until a wave of vertigo sent me tumbling back.

Fuck!

I saw the irony, considering he was two steps through the door the moment he sent it flying into my face. I just didn't care to acknowledge it. Keeping my feet firmly planted in the delusion seemed like the medically sound route to take right now.

"More like the fact that it would be so much more fun to keep you alive, so you could watch..." he trailed off, and I didn't have to see his face to know that he was gloating.

"Watch what, Tate?" I indulged him. Because the only thing that was going to get me standing again was time. Something I didn't have.

Instead of answering, he stomped back towards the door and slammed it closed. And then I heard the unmistakable thud of a padlock clinking into place.

Motherfucker...

40

MARISELA

"He ain't coming, ya know?"

"Who?" I didn't bother looking back. I recognized the kid's voice as much as I recognized the clanking of his wheels and the popping of his chewing gum.

Pop. Clank. Pop. Clank. With the occasional high-pitched squeak that had you shoving a finger into your ear. The kid could use an upgrade, seeing as that chair was likely older than the first layer of lead paint that coated these walls.

He was also the only one who didn't just barge into my room whenever he was feeling like a creepy little shit. Though something told me that had more to do with the difficulty of navigating the small space and not because he wasn't just another *creepy little shit* in a building chock-full of *creepy little shits*.

No one gave a damn about manners when you had a grocery list of diagnoses scrawled out under your name or a few letters behind it that somehow gave you a god complex larger than the balls you thought you had.

Not that I cared much for manners to begin with. Which was exactly why I continued to peer out the window. Rubbing a thumb over the one person in the room I *didn't* recognize. The girl staring back at me as I traced a broken nail over the growing spider vein in the glass. Mesmerized by the pretty little cracks that splintered off this way and that, while missing the bite of jagged edge against my skin and feeling nothing thanks to the double pane that kept my fingertips as smooth as the spot where my hair was thinning out and falling off in clumps.

My twin didn't feel anything either as she returned my vacant stare. Her eyes sinking into her skull and her lips more cracked and peeling than soft and plump. She'd been aged nearly a decade at the same time her mind was reduced to the complexity of a toddler. Her coordination not much better. Itty-bitty baby steps and the shuffling of feet that meant there was no running away. Feeling as if the world was tipped upside-down or spinning a little too fast so that everything else seemed a million times slower in comparison.

She was still nice to look at though. Like a vintage doll you could bring back to life with a little bit of elbow grease and a touch of paint. Something to prop up on a shelf or perch behind a piece of protective glass when there wasn't much else you could do with it. Like my mother... until even a comb and a bit of makeup wouldn't help her...

I didn't know where she was, what happened to her

after that night. Just that she wasn't here. Or there. At the house with my father. And that was better for both of us. I mean, what good was a doll you couldn't dress up and put on display anymore?

I blinked twice when the little raindrops dotting the glass blurred her image. The girl who'd morphed into a woman who'd morphed back into a version of a girl again, forcing my focus behind me. To the boy in the chair.

"Whoever you're waiting for. 'Cause you're definitely waiting for someone." He seemed to muse to himself before commenting with a *tsk* of his tongue, "You still got that look in your eyes."

"What look?"

He shrugged a single shoulder, a small movement that caught my eye and not much else. Because turning my head took too much effort. "Hope. Like ya still think someone is gonna come riding up that driveway on a white horse or some shit. Is that who you're waiting for, princess? Your knight in shining armor? A hero in a world overrun by villains?"

"There's nothing wrong with hope," I pushed out a reply in one long breath, and another wave of exhaustion settled itself on my shoulders. As if some physical force was weighing me down so that even the air seemed heavier. Thicker. "Don't you ever hope for something?"

I could see him staring at me through the window, his blonde hair more like a bright-white dot. His head canted and his mouth kicking up to one side. A permanent smirk meant to both put you at ease and intimidate you, depending on the day's objective. Until another raindrop made his reflection just as invisible as my own.

He didn't answer. Like the answer should be obvious. Or maybe it was more *ominous*. Maybe it was a way of calling me naïve without ever having to say the words. Because despite the several years I had on him, I was the one who had trouble facing the reality of my fate. *I* was the one who had trouble accepting it. And the realization that neither one of us was walking out of here. For two very different reasons...

I didn't believe in old souls. That was something pedos liked to say to excuse their behavior. What I did believe in was trauma, and this kid had more than enough of it to pass around like candy-flavored sedatives.

Honestly, those didn't sound so bad right now. I'd shove a handful down my own throat if some part of me weren't put off by the idea of being just another name on the broken crosses I was counting again.

When I glanced from the window, back to the door, the kid was gone. Just the ghost of his bouncy ball echoing down the halls and the squeaking of his rusty wheels.

I was starting to wonder if the blonde boy in the wheelchair was another figment of my imagination, dug up and fleshed out by a mind that was slowly liquifying as time went on. Then again, I wasn't sure that it mattered. Not when his company was the only thing keeping me sane.

If I could even call myself *sane*... Wasn't entirely sure I could...

41

ADRIAN

It was funny, the shit you picked up from an elective you decided to take on a whim. Shit like the fact spiders contained nearly one-hundred and thirty percent of your daily protein requirement, crickets thirteen percent, while termites maintained the highest caloric intake at over six hundred calories each—you only needed a handful of those crunchy sons of bitches to sustain the human body for an extended period.

In my case, *days*. At least four. Maybe five. Had plenty of termites during that time, the occasional cricket and a fat spider or two. But cockroaches were where I drew the line. Couldn't stomach them. They were also faster than you'd think. Scurrying past me and dipping into little crevices in the stone. Never realized how many room-mates I had until I had to start hunting for ˊem.

I scrunched my nose and swiped my tongue over the film on my teeth, trying to loosen some of the breakfast particles that embedded themselves in my cheeks. What they didn't tell us in that entomology class was how the tiny legs liked to stick to your gums. And forget swallowing the fuckers whole. Without more than the condensation from the stone walls to force them down, you'd end up with a throat full of thorax pieces and antennae. A scratchy feeling that—believe it or not—was far worse than the earthy aftertaste they left in your mouth. A mix of old basement and fresh insect guts.

There was no part of me that believed big brother *didn't* intend for me to die in here. The same way I had no doubt he didn't just "forget" to feed his pet parrot a few years back. Seven days in a row. Without fail. Strange, considering Louie IV knew how to talk and had no problem yelling out whenever he was hungry. The fucker's squawking carried through the vents and echoed down the halls upstairs. To the point I had to sleep with a pillow over my head some nights.

Didn't last more than a week, the squawking and the bird that should have had a lifespan longer than the rest of the household, seeing as the poor thing had resorted to eating its own tail feathers and pseudo-cannibalism before Justine finally found him ass up at the bottom of his cage. Oddly enough, Tate hadn't forgotten to fill the water bowl. Almost as if the sick fuck wanted to watch the damn bird wither away.

Big brother wasn't as *kind* to me, though. I wasn't given the luxury of a bowl or even the spit pooling at the base of one of his leftover water bottles. I also didn't have the foresight to stash much of anything besides a few drug vials. Which meant dehydration was likely to get me long before starvation had a chance to set in. My kidneys giving in before my heart gave out. Of the two, it was the more physically painful way to go.

I'd give Tate credit for his new level of sadism if I weren't sure the outcome was a stroke of luck rather than part of some sort of master plan of his. Fucker was the very definition of an opportunist. The type to jump at the chance instead of making his own way. And that was something I had on him. I knew how to bide my time. I knew how to analyze without acting. I knew how to survive.

And I would survive this shit too. I just needed to clear away the brain fog long enough to think.

I looked around, taking in the four corners I knew better than the underside of my own hand, which was saying something—*my palm and I were well acquainted over the years.*

But these walls were a different story.

They'd stared back at me the first time I'd opened my eyes. They were my sanctuary as much as my prison. They weren't about to be my tomb. I'd already nixed trying to pop the bolts out of the hinges, seeing as they were conveniently located on the other side of the door. I had no doubt that shit was intentional too. Built to my old man's specifications. The sort meant to keep you in and not let you out.

Apparently, sadism was an inherited trait. That didn't leave much hope for me, now did it?

Hope. I laughed at the fucking word. Probably because the delirium was getting to me. But also because that feeling was as useless as it was essential. Hope alone didn't get ya anywhere. But sprinkle it on top and suddenly a shit sandwich was a little easier to choke down.

It was also all I had at the moment. Hope and a burning rage. The kind that had me pushing to my feet, sweeping an arm across my desk and sending everything crashing to the floor, before I stomped over to the bookcase and shoved it onto its side. The bed was in my sights next when the creaking of a hinge had me spinning on a heel and glancing around an empty room and a still-closed door.

I was losing my goddamn mind. Hearing things. It wasn't unexpected, just inconvenient.

But then I heard it again, a creak followed by a small voice calling out to me. "Adrian?"

I spun around again. And again. Until I was making myself dizzy, leaning my back against the closest wall and sliding onto my ass. My feet spread out in front of me, my head pounding and my heart racing. More symptoms of dehydration.

I could feel my eyelids growing heavy, the stonework cool against my spine as a thin sheen of sweat dried across my forehead—moisture I couldn't afford to lose.

The first slow blink had me looking back at nothing. The second the same but darker as my vision started to tunnel while the third had me scratching at the floor. Trying to pull myself up as I stared into the face of a woman I'd only seen in photos.

A ghost. My mother.

42

ADRIAN

Her eyes were haunting. A chocolaty brown with flecks of honey color no photo could capture right. Her hair long and dark, though it was usually pulled tight and piled high on her head, and her smile tense. The kind of smile that held back far too many secrets with a taut jaw that suggested she was afraid of them tumbling free.

My mother was a stranger to me, a fairy tale I both idolized and despised over the years. But this girl wasn't her. She just *looked* like her. For a brief moment when my brain made the mistake of filling in all the holes with something familiar. Like a childhood memory turned nightmare. Except it was hard to remember shit when you never met the woman.

"Adrian, are you okay?" Trixie whispered as she took a blurry step in my direction.

"Yeah... no..." I lifted a hand to my head, rubbing at

my temples as I tried to orient myself. "How'd you get in here?"

The girl tugged on my sleeve, urging me to stand as she dragged me off the floor and over to the other side of the room. Then I watched in stunned silence as she used all seventy pounds of her body weight to push my bed away from the wall. By the time she was finished, I was staring down at a rolled-up portion of the area rug and an open trap door.

"Don't tell Mama..." Trixie looked at me from over a shoulder, those brown eyes wide and pleading. "I heard a bunch of banging and I got worried something happened to you..."

Didn't know why she gave a damn about me. Sure, I was friendly with the kid's mother. The way you were friendly with someone who shared the same hell you were cursed to live inside. You didn't know much about 'em other than the fact they were just as fucked as you were. Guess that could be comforting in a way. Not that I ever really stopped to think about it...

I didn't have time to think about it now either.

I braced a palm on a bedpost as I peered into the square-shaped hole in the ground. I couldn't make out the bottom. Just a long stretch of blackness that told me the tunnel went deep. And far. Under the entirety of Prescott Estates, if I were to hazard a guess.

I sucked a steadying breath into my lungs, forcing it out before glancing back to the girl. "Where's that go?"

Trixie shrugged, twisting her yellow sundress between her hands while gnawing on her bottom lip.

"All over. Mama said we were only supposed to use it if Mr. Prescott came looking for us."

Tate, not my father. The old man didn't have it in him to go around skirt-chasing downstairs anymore. Mostly because it was *downstairs*. And the fucker's failing health couldn't handle all that cardio. Install a freight elevator and I was sure Daddy Dearest would be back at it again.

Though Justine's girls were young even for his tastes. Trixie was almost twelve, small for her age, a little naïve too. In and out of doctors' offices and hospitals for most of her life. No one seemed to know exactly what was wrong with her, and she was locked up in that room too much for me to try to figure it out for myself. Not that her mother would let anyone with Prescott blood in their veins touch the kid. For reasons that didn't need mentioning. And Alice? The girl was sixteen going on thirty. At least she thought so. She was also exactly how my brother liked 'em. Pliable, with the body of an adult and the mind of a child.

I saw the hypocrisy when it came to my infatuation with a certain schoolgirl. I just didn't care. Shit wasn't as easy for me as it was for Tate. I deserved to be selfish once in a while.

I also wasn't attracted to Marisela because of her age. Because of a power dynamic that meant she couldn't say *no* to me. I was attracted to her because of how much of a challenge it was to manipulate her to say *yes*. To scream it. Over and over.

Trixie tugged on my sleeve again, breaking me from the kind of thoughts I shouldn't be having in the same room as a child.

"Your head's bleeding." She lifted her chin to look up at me. One eyebrow raised like this kid was somehow judging my life choices.

She was also wrong. I wasn't bleeding. Anymore. Coagulation set in days ago. What I did have was a large door-shaped indent in my scalp that probably wouldn't heal right without a few strategically placed stitches.

I scraped some of the dried blood off my skin before gesturing for Trixie to climb down first. She got herself here. I could only assume she could get us both *there*. Outside this room, if not outside these walls.

It took Trixie less than a minute to slide down the metal ladder, and I shimmied the trap door back in place before following her. I'd have to worry about covering my tracks later, because there was no way my ass was fitting under the bed if I tried to reposition the furniture how it was.

A few quick turns, as I held on the wall to keep myself upright, and then we were popping up on the other side of the servants' quarters. Most of the old man's employees lived onsite, and it wasn't because Tate Prescott was the generous type. It was because he liked holding it over your head. Controlling all aspects of your livelihood. A *do as you're told or you'll be out on your ass* sort of thing. It also kept you close enough to answer his every beck and call at a moment's notice.

I left the troublemaker to her own devices as I slipped

out Justine's bedroom door, glancing down each side of the corridor before creeping towards the kitchen. As much as I wanted out of this house, I needed something in my stomach first or I wouldn't make it past the threshold.

My fingers had just closed around the handle of the pantry door when a solid palm slammed down on my shoulder, freezing me in my tracks.

"Where have you been, boy?" Prescott's voice boomed from behind me. He didn't care to wait for an answer before grabbing me by the back of the neck and guiding me towards the stairs. "Borrow one of Tate's old suits. We have a special guest coming for dinner tonight and the whole family's invited."

43

ADRIAN

I brushed a loose strand of dark hair over the gash in my forehead as I eyed myself in the mirror. Smoothing the black tie along the seam of the matching vest, the silver glint of the polished buttons catching the light as I adjusted each of the sleeves of my black dress shirt and secured the cufflinks. As much as the thought of stepping foot in my room sickened me, I refused to wear someone else's throwaways. Especially when that someone else was the twisted son of a bitch looking to starve me to death like a discarded pet he couldn't be bothered to euthanize.

At the same time, I wasn't naïve enough to think the old man didn't have some ulterior motive behind tonight's dog and pony show. We didn't do "family dinners." At least not where they concerned me. I was no more part of the Prescott family than the used tube socks tossed around Tate's en-suite bathroom.

But if the old man insisted I dressed for whatever

bullshit he had up his sleeve tonight, it would be in a three-piece fitted suit I had custom tailored to my measurements... in exchange for a few sexual favors with a local seamstress. Her handiwork was impeccable. *Mine was better.*

Either way, the widow's lax bartering system served to keep my closet fully stocked over the years without having to dip into my savings. If I needed new shoes, I'd slide a handful of tranquilizers under the right salesman's door while a few bottles of pills gave me free rein over most of the local clubs. Drug use might not have been tolerated but it sure as fuck was enjoyed by the occasional rule breaker at Original Sin.

And when I stepped through those doors, my mask in place and my identity as obscure as my sexual preferences, I wasn't the bastard son of Tate Prescott anymore. I was "the doctor," thanks to my choice of profession and face-wear. A few more years, and I'd be upgraded to the rich folk's favorite plastic surgeon. Spending my days pumping tits with silicone and foreheads with Botox while lining my pockets with the fuckers' cash.

That was what I reminded myself as I shoveled another protein bar into my mouth, glanced at my reflection one more time, and then strolled back upstairs with my hands in my pockets. Appearing as unbothered by big brother's cheap shot as he was *bothered* by my existence.

The jingle of the silver chain of my pocket watch announced my presence before I stepped foot in the formal dining room, set for four when there were only three of us in attendance. Tate leaned an arm over the mantel. A small white bandage covering the incision on his nose as he grinned in my direction. His eyes flicked behind me, then back again. Until I had no choice but to spin around to see what he was seeing.

My gaze dropped to a set of modest heels. Raked over two long stocking-covered legs and the flowy hem of a rose-petal pink dress before hinging on a silhouetted waist that curved outward to cradle a perfect set of tits, a gold pendant necklace, and a few loose curls of dark hair. And then my focus was forced up to a pair of green eyes. Eyes that had lost that last flicker of life I was certain I'd seen there a few days ago.

I was too far gone to notice Tate had stepped up behind me until his arm circled around my neck in a headlock as he pushed up on his tiptoes, lifted his mouth to my ear, and whispered, "Pretty little thing, isn't she?" He smirked. I could feel the tightening of his jaw muscles against my cheek. "*Mary*, this is Adrian, our houseboy. Whatever you need, the good man will be sure to get it for you." He tapped the back of a hand on my chest before shoving me a step forward. "Adrian, I'd like you to meet my fiancée, *Mary*. But you'll address her as the future Mrs. Prescott."

PART THREE

Chicago Tribune

ARRANGED MARRIAGES

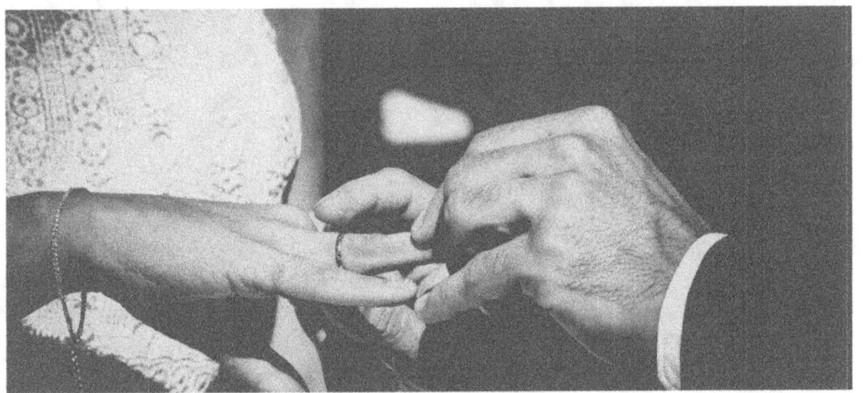

Politicians and wealthy backers joining families instead of shaking hands.

NEW TREND OR TIME-HONORED TRADITION?

Divorce isn't an option with more than marriage on the line.

In recent years, a notable shift has occurred within elite circles: arranged marriages, once considered a relic of tradition, are experiencing a resurgence among the wealthy. This trend is becoming more evident in the United States amongst prominent Chicagoan families, where modern matchmaking services are blending traditional practices with contemporary values as well as creating political alliances amongst the city top candidates.

The landscape of arranged marriages has evolved significantly. Professional matchmakers now utilize sophisticated algorithms and psychological assessments to pair individuals based on compatibility, education, and family background. In cities like New York and London, high-end matchmaking services cater to affluent clients seeking partners who align with their social status and values—and now their voting status.

CONTINUE READING ON PAGE 12

44

MARISELA

The sun had just crested over the hill, the sky a rosy pink that reflected onto the little plot of white crosses then flicked back up towards the window, when four men in matching blue scrubs had burst through the hospital room door. I'd barely turned around before one of them was pinching my jaw open while the other shoved a handful of drugs down my throat, strapping me to a gurney and shooting something else into my veins when I'd spit most of the pills back up the way they came.

Couldn't do much about that one. Though if you were to put a razorblade within arm's reach, I might have found a way to cut the liquid out of me.

Then again, whatever it was made it so I didn't care. So that the colors were both brighter and duller in some fashion. My skin heating up while also cool to the touch.

And I smiled, without making any expression at all. My lips just pulled taut, like someone else was tugging on an invisible puppet string that kept my legs perfectly crossed and my hands resting neatly on my lap.

In a matter of a few hours, I'd been discharged, washed down and dressed up, and then deposited on another doorstep. A whirlwind of activity that had me feeling like I was standing still while everything and everyone else darted around me. Except I wasn't standing at all. I was sitting. In some sort of parlor that smelled like the inside of the boys' lavatory. Musty with more testosterone than oxygen, and a stale odor that hinted at the fact that several types of bodily fluids had been left to dry where they'd landed.

The gray hospital room had faded away. Replaced by darker, richer hues and coordinating wallpaper. The cold floors morphing into warm hardwoods and plush area rugs. The blue scrubs traded in for starched dresses and pleated pants. The faint screams growing more melodic...

I blinked at the sound of an old grandfather clock chiming from somewhere down the hall, announcing the fact that it was nearly time for dinner and I'd yet to move from the spot where the woman in the black-and-white maid uniform had left me, while the ornate fireplace crackled in the background. The orange glow bouncing off the crystal accents and vaulted ceilings, dusty book-shelves and decorative vases, occasionally lighting up the taxidermized animal carcasses and ancestral portraits that each bared little resemblance to whatever creature they were trying to emulate.

Just wall upon wall of deadened eyes and similarly

forced smiles. Some stitched in place and others bogged down by lead paint and an artist's quick brushstroke.

I couldn't help but feel as though they were all staring down at me while at the same time wondering if they were inviting me to stay or warning me I might be the next stuffed head to join them...

Until a thunderous bang had me sinking deeper into the sofa cushion that was more stiff than forgiving as I bit back a yelp. A storm was brewing outside, thrashing against the rooftop so that all I could hear past my own morbid thoughts were the low grunts and mumbled words of the two men in front of me. Talking in hushed whispers meant for their ears only and certainly not for mine.

I watched them anyway. Studying how the flames cast an eerie shadow over my father's unfurled arm, obscuring his face entirely, while making the appendage somehow appear more cephalopod than human in the dreariness of the smoked-filled air that seemed to curl around them like a python ready to strike.

A few curt nods and then he was clasping a tentacled hand around an equally slimy palm. Squeezing until his knuckles were as white as the generational wealth seeping out of every crevice of this room.

It was a gentleman's agreement, made over cigars and whiskey-laden tumblers, while neither of the shadowy figures was forthright when it came to what the other was really getting out of this deal. Because it sure as hell wasn't whatever it appeared to be. A daughter for some political backing didn't make much sense.

Not when there was no such thing as a one-for-one trade between men like Mr. Prescott and my father, which meant someone thought they were coming out on top. I just had yet to figure out who that someone was. Or what it was they thought they were getting.

I had plenty of time for that, though. Seeing as Papa didn't so much as glance at me over a shoulder as he slid into the back seat of his town car and pulled off down the driveway a few minutes later, disappearing past the gates of Prescott Estates. My new home. Where I'd be groomed to take on my role as lady of the house. A title that was just one step up from being my soon-to-be husband's fuck doll—though it was probably just as mind-numbingly dull.

And then I watched from a slightly more gilded window than the one I used to stare out at Briarwood as the clouds blanketed the night sky, the occasional bolt of lightning shattering the silence of the tomb-like room in the mausoleum-like house I was told would be mine in a world where I was made to remember I didn't *own* anything. Certainly not this estate or the last name that would replace my father's in a few months' time.

Being the wife of Tate Prescott meant more than slipping out from under one thumb, only to be oppressed by another. It meant giving up the girl I *was* to wear the mask of the woman they wanted me to be...

45

MARISELA

He was pretty. Prettier than any grown man should be. With long, dark lashes. Deep brown eyes and a square, shaved jawline. Medium-toned skin that told me he was mixed with... something. A strong nose and a prominent brow. The type of sharp features that meant you could *feel* it when he looked at you. Like he could somehow peel back every layer of clothing on your body without ever touching it.

It was the most I'd felt of anything in days. Familiarity with a smattering of confusion. An odd sense of being comfortably exposed while I fought the instinct to cross my arms over my chest.

But that wouldn't be ladylike. The voice whispered in my ear. *Ladies kept their hands at their sides, a smile on their lips and their legs closed. Tight.*

As tight as the constricting of my throat as I tried to swallow past my anxiety. I wanted to shake the noise out of my head. But they'd dug a hole. Fed and nurtured the insanity until it took root. Until it sprung free on its own and twisted itself around my common sense. Like a parasitic vine in a rose garden. Taking over to the point trying to rip it free would do more damage than good.

They'd played those tapes over and over again. And then it all mingled together so that I didn't know the difference between my own voice and theirs. My own thoughts and the ones they'd implanted.

Exposure therapy I'd heard them say. But torture is what I would have called it. A slow, methodical torture as disembodied chatter took over the silence. I didn't know what silence was like anymore. Just the white noise of static and the buzzing of the electrodes on my forehead.

What I did know was that those dark eyes were looking at me again. Staring at me from across the table. Watching me. Calling me forward to the point my toes were dancing in my Mary Janes while the man beside me —the same man I was supposed to marry—didn't spare more than a glance in my direction.

Which was fine. I didn't care much for him either. Mutual disgust wasn't the worst way to coexist.

I blinked and suddenly the clinking of silverware and glasses alerted me to the time. Dinner was over and I didn't even remember eating. I couldn't be certain I ever did. Just that the table was being cleared and I was being shuffled towards the parlor door, where tea and coffee were now being served.

I cleared my throat, trying to force out a full sentence and coming up with a handful of words. "The powder room...?" All eyes turned my way as I did my best to appear more human than doll. But not so human that I insulted the self-importance of the men surrounding me. "May I please use your powder room, Mr. Prescott?"

The older man in the navy-blue jacket with gold buttons eyed me for a moment, a sour expression twisting up his lips though I didn't know why, before he waved a hand in the air. "Make it quick."

"Yes, sir." I dipped my head into a polite nod, slowly turning on a heel and walking out of the room.

I couldn't breathe. Not with all of them looking at me. Not with *him* looking at me. I felt like I was drowning and dying of thirst at the same time. Like I was both trapped inside my body and floating above it. As a bunch of rich fuckers in stuffy suits discussed their plans for me.

I grabbed the powder room door and wrenched it open, prepared to slam it closed again when a polished shoe forced its way inside, followed by the body it was attached to. I recognized that shoe. The Italian leather and hand-stitching. But more than that, I recognized the way his voice dropped an octave when he spoke to me. The way he tasted my name and the heat of his palm as he brushed it over my cheek.

"I know you..." It was a statement, even if it sounded more like a question.

He stepped forward and I stepped back. Not because I was afraid. *I wasn't afraid.* More like trapped. And I couldn't stand the thought of being trapped again.

"What did they do to you, little lamb?" He might have been looking at me, but he was talking to himself.

My eyes widened before I schooled my features again. *Ladies didn't emote.* The voices were quieter now, looming in the background instead of the forefront of my mind, as the smell of his cologne wrapped itself around me. Creating a cloud of a different kind.

He clicked the lock on the door in place, and then he was stalking forward again. Closer and closer until I was pressed against the corner of the powder room.

"Where's the mask?" I hissed, unable to keep my own from slipping. I was angry, hurt, and angry again because I didn't like feeling hurt.

He tilted his head to look at me for a moment, his dark eyebrows pinched together as he reached out a hand to brush a stray curl out of my face. I flinched. Human touch was an odd sensation nowadays. Alien when it used to be the only thing that let me know I was alive.

His lips pursed, like he was chewing on the inside of his cheeks as he watched my reaction. "Don't think it really matters anymore, does it, Marisela?"

"You're right. It doesn't." I clenched my jaw, my eyes flicking behind him as I waited for the door to pull open at any moment. Surely someone would come looking for us. For me, at least. I didn't have the luxury of even pissing on my own. "You were working with them the whole time, weren't you?" I shoved at his chest. *Adrian's* chest. Because I had a name to go with my shadow man's bullshit now. A face too.

"No." A one-word reply. No more explanation than that.

"Yes," I hissed a little more forcefully. "After we…

after *you*...” I shook my head. “You told me to wait in my bedroom that night. Promised me you were coming back for me. But you never did, did you?”

“No,” he agreed, but it didn't matter because I was already speaking again.

“And do you know what happened next?” I didn't wait for him to answer me. “Papa found all that blood in the hallway, called his friend and told him Mama attacked me. That she ran off so he could send me to that place *to recover from the shock.*” I was shaking, my chest heaving and my fists flexing at my sides. “No one even bothered to question where the blood came from or why I didn't have any wounds on me. Then again, I'm sure they were paid not to ask. *You* were paid not to ask,” I spit the accusation in his face.

He didn't blink. “No.”

“*Yes!* You were there. At the hospital. I remember those eyes. Your voice. You helped them bring me there, and then you didn't come back.” I pounded on his shoulders as he dropped to his knees in front of me, tightening my grip on the exhausted tear that wanted to break free and channeling the rage instead. “Why didn't you come back?”

“No,” he repeated, as he stared up at me, and then he was lifting up my skirt and tugging down my stockings before I could register what this man was doing on the bathroom floor.

46

MARISELA

My palms shot out and slapped against each side of the wall, as my head tipped back and my spine arched with the first swipe of Adrian's tongue. The next few had me digging my hands in his hair, clawing at his scalp as I guided him left and then a little right, before that nimble appendage was twirling itself inside me and I was riding his face like it was a one-way ticket out of the hell that had become my reality.

Except it wasn't. It was just a short reprieve. I wasn't saved. I was just vacationing in the land of euphoria. Biding my time until the demons were ready to drag me back through those iron gates again.

I shook my head, trying to shake the negativity away too. Because I needed this. I needed to escape for a little bit. I needed my thighs trembling. I needed my brain turned to mush. I needed that tingly sensation rushing through my every nerve ending and I needed the nothingness that followed it.

It didn't come, though, and neither did I. Almost as if my body didn't understand what it was supposed to do anymore. Like it'd forgotten how to reach that peak or how to jump over once it got there. Like some connection had been severed and was as limp as the old fucker who'd forgotten to take his little blue pills before dropping trou.

Thing was, I didn't think there was a pill for this. For my problem. For men, yes. But the scientific world didn't seem to care if us girls had an issue reaching climax. Instead, we were meant to lie back and wait until it was over. Pretend that it felt good.

And, right now, it did feel good. It *all* felt good.

Adrian's grip on my thighs, the back-and-forth motion, that thing he did with the tip of his tongue, how he alternated between quick flicks and slow laps. How he buried himself up to his nose with no regard for his ability to breathe past my clit. The feel of his hot breath on my skin and the chilled breeze that followed each inhale. How he didn't stop, no matter how much time had passed. The obnoxious sounds he made, a mix between a moan and whimper, and the way he drank me down like he couldn't get enough. Like he'd never tasted anything better.

I could feel him watching me, flicking his eyes up to look at my face, which I was sure was contorted in some kind of way. My nostrils flared and my brows creased. My lip drawn between my teeth and sweat dotting my forehead as I did my best to grind down each time he plunged upward, using his chin to add a little more friction.

I gave myself a few more minutes, a little more suction and a couple more licks before I was shoving at Adrian's shoulders and landing him on his ass on the black-and-white tile.

"I can't," I huffed in a breath, my chest heaving for a different reason as I tugged my stockings and underwear back up my thighs and flattened my skirt in place. There was no fixing my hair now that it stuck to my cheeks, which were at least three shades darker. Something I didn't need a mirror to tell me when I could feel the heat radiating off my skin.

The only thing worse than facing a room full of people looking like I'd had my soul sucked from my clit was the fact that I hadn't. That I was painfully frustrated and unsatisfied.

Adrian canted his head to one side, not bothering to stand upright as he eyed me from the floor. His palms splayed out behind him and his legs spread out in front of him. "What do you mean *you can't?*"

"I mean, *I can't*," I repeated as I stepped over his arm on the way to the door.

He reached out a hand and wrapped it around my ankle, his voice low and bitter when he asked me, "Is it because you know who I am now?"

The question was vague. But it didn't take me long to figure out what it was he meant. He thought it was because of his station in life. Because I was literally standing above him. Because he was a houseboy and I was an heiress.

And I laughed before I could stop myself. It wasn't funny. It was pathetic. It was also so far from the truth it might as well be one of the promises Mr. Prescott made to my father in the back room when they didn't think I was listening.

"No, it's because I'm broken, Adrian. They *broke* me. And there isn't shit either of us can do about it now." I didn't wait for his reply as I tugged the powder room door open and slammed it shut behind me.

Fuck him. Fuck all of them. Because they didn't just take my freedom away; they took the only escape I had as well, and I wasn't sure there was any drug on this earth that could fix me. Or at the very least, help me forget.

47

ADRIAN

She wasn't moving, her supine figure sprawled out in the middle of the king-sized canopy bed. Her toes pointed outward and her arms tucked neatly at her sides. But I knew she wasn't sleeping either. She was just staring. Looking up at nothing, almost like her brain had forgotten what it was like to rest.

I could help her with that. Mix together something that would knock her out long enough for her body to start to relax and begin to repair itself. But I had a feeling that wouldn't be the best way to go about getting her to trust me again. And I would get her to trust me.

That's all she needed to be able to let loose, to give in to all the dirty things she enjoyed me doing to her. Finding out who I was, was a shock to her system. She just needed another chance to forget. We both did.

My little lamb wasn't broken—I refused to believe that—but she was... cracking. Coming apart in a different kind of way, and I just had to figure out how to piece her back together.

I watched her for a few more moments. Tucked up behind the portrait of some old woman several generations down the Prescott line, my face covered by my favorite mask and my hands shoved into the pockets of my sweats. It was the only thing keeping me from reaching out and touching her. From trying to prove to her and myself that birth order didn't mean shit when you had other... attributes.

Marisela had options and my brother wasn't one of them. He might have had the last name and the inheritance that came with it but that was about all the fucker had. No drive, no brains, not even size to make up for it. Tate was just a placeholder, someone who could be swapped out for someone else with just as many zeros in their bank account and no one would know the difference. Whereas I had everything the fucker was lacking. Everything but the pedigree.

At least not part of it, and apparently that was the only part that mattered.

I took a deep breath, holding it for as long as I could to avoid breathing in the odor of stale air and rodent droppings before forcing it out through my nostrils as quietly as I could. Thanks to Trixie, I'd found my own uses for these tunnels the staff had done their best to keep secret over the years. I understood why, of course. I just didn't like being placed in the same category as my brother and the old man.

Ironic, considering I wasn't one of them but close enough that their sins were mine too. It was like toeing an impossible line that meant you never belonged on either side. Like they couldn't decide what box you fit in so they excluded you from both.

I waited until the clock started counting off the hour, using the loud chimes as cover as I slipped out from behind the hidden door and slowly made my way towards the bed. Either Marisela couldn't hear me or she didn't care enough to look as my fingers inched forward to brush the stray curl from her face. Staring in horror when it came away with my hand.

"That happens a lot."

I glanced down at the chunk of hair still wrapped around my fingers before returning my focus to Marisela. She wasn't looking at me, even as she spoke. Something I was used to and increasingly irritated by. I grabbed her chin, pinching her jaw until she had no choice but to turn her head.

"Do you feel better?" she asked, one eyebrow cocked and her tone as dry as the pussy I could just make out through the thin fabric of her nightgown.

"No. Do you?" I threw back at her.

She tugged her face out of my grip, and I let her. Now that I had her attention, whether or not she was looking at me didn't matter. "What do you want, Adrian? Why are you here?"

I lifted a shoulder into a half shrug, my hands tucked back into my pockets, along with her lock of hair, as I rocked on my heels. "Just trying to get to know the future lady of the house better," I grunted.

"By creeping on her when she's sleeping?"

"Maybe. Except she wasn't sleeping." Another shrug,

this time accompanied by a grin as I took a step towards the bed. "Tell me, why aren't you sleeping, little lamb?"

"Why aren't you?" She tried deflecting again. It wouldn't work.

"Because dreaming about that tight cunt of yours isn't nearly as sweet as the real thing. Because tasting you again wasn't nearly enough to satisfy either of us. And because I refuse to let Tate try his hand at something I didn't get to finish first."

Marisela pushed herself upright on the bed, so that I could now see the outline of her perfect breasts—thanks to the moonlight streaming in from her window. "If you're here just to prove that you measure up to your boss, you can find one of his whores for that."

"I don't want one of his whores." I placed a knee on the mattress before swinging my other leg over Marisela's body to straddle her. Then I leaned forward while stretching her arms high over her head as I pressed my lips to her ear. "I want *my* whore."

"I'm not your whore," she hissed back.

"No, but you want to be, don't you, princess? You enjoyed sneaking around, playing our little game of cat and mouse. You enjoyed fucking yourself on my mouth and the way my tongue was rammed so far up that cunt of yours, you couldn't be certain you were a virgin anymore. You just need to relax and remember what that feels like again. Remember what it was like to be strangers who knew each other more intimately than friends."

She threw her head back, her body shaking so forcefully it was shaking me too. She was laughing at my expense for the second time in a matter of hours. "It's so sad it's funny," she wheezed in a breath. "You think you're so different from the rest of 'em. So much smarter, more evolved. When the truth is... you are exactly the same. Maybe worse, because at least Tate embraces the fact he's an egotistical maniac while you're clearly still in denial that you're one too."

<h1 style="text-align:center">48</h1>

MARISELA

I watched Adrian tug the mask off his face and toss it aside. A single strand of dark hair breaking free and clinging to his forehead as he glared down at me with more than a hint of irritation knitting his brows and tightening his jaw. He was pissed, his self-esteem taking a back seat to whatever repressed insecurities he had underneath that composed surface of his. And I needed more of it.

I needed the angst, the push and the pull, the fight. Something, anything to make me feel... *anything*. I also didn't care much for self-preservation anymore. I just wasn't ready to admit that part aloud. I wasn't ready to admit how good giving up sounded.

I wasn't suicidal. I didn't want to die. I just didn't want to live like... this. I didn't like the idea of someone owning me... even if in some way, they always had.

Adrian's palm shot to my neck, squeezing just enough as he pinched my mouth open with his free hand. And I sucked in a strangled breath at the same time his tongue darted inside. Tasting me from throat to teeth before ending the kiss on a groan.

And then, just like that, the tension was gone. His lips quirking into a half smirk and his expression softening as he dropped his grip on my cheeks and used that hand to caress the same skin he'd brutalized a few seconds ago.

I'd provoked him, coaxed the rage to the surface, only to have something else tamp it down again. What? Couldn't tell you. All I could say was that this man went from wanting to choke the life out of me to looking at me like if he squeezed too hard I might break. And that fact bothered him almost as much as his backing down bothered me.

"You still want me," he hummed, like it was an observation he was making to some invisible spectator rather than a question he was directing at me.

"What I want is a goddamn orgasm," I hissed in reply. It was the truth. It was also an impossible feat. Believe me, I'd tried. Over and over and even my own fingers had failed me. It wasn't a fluke. I was legitimately broken, the lust I enjoyed ripped away so that I felt like I'd lost the same femininity they wanted me to embrace.

Being a woman didn't mean being innocent, soft-spoken, obedient. At least it didn't have to mean that. It was just easier to handle us that way. And right now, I didn't want to be handled. I wanted to be *man*handled. Thrown up against a wall and fucked until my legs were jelly. Treated like a reinforced fuck toy instead of a china doll.

I was pretty sure that was what I wanted, even if I hadn't experienced it before. Point was, I wanted *the chance* to experience it. The option to be more than arm candy to some spoiled little rich boy.

"How about several?" Adrian lifted a questioning brow as he slid down my body and pressed himself between my clenched thighs. Didn't matter how much friction I tried to create there. I barely felt it or him. Or his mouth when he lifted up the hem of my nightgown as he started kissing me in a much more salacious way.

"I already told you I can't..." I groaned as he probed his tongue so deep inside me I could hear his jaw crack. His nose pressed against my pubic bone and his nails digging into my thighs.

It was a slightly more sensual repeat of our little tryst in the powder room, except this time I was grabbing onto a headboard instead of a wall. His movements slow instead of frenzied. His posture relaxed instead of agitated.

And just like in the powder room, it felt good. Slightly less intense but good. Just not good enough. It was as hard to explain as it was to accept for someone who'd always been over-sensitized. Because it wasn't a matter of skill or time or interest. And it wasn't like I didn't know what I was looking for. All those little signs and signals my body made right before it... Got. Me. There.

No, I wasn't fumbling around in the dark, trying to find something I didn't recognize, even though we were quite literally *fumbling around in the dark*. Rather, I was searching for something that just didn't want to be found. So that as soon as my fingers closed around it, it wiggled free and I was left empty-handed.

There was that building sensation I remembered like a long-lost friend. Slightly more distant, somewhat less defined. The instinctual tightening and loosening of muscles and the quickening of breaths. And then, just when the roller coaster should be making its quick descent, plummeting to the bottom while the wind blew through my hair, there was... nothing. The tracks evened out and the cart pulled to a stop. And before I knew what was happening, some guy in a polo shirt was pulling me out of my seat and asking me if I enjoyed the ride.

While I was left asking, "What ride?"

It was disappointing. Depressing. Frustrating in the worst possible way. I wanted to punch something and I wanted to cry. Didn't matter if it was both at once or not.

I pushed up from the bed, and Adrian shoved me back down again. "I get it," I huffed. "You feel less like a man if you can't get me off. But this isn't about you."

He glanced up at me from between my thighs, moving his mouth away just long enough to reply. "You're right. It's about *you*. Because if it was about me, I'd be fucking you into that mattress right now instead of giving myself lockjaw."

"No one asked you to do that."

"You never have to ask me, princess. I'd sooner sever the muscles than risk stopping now."

49

ADRIAN

I couldn't fuck her. Not until I was sure we'd get there together. Otherwise, all the chemicals in her brain would associate sex with disappointment and frustration, making it that much harder for her to achieve climax the next time. And the next.

It was an amazing organ, the brain, shaped by external stimuli and emotion in a way no lump of tissue should be. It was also what made it so complex, so infuriatingly difficult to navigate. Because what worked like a well-tuned clock one moment could be suddenly out of sync. Like someone had hit reboot. Except instead of a factory reset, we were looking at an entirely different model.

It didn't matter, though. Because the thing was, I loved all of them. I loved Marisela, every model, and in all forms. Loved. *Not liked.* And she loved me too. She just hadn't figured that out yet.

I could tell my little lamb had enjoyed what I'd done

to her in that bathroom, what I'd done to her again that night, what I was doing to her several more nights later after each time I crept into her room. She enjoyed the way my tongue swirled around her clit, gently so as not to overstimulate her. How I alternated between the heat of my mouth and the cool air of my breath. How I kept my glands salivating and her body hydrated and how I shaved extra close to ensure my face remained smooth against the softness of her thighs.

The repetitive ECT treatments just dulled that enjoyment over time, messed with her neurons.

Practice was key. Rewiring her brain so that it remembered what it liked or discovered it liked something else. Didn't matter to me one way or the other as long as I got to see her face when she finally gave in. Those sounds she couldn't stop herself from making...

I was addicted to it. And to her. Her taste. Her smell. All of it.

Which only added to my growing annoyance whenever I had to watch her with Tate. Not that the fucker seemed all that interested in the actual engagement. Just in making me squirm. Almost like he knew something he had no way of knowing.

Speaking of squirming...

Marisela began bucking her hips, moving them in time with my slow laps and urging me to pick up speed as her freshly-painted nails clawed themselves against my scalp. I waited until she was panting, climbing but not too high, before I removed the suction toy I'd brought with me from a pocket. Replacing my mouth and tugging her thighs higher on my shoulders. She wasn't expecting it or the feel of my tongue flicking around and then carefully piercing the tight little ring of muscle around her asshole.

There were so many things my girl had yet to experience, so many nerve endings I'd yet to light up. I just had to be patient. We had to be patient. And there was nothing wrong with being patient. It didn't make you weak; it made you determined.

Her legs were trembling, her toes curling against my back as I plunged my tongue deeper into that forbidden hole. Coaxing her orgasm to the surface with a mix of double penetration with my fingers and stimulation of the toy and my mouth. Her spine arched off the mattress, her body twisting and contorting like it was possessed.

And it was. She was. She was mine and so was every bit of her I was drinking down.

I didn't stop my efforts, didn't change them in any way either. Worried that the slightest deviation would send her spiraling in the wrong direction.

I grunted against her skin, not caring how loud either of us sounded or if the noise carried down the hall to Tate's bedroom as his bride fucked herself on my tongue, until Marisela slammed a palm down on the mattress. Her leg yanking back off my shoulder as she pressed a bare foot on my face to pry me away.

Her juices coated my cheeks, dripping down my chin and hands so that I couldn't help but continue to smell her, no matter how much distance she was presently trying to put between us.

"Enough, Adrian." Marisela shook her head as she

paced back and forth across the bedroom floor. "It's over. I'm done."

I eyed her for a moment. Taking in how wild her hair was, even with a few patches still missing. How puffy her cheeks were after she had been biting on them for so long. And how beautiful she looked in a state of *almost* undress. Like a present you were too eager to unwrap all the way.

"It's done when I say it's done, little lamb." I kept my tone calm, controlled. "And we are not done."

She crossed her arms over her chest as I stood from the bed and took two long strides towards her. I could see the distress in her eyes, the desperation and despondence too. It wasn't just about sex, some form of it at least, or about orgasms. It was about what Briarwood had taken from her. What they had taken from me too. Because getting lost in this woman was more satisfying than anything I'd ever felt before.

Pain. Self-gratification. Revenge. Someone else's blood on my hands... nothing compared to the feel of her coming on my lips.

"We are done. We have to be done," she tried again.

"Why?" I lowered my mouth to hers, forcing her to taste herself as I kissed her soft again. She melted into my arms but only long enough for her stubbornness to settle in as she attempted to shove me back. I didn't let go.

"Because I'm broken," she whispered, repeating that same mantra she'd been telling me for weeks.

"Then let me fix you," I whispered back as I forced her chin up to look at me.

"Sometimes you can't fix people, Adrian." She was wrong. I could fix people. I had been fixing people. "Sometimes it's better to just put them down."

It took me a moment. A moment too long to realize what she was asking of me. The same thing she'd asked me that night in her room... the sudden blur of images confirming what the DNA tests had told me a few days ago. The body I'd tossed in that well was her mother. And I'd sliced her throat because my little lamb couldn't bring herself to do it. But I could. I'd never even questioned it.

And now I could feel her grip on the knife in my pocket, stroking it like I wanted her to stroke me. I grabbed Marisela's wrist, squeezing until she had no choice but to pull her hand away.

I wouldn't do it. I refused to do it. "Don't."

"Don't what, Adrian?" she huffed.

"Don't ask me to do that. It's not going to go the way you think it is," I warned her.

"And what way is that?"

"You already know I'm willing to kill for you. What do you think I'm willing to do to ensure you stay alive for me? To ensure I get to keep you?" I watched her eyes widen. "Whatever you're picturing, yeah, I promise you it's much, much worse."

"I'm not yours to keep, Adrian. I'm getting married. To your boss. In less than a month." She sighed. "And I'm pretty sure he's gonna notice some creep crawling into our bed at night."

She was trying to be funny. She wasn't.

"Not my boss." I shrugged while twirling one of her

curls in my hand. Careful not to tug it too hard. The vita-mins I was slipping into her orange juice were doing wonders to bring my girl back to life again.

"What do you mean?"

"Tate's not my boss, little lamb. He's my brother." I didn't give her a chance to respond before I was silencing her with another kiss.

50

MARISELA

He's my brother. I didn't know what to make of that.

They didn't look alike, sound alike, or even move in the same circles. Which wasn't uncommon for half-siblings. Especially when one of them was illegitimate. Still, Adrian and Tate couldn't be more different for two people who supposedly grew up in the same household. Almost as if upstairs and downstairs were more than separate floors. They were separate planets.

Whereas Tate barely acknowledged me, I was Adrian's entire world. Neither was healthy. But one was certainly much more appealing.

Even now, as my future husband and I were ushered around from place to place. Making all the last-minute arrangements for an event we were somehow equally blasé about attending, I could sense Adrian's eyes on me while Tate's were glued to Barbie's ass. Our wedding planner.

That wasn't the woman's name. But I didn't care to learn it. I didn't care about any of it, if I were being honest. What I did care about was how bleak my future felt.

It was probably why I continued to let Adrian slip into my bed at night, why I didn't push back when he said we weren't done. It was the thrill of doing something I wasn't supposed to be doing that kept me from finding the highest point of this building and plunging off.

"What do you think, dear?" Tate turned to me, tugging my body closer to his side. One hand around my waist, the other gesturing to Barbie. Whose impatience—and annoyance—had her tapping a heeled foot on the tiled floor in front of us.

Tap, tap, tap. The woman was giving me a headache.

"Whatever you think, darling," I replied through gritted teeth and a forced smile. Truth was, I didn't even hear the question.

"That's my girl." Tate pinched my ass through my skirt before shoving me aside again. And then he was following Barbie, practically salivating every time she flipped her hair over her shoulder and giggled in his direction. They prattled on about color schemes and linen choices until their voices dropped off when they turned a corner.

He was going to fuck her. Right now. In some supply closet or prep room. Probably not for the first time. And all I could think was: *Better her than me.*

I rolled my eyes as I strolled towards the middle of the empty ballroom, my shoes clacking across the floor, as I tried to envision what this place would look like filled to the brim with hundreds of people I didn't know. Flowers in every corner and soft music playing in the background. A fairy tale for most, a tragedy for some.

I didn't make it more than a few feet before a palm was wrapping around my wrist and tugging me back.

"What are you doing here?" I hissed, refusing to admit I knew he was watching us, long before he yanked me into a room off the hall.

Adrian locked the door behind him, his hands shoved into his pockets like they often were as he leaned against the frame. "What do you think?" He took two steps forward, expecting me to step back. I didn't.

"I think you want to get caught."

"By whom?" Adrian lifted a questioning brow before chucking a thumb over his shoulder. "Him? Not worried about that. Fucker is already balls-deep in that blonde with the big tits." He eyed me for a moment. Waiting for some sort of reaction when I had none to give. It was hard to be jealous over someone you didn't give a shit about.

Then again, I didn't think this was about me. It was about him. My shadow man and that ego of his again. His own jealousy and not mine. He wanted to see if it bothered me. The thought of my fiancé and someone else.

If my brain wasn't sunny-side up, I would have played along. Pretended to be disgusted, put on a good show and maybe even shed a few tears. But I didn't have it in me today. Most days. I could feel that fire dying, almost as if some spark had been extinguished as I slowly became more and more like my mother.

And maybe that was the punishment I deserved for killing her...

I'd barely begun to wallow in my self-pity before Adrian popped up in front of me, his hand closing around the back of my head and tipping me forward as he dropped his mouth to mine. I had to admit I did like kissing him. I liked the way it felt like he was devouring me. And then he was yanking up my skirt and fumbling around with my underwear.

I knew what he was doing, at least what he was trying to do. I also knew he would fail again and I wasn't interested in more disappointment. Not when I wanted some semblance of control.

I swatted his hand aside and shoved at his chest until I had him backed against the door. He didn't stop me. He could if he wanted to. But this man enjoyed getting knocked around a bit. I'd felt all the raised marks on his back, the healed scars, and the freshly broken skin. He enjoyed a bit of pain. It was a need I recognized.

I waited until his spine grazed the handle, causing his eyebrows to knit, before I ripped his belt from his pants, grabbed his wrists and looped them together. Adrian didn't say a word, just watched me and obeyed when I gestured to the little peg above his head.

"I'm at your mercy, princess." He grinned as he hooked himself in place. Arms raised high and feet spread wide.

I didn't reply. What was coming out of his mouth

didn't interest me. Not when I was more focused on what was straining between his legs. What I wanted to do to it, the way he whimpered at my touch, and how the sound of him begging for me made me feel when it was so hard to feel anything anymore.

51

ADRIAN

uck. Me. It was the first thought to enter my mind as I stared down at the pair of tits that were perfectly level with my cock. And pressed so close together in that dress of hers I wasn't certain anything else could fit. But I sure as hell wanted to try. I wanted to watch the tip disappear between two globes of tan flesh. A little spit hocked on my palms and I could make that happen. A little bit of force and I could...

"Oh, fuck!" I grunted the moment the chill of the air on my balls met the warm, wet heat of her tonsils.

My little lamb was on her knees in front of me, her curls piled high on her head with the help of a hair tie she'd pulled from god only knows where. Her cheeks suctioned in and streaked with tears, and her knuckles white as her mouth bobbed up and down on my cock. Her grip on the base was probably tighter than it should be, tighter than was good for me or my circulation, but I wasn't about to tell her that.

Not with how fucking good it felt. And it felt *fucking good*. She could twist it off for all I cared, as long as she didn't stop what she was doing. And what she was doing was giving me the type of blow job that could make a grown man weak in the knees. Could and *was*.

Because I had no doubt that if it weren't for the tensile strength of the leather in this belt currently bearing the full weight of my body, I'd be a puddle on the floor. My abdominal muscles clenched and my spine nursed straight.

This woman's mouth was more powerful than any aspirator in any operating room I'd ever seen. More accurate too. She didn't need me to guide her—something I couldn't do anyway with my arms looped above my head. She didn't need me to tell her when to speed up or slow down either. She read my body, the way I used to be able to read hers. Adjusting her rhythm each time I sucked in a sharp breath or groaned in a way she liked. Her palm working in tandem as she fluctuated between long, languid strokes and quick jerks of her wrist.

I wanted to watch her. To strain my neck muscles and lean forward so that I could see when her nostrils flared on a staggered breath, when she swallowed down the saliva pooling in her mouth and dripping down her chin, when she went too deep and had to pull away to keep herself from gagging. But my head had a mind of its own. Tipping back and knocking on the door as my eyes rolled up towards Heaven.

It was the closest a guy like me would ever get to those pearly gates, and I had to sin in order to do it. *Fuck if that wasn't irony for ya.*

Good thing I didn't believe in that shit. Or I might have felt the tiniest bit guilty when Marisela drew her mouth almost back until the only thing wet was the tip. Circled her tongue around me once, twice, before relaxing her esophagus enough to choke me down. I groaned, much louder than I should, and clenched my ass cheeks to keep from coming.

A gentleman would have finished right there, balls-deep in her throat, where she couldn't taste it. He would have ended it quick, allowed his girl to tap out and stop putting so much pressure on her knees. He would have let her know what a good job she was doing being his perfect little slut.

I was no gentleman. Even if Marisela was everything a lady should be. I was also well-acquainted with edging myself, which meant I could draw this out for hours if I wanted to. And part of me did *want* to, while another part wanted this woman's face covered in so much cum she'd have trouble opening her eyes without feeling the burn of her lashes.

At least that's what I thought before she choked me down again, like some sword swallower in a sideshow, her finger creeping its way towards my ass. Then, the next thing I knew, she was massaging my prostate at the same time she milked my cock dry.

My head was spinning, dizzy and detached, as I tried to blink myself back to consciousness. Which was no easy feat after some she-devil in a powder-pink dress syphoned your soul from your body through the tip of your cock.

Marisela grinned at me with pouty lips—much

poutier after all the friction—while dabbing at the side of her mouth with a manicured hand. There was no reason for it other than dramatics, seeing as my little lamb hadn't spilled a drop. But who was I to call her out with the one-woman show she put on for my benefit?

"Just because I've never been fucked, it doesn't mean I don't know how to fuck," she whispered against my ear, pushing herself up on her tiptoes to reach it. "Watching porn used to be one of my favorite pastimes."

I lifted a curious brow, while wishing like hell I knew a tech guy I trusted enough to pull up her browser history. "Used to be?"

Her smirk dropped, tugging into a frown before settling on neutral. "Don't see much of a point anymore." She shrugged as she shoved me aside, grabbed the door handle, and yanked it open. Forcing me to shuffle forward a few steps to give her space to slip through.

I wanted to follow her, to watch and see if Tate could smell my cum on her breath. If he cared enough to notice the bruises on her knees or how flushed her cheeks were. But I couldn't do any of that until I found the energy to unhook my arms and tug up my pants. And I was still looking for it... The energy to move and the strength to stand upright.

52

MARISELA

I rinsed the taste of cum from my mouth with a sip of hot tea while Tate did the same with the pussy juice I could still smell on him, and realized this was what my life would be. It could be worse, though.

There were worse things than living in a lavish mansion with maids and butlers attending to your every need. Worse things than marrying someone who cared less about what was in your head and more about getting it from someone else. On that same note, there was a sort of freedom that came with knowing the man at your side didn't give a damn about what you did in your spare time—as long as it didn't affect him.

It was something we could both agree on. At least I was pretty certain we could.

I cleared my throat, waiting for Tate to look up from whatever piece of ass he was currently messaging on his phone. Because I had no doubt that was what he was doing. He locked the screen before shoving the device into a pocket, crossing a leg over a knee as he sank deeper into the cushion of the large wingback in the parlor. We'd just returned from the ballroom, barely speaking two words to each other during the drive back to Prescott Estates.

"How was she?" The question was nonchalant, like I was asking about the weather and not the woman my fiancé was fucking before we got here.

He was quick to drop his gaze, staring at his nail beds as though he was suddenly more interested in getting a manicure than what I had to say, and not because he was ashamed. Men like Tate were not ashamed of the shit they did. He just didn't want to deal with the consequences.

"Who's that, my dear?" he hummed.

"The blonde you just fucked."

He paused for a moment, his eyes narrowing as he searched my face for something he wouldn't find. Jealousy. "Which one?"

I shrugged. "Honestly, the answer doesn't matter. I was just trying to get your attention."

"And now that you have it, what are you going to do with it, sweetheart?" Tate grinned, steepling his hands while leaning back so that his crotch was in my direct line of sight. Like he was expecting me to get on my knees or something.

"Not that kind of attention." I shook my head.

"Shame. I do like getting my dick sucked after a quick fucking." When it was clear I wasn't getting the hint,

Tate huffed. Pushing to his feet and storming off. But instead of leaving, he slammed the pocket doors shut. Latching them closed before turning back towards me. "What do you want, Marisela?"

I wasn't holding my breath. But I also wasn't ashamed to admit I *was* looking for something I could stab him with. If it came to that. "The same thing you want, Tate."

"And what's that?" He took three slow steps in my direction. I didn't bother turning around to look at him. But I could sense him looking at me. Like a lion hunting a gazelle. Except he failed to realize who was who in this scenario.

I had nothing to lose. I didn't give a shit if he killed me. But he did. Which also meant I had everything to gain. "For you to be able to fuck whomever you want, whenever you want. Without worrying that your wife might find out," I explained.

Tate heaved out a loud laugh, closer to a howl, as he threw his head back. He was standing in front of me now. Slowly lowering himself onto the coffee table so that I was trapped between his spread legs and the sofa. "And why would you want that, sweetheart? I mean, I know why *I'd* want that but why would you? What's the catch?"

He reached out and grabbed my chin, a little too rough for my liking. I tugged it free and shifted back on the cushion. "No catch. I don't care what you do, Tate. Or who you do it with. And I have no intention of pretending like I do."

It was the truth. At the very least, it was close enough to the truth that I wasn't lying.

"No." One word, and that was it. Tate stood to his full height before strolling back towards the door again. This time I watched him go.

"What do you mean *no*?"

"I mean, no, I don't believe you. I don't give a shit either." He grinned as he crossed his arms over his chest and leaned a shoulder against the door. "Let's get one thing straight, Miss *Cruz*. I'm going along with this whole thing for one reason and one reason only."

"Your fath—" I started to say, only to have Tate rush forward and spit in my face.

"*Fuck* my father. He's two steps from his grave and too fucking stubborn to jump in it." Tate lifted an arm and grabbed my cheek, pinching as he leveled me with a glare. "But don't you worry your pretty little head about that. When the time's right, I'll give him a nice little shove. And then it's just you and me, my darling bride."

He dropped his hand and I rubbed the sting away. "If not your father, then what's the reason? Why me?"

Tate paced across the area rug, stepping over the corner he kicked up with his shoe instead of fixing it. "You know what? You're right. If we are going through with this whole thing, we should be on the same page. United front and all that. I don't need to be the enemy, Marisela. In fact..." He closed the distance, shoving me down on the sofa as he slid a knee between my thighs. His mouth closing over mine in a sloppy kiss that consisted of too much tongue and not enough toothpaste. "We could even be friends."

I shoved him off me and wiped the remnants of his saliva from my lips. Secretly hoping some of Adrian's cum didn't make it down my throat. The asshole deserved the salty taste of his brother's backwash.

"I don't think so," I grunted, and Tate laughed.

"Suit yourself." He shrugged. "But these are my terms. Take them or leave them. I will fuck whoever I want, whenever I want. And you'll keep your mouth shut about it."

"Those aren't really ter—"

Tate lifted a finger. "I'm not done. Now, as I was saying, you'll keep your mouth shut about what I do. And I'll go as far as to turn a blind eye at whatever it is *you* do."

"As in?" I pressed.

"*As in,* I don't give a fuck who you fuck, Marisela... as long as it isn't my brother." He smirked, watching my face again. Waiting for my reaction.

"I wasn't aware you had a brother," I countered, meeting Tate's seething glare with one of my own.

He *tsked* his tongue. "Come now, we both know that's a lie, sweetheart. Why do you think you're here if not because of the special interest he took in you?" When I didn't respond, he sighed. "It's simple as this: fuck my brother and I'll make sure your ass is tossed back in that looney bin quicker than you can say *kum...* quat. But keep those legs closed and the world is your oyster."

"One condition," I countered. "I want a job. A permanent position at Prescott R&D."

He watched my face for a moment.

"And I don't want to be forced to raise your little

bastards. No children outside this marriage." I took a deep breath before adding, "Push them down the stairs, take a coat hanger to their uteruses—I don't give a damn what lengths you have to go to. Just ensure it doesn't happen."

I could see the wheels spinning in his head, his eyes crinkled at the sides and his jaw set tight. Tate didn't know if he should be pissed off or impressed. What I did know was that the asshole was turned on again. His poor excuse for a dick pressing against his zipper as he rubbed himself through his pants before one side of his mouth started tugging upwards.

"You want to work? Then work until those boney fingers are nothing but nubs, darling. Make yourself the COO, for all I care. I don't give two shits about what you do as long as it isn't *him*."

Tate was on his feet again, straightening the seam of his pants and buttoning his jacket before stalking towards the door. I sighed under my breath, more pleased with myself than I should be before he called over a shoulder.

"Oh, and, Marisela? It's in your best interests not to disappoint me on our wedding night. A groom expects his bride to be... *intact*. I mean, think about it. What's more binding than a blood oath?" He took note of the confusion on my face. Probably the disgust too, whether or not he realized it was there was beside the point. Seeing as whatever he was thinking only had him grinning wider. "Make no mistake, dear. Regardless of where I'm getting my dick wet, you will be performing your wifely duties."

I schooled my features and steeled my spine. "I'm not sucking you off, Tate."

"Of course not. That's what the *whores* are for. But you will do everything in your power to provide me with an heir. Must carry on the Prescott name, after all..."

53

ADRIAN

"Do you think it's possible?" The white surgical mask clung to my lips each time I sucked in a breath. Usually I enjoyed the feel of it. The biting odor of the antiseptic tinged with the copper scent of fresh blood. But right now, my mind was somewhere else. Focused on someone other than the patient cracked open in front of me.

"Do I think *what's* possible?" John huffed through the mic in my ear as the instruments in my gloved hands peeled epidermis from muscle and muscle from bone.

I'd forgotten he was listening from where he'd propped himself up in the adjacent room again. Always heard and never seen.

"Nothing. Just thinking aloud." I shook my head and returned my attention to the mess of metal plates and protruding screws. Tracing a blue fingertip over each of the vertebra along the kid's spine.

I'd already fashioned a few rough prototypes using a

mixture of synthetic materials and ground cadaver bone. The implant had to be sturdy but flexible. Permanent but easy enough to repair or replace if needed. This kid had become my passion project, when I wasn't too busy burying my face between Marisela's thighs. Almost as if part of me thought that if I fixed him, I could fix her too.

And maybe I was that naïve. But naiveté incited ingenuity and ingenuity was the foundation of progress. Right?

"You've got something up your sleeve, don't ya, Doc?" The kid yawned, causing his chest to inflate and rise enough to have me nearly nicking an artery.

"Don't move. Unless your idea of a good time is bleeding out on my table," I grunted, and he moved again. Shrugging his shoulders just to spite me.

"Maybe it is. Maybe it isn't."

The muscle relaxant must have been wearing off. Which meant I had to either hold him down or stitch him up until I could mix together another syringe. An IV drip would have been a better option, if I had a compliant patient and another set of hands to monitor the device for me. I didn't have either of those.

"You're all talk, you know that?" I shook my head as I started piecing the kid back together again. One layer at a time.

"Nope. I'm action too. A lot of tongue action. But according to you, that ain't your thing."

"Bullshit." I tugged harder than I needed to, looping the first subcutaneous stitch before moving on to the next. "You're a smart kid. If you really wanted to take yourself out, you would have found a way to do it already."

"Easy for you to say from that pedestal those two legs are standing on," he muttered against the face-rest.

"Sure is. Easy for you too, with all those pills you got stashed in your room. Why not just take a handful and see where it lands you?" I lifted a challenging brow for no one's benefit but my own. It also helped push back some of the sweat that was beading across my forehead. The hospital lighting was harsh and the room stuffy, so that even a few minutes in here had you feeling like you were sitting in a sauna.

"How do you know about those?" he asked me.

And the answer was... *I didn't.* It was just an educated guess, considering how quickly he metabolized everything I tried to flush through his system. Kid wasn't just immune to pain; he'd also developed a tolerance to most sedatives. It was probably why he didn't consider overdosing an option.

He didn't need to know how or what I knew, though. It was better to keep him on his toes—*okay, maybe not the best choice of words.*

"He's gone, you know," he whispered after a few more moments of awkward but pleasant silence.

"Who's gone?"

"Whoever you had in your ear," the kid clarified. "He ain't listening anymore."

"Okay."

"I heard the door shut, followed by the swishing of his pants down the hall."

"Okay," I repeated.

"*So* now you can tell me what you're really doing with my back."

Like I said, the kid was smart. "What makes you think I'm doing anything?" I countered, and he shrugged another shoulder.

"I don't think. I know. You're taking measurements. None of the others ever took measurements. Just poked and pulled and sliced and screwed. And you're being careful. None of them ever cared enough to be careful either. Which means you're up to something."

"And what if I am? You gonna rat on me?" I questioned him.

"Do I look like a rat to you, Doc?" he fired back.

"Nope. But you do look like someone who will do whatever suits him."

"You're not wrong." He grinned. Even though I couldn't see his face, I knew the way his tone changed when he was grinning. "And what suits me right now is introducing you to a friend."

"I didn't know you had any?"

"Oh, I have plenty of friends, Doc. Plenty of enemies too. But we can take care of those fuckers another day."

We? It was on the tip of my tongue to say since when the fuck are *we* a *we?* But I couldn't deny that I was curious. Which also went hand in hand with that progress I mentioned.

"You know what? Why the hell not?" I tugged off one glove at a time before tossing them into the red bin. "Introduce me to your friend, kid."

"Kaz, Kazimir Markov."

"Hm?"

"That's my name. Not *kid*," he corrected, his tone more level than I'd ever heard it before. More Russian too. Almost as though he had a slight accent he'd forgotten to hide. "But *my friends* call me Casper. Like the cartoon ghost. You should catch on, since you're about to be one of ' em."

"I'm about to be your friend? Or a ghost?" I attempted to clarify.

"You're about to be my *best* friend. You'll see."

54

ADRIAN

Two steps into the hall and the stench of urine smacked me in the face, hard enough to have me stumbling back. I was more than used to the odor of rotting flesh and human meat patties. But this was something else. Sharp and musty in a way that had my nostrils watering and my eyes tearing up.

I looked over at the kid in the chair, his hospital gown ballooning slightly at the hem each time the AC kicked on, and he grinned back at me. Didn't know where he was taking us. Just that it required us using an elevator before we were navigating what appeared to be the lowest level at Briarwood. A basement.

It was more than that though. It was its own separate ward. More zoo than hospital.

"There ain't much you can do about most of 'em." The kid shrugged, as he continued to guide me around various cages, arms stretching towards us and fingers clawing at the metal bars. "But I think my friend over there has real... potential. Might be able to help you do whatever it is you're trying to do here."

I eyed the man in the far corner, hunched over in a ball and talking to himself as he rocked back and forth. So forcefully he was shaking the floor beneath him too. His mannerisms infantile while the rest of him... *wasn't*. The fucker was nearly seven-feet tall—my best guess going off what I could see of him—the muscles in his arms larger than his head and his shirt so tight it was ready to bust off his torso. But it was all the chains that caught my eye. Wrapping around him like a snake and keeping him from getting farther than a few steps from the concrete wall.

"Don-Don misses the voices." The blonde kid leaned over in his seat to whisper in my direction. "They haven't been back since they cut into his brain."

"Don-Don?" I lifted a questioning brow without taking my glare off the man in front of us.

"Yep, *Donnie*. Don't know his real name. None of us do. But figured it was fitting for a schizo who prefers imaginary voices over real people."

I nodded, and not because I understood the reference but because I understood the significance of carving out your own identity. What you called yourself, *what other people called you*, was all you had when they stripped everything else away.

I was a Prescott by birth. But I was Adrian Lambert by choice. A last name I'd picked out of an astrology book as a kid after I was told I needed one for the old man to register me in school. Something he never considered until the fucker realized I'd taught myself to read.

I might have not had any respect for my father. But at least he was smart enough to pick up on the fact Tate would never be anything more than a breeder. A cum deposit filled to the brim with useless DNA. But me? The old man could use me. Shape me. Mold me into something worth investing in.

Point was, if the kid wanted to be named after a *cartoon ghost*, it wasn't on me to tell him it was a dumb idea. Guess it made more sense than a five-year-old idolizing some French mathematician.

"How long's he been down here?" I turned back to Casper, my voice raised enough to carry over the continued clanking of metal and constant wailing.

"As long as I've been here. Probably longer."

I flicked my eyes towards Donnie again. "And what do you expect me to do with him?"

Another smirk, followed by another lift of a shoulder. "Fix him. Or don't. I don't really care. But at the very least you should use 'em."

"For what?"

"To scratch your balls, dumbass." Casper shook his head. "To take over. Think it's time for new management. And something tells me you're the guy to do it, Doc."

I threw my head back on a laugh. It was all I could do, seeing as the kid wasn't just antisocial. He was delusional too. "First of all, why the fuck would I want to take over..." I gestured around the room. "...this place? Second, even if I wanted to, how is that guy..." I threw a thumb towards the giant-sized ball of fluff one quick blow away from crying out to his mommy. "...supposed to help me do it?"

Casper's lips unfurled like a spool of yarn accidentally tossed down the stairs. The transformation just as quick too. Until I was staring at nothing. Not a smile. Not a frown. The type of blankness you see on a corpse before you cut into it to look at what's inside. And then he twisted his neck to the left, calling out, "Hey, Don-Don, that pretty nurse you like is back!"

He'd barely gotten the words out when the pile of muscle and limbs rose from the dead and started yanking against the chains, bending metal and causing the ceiling above to start to cave in. Splintered wood twirling through the air as the rafters creaked and cracked with the force of Donnie's blows.

I should have been running in the opposite direction or at the very least calling up for help. Instead, I was transfixed. Riveted. And so very fucked the moment the man in front of us broke free of the chains around his hands and ankles. While the kid beside me appeared more amused than fazed.

"Don-Don fucks like a rabbit in heat. Problem is... he's much larger than any rabbit I've ever seen," Casper mused. "The last girl he got his paws on ain't doing so good. But that shit sure is a great incentive in the right hands..."

"I bet it is," I agreed on a hum, glancing to my right when I felt a quick tug on my lab coat, which was now scrunched up in a palm five times the size any human palm should be. One closed-fist punch to the face, and Donnie wouldn't be the only one suffering from brain damage. This guy could literally bend my body in half and not break out in a sweat. But for some reason, he seemed to trust me. Or maybe just trust that I was his key to getting some pussy.

"So, Doc, are yours the right hands?" Casper asked.

I didn't reply, all the possibilities bouncing around in my head, as part of me was settling on the reality that this kid might really be on to something.

Maybe Briarwood was what I needed. A way for me to make a name for myself, without the story of how *I came to be* following me around like the ghost of a woman whose legacy ended shortly after she opened her legs for the last time.

55

MARISELA

Give them all something shiny to look at and they'll forget to look anywhere else.

It was a lesson I'd taught myself over the last few weeks and the best weapon I had at my disposal when I didn't have a pocketknife hidden on me. And right now, the only thing shinier than my sparkling personality was the diamond pendant sliding along my collarbone and catching the light as I tipped my head back and laughed. Forced, because nothing these fuckers said was funny.

I raised my arm, mindful of the chilled champagne sloshing around the flute without spilling over, as I offered our guests a polite cheers. Dr. So-and-so and his wife, Such-and-such. Politicians and their backers. I didn't know most of their names. And it didn't matter, because tonight I made sure they knew me. I made sure they took notice of me.

They weren't the only ones, though. His glare was tracking my every movement, each step I took across the room and every smile that was aimed at someone who wasn't him. Like if he stared long enough, the invisible leash he had wrapped around my neck would tug me in his direction. Like he could strangle me with that stare.

Not all that long ago he probably could too. But not now. Not when I had a hand in the game.

I saw him, felt him, without ever having to look at him as he tipped the whiskey glass towards his lips and downed the contents. I could also smell him or more I could smell the alcohol wafting off his breath as he stalked towards me. His steps just as determined as the annoyance curling his lips into a scowl.

Like I said, I was used to being dissected from afar. Being leered at until my skin crawled. What I wasn't used to was it coming from my fiancé instead of his brother. The same fiancé who claimed he didn't care who I fucked, when what he really meant was he cared a whole lot about who wanted to fuck me. He also cared about what it looked like. Especially to everyone else. Which meant I needed to look like the adoring bride at all times.

Tate tugged me to his side, one arm wrapped around my back as he dropped his mouth to that spot just above my ear, his voice low and harsh. His grip on my waist possessive and *harsher*. "What do you think you're doing?" His eyes flicked from the group of investors I'd been chatting up, back to me and the way my chest was nearly popping out of my neckline.

This wasn't jealousy. This was a kid not wanting to play with a toy anymore but not wanting anyone else to play with it either.

"Getting you another drink now that I see your glass is empty, my love." I grinned past my disgust, slowly spinning into his hold rather than pulling away from it, as I placed a gentle palm on Tate's chest.

I could feel his pulse racing, the vein in his forehead throbbing and the bulge in his pants doing much the same.

Tate had a temper, enjoyed drinking almost as much as he loved golfing—he was good at neither, mind you—but he was also pliable. Like a stray dog who was one deep ear scratch from showing you his belly. As long as you weren't afraid to risk a hand trying.

At this point, the fucker could gnaw my whole damn arm off, and I wouldn't bat a lash.

I pried the tumbler from his fingertips, pushing up on the tiptoes of my flats because Tate's dick size somehow grew the more I didn't, and pressed a kiss to his cheek. It didn't take his gaze more than a few seconds to wander from my ass to the pair of tits in front of him. A redhead this time. With a forehead so tight it didn't move. She was someone's wife and someone else's mistress. I didn't care to figure out who was who. Just paid enough attention to the way Tate eyed her.

Another thing about my soon-to-be husband was the fact he didn't have a type. If it had holes, he'd fuck it. What he did have was a competitive streak. The need to have whatever it was someone else wanted. A need that was easy to manipulate once you understood it. And I understood it better than anyone else.

It was the one benefit of growing up surrounded by monsters. While most people tried to avoid them, I learned how to blend in and live amongst them. And I wasn't just living. I was thriving. Navigating this engagement party like I was born to do it. So that everyone was eating out of the palm of my hand.

Almost everyone.

I chanced a glance behind me. Over to where Adrian had positioned himself on the other side of the room. Dressed head to toe in black. A black dinner jacket, black slacks, and a matching black button-down shirt. Open at the collar to reveal skin a shade darker than everyone around us. A guest in a space meant to be his home. Introduced as employee and never son.

I could only imagine what that was like. Then again, I knew exactly... Maybe I'd never been my father's employee but I had never been his daughter either.

My shadow man hadn't looked my way all night. And not because he wasn't watching me. But because he was better at hiding it than I was. Better than Tate too. Which left me to wonder what my darling fiancé *thought* he knew. I was certain it was nowhere near as off-putting as the truth.

By the time I made it back over to where Tate had been standing, he was gone. And so was the redhead. While the remaining guests all appeared too drunk or too self-absorbed to notice.

I sculled back the glass of whiskey in my hand, allowing the liquid to warm me from inside out before something else warmed my waist. A palm pressed almost too low to be decent and a mouth hovering over the nape of my neck.

"Only an idiot would leave his woman alone in a room full of fucking predators."

56

MARISELA

"Is that how you see yourself, Mister...?" I might have known who his father was but that didn't mean I knew his last name. Though something told me it wasn't *Prescott*. At least not on paper.

It wasn't the way things were done when people wanted the skeletons kept in the giant walk-in closets those same piles of bones afforded them. And the man with a suit much richer than he was, was more than a skeleton. He was a black mark on the legacy that built this city. Which left you to wonder why he was even here. In this room. This house. On this earth. Still breathing. When it was a lot less risky to bury him.

"Just Adrian to you, little lamb." He grinned against my ear, his glare on everyone else while his hands remained on me.

I spun around, putting a polite distance between us. In case Tate happened to be watching. I doubted it. Considering he much preferred to watch the ass cheeks jiggling in front of him as he pounded them from behind. Something I had the misfortune of seeing firsthand when I walked in on him with one of the maids.

I shook the image from my head, returning my focus to the pair of dark eyes staring back at me instead of the blue ones that would rather linger on whatever pussy was closest.

"Okay, then, *Adrian*. Is that how you see yourself? As a predator?" I lifted a challenging brow, repeating the question he seemed hesitant to answer.

Adrian's gaze flicked behind me, then back down again as he canted his head to one side. "Oh, no. I am well aware I don't belong here. But you do, don't you, Marisela? You live for this shit."

"If not a predator, then what are you?" I asked, ignoring the implication while issuing one of my own.

"I'm the prey. To all the leeches in this room, I'm nothing but something for them to latch on to and bleed dry." Adrian shrugged. "I'm the same to you too, you know."

"You are n—"

He waved a dismissive hand. "I am. But that's okay. Because for you, I'd do it willingly. I would give you every last drop in my vein just to watch the way you feed off it. To see your pupils dilate and your heart beat faster. I would get on my knees and let you consume me, if only to know it'll make me some part of you."

"That's deep." I snorted at his ridiculousness, quickly cupping my palms over my face to cover the sound.

Adrian chuckled and stepped forward. A few inches that might as well have been several feet. At least that was how it felt. Like the walls were closing in on me at the same time he did. "Take me to your bedroom and I'll make it deeper," he offered. His voice so low I might have imagined it.

"I have to take you there now? Pretty sure you know where it is," I countered.

"That's not a *no*, Marisela."

"It's not a *yes* either, Adrian." My back brushed the edge of a cocktail table, forcing my eyes to bounce around. Glossing over face after face. None of them turned this way. Somehow, we'd remained unseen in a room full of people. I was surprised. Adrian wasn't. He was used to it. To being invisible. Whereas I was used to wishing I could be.

His palm landed on the table behind me, just one, so I had a way out if I wanted it. I wasn't sure I did. And then he was leaning forward. Our lips almost touching but not quite, before he lifted a hand to rub the pad of his thumb over my bottom lip.

"This color looks good on you, but it looked so much better on my cock the other day." He grinned, pushing himself back and shoving his hands into his pockets. His sleeves rolled up just enough to show me how much the muscles in his forearms were straining.

He was holding back, keeping himself from touching me. That was why he did it. Why he was always tucking his hands away.

It was the moment I realized I was wrong. Because this man wasn't just eating out of my palms. He was practically gnawing his own off. Just to get at me. I should have seen it before. He told me as much himself.

Showed me when he pressed that blade to my mother's throat. Watching me as he did it. But this was different. This wasn't cheapened by drugs and adrenaline. It was raw and uninhibited.

It was also a power dynamic I wasn't used to. But I liked it. It was more than when he would hide in the trees and look up at me through my window. It was more than curiosity. It was dark and it was primal. It was hunger and it was desperation.

And I could work with that. Coax it to the surface and play with it. As long as I didn't let myself get lost in it. Because this thing between us was temporary. Especially when I'd given my word I wouldn't fuck him—*my fiancé probably should have been more specific. Clarified his definition of sex.* I purposely didn't. Tate would get the virgin he wanted on his wedding night. What he wouldn't get was my innocence.

That was gone a long time ago.

"You're right. It did." I leveled Adrian with a glare. "Almost as good as your blood looked on my hands that time I gutted you."

57

ADRIAN

My little lamb talked about stabbing me like it was an art form. My body and blood, her canvas and paint. Put us together and the result was as beautiful as it was dangerous. Disastrous.

I was too smart to throw it all away for a woman. Too talented to risk everything I had planned for myself on a few stolen moments in the shadows. Yet here I was. Sneaking off with my brother's bride. At their own damn engagement party. Taking her by the hand and dragging her through the halls and into the first empty bedroom with a lock on the door.

It wasn't by chance either. It was by design.

The handful of sedatives I'd tossed into Tate's glass thirty minutes ago meant big brother was ass-up before his pants made it around his ankles. His face buried in his mattress and his cock buried in no one. Fucker deserved more than a bad case of blue balls. But I didn't want to think about him when I could be thinking about *her*.

About the woman whose darkness matched my own. Who was as sanctimonious as she was sadistic. As smug as she was savage. Her arms crossed over her chest and her hip cocked like I was an inconvenience. Like she didn't want me.

Marisela was good at pretending. I'd seen her do it all night. What she wasn't good at was believing her own lies. Which meant her body betrayed her.

That's what my game had been about downstairs. Why I'd risked us being seen together. To prove to her— and myself—that she wasn't as unaffected as she tried to appear.

I pulled her little red pocket knife from the lining of my vest. Jerking it open and locking the blade. Watching Marisela's eyes flick from my hand back to my face as I took a step forward and flipped the handle in her direction.

"Go on, take it." I grinned.

"Why? What is it that you really want from me, Adrian?" she questioned, her fingers wrapping around the hilt and tugging it free without much resistance.

"Nothing, everything." I shrugged, my hands finding their way back to my pockets. "Whatever you wanna give me."

"What if all I want is for you to fuck off?" She didn't mean it. She wasn't angry at me. She was angry at the world. At how it'd wronged her. More than that, she was testing the waters. Seeing if there really was anything I wouldn't do for her.

"Mmm, can't do that. What else you got?"

"Fine, what if I want your head on a spike? Would you give it to me?" She stalked forward, close enough to press the tip of her blade to my throat. And I leaned into it until she drew blood.

"No..." I told her before dropping to my knees. "But I'd let you take it. I would let you saw through flesh and bone, tendon and muscle, and I wouldn't do shit to stop you."

"Why?" Now that was a fair question. It was also one I didn't have an answer to.

"I have no idea."

"Well, at least you're honest." Marisela lowered the knife to the collar of my shirt, wiping it clean before snapping it closed again.

"With you, always."

"Always?" She lifted a challenging brow and I couldn't suppress another grin.

"Almost always," I clarified.

She was studying my face, like she was trying to figure out what I wasn't telling her. As if the possibilities were far more exciting to her than the reality. They probably were, but that didn't mean I was ready to reveal all my secrets to her. Not yet. Not until every last piece was positioned just right.

And then she was pressing on my shoulders, shoving at my chest until I was sprawled out flat on my back while her hands tugged at the buttons of my fly. Her palm soft and warm as it wrapped itself around my cock. Yanking almost too hard but not hard enough that I didn't enjoy it. Or maybe so hard that I couldn't help but enjoy it more.

I wanted to touch her. To flip her ass around so that she was riding my face at the same time she was gagging on my cock. But I also wanted her to maintain her control. Use and abuse me and my body until she found a rhythm that had her screaming my name again. Until she found a way to fix herself.

I would be whatever this woman wanted me to be—her test subject, her fuck toy, her oral fixation—as long as she kept doing that thing with her tongue. The thing that had me biting on a knuckle and lifting my hips to meet her lap for thrust. That had the muscles in my thighs vibrating and my balls contracting so tight against my body they were practically inside me again.

Marisela didn't just suck cock. She worshipped it. Punished it. Soothed it. She used her tongue like it was an extension of her palm. Like it could wrap around and grip me. Her teeth like a prod. Meant to sting and mark me so that the neuropathways that distinguished pain from pleasure didn't know which way to go anymore. Alternating between fast and demanding and slow and torturous. Switching it up whenever I was dangerously close to coming.

This was about her, not me. Even though it was so very much about me. And bringing me to that brink. To controlling when I would be tossed over it.

I was so distracted by the feel of her warm wetness twisting itself around my cock I nearly missed the most important part. The fact that Marisela had her free hand pressed between her thighs. Her fingers working in sync with her mouth as she circled her own clit. Choking me down at the same time she fucked herself.

58

MARISELA

As good as it felt, as much control as I regained, it wasn't enough. It was never enough. It was something I would have to come to accept. That part of my life, how much I enjoyed my sexuality, it was over.

Truth be told, it was probably for the best. It meant I could stay focused, instead of being so lust drunk on a man I was supposed to be avoiding. It meant I maintained the upper hand when it came to my fiancé *and* his brother.

That didn't mean I was dead. It also didn't mean I didn't appreciate the way Adrian whimpered for me. The way he looked at me whenever I dropped to my knees and stared up at him through my lashes. How he clawed and begged. It was a different kind of satisfaction. An indulgence I enjoyed as the wedding date crept closer and closer. Until it was nearly here. Less than twenty-four hours and I would wear the burden of a ring that would lock a chain around my ankle at the same time it offered me the key.

I'd gotten it all down on paper. I wasn't so dumb as to take Tate for his word. A prenup as well as a contractional agreement that gave me forty-nine percent stake in his father's company... upon the old man's demise. And gave my soon-to-be husband the right to fuck whoever he wanted, including me, as long as it didn't affect the Prescott legacy, any of the shareholders, or the combined profits—legalese for *be careful where you deposit your sperm*. With one stipulation, my virginity to seal the deal.

Something I never had any desire to keep and didn't care if I lost anymore. The fact gratification was removed from the equation just made it that much easier to give it away to a man I could barely tolerate. In exchange for everything I would get in return.

Tomorrow was the day. I glanced around the small bridal suite, dragging a comb through my loose waves as I stared at the girl in the mirror, who appeared as anxious as she was resolute. Until a tapping had me looking towards the door.

I slipped off the seat, the hem of my nightgown clinging to my thighs as I crept closer to the sound. Wrapped my palm around the handle and started to twist before the door was already pushing forward in my direction.

"What are you doing here?" I hissed as Adrian quietly clicked the door closed behind him, his hair tussled and the sleeves of his white dress shirt rolled up to his elbows. He set a small duffle bag down on the floor by his feet, his eyes never leaving mine as he rose to his full height again.

I didn't know how he did it. How he could appear both disheveled and relaxed at the same time. Eerily calm yet feral.

He didn't answer me, taking two steps forward and dipping his head, his lips brushing mine. Like he was tasting me instead of kissing me. Like he hadn't tasted me a million times before. When he pulled back again, I could see how dilated his pupils were. He was on something. Or he'd been drinking. Maybe a mixture of both. It was hard to tell. Adrian just had this way of keeping his guard up unless his pants were down and then I could read him like a picture book.

"You wearing that for me *or him*?" Adrian quirked a brow, jutting his chin towards my silky nightgown. A pearly white against my dark hair and skin.

I rolled my eyes. "You're being dramatic. *He's* my husband. At least he's going to be in a few hours. And you're going to be my very platonic brother-in-law. You're just going to have to accept that." I shrugged, turning on the ball of my foot and throwing over a shoulder, "I have."

"And what if I don't?" he grunted in a way that had me turning back to look at him. Something was off. His tone, his demeanor. It was all off.

"What if you don't *what*, Adrian?"

"You asked me what I was doing here. What if I told you there was a way out? A place for us to go. Without having to worry about your father, Tate, any of 'em. What would you say?"

"I would say you should probably go and find some-where to sober up. Somewhere that's not here." I crossed my arms over my chest and pinned him with a glare. The man was talking nonsense. He was also mistaking what-ever was going on between us for more than it was. Which was nothing.

Neither of us had the luxury of making it more than that.

"I'm not drunk, Marisela. Just shot up with enough adrenaline to take down a small horse. Needed it in case those guards of yours put up a fight." He grinned. More like snarled. "They didn't by the way. Didn't even know what hit 'em before the sedative was already working its way through their systems. Must have been drinking on the job."

I looked past Adrian towards the door again. As if I could somehow see through it and out into the hallway. I couldn't, but I couldn't stop myself from trying either. "What do you think is going to happen here?"

Adrian opened his mouth to speak, and I quickly cut him off. I didn't really want him to answer anyway. I didn't need him to. I knew what he was thinking just by looking at him.

"You honestly thought you would come in here and what? Save me? Wait until the last possible minute and then swoop in on your white horse and save me from myself? Is that really what you thought? Are you that delusional?"

He didn't move, other than to tilt his head slightly to one side to look at me. "Some things take time, Marisela.

Planning. I was never going to actually let you go through with this shit."

"Let me?" I forced a laugh, so loud and jarring it had Adrian scowling before his mask dropped back in place again. "Who are you to let me do anything? This is my decision. One that I didn't have a hand in making. Not at first. But one I have come to accept is what's best for me. Marrying Tate, that is what's best for me." I didn't explain further. What happened between me and my husband wasn't his brother's business anyway.

It was like watching an animatronic power down, some sort of robot that had been overloaded and couldn't compute. Like we were speaking foreign languages and all Adrian could hear was nonsensical chatter. Until only one concept seemed to land.

"He's going to want to sleep with you. He's going to want to fuck you, Marisela." He was pacing now, my gaze bouncing towards the duffle bag just out of reach as part of me started to question the contents.

"And? You don't think I can close my eyes and pretend I'm somewhere else for a couple of minutes? I've been doing it every day for my whole damn life!" I shouted back.

Adrian stopped dead in his tracks. His eyes darker than I'd ever seen them before. More black than brown, so that I felt as though I was now staring into a pair of lifeless pupils. "I'm not going to let him have you."

"You don't have a choice!"

"That's where you're wrong, princess." Adrian growled in my direction before storming towards me. His jaw set tight and his nostrils flaring. And suddenly, he wasn't a robot anymore. He was a beast.

59

ADRIAN

Some monsters were born. Others were carefully curated. I guess you could say I was a little of both. But it wasn't until this moment that I finally realized it. Embraced it. As I cornered Marisela, reaching out and tugging her back by her hair when she tried to escape me. I'd never been violent with her before. I'd never been more forceful than she needed me to be.

But I'd be lying if I said the way she was looking at me didn't turn me on. Feed some deeper need I'd been doing my best to tamp down over the years, while I pretended to be better than the men around me. When, really, I was just like them. Just as dark. Just as depraved.

I could feel her hatred radiating off her skin, her disgust, and I... liked it. I'd been running from it for so long. Only to realize I needed it. I craved it. I fed off it.

I was so hocked up on the artificial adrenaline, on the natural adrenaline mixing with it and coursing through my veins, I didn't feel the bite of Marisela's nails digging into my skin. I didn't feel it when she lashed out and struck me across the face. I didn't feel the blood streaming down my nose, even though I knew it was there.

What I did feel was the throbbing urge to make her submit. To claim her before someone else could. Before *he* could fucking touch what was always meant to be mine. Before she let him.

And the rage. I felt that too.

The idea that she was *choosing* him over me awakened the most twisted parts of my psyche. The same insecurities that constantly whispered in my ear, telling me I'd never be good enough. I'd never be *them*.

And if I couldn't be them... If I couldn't be *him*, I'd be worse.

I shoved Marisela onto the bed, watching her bounce off the mattress before swatting at my chest. I grabbed her wrists in one hand while reaching for my zipper with the other, yanking it down, only to have her slip out of my hold and make a mad dash for the door.

She didn't get more than two steps before I was tugging her towards me again. And then I was walking her backward until her spine was pressed up against the wall. Her teeth gnashing in my direction and her white nightgown stained with my blood.

"Let me go, Adrian," she hissed, saliva splattering against my face along with the venom she plied it with. Both tasted as sinful as my little lamb looked squirming beneath me.

My lips tipped up until I was grinning so wide my

cheeks hurt. Or at least they should. I still couldn't feel them. "Never."

I watched her eyes widen when she realized where my hand was going. What I'd taken from my pocket and was clutching between my thumb and forefinger.

Drugging her was the last thing I wanted to do to her tonight. Fucking her was the first. But she didn't leave me much of a choice here. The noise was bound to draw someone's attention and then we'd both be shit out of luck.

I lowered the tip to Marisela's jugular, my grip too shaky for a quick administration, and she slapped my arm aside. Sending the syringe to the floor as I pressed more of my body weight against her much smaller frame.

I always knew my girl was a fighter. But so was I. I just never had a reason to fight her before. And now I had more than a reason. I had a need that was stronger than either of us.

She cursed my name, called me every insult she could think of as I lifted the flimsy material of her nightgown over her head, using it like a cloth hood to muffle her screams. Each time she sucked in air, more of the soft fabric shoved its way inside her mouth while my hand worked over her pussy. Thrusting in and out until my palms were sticky with her cum, until the air smelled like her and I couldn't hold back anymore.

I leveled my forearm with her throat, compressing her larynx while I fumbled with the opening in my boxers and pulled myself free.

I'd been waiting for this moment for so long it seemed wrong to rush it. But it also felt so right. Especially when I gave myself a few quick strokes, Marisela's nails scraping away at layer after layer of skin as she tried to peel my arm back.

There was no moving me. Not unless I wanted to be moved. And right now, there was no place I would rather be than here. With this woman. Inside her.

I kicked her feet apart, spreading her thighs wide before I lined myself up and broke through that barrier with one, quick upward grind of my hips. Marisela whimpered. I think I did too. I didn't know whose sounds were whose. Just that they were absolutely obscene. Unhinged and guttural. And so was the pounding of flesh against flesh against solid wood. The knob jiggling in the frame each time I slammed myself farther. Deeper. Each time she arched her spine only to have me force it flush again.

I swiped Marisela's nightgown off her face so I could look her in the eye. So she could look *me* in the eye as I continued to fuck her up against the door, where we'd finally landed.

It felt better than I thought it could. Better than I imagined. Her cunt clamping around me like it knew I was meant to be there even if Marisela didn't. Even if no one else knew. I knew. I knew she was mine. No matter whose last name she wore. She would always wear mine. In some fashion or another.

This wasn't just sex. This was me refusing to let her go. This was me choosing us, even if she didn't choose me.

My thrusts were becoming staggered, less refined and frenzied and more languid as the stress hormones seeped their way out of my pours and sweat began to trickle down my forehead. She felt too fucking good to keep going but I didn't want to stop either. I couldn't imagine stopping.

A thought that had my palm smacking against the space behind Marisela's head as I braced our combined weight. Her leg slung over my hip, where I was holding it in place, and her hair clinging to the dried tears on her face. A dozen or so more long, angled strokes and I couldn't do it. I couldn't hold back. I couldn't bring her there with me and I couldn't keep myself from going there alone.

Because that was what this woman did to me. Turned me into... this. Not by making me into something I wasn't. But by peeling back the exterior and revealing the monster that was always there. Allowing me to be who I always was beneath the surface.

60

I didn't have to look over to know that he was sleeping. Knocked-out by an orgasm-induced coma I didn't have the luxury of having myself. I didn't have to look because I could hear him. The slow, even breaths that had his chest lifting and falling in rhythm with his exhale. The thin sheet he had wrapped around his torso doing the same.

I could feel him too. The eerie stillness that had his arm finally slipping off my hip and drifting to his side. The way his body heat radiated off him and warmed my exposed skin.

It all seemed so... intimate. Except it wasn't.

I was never more alone than I was right now. Contemplating who I hated the most, the man beside me or his brother, at the same time I realized I would never escape either of them. Not unless I put an end to this for good.

I inched myself to one side of the mattress, draping

my legs over the edge so that I was standing. Then I crept across the room, silently brushing the pads of my feet along the carpet until I stepped on something sharp. The needle Adrian had brought with him. I didn't know what was in it. Just that it was slightly cloudy and was probably meant to incapacitate me.

I could leave now. Take whatever was in his duffle bag, pray that it included some cash, and not look back. But the truth was, I had nowhere to go. Nothing of my own. All I had was whatever was waiting for me at the other end of the aisle. Without the bargaining chip I'd been holding over his head.

It seemed as dumb as it felt. As hopeless as it was. I also refused to let it be either. Because I was too smart to be dumb. And too jaded to rely on hope anyway.

If my time at Briarwood taught me anything, it was that hope was for the people waiting around to be saved and I was tired of waiting. Especially when I could do the saving myself.

I carefully tugged on the zipper on the bag, scrunching my eyes each time it caught before reaching a hand inside. My fingertips dancing across shiny metal that reflected off the moonlight. Various knives and vials all lined up along the bottom of a psychopath's toolbox. I grabbed the biggest blade I could find and crept back over to the bed. The syringe in one hand and a knife in the other.

He looked so peaceful. So proud of himself. So smug. All it would take was one quick jab. Aimed at the middle of his chest and slightly to the left. And he wouldn't be so smug anymore, now would he?

But something held me back from being able to do it. I didn't want him dead. I wanted him to suffer. I wanted to take from him like he'd taken from me. I wanted him to never be able to get it back again either.

My glare flicked down, over to where his semi-hard cock was sticking to his thigh. It would be easy enough to sever it. Just muscle and tissue. No bones to saw through. I considered it for longer than I'd like to admit, dismissing the idea when I realized it was the one part of him I could always control. The one part of him he couldn't. Otherwise, he wouldn't have left himself in such a vulnerable state right now.

Before I could think better of it, I pressed the syringe to the largest vein in Adrian's neck and pushed my thumb down on the other end as I forced the fluids out the top.

His eyes shot open, his brows knitting together and his mouth parting on a silent gasp that lasted a few seconds. And then nothing. No sound. No screaming. No fighting. His lids dropping closed and his expression deathly still.

I flicked on the light, swiped up the blade I'd left on the nightstand, and poked Adrian with the tip. Waiting a few seconds before I poked him again. He didn't move, even when I pushed down so hard blood began pooling on the surface of his skin. Even when I tugged off the sock of his left foot, wrapped a hand around his pinkie toe, and began sawing through flesh. And yellow meat. Having to adjust my aim when I hit solid bone instead of a break in the joint.

It was more difficult than filleting a fish, more

complex than deboning a steak. It was also much more satisfying.

I held the chunk of human tissue up to the light, blood dripping down my fingers, my wrist and forearm. Curling around the bend in my elbow before splattering onto my bare feet. And grinned. It was like collecting the prize at the bottom of the box after weeks of eating the same bland cereal.

I glanced back towards the bed, taking my little trophy with me as I made my way into the en-suite bathroom. I didn't know how long Adrian would be out for. Especially if that needle was meant for me. We weren't exactly the same body weight. Which meant I had to be quick. I didn't have time to cover up my tracks, only to rinse off and head downstairs to meet up with the rest of the bridal party.

It was my wedding day after all. I had to look picture-perfect, especially if I was planning on convincing my new husband that I was still a virgin.

I changed into a pair of shorts and a tank top before shoving my arms through the sleeves of my silky bridal robe, securing the tie around my waist with a loud huff. What I really needed was a shower but this was as good as it was gonna get. My hair piled high on my head in a loose bun and my skin reeking like another man. I sprayed enough perfume on my body to have myself smelling like a cheap whore and took one last glance over my shoulder at the figure on the bed. Then I clicked the door closed without ever looking back again.

PART FOUR

Chicago Tribune

Briarwood Sanitorium first opened its doors in 1915 as a treatment center for tuberculosis.

BRIARWOOD MASSACRE

SOUL SURVIVOR SPEAKS OUT

Once an esteemed treatment center, the name Briarwood Sanitorium has become synonymous with the medical atrocities that were discovered there late last week. The institution is now being referred to as a modern-day "Bedlam" with patients found to be subjected to neglect, abuse, and systemic torture. The horrors of Briarwood were brought to light by Dr. Adrian Lambert, a physician and advocate for holistic care as well as the only surviving employee, after the murder of his colleagues drew his attention to the facility's basement, where patients were found locked in cages and chained to the walls.

WHAT REALLY HAPPENED TO THE EMPLOYEES OF LOCAL SANITORIUM?

"Basement of Horrors"

It's unclear who initiated the massacre of the sanitorium's long-term staff while some claim the vigilante-style justice was warranted. Briarwood first opened its doors as a tuberculosis treatment center before transitioning to general patient care. Its residents, which include children and adults with intellectual disabilities, show signs of physical and sexual abuse, medical incompetence, and neglect. Many deaths occurred under suspicious circumstances, and a mass grave containing skeletal remains was discovered on the grounds, along with individual gravesites marked by wooden crosses.

The facility's closure followed a federal judge's order, strengthened by Dr. Lambert's detailed report of the ethics violations he witnessed firsthand under the employ of Dr. Hare and Dr. Burke (now deceased). These cases underscore a grim history of abuse and neglect in mental health institutions worldwide. While many of these facilities have been closed or reformed, the legacy of their atrocities continues to impact survivors and their communities. Acknowledging these dark chapters is crucial in preventing such abuses in the future and ensuring that mental health care prioritizes the dignity and rights of all individuals.

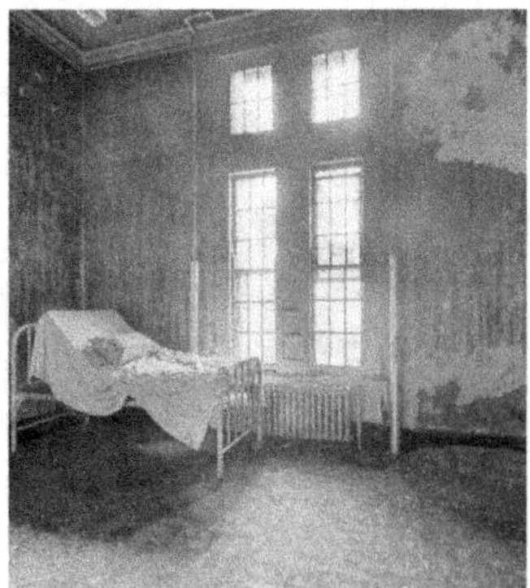

Patients found in cages and chained to walls and metal beds.

61

ADRIAN

ONE YEAR LATER

"Catch." I tossed the soft vinyl mask in Casper's direction and waited for it to land. He eyed it for a moment before looking up at me. "They were all out of your favorite ghost. Figured it was close enough." I shrugged.

He didn't say anything, and I held my breath. Never knew when one of his hissy fits would rear its ugly head but it always started like this. A long moment of quiet, followed by a teenage-sized tantrum.

"It's perfect." He grinned, scooping it off his lap and dropping the hood over his head before staring back at me through the slits of the 90s' style Scream face. It was hard to find in the off season but the kid deserved something with how patient he'd been over the last year.

The fact he couldn't feel me digging around his spine didn't mean that shit was any less uncomfortable. Especially all the sitting still. Which was like hell for an under-medicated hyperactive. But I wasn't about to force more drugs down his throat. Not when he was finally starting to trust me.

All the patients were. And it wasn't because of my bedside manner. It was because I was honest with them. I didn't tell them it wasn't gonna hurt when we both knew damn well it would. I didn't make promises everyone knew I couldn't keep. What I did do was give 'em a choice. Me or *them*. Hare and Burke. And somehow I turned into the lesser evil.

Despite what Marisela might tell ya, I wasn't a bad guy. I just did bad things. When it suited me.

I positioned myself behind my desk and glanced down at the computer screen. At another email left unanswered. She was avoiding me. Pretending like I didn't exist.

GOOD MORNING LITTLE LAMB,
DO YOU MISS ME YET? DO YOU THINK ABOUT ME WHEN HE'S FLOPPING ON TOP OF YOU LIKE A FISH TRYING TO FIND LAND? DO YOU CLOSE YOUR EYES AND WISH IT WERE ME INSTEAD?
YOURS,
A

I would love to say I regretted it. That I felt some sort of guilt for the way things turned out that night. But I didn't. I didn't regret a single moment I spent with the woman.

Did that mean I had more of my father's blood

running through my veins than either of us would like to admit? Maybe, but I did not care.

Because this wasn't about him. It was about me. He brandished his cruelty on numerous women and I only wanted one.

It was the sort of justification that came with the sociopathy I was more than self-aware enough to recognize. Diagnose but not treat. Because it was what motivated me. The need to have her no matter the cost to anyone else. Even her.

The fact that she severed my toe and took it with her just made it that much better. Like I said, I wanted her to have a piece of me with her always.

I wiggled the phantom appendage around in my shoe. A little reminder that she was always with me too. That she cared enough to tie off the end with some dental floss to ensure I didn't bleed out. It wasn't likely but she didn't know that.

Before I knew what I was doing, my fingers were flying across the keys again. Another email. Reassurance that I was here. That I hadn't forgotten about her and neither had my cock. Nothing could compare. I'd thought about it. Considered my options. But my appetites had been spoiled. Once you had your first taste of fillet mignon, a McDonald's cheeseburger just wouldn't do.

That was the problem when it came to this woman. I wasn't impatient. Or impulsive. But I was crazed.

I'LL TAKE YOUR SILENCE AS A YES. THAT'S OKAY. BECAUSE I THINK ABOUT YOU TOO. EVERY TIME I'M ALONE IN MY BED, MY HAND GRABBING THE BASE OF MY COCK AND TUGGING HARD. I CAN STILL FEEL YOU THERE, YOU KNOW. GRIPPING ME SO TIGHT IT'S ALMOST LIKE YOU DON'T WANT TO LET ME GO.

YOURS,

A

I had no doubt this message would go unanswered. Just like all the texts she'd left on read and the letters that had been returned to sender. Point was, she did read them. She was curious enough to open them. That wasn't rejection. It was stubbornness, pure and simple. And I could work with stubbornness. It was one of my favorite things about her after all.

I didn't have to look up from the screen to know Casper was watching me. Most would find it creepy. How interested he was in everyone else's business. I called it observant. It was useful too. Nothing went on inside these walls without this kid knowing about it. And he was quick to pass that information on to me. For a price.

The mask was the latest reparation. In a long list of toys and treats and the occasional weapon. Shit I was sure he traded for booze and pills as much as he kept 'em for himself. Not that I gave a damn what he did with the goods after they exchanged hands. Everyone was privy to their secrets.

I sure as hell had my own.

"She still ghosting ya, Lambo?"

Okay, maybe I didn't.

I quirked a brow at the nickname. Which was honestly tame compared to the rest. "Who?"

"The princess with the nice tits?" He lifted a shoulder and the black-and-white mask bounced with the sudden movement.

I pushed back in my desk chair and steepled my hands. "How do you know what her tits look like, Markov?" I grunted between clenched teeth. *It wasn't the first time he'd mentioned them.*

"Just assuming. You don't seem like the type to simp over a chick who didn't at least have nice tits."

He was lying. But I wasn't about to call him out. It meant he feared me enough to lie. Sure, trust and respect were great. But fear was earned too. It also held a lot more weight. Not everyone had someone they could trust or respect. But everyone had something they feared. Even me.

62

My phone dinged with another incoming notification. I didn't have to look to know who it was. Because it was always *him*. No matter how many times I blocked his number, username, *existence*... No matter how many notes I dropped in the trash bin or sent back with the courier... he never gave up.

Ignoring him wasn't working. Responding was worse. Pretending was all I had.

Pretending I didn't read every word. Pretending they didn't affect me. Pretending I wasn't miserable. Pretending I enjoyed the life I'd chosen for myself—as much as I could have chosen anything.

Let's be honest. I hadn't chosen shit. I just stopped fighting the inevitable.

I glanced over a shoulder. To where Tate was passed out in our marital bed after deciding to crawl in beside me last night. An occurrence that was as rare as it was unwanted.

My husband wasn't just a philanderer. He was also a drunk. Good thing too. It made it easier for me to empty one of the vials I'd stolen from his brother's bag into his drink the night of our wedding. Easier than that to convince the dumb fuck that the blood on the sheets was mine when he woke up the next morning.

Did I have to suffer through a few minutes of friction burn before the shit took effect? Sure did. But then it had just been a matter of shoving him aside, smearing some of Adrian's blood on the virgin-white sheets, and sinking into a steaming-hot bath. Where I stayed until my skin was wrinklier than his balls. Which were on full display right now.

I scrunched my nose, trying not to gag at the thought. Until my phone dinged again. Drawing my attention to the screen. A text message after the two emails had gone unanswered. It had barely been an hour.

UNKNOWN:

I could do something about his snoring, you know? Just say the word and I'll bring my scalpel.

My lips quirked up into a smirk before I forced them down. My eyes flicking around the room as if I could spot him. I couldn't. Not unless he wanted me to. But I had no doubt he was watching me. Lurking and listening. From somewhere behind the walls.

At the very least he was recording me.

He could have been bluffing. Making educated

guesses. But something told me there was more to it than that. There were too many coincidences.

Like how he always knew what I was wearing, what I'd eaten or more often than not what I'd moved around the plate before leaving it on the table, when I went to bed, when I didn't sleep... He knew it all.

I might have left the barred windows and medical devices behind but I was still under the microscope now as much as ever.

I adjusted the pleats in my skirt, smoothing out the hem, and then grabbed my textbook from the dresser. Leaving Tate to sleep off whatever or whoever he'd gotten into last night.

Attending classes wasn't an option anymore. My place was by my husband's side, whether that be in the office or in the home. But being a college dropout wasn't a good look for the Prescott name either. So private tutoring it was. Enough schooling to make me an asset but not a threat. Even if I was more than prepared to be both.

I navigated the double staircase with ease, turning the corner as soon as I hit the landing, only to pause in my tracks. My textbook tumbling out of my grip and onto the floor.

A hand reached out to grab it, a set of shoulders rising higher and higher until a pair of dark eyes were staring down at me.

My father-in-law cleared his throat, drawing my attention his way. "She's a clumsy little thing, isn't she?" He clamped a hand down on Adrian's shoulder, forcing him back a step at the same time he maneuvered himself between us. "Shouldn't be too much trouble for you, though."

"No trouble at all," Adrian replied, never taking his eyes off my face as he passed me my textbook and I pressed it tighter to my chest.

It was so much easier to ignore someone when they weren't standing right in front of you. It was much easier to pretend they didn't affect you too.

I plastered a smile on my lips, polite with an edge of something else underneath, and extended a palm. "So good to see you again, Adrian."

"Mr. Lambert," he corrected. "Best we keep the tone professional. Considering the circumstances."

I lifted a curious brow, not realizing I was doing it until it was too late. "Circumstances?" I parroted, my glare flicking between the two men in front of me.

"Adrian is going to be tutoring you. Boy could use the extra cash." Mr. Prescott smirked in a way that told you he was being condescending, in case his tone didn't get the message across. "Couldn't you?"

"And what happened to Miss Whittaker?" I asked, knowing I wouldn't like the answer.

"Unfortunately, Miss Whittaker won't be returning."

Neither would Miss Benton, Miss James, or Miss Kent. Four tutors in twelve months. Five if you counted *Mr. Lambert*. At least if this one didn't return, I knew it wouldn't be because my husband got bored with fucking him. Because that was exactly what had happened with the rest. Guess my bastard brother-in-law was their last resort. Mine too if I wanted to continue with my schooling.

I nodded once. "A shame." The socialite's way of saying: *I know more than you think I know.*

"It is," Mr. Prescott hummed. His way of telling me to keep my mouth shut and not ask any more questions about what *I knew.* Which was actually something we could agree on. I didn't care to ask and he didn't care to tell me. "Right, well, I'll leave you to it. Adrian, *Mary.*" He dipped his chin and exited the room. His heavy steps trudging down the hall before dying off completely.

I waited a moment, keeping my voice low and my glare narrowed as I turned it on Adrian. "What the fuck are you doing here?"

He tucked his hands into his pockets, his stern expression melting into a grin. "Like the old man said, little lamb. I'm just here to teach you a thing or two."

63

ADRIAN

"Lambert?" Marisela asked.

She didn't have to say more. I saw the question in her eyes—rather the realization—and I couldn't keep myself from touching her. Even though I knew I shouldn't. That she shouldn't let me. My hand moved towards her face, the pad of my thumb brushing against her bottom lip. Remembering what those lips tasted like. How they felt against my cock. How perfect they looked pursed together and covered in my cum...

A day, a month, a year... it didn't matter. There was no forgetting this woman and the way she altered my brain chemistry. The way she altered me and the way I'd altered her in return. We didn't fit together. In the same world, in the same room.

I didn't care. I'd shave down all our edges until we'd click into place. Until she became that piece I'd been missing since the first time she looked down at me from her window.

"See that?" I lowered my mouth, close enough to breathe her air, without actually making contact. The anticipation was everything. At least for me it was. It just seemed to infuriate her. "I gave you my name long before you took my brother's, little lamb," I whispered. Quickly dropping my hand to my side. Stepping back and putting a few feet of distance between us.

It was all I could do to keep myself from doing something stupid. Something gratifying but so very stupid. It was ironic, how often those two crossed paths. How something could be wrong and feel so right.

Not to say anything about her being mine was wrong. It wasn't. The timing was. I couldn't rush it.

Marisela set her textbook on the coffee table and crossed her arms over her chest, the way she often did when she was trying to put her guard up around me. "Does Tate know about this?"

"It was his idea," I admitted. Technically, it was mine. He'd just been too dumb to figure that part out.

"Of course it was," she groaned, plopping down on the sofa. Her eyes rolling towards the ceiling before flicking towards me again. She paused a moment, then cocked her head to one side. "How's the foot?"

"Significantly lighter. How's that pretty little pussy?" I watched her smirk drop.

"You took something you had no right to take, Adrian."

"Mr. Lambert," I reminded her. "And so did you."

"That was different."

"The way I see it, it was very much the same."

She was fuming now. Her brows knitted in the

middle and her lip curled slightly at the top. "Mine is gone forever. Yours is sitting upstairs in a jewelry box."

"Do you plan on returning it, Marisela?" I lifted a challenging brow.

She shook her head and hissed, "Never."

"Do you regret it?" I continued to press.

"Not even a little bit."

"Me either." I shrugged. "See? Same." She opened her mouth to reply and I raised a finger to stop her. "I suggest we use your time wisely. Unless you'd rather wait and see what other warm bodies your husband can dig up? But I can assure you their qualifications won't be anywhere near as good as mine are."

"Fine," she grunted. "Show me what you got, *Mr. Lambert*. Just remember, a day will come when the student surpasses the teacher. It always does."

"I have no doubt," I told her.

Truth was, I was looking forward to it. There was nothing sexier than a woman who could bring a man to his knees. And I was practically crawling.

Several weeks passed and Marisela still wouldn't let me touch her. Which was smart on her part. I'd seen the morality clause in their prenuptial agreement. Just the hint of a scandal, and she'd lose everything. And what was more scandalous than having an affair with your bastard of a brother-in-law?

It was why I was here. Why Tate allowed it. Why he didn't fight the suggestion I made and the idea he thought he had. To tempt her. To torture me. It was another game to him. One that was easy to play when you had the dealer in your pocket and all the cards in your hand.

It was also why he would lose. Why I would do whatever needed to be done to ensure Marisela would win.

She hadn't realized it yet. But we weren't on opposing teams. Fighting was just part of the sport. The more she hated me, the more driven she became. And fuck if she wasn't driven to hate me.

She chewed on the end of her pencil, so lost in thought she didn't feel me watching her. Relaxed. More relaxed than she should be in my presence. Considering all the things I was picturing doing to her right now. She was also hyperfocused. Her legs curled up under her ass, one elbow propped up on the arm of the sofa. All her concentration on the chemistry problems in front of her.

The woman wasn't just smart. Plenty of people were smart. She was cunning and curious and unapologetic. She knew how to read the room, how to work it in her favor, how to adapt. It was survival of the fittest. It was also something you couldn't teach.

She scribbled down a few more equations, checking her math before shoving the paper in my direction. I grabbed it out of her hand and set it aside.

"Aren't you even going to look at it?" She sighed. "Make sure I'm right."

"Don't need to. I know you're right," I explained.

"How? How do you know without even looking?"

"I looked at what mattered." I lifted a shoulder. "Your face told me everything. You know you're right. I am not going to waste the effort proving it for you. You don't need outside validation. Trust your gut, Marisela."

"Even when it's telling me I should take this pencil and shove it through your eye," she grunted, and I grinned.

"Especially then."

64

The slight chill in the air had me reaching into my jacket pockets, attempting to keep warm at the same time the vibrating of my phone sent a different kind of shiver down my spine. The kind you got when you knew you shouldn't be sticking your hand inside the cookie jar even as you were licking the crumbs off your fingertips.

I held my breath, propriety warring with curiosity as I tugged the device out and skimmed the notification across the top. An email I shouldn't read, especially here, but couldn't stop myself from devouring either. Every word latching on and feeding my tendency for self-sabotage. My ego too, if I were being honest. Because I enjoyed the attention nearly as much as I despised the man giving it to me.

My Dearest Marisela,

You looked particularly beautiful when you were leaving the house this morning. Sad but beautiful. What can I do to turn that frown into a smile? Would my mouth lapping at that sweet cunt help? My face is yours for the taking.

AL

I shook my head, swiped the email from my screen, and sent it directly to the recycle bin before emptying that too. Out of sight, out of mind. Except he was never really out of my mind. He made sure of it. He continued to make sure of it. No matter how long I'd been married to his brother. No matter how many times I turned down his advances over the years.

Still, for as much as he claimed to know me, he was wrong. I wasn't sad. I was caught off guard. Shocked, I guess?

It had been sudden. At least it felt that way. Or maybe that was just something that had been so ingrained in us to think. To say. That death was sudden. Even though that wasn't always the case. Even though sometimes death was expected. Appreciated. Like my mother. Like the man in the casket in front of me.

Maybe *he* didn't appreciate it. But I sure did. And so did my husband. Who'd been left everything in the will. It was all his. Mine by proximity. The company, the estate, the cash flowing out of the multiple bank accounts...

It almost seemed too easy.

I looked up, peering past the giant hole that sepa-rated family from friends. My black veil fluttering in the wind and my hem whipping against my knees as my glare honed in on Adrian. Who hadn't been there a moment ago. Who wasn't even named in the obituary. The prodigal son treated like a stranger at his own father's funeral. Not that he seemed all that bothered by Mr. Prescott's death. More bored than anything else. And that's when it occurred to me. He wasn't here to mourn. He was here to see it for himself. To watch the casket get lowered into the ground, the dirt get piled on top. To ensure those bones were as forgotten as the secrets they kept.

Or maybe I was wrong about that too. Maybe he had another reason to be here. I could only guess, consid-ering the man flipped between hot and cold, between sending me dirty emails in private and insisting I address him appropriately in public.

Mr. Lambert was...

Well, I didn't know what he was. Only that some days I hated him and others I hated him *less*. I wasn't sure what category he fell into today. But I had a feeling I'd figure it out soon enough. Seeing as the crunching of grass announced his presence before he did. Then again, I would have felt him even if it hadn't. Somehow, the air always increased a few degrees whenever the man was near.

I spun on a heel, grabbing on to Tate's arm to keep him from toppling over. He smelled like booze and Botox. He overindulged in both.

"My condolences." Adrian dipped his chin to his

brother, then leaned forward to press a kiss to my cheek. Lingering a few seconds before pulling back again.

I quirked a brow. "To you as well, Mr. Lambert."

"Doctor," he corrected me, which seemed to be one of his favorite things to do.

"Right. Of course, my mistake, *Dr.* Lambert," I replied, my tone sharper than the tips of the long red nails now digging into Tate's elbow. He was too drunk to feel them. "Congratulations, by the way."

"For what?" Adrian tilted his head, the light rain splattering against his glasses while he did nothing to stop it. Nothing to wipe the droplets away. Unbothered and so fucking arrogant.

"Briarwood. It was a shame, the atrocities they said went down there. Heard you had a hand in shutting them down." Another polite dance laced with double meaning we both understood. "You're lucky to have made it out alive."

"It was a... team effort." Adrian shrugged, the gesture more nonchalant and less boyish charm as the years passed between us. The way he carried himself and spoke now, much the same. I wasn't the only one putting on a show for everyone around me.

"Isn't it always?" I pressed my mouth into a fine line, neither a smile nor a frown. And tugged a little harder on Tate's arm. "Well, as usual, it's been a pleasure, Dr. Lambert. But I think it's time my husband and I mourn in private. You understand."

"Of course. I can only imagine what it's like to bury a parent. Call me if you need anything. Either of you."

Adrian held my glare for another moment before stepping aside, allowing us to brush past him.

I didn't look back. I didn't have to. It wouldn't tell me anything I didn't know. Because once again, I could feel him watching me.

I kept my spine straight, my gait steady as I guided Tate down the path towards the stretch limousine. Though he was barely conscious by the time I shoved him inside. And it wasn't because he was heartbroken over the loss of Senior. It was because he was out late celebrating our financial gain.

Tate's head slumped against the tinted window as he swiped up a bottle from the minibar. This time, I didn't care to stop him. If I was lucky, maybe he'd drink himself into an early grave.

It wasn't like it would be a hardship to toss another body in that hole. *And wouldn't you know, I was already dressed for the occasion.*

65

ADRIAN

I didn't remember what it was like to kill my father. Not in the moment, just the feeling that came after. Like being stuck underwater for so long you were close to accepting death, only to pop up at the last second and take a large gulp of air. The realization that he was gone was that air. Relief and freedom all rolled up in one.

Except I wasn't really free. Not until Tate joined him and I couldn't get rid of big brother without risking losing the woman I loved. It wasn't like being stuck between a rock and a hard place. It was like being spit-roasted over a fire. The farther you moved away from the flames the deeper you drove the stakes, and the closer you got, the more you felt the burn. Either way, you were suspended there. In agony, until one or the other did you in.

Then again, it was hard to remember something that didn't exactly happen. Because I didn't actually kill the old man. The gravediggers did. Or maybe the real culprit was all the dirt they piled on top of him.

I stood at the edge of the eight-by-four hole, the weight of my shoes sending a few loose clumps of dirt toppling inside, and gestured a hand at the two men standing beside the casket. Signaling for them to pry it open wide enough to have the fucker's dead eyes staring back at me.

He didn't get the luxury of resting easy. Of dying easy either. Which was why I went to the trouble of having him buried alive. Injecting him with a cocktail of sedatives and paralytics that kept his heart beat slowing but not stopping. Paying the ME and a couple of morticians for their silence.

They were happy to do it too. Happy for all the work I promised them in the future. All the bodies I planned to store in their freezers until I had Briarwood fully operational again. My little lamb had been right when she said I was responsible for getting their doors closed. But she was wrong if she thought that shit was permanent.

Hare and Burke might have been a few spots over from where I was standing. Or at least what was left of them was. But I had plans, and now that the old man was done paying for med school, I had the actions to back 'em up.

I glared at his lifeless face for a few moments longer, rolling the eye caps around the palm of my hand before pocketing them. I'd removed those myself, ensuring the old fuck had nothing to look at but the overpriced satin that lined the underside of his casket. And then I watched them shovel pounds of dirt on top. Digging him back up a few hours later so I could see it myself. See the way his face had contorted after the cocktail began to wear off and the only thing he could do was scream and claw and cry out for help that wasn't coming.

And now that I was sure it was over, sure that he'd rot in that hole, I could move on with everything else I had in mind for myself. Everything I had in mind for Briarwood.

You'd think it would get to me. Make me angry or bitter. All the years of seeing them together. Knowing he touched her whenever he felt the urge. Knowing she'd let him because it was her wifely duty. Or the more likely reason: *because* she knew it irritated me. But I wasn't bitter. I was intrigued. Obsessed. Inspired.

I pressed send on my latest email, encrypted thanks to the tech genius now under my employ, and pushed back in my office chair. She wouldn't answer me. But it didn't matter because she would read it. And I would receive a notification the moment she did.

ARE YOU SLEEPING WELL, MARISELA? YOU SEEMED TIRED AT BREAKFAST TODAY. IT'S HIS SNORING AGAIN, ISN'T IT? I KNOW HE ISN'T KEEPING YOU UP IN OTHER WAYS. BIG BROTHER NEVER DID HAVE MUCH STAMINA.

HOW DO I KNOW, YOU MAY ASK? THOSE

WALLS HAVE EARS, PRINCESA. IT'S HOW I ALSO KNOW YOU REQUESTED SEPARATE BEDROOMS. IS THAT YOUR WAY OF ASKING ME TO JOIN YOU?
YOURS,
AL

My computer dinged. A little *open* icon popped up on my screen and I grinned. Picturing her face. The way her cheeks would heat up and turn a shade darker, how she would try to hide it even if she was alone. Biting the inside of her cheek and pressing her lips together to keep from smiling. Because god forbid my little lamb give into her urges.

The same urges that had me loosening my belt buckle and reaching a hand inside my boxers. My legs spread wide under my desk as I remembered the way those lips sucked me off. The perfect balance of tongue and teeth and throat. Of suction and saliva.

I gripped my cock tighter in my palm, stroking up and down until it was throbbing. Begging to be inside her again. To fuck her until she was screaming my name. *My name,* not his.

My own hand was never enough. But envisioning hers? It had me fucking my palm like I was a goddamn teenager again. Clenching my ass cheeks, lifting off the seat, and meeting my wrist thrust for thrust.

I used my free arm to fumble around with the desk drawer—I didn't have to stop to find what I was looking for—swiped up the mask and brought it to my nose. Breathing the scent of her cunt deep into my lungs while a phantom hand continued to work my cock. I could almost feel her. Almost taste her. Though I was afraid to try and accidentally lick it clean.

The chair continued to shake and squeak with my movements, one palm pressing the leather almost flush against my face at the same time the other stroked me from base to tip. From tip to base again.

And then I was coming, drenching the underside of my desk and the crotch of my pants with everything I'd saved up for her.

The woman who was mine and wasn't. Yet.

66

BUGS

I squeezed my eyes shut, attempting to relieve some of the pressure. It only made things worse, though. The left side of my head tender to the touch, the right doing its best to compensate for the change. But it was the random twitching that really got to me. The way the muscles in my face seemed to have a mind of their own.

Still, I was grateful. A little bit of pain was better than the silence. Than being ignored. Most of the time. Sometimes blending into the background had its benefits. Made it easier to grab a few extra pudding cups, swap out some batteries, or plant the occasional camera. To watch the crap going on behind the curtains and read lips. I didn't need to hear what they were saying, not when I could see it up close. Not when I could study it and their mannerisms.

The human body told ya a lot more than their words. Every fucking time. Except when it came to the real psychopaths. Then it turned into a bit of a guessing game.

Either way, technology was my lifeline. Gave me more than human interaction ever could. Kept me in contact with my brother when they did everything in their power to separate us. It was also the answer to bringing us back together. He needed his brain fixed and I needed another implant. Might not have had the cash but what I did have was the skills to get it from someone who had plenty of that shit to go around.

I glanced at my reflection on the black screen. I looked like a dog tilting his head, like someone was blowing a whistle and I was trying to find the source. The imbalance was driving me fucking nuts. Then again, I suppose I was in the right place for it.

I tapped a key before entering in my password. Never needed one until Casper started flooding the hard drive with viruses. Kid liked porn more than I liked my dick. Which was saying something.

My shoulder jerked upwards, tapping my temple at the sudden crackling sound, like Pop Rocks going off in the back of my throat, except this shit was all in my head. The slight ache radiating from the middle of my ear and down my jaw. I wasn't used to the implant. Or all the noise that came with it.

It was a constant sensory overload. Everything making some sort of sound. The buzzing of the light-bulbs, the humming of the computer screen, the rattling of the glass in the window frame.

It was hard to focus on anything when I was focusing on everything. I powered down the sound processor, shrugged the tension out of my neck, and returned my fingers to the keyboard. It didn't take more than a little bit of coding to bypass the hospital's security system, hack into their cameras, and stream the live feed.

I didn't know what exactly I was looking for, just that it needed to be incriminating. Blackmail usually was. Which meant hours of watching this shit in real time. Not that I was squeamish. It was just boring. No better than watching a goldfish swim laps around the same bowl. Until that goldfish slipped a fin into his pants and started jacking off.

I sat straighter in my chair and hit record. And not because I was a fucking perve. Guys weren't my thing. But doctors behaving badly certainly were. Especially when this doctor in particular was worth more than the gold watch sliding up and down on his wrist.

It was weird. Walking freely through the empty halls. Not having to worry about tiptoeing past the orderlies or pretending I was too slow to know what they were saying. The sounds were weird too. The dripping of rusty pipes and the creaking of the foundation. How the stale air seemed to whisper around you.

I didn't believe in ghosts. But if I did, Briarwood would be chock-full of 'em.

I turned another corner, stepped over a pile of construction material, and pushed my way inside Dr.

Lambert's office. He looked up from his computer screen just as I was tossing the thumb drive onto his desk.

"You know I have eyes everywhere, right?"

He quirked a brow, waiting for me to clarify.

"You might wanna think twice before going to town on yourself. Could ruin that squeaky-clean reputation you're trying to maintain around here." I smirked.

He swiped out a hand and grabbed the drive, not bothering to deny what we both knew was true. "What's this?"

I lifted a shoulder before turning around and making my way back towards the door. "Just a little insurance. In case the premiums go up."

67

ADRIAN

I popped the flash drive into the side of my computer and waited for it to load. Not the tiniest bit shocked when a video file appeared on my screen. There was a reason I went out of my way to provide the kid with whatever gadget I could get my hands on over the years.

It was a lot better to have him on your side.

I refastened the button on my pants. Sat back in my chair and pressed play. It took me a few minutes to realize exactly what I was staring at. Besides an active operating room. Two attendings elbow-deep in some girl's guts. A routine appendix removal by the looks of it. Until my focus shifted to a face I recognized. The camera lens zooming in on what he was doing with his free hand when the feed should have been locked on the incision site. They claimed it was for educational purposes when they had you sign off on being recorded—really it was the hospital's way of covering its ass in a malpractice suit.

Funny how quickly those tapes disappeared when the surgeon went a few centimeters in the wrong direction and caused the patient to bleed out. But that was beside the point. Seeing as I didn't give a shit about working the system on the up-and-up. Not when there were much more lucrative options on the black market. Organ trafficking, forged scripts, even the occasional hit...

That last one was Casper's specialty. All that energy needed to go somewhere. Who would have guessed the kid was good with a gun? Even better in close combat with a knife. His new spine had him twisting himself up like a pretzel, slipping through doors and windows. The challenge fueling his need more than the drugs and alcohol ever could. Not that he'd given those up entirely. But I wasn't his father. Even if the fucker liked to call me *Daddy* just to watch my face contort with disgust.

Right now, though, I was grinning. We were in desperate need of upgrades if I planned on getting this operation off the ground anytime soon. And I wasn't a fan of taking loans I couldn't pay back. Especially when those loans ran the risk of having someone showing up at your door looking to collect. And taking your hand when you couldn't.

My little lamb was the only one allowed to have a piece of me, and I drew the line at anything below the wrists. Wouldn't be much use to her otherwise.

But there were other methods of getting large sums of cash. And quick. Blackmail was at the top of that list and this little five-minute tape was worth millions to the fucker behind the surgical mask. Which meant it was priceless to me.

Sure, he could argue that it wasn't him. The schedule and patient chart would prove he was lying. And either way, the tape would become part of the hospital record. *Public* record if it was accidentally released to a certain media outlet with a hard-on for the growing healthcare crisis. It was much safer for all this shit to go away. For everyone involved.

I typed out a quick ransom demand. Short and to the point. *Pay us or we release the tape.* And then I hit send. While Bugs did his work behind the scenes, spoofing the account so that it appeared as though the *call was coming from inside the house*—as Casper would say.

Kid loved his horror movie references almost as much as he loved dressing up like every day was Halloween. A classic case of Peter Pan Syndrome to go along with the rampant ADHD and those pesky psycho-pathic tendencies of his. But that wasn't my problem. Same as I wasn't his daddy, I wasn't his doctor anymore either. Though I had to admit he'd grown on me.

Like a weed you just couldn't kill. Still, I had a soft spot for the kid. Things wouldn't be moving as fast as they were without him. And they were about to go a whole lot faster. Once this deal came through.

But right now, it was more of a waiting game as our frisky little friend here scrambled to track down the sender, accepted he wasn't gonna find him (probably because he didn't exist), and then finally agreed to make the drop. Unmarked bills in exchange for the original thumb drive.

We'd have copies. Plenty of 'em. But he wouldn't know that. What kind of businessman would I be if I didn't see how long I could milk the fucker dry?

Until then, I had a lot of time on my hands. Time that I would much rather have been spending with *her*. If she ever decided to reply to one of my messages.

> GUESS WHO?
> DID YOU LIKE THE FLOWERS I SENT? THEY REMINDED ME OF YOU. BRIGHT AND VIBRANT WHEN WET. AND DULL AND LIFELESS WHEN DRY. BE SURE TO STAY NICE AND WET FOR ME, MARISELA.
> YOURS,
> AL

I knew Bugs was somewhere hacking into my emails. Both business and personal. Making sure I wasn't going to screw him over. Probably rolling his eyes or maybe he'd finally smartened up and started taking notes. God knew he needed to get laid after spending most of his teenage years locked up in here.

I mean, even his brother found a way to get his dick wet. And that was after having his brain tossed into a blender and his waist chained to a wall. Not saying it was entirely consensual but Donnie worked with what was within his reach. And what was in his reach happened to be a bunch of less-than-willing nurses.

Then again, it was no real surprise Bugs had never had a girlfriend. Besides the lack of a social life, guy had real trust issues. Not that I blamed him with the shit they did to his hearing. It was why I didn't bother trying to hide anything from him. He'd find it anyway and then I'd have to hire another tech guy. Specifically one who wanted something from me, enough to work for room and board and not much else. Because until that payment landed in our accounts, I didn't have much else to offer.

68

A loud bang had me looking up from the stack of files on my desk just as my office door was swinging open. Hitting the wall with a thud and more than likely denting the new drywall. I tossed my glasses aside and rubbed at the bridge of my nose. Reminding myself it wasn't Donnie's fault. Fucker didn't know his own strength. And he really was making progress. Speaking almost full sentences without nearly as many violent outbursts.

As for the sex addiction, couldn't do much about that. He was a prisoner to his dick. I glanced over at the email I'd just sent to Marisela.

Okay, maybe he wasn't the only one.

"What is it, Donnie?" I paused, giving him enough time to process the question and try to formulate an answer. Press him too hard, too quick... and something was getting smashed.

"Man here. For you."

I nodded once. "Send ' em in."

Donnie stepped aside, and I realized he meant literally here. As in, right outside the door. But that wasn't the curious part...

I kept my expression neutral, gesturing to the chair in front of my desk. "It's been a long time. How can I help you, John?"

He was sweating. His knee bouncing up and down while his right hand tugged at his collar. Obvious signs of distress, mixed with a touch of guilt and desperation. "I need a favor."

I clasped my hands together and leaned forward. "As in a consultation? A patient giving you trouble?"

He shook his head. "This is, ah, more of a personal matter."

"Are you ill, John? Please tell me it's nothing serious."

"No, nothing like that." He glanced from side to side, like he was afraid he was being watched. He was, of course. Bugs wouldn't have it any other way. "It has to do with my finances."

I *tsked* my tongue, and he shrank back in his seat. "Now, John, we both know I am not in the business of dishing out loans."

"No... but someone mentioned you were in the business of... something else."

"Someone and something...? You're going to have to be more specific than that." I quirked a brow.

"Like taking someone out. Like making sure they can't talk," he said cryptically.

"Once again, I need specifics, John. Or else stop

wasting my time. Someone who? And what is it you're afraid of them saying?"

"A colleague. A student—"

"You want me to murder a kid for you?" I lifted a palm to my chest and did my best to appear offended. When really I was just fucking with him. Enjoying the way he cowered in on himself. In my office. In my facility. In my city.

"No! He's a resident. An adult," John was quick to clarify.

"Right, okay then, what did this adult do to warrant you wanting to off him?"

"He's blackmailing me. Threatening me, threatening everything I've worked for."

"I see... and what does he want?"

"Money."

"So give it to him." I shrugged. "I don't see the problem, John. Pay him to keep his mouth shut and I'm sure this will all blow over without us having to resort to cold-blooded murder."

"I did! I have been!" John was yelling now, up on his feet and pacing in front of my desk. "He just keeps asking for more. It's been months. It's not gonna end, Adrian. I can't sleep. I can't eat. It's never gonna end."

"I see. You're right. That is a problem." I nodded.

"Okay! So you get it now. I don't have any other choice."

"And you're sure it's him. This student of yours?"

John raked an agitated hand through his hair. "It couldn't be anyone else. No one else knows about me...

about what I... about my preferences. No one except him... and you. But you aren't—"

"I'm not what, John?" I grunted, daring him to give me a reason. Just one fucking reason to jump across this desk and wrap my hands around his throat.

"Not *ya know*."

"No, I don't know so why don't you explain it to me?"

"Not like that." He gestured a hand in the air. "You're... loyal."

I twisted my scowl into a polite smile. "You're right. I am loyal, John. To those around me, those in my very tight circle. To those I respect and admire and trust with my secrets."

"Exactly!" He clapped his hands together, relief dripping down his face and moistening the edge of his collar. "Did I ever tell you that you were like a son to me, Adrian?"

"No," I forced out between clenched teeth. "Never. Not once. But you know what? You sure as hell always treated me like a father." I didn't give the words a chance to sink in before adding, "I'll tell you what... I'll take care of this little problem for you. For a price."

He nodded, his glasses shifting up and down on his nose each time his chin tapped his chest. "Yes, of course. You name it. But... it needs to look like an accident. Can't have this leading back to me."

"Accidents take time, John," I sighed. "Planning, research... What's this guy's routine? Does he have any hobbies? A girlfriend?"

John just stared back at me. "Uh, I don't know. I don't think so. Maybe?"

I didn't bother responding, jabbing a finger against the intercom that I knew was already on and listening. "Bugs?"

"Yes, Dr. Lambert, how can I assist you?" the kid replied, much more formally than usual. It was all for show. A way to ensure our customers got the full experience.

"Dig up everything there is to know about a Mister…." I looked to John, waiting for him to fill in the blanks.

"Michaels. Cohen Michaels."

I dipped my head in acknowledgement. "Dig up everything there is to know on a Cohen Michaels, a med student with a residency at Northwestern."

"Got it, boss," he signed off, and I returned my attention to John, who was staring at me with a puzzled look on his face.

"Bugs?" he questioned.

"Best if we keep things impersonal. Plausible deniability and all that," I explained. "Now that that's settled, we have to go over a little housekeeping. We only accept cash. Upfront. I am sure you understand the reasoning."

I waited for John to slip back out the door with his tail between his legs before calling the boys into my office. Bugs was the first to appear, probably because he never stopped listening.

"So let me get this straight..." He leaned a shoulder against the jamb, arms folded over his chest and ankles crossed. "The guy we've spent close to a year blackmailing, just dropped in to the place he helped pay to upgrade, offering to give us a ridiculous amount of cash to take out the wrong guy?"

I lifted a noncommittal shoulder, allowing the smirk to spread across my face. "In our line of work, we call that double dipping."

Instead of replying, Bugs stumbled forward as Casper barged his way inside the room, tossing a thumb behind him. "Who was that?"

"That was John... Dr. John Rath. Our newest client."

Casper glanced towards the door before looking back at me again. "Kinda looks like a weasel."

"That's because he is one."

69

MARISELA

"Did you figure it out?" I shot my glare at the kid sitting in my office chair, his dark shaggy hair pressed behind his ear by one of those hands-free devices while his fingers clicked away at my keyboard. The sound loud and annoying when it wasn't coming from me.

It took a moment for his bright-green eyes to flick in my direction, landing on my scowl before flicking up to my face again. *Fucker better keep it in his pants if he doesn't want one of my heels shoved up his ass.*

"I'm sorry... Did you say something?"

Hard to hear when you're too busy staring at my mouth, huh? Then again, that was why I preferred red. Men weren't exactly bulls but they were easily distracted by shiny objects. And today, *I* was that object. I needed to be if I wanted anyone to pay attention to me in that boardroom.

I huffed my annoyance, my heels clanking across the

floor as I paced back and forth in front of him. "*I said* did you figure it out?"

"No, sorry, ma'am. Whoever's on the other end of this, they're good. Like tech-genius level good. Each of these correspondences is being diverted and filtered through another IP address. We can't track it or keep the emails from coming—unless you want me to block all senders outside the server…?"

"Meaning?"

"Meaning all emails would be internal…" he explained, and I lifted a questioning brow. "Employees only, basically. But even then, if someone knows what they're doing, they can spoof the domain name…"

I shook my head. "Doesn't matter. Seventy-five percent of what I do is outsourcing. It's not feasible anyway."

"Sorry I can't do more, Miss Cruz." The kid sighed.

"Mrs. Prescott." I eyed him for a moment before gesturing a hand in his direction. He was pretty. A little too pretty for a computer nerd. "Who are you again? What's your name?"

He grinned, one side of his mouth punctuated by a dimple. "Elliot Walker, ma'am. Your husband brought me on last week. Guess they're still working on my name tag." He chuckled.

"Right, well, you can remove yourself from my seat now, can't you." It wasn't a request. I didn't pretend that it was either.

"Ah, yeah, sorry." That dimple sank deeper as *Elliot* pushed himself up from my chair and maneuvered around my desk, rubbing at the back of his neck and drawing my attention to the way his muscles pulled the material of his dress shirt taut. It wasn't unusual for Tate to hire someone based on their looks. But it was unusual for that someone to be male. "Just, ah, let me know if you need anything else," he added while peering at me over a shoulder.

"Sure." It was one word but it might as well have been two. *Fuck you.*

I huffed again, listening to my office door click closed before lowering myself back in my seat. My anger was misplaced. I knew that. It wasn't the kid's fault. It was Adrian's. And whoever he had on his payroll, because I knew this shit wasn't him. Dr. Lambert liked his antiquities—*tech had never really been his thing.*

I scooted myself closer to my desk and glanced down. His latest email taunting me from my computer screen.

LITTLE LAMB,
You can't ignore me forever. We're family after all. Bound by blood. And so much more.
Yours,
AL

I'd spent years trying to ignore him, even when he was in the same room with me. Years avoiding him and refusing to give in. And maybe that was just what he wanted. Maybe he wanted the chase. Maybe he needed something to fantasize over. Maybe indulging him would be enough. And maybe responding was what we both needed to move on.

I flexed my fingers before brushing them over my keyboard. Typing out a curt reply that I had no doubt I would regret at the same time I did nothing to stop myself.

> MR. LAMBERT,
> SEEING AS THE TECH DEPARTMENT HAS INFORMED ME THAT IT'S IMPOSSIBLE FOR THEM TO BLOCK AN ENCRYPTED IP ADDRESS, I WOULD APPRECIATE IT IF YOU WOULD REFRAIN FROM USING SUCH VULGAR LANGUAGE IN YOUR CORRE-SPONDENCES.
> SINCERELY,
> MARISELA CRUZ-PRESCOTT

A new email landed in my inbox almost immediately.

> DR. LAMBERT... IF YOU INSIST ON FORMALI-TIES, MS. CRUZ. AS FOR VULGAR, WE BOTH KNOW IT DOESN'T MATTER HOW PRIM AND PROPER YOU TRY TO ACT... YOU'LL ALWAYS BE MY DIRTY LITTLE SLUT UNDERNEATH IT ALL. I BET YOU'RE TOUCHING YOURSELF RIGHT NOW AS YOU'RE READING THIS. ARE YOU WET FOR ME, PRINCESA?
> YOURS,
> AL

"You have got to be kidding me..." I cursed under my breath, too irritated to consider the ramifications before slamming down on the keys again and quickly pressing *send.*

> DR. LAMBERT,
> I WOULD NEVER DREAM OF DOING SUCH A THING IN THE OFFICE. ONE OF US IS A PROFESSIONAL. ONE OF US ALSO HAS ACCESS TO A RATHER LARGE AND LITIGIOUS LEGAL DEPARTMENT.
> SINCERELY,
> MARISELA CRUZ-PRESCOTT

It was an idle threat. And we both knew it. The burden of proof would be on me and I had nothing that actually proved Adrian was on the other end of the screen. And neither did our IT department apparently.

> MY DEAREST MARISELA,
> PLEASE DON'T THREATEN ME WITH A GOOD TIME. ACTUALLY, I TAKE THAT BACK. PLEASE DO. I'D LOVE TO SEE YOU ALL DOLLED UP AND SITTING ACROSS FROM ME IN ONE OF THOSE TIGHT-FITTING SKIRTS YOU LIKE TO WEAR. A TEAM OF LAWYERS AT YOUR BECK AND CALL WHILE YOU HURLED EVERY ACCUSATION IN THE BOOK IN MY DIRECTION BEFORE I CLEARED THE ROOM AND FUCKED YOU IN THE MIDDLE OF THE CONFERENCE TABLE. JUST TELL ME WHERE AND WHEN, LITTLE LAMB.
> YOURS,
> AL

Fucking hell!

NOWHERE AND NEVER.

No address or sign-off. Short and sweet. Anything more and I would be tossing my computer across my desk just to watch it shatter.

ALWAYS AND FOREVER.
YOURS,
AL

70

ADRIAN

"Do we have any intel on the girlfriend? Is she someone we have to worry about?" I looked over at Bugs, who was sitting cross-legged in front of me. A tablet on his lap and a stylist pressed to the screen.

I didn't like complications. More than that I didn't like loose ends. And I wasn't above throwing in a freebie if it meant the job got done right. There was collateral damage in every business. Mine just happened to include spare body parts. Which were in high demand by the way. Especially to the right buyer. A win-win if you asked me.

"She's pretty." He shrugged. "But irrelevant. No family, no real social media presence, newer relationship... My guess is she'll just assume he's ghosted her. It's kinda his MO."

"You like her..." I watched his face for a moment while he pretended to watch his screen and not hear me.

We both knew he did. I'd tested the new implant and it was working perfectly. This was just Bugs's way of coping with shit he didn't like. And it'd worked for a long time. That time wasn't now, though.

Realizing I wasn't about to drop it, he finally looked up and narrowed his gaze. "I don't like her. I don't even know her," he grunted.

"Except you do. You know everything there is to know about her, don't you?" I countered.

"That's my job, isn't it? Finding out everything there is to know about the target."

"The target, yes." I lifted a shoulder. "The target's girlfriend, not so much. We just need the basics, not her life story." *Our boy had a crush.* It was cute. It was also dangerous. "Stay away from the girl. If she really is irrelevant, be smart and keep her that way."

He nodded once before returning his focus to his tablet. I wasn't dumb enough to think that was the end of it, though. These kids weren't exactly the listening type. But they were loyal. And more than that, they were predictable. Which made it easy to figure out what kind of trouble they were going to get themselves into and prepare for it.

Besides, keeping tabs on the girlfriend wasn't exactly a bad thing, if he was discreet about it. Meant we would be the first to know if she became a problem.

"I'm thinking a car accident..." I broke the silence, waving a hand in the air as I tried to picture it. It was a waste of good organs but our client wasn't paying for a disappearance. Rath wanted a body. Proof. And customer satisfaction was always my top priority. "Something messy but not uncommon…"

Bugs shook his head, his eyes lighting up like they did whenever I ordered him a new piece of tech. But we weren't talking tech right now. We were talking murder. "I got a better idea."

I shifted in my seat, leaning closer as I waited to hear him out. This was a group effort after all. "I'm listening."

"Guy owns a bike. Yellow and flashy. The kind people like to ride a little too fast… the kind that're easy to track in the dark… The kind that are prone to spinning out and hitting a guardrail without anyone asking why…"

Bugs met my glare from over the top of his computer screen, dipping his head in a curt nod. And I used a burner phone to dial Casper. Letting it ring out three times before hanging up. He would know what it meant.

Our target was in position. The perfect combination of factors that would have this whole thing appearing like a tragic accident. A guy at the prime of his life taken out by too much confidence and adrenaline.

Really was a shame, though. I recognized what John didn't. The fact that his pupil was as depraved as he was. Maybe more so. Cohen Michaels wasn't just any surgical resident. He was a serial killer in the making. Lacked empathy and couldn't see past his own ego. I could work with that. I could manipulate it into being exactly what I needed. If only his head didn't come with such a high price tag.

Unfortunately for Dr. Michaels, he was worth much more to me dead than alive.

Thirty minutes later, my phone lit up with an incoming call. A call meant there'd been a complication. It was more of a *no news was good news* kinda thing. I swiped answer and pressed the device to my ear, waiting to hear who was on the other side before speaking.

"Minor hiccup," Casper grunted into the receiver. "Fucker just doesn't want to stay down. Should I take care of it?"

I considered our options before landing on one that had me grinning. "No."

I'd let fate decide for us. If things didn't go exactly according to plan and Dr. Michaels was able to bring himself back from the brink of death, then I'd give him a second chance. Fix him up and use him. If not, then so be it. Either way, we were getting paid. That's what liability clauses were for. Nothing was guaranteed when our client insisted on it looking like an accident—he signed a contract saying as much. Whether or not John read it wasn't my problem. It was his.

"You sure?" Casper pressed, and I could hear the apprehension in his voice. He didn't like leaving shit unfinished. He'd be too ramped up to let it go, which meant I would be getting another call after he drank himself into oblivion tonight. Then again, he'd probably do that anyway.

"Yes." I hung up without bothering to say more. He would do as he was told. Kid had learned the hard way what happened if he didn't and now we had an understanding. We all did.

I wasn't a dictator. I just did what it took to keep everyone in line. Other than that, the residents of Briarwood had free will. It was a fair trade. At least it was more fair than they'd get from anyone else.

71

ADRIAN

I recognized obsession when I saw it. I had my own to deal with after all. I also understood how much of a weakness it was. To both of us. Good thing *our friend* here didn't know about mine.

I knew all there was to know about his, though. About how he followed her everywhere she went. Watched her from a distance—something else we had in common. How losing everything in a matter of a few weeks meant the only thing he could focus on was her. Her and the child he thought they were going to have.

The folder in my hand told me otherwise. I flicked through a few pages before rolling it up and tucking into my jacket pocket. Memorizing just enough to grab his attention and likely send him spiraling. Medical jargon I knew he would understand but probably not absorb, seeing as part of him already blamed the girl for his misfortune. Blamed her for luring him out onto the street and right into our trap. Even though the poor thing didn't know that's what she was doing.

He didn't know either.

But it didn't matter. Narcissists didn't care whose fault it was. Just that it wasn't their own.

I was curious how he would take the news. One more thing ripped out of his severely-mangled hand. One more disappointment life had dealt him.

There were really only two options. It would either break him or motivate him. And I had a hunch it would be the latter. Suicide was far too self-reflective for a man like Cohen Michaels. But revenge wasn't. And revenge was an even greater motivator than love. Though one usually fueled the other.

I stared at him from behind the foggy glass of the bar window. Waiting on the sidewalk with my hands tucked into my pockets and Bugs standing at my back. Casper was a wild card, one I couldn't risk with situations as... delicate as these. Besides, I didn't think he would be able to contain his excitement after he saw what our little "accident" did to our former target's face. What some sloppy surgeons had done to piece it back together not so tactfully.

A waste of skin and tissue. Good thing it wasn't his looks I was interested in. It was what he could or couldn't do with his hands. What I could do to fix them and then what he would do to pay me back.

I waited for the girl to leave—Emily Shaw was her name I'd come to learn—and stepped up behind Cohen's back just as he moved to follow her. Clamping a hand on his shoulder and shoving him down again.

"Dr. Cohen Michaels, it's a pleasure to make your acquaintance." I grinned.

He didn't. But that was because he didn't know about my proposal yet. He would soon. And he would accept it or I would be forced to finish what I started.

Like I said, I didn't like loose ends. But I sure as hell enjoyed tying them off.

It took longer than I preferred for Dr. Michaels to get onboard with all that Briarwood had to offer. And not because the shit we did here bothered him. I saw the way his eyes lit up when they swept over my surgical table. How feral he looked when the scent of blood penetrated his nostrils. The fucker came alive with a scalpel in his hand. Even if he struggled to hold it.

No, the problem he had was the fact he wasn't in control. I was. And I always would be too. My boys would make sure of it.

See, that was the difference between me and Cohen. He didn't play well with others. Didn't know what it was like to think about anyone but himself. Didn't know what it was to set your own desires aside in favor of someone else's. But I did. Even if it was all in favor of getting what I wanted in the end.

If I were being honest, and I usually was, I'd admit that I saw a part of myself in each of the men I collected over the years. The good and the bad. The advantageous and the toxic. It was funny when you recognized yourself in someone else. It was less funny when that someone irritated the hell out of you.

Casper was playful and indulgent, the way Marisela made me feel during all those months we were sneaking around.

Dr. Michaels—Frankie, as the others liked to call him now—was egotistical, to the point it was to his detriment. A lesson I'd learned the hard way.

Donnie was... broken. Like the boy who grew up in a basement without a name. We had that in common. I just hid it better because my scars weren't as easy to spot.

And Bugs... he'd sacrificed everything for the person who meant the most to him in the world. For him, that person was his brother. For me, it was Marisela. They reminded me of the worst parts of myself. The parts I hated. And missed. The parts I was smart enough to rise above and the parts I would tuck away until the time was right.

I just had to keep reminding my little lamb I was here, waiting, until that time came. I pulled out my phone, deciding a text was more appropriate than an email right now.

ME:

Did I ever tell you what I noticed about you first?

ME:

> It was your hair. Long and dark, flowing down your back. Bouncing when you shoved past me. Some people would think you were stuck-up. Not me. All I could think was how do I get that girl's attention? How do I make her see me? Do you see me, little lamb? Because I see you.

If I knew Marisela as well as I was certain I did, she would spend the afternoon sawing away at her curls. Short enough that the only thing to bounce would be the ass they no longer brushed against.

It would be just another sign that she was as affected as I was. You didn't do shit like chopping off your hair out of spite unless you cared. And my guess was she cared more than either of us realized.

It was my guess *and* my hope.

72

MARISELA

I knew what it looked like. It looked like I was seeking *him* out. I wasn't. I was merely curious. Bored. Complacent. *Very married.*

Honestly, I didn't like the version of me I saw in the mirror anymore. The version I'd worked so hard to curate. The version that had become unrecognizable the longer I stared at it. All hard lines and jagged edges without any softness in sight. Nothing to use against me. Nothing to grab on to and control. Especially with the shorter bob that barely reached my shoulders.

I shook my head from side to side, the straightened ends brushing against my cheeks. I hated it. But I'd been impulsive. I needed a change. To be someone else if I couldn't be myself. The thing about playing a part was that sooner or later you realized you weren't playing anymore.

Because at some point, you'd crossed that line of

playing and started becoming... And the person I'd become was stale and lifeless.

I dropped my red mask back over my head, fanning out my lighter locks so that they fell perfectly across the sides of my face. My matching lipstick just barely visible beneath the shadow of the protruding nose.

Adrian would recognize it. And me. But no one else would.

I pushed out of the ladies' room door, the heady atmosphere of Original Sin greeting me on the other side. My heart nearly beating out of my chest as my eyes couldn't help but scan the crowd.

It was like that first time all over again. It was also completely different. Like stepping into an alternate universe where both things could be true at the same time.

I stepped up to the bar and raised two fingers, only to have a double shot of bourbon dropped in front of me. I glanced at the glass, then back at the man who'd put it there.

"I didn't order this..." I cocked my head at him. It was a condescending thing to do. I know. But it was a habit. Couldn't stop myself if I tried.

"Courtesy of your friend." The bartender gestured behind me. I didn't have to look to know who it was, though. I could feel him. His glare on my exposed back, grazing lower to the barely-decent dip of the silky material that started just above my ass. Hugging each cheek so that one wrong move would give everyone an eyeful.

Sure, sometimes the fantasy was better than the reality. But not this time. Not when I'd had years to fill out. To embrace my curves and use them to my advantage.

He continued to study me for a moment, as I lifted the glass to my lips and took in the smokey flavor. Michter's. I'd recognize it anywhere. It was my father's favorite. It was also too expensive to be on the menu. Which told me it was from *Dr. Lambert's* private stash.

I lifted a hand and ordered another. I'd drink the whole bottle, if only to spite him.

By the time I heard him step up to me, it was too late. His right hand was already around my waist while his left shifted the bourbon from my lips to his own before he lowered his mouth to my ear. "It's good. But your cunt tastes better."

I slid onto the closest bar stool, spreading my thighs wide enough to glide a fingertip over my pussy, coating my skin up to my knuckle. Then I raised my hand to my lips and licked it clean.

"You're right. It does. Too bad I don't share." I swiped my glass back and downed the rest of the contents before Adrian could stop me.

He swung out a hand and grabbed my wrist. "Neither do I," he grunted.

It was a nice sentiment. The fact that he thought fucking me first meant he owned me. But that's all it was. A sentiment. A flag impaled at the peak of a mountain until the next climber replaced it with their own.

I wasn't about to tell him that, though. Not now. As nice as it would be to see his *flag* deflate, I enjoyed our games too much. I needed them. I needed to feel wanted by someone. Even if I would never admit it.

He released his grip on my wrist just to raise his arm, combing his fingers through what was left of my hair. "You cut it." He was grinning, the way his mask shifted upward telling me as much. And something else told me that was what he had wanted all along.

He wanted to manipulate me. Predicting I would zig if he asked me to zag. And he was right. Because I did.

I wouldn't make that mistake a second time. Then again, maybe I would. Maybe it was the defiance he brought out of me that I enjoyed, more than his company.

It made sense. Seeing as the next thing I knew, I was rubbing a palm against his crotch, forcing Adrian to tip forward. A stack of papers plopping out of the inner lining of his pocket and onto the floor.

He didn't notice but I did. He was too busy leaning into my touch. Enjoying the way I stroked his cock like it had been minutes instead of years. His bulge biting against his zipper in an effort to get closer to me. To get inside me. To fuck us both into an oblivion *one of us* couldn't reach anymore.

But the other could. And there was just something about making a man come in his boxers that was so deliciously degrading. Something about reducing him to a teenage boy humping your hand, in full view of everyone else in the room, that was nearly as satisfying as the orgasm I couldn't achieve.

A few more rough strokes in the right direction and Adrian slapped a palm against the bar top, grunting as his bodily fluids continued to seep through the front of his pants. Dampening my fingers enough to know that my job here was done.

I stepped off the bar stool, my purse slipping from my grip and landing on the floor. I quickly swiped it up, along with the papers he'd dropped, and pushed out the closest exit.

Adrian didn't follow me. And I was as grateful for his indifference as I was annoyed by it.

The moment the door clicked closed, I lifted a brow. The effects of last night's liquor had worn off, but my irritation hadn't. "I assume you know the importance of discretion, Mr. Walker."

The kid adjusted the frames of his glasses and cleared his throat, shifting his weight from one foot to the other. "Um, yeah. I mean, *yes*, of course, Miss—Mrs. Prescott."

"And by discretion, I mean whatever happens in this office, whatever is discussed in this office, whatever anyone is instructed to do for me *in this office...* stays in this office. Do you understand me?"

I watched his Adam's apple bob in his throat as he swallowed. Or tried not to vomit. I could never be sure. Before he nodded once.

"Good." I tossed the rolled-up file across my desk. "I need you to find everything there is to find on this woman. Then I want you to doctor up a resume, make it look good but not too good. I want it to appear realistic before you fast-track it through our hiring process."

"I'm not really… I'm not…" he started to mumble while scratching at the back of his head.

"You're not what, Mr. Walker? Smart enough? Skilled enough? *Competent* enough?" I challenged.

"*HR* enough," he replied with a shrug.

"You are whatever I say you are."

He swiped the file from the top of my desk and glanced down at the name. His mouth pulled taut for a moment, and I wasn't sure if it was out of recognition or confusion. I didn't care to find out either.

"No problem. I'll get right on it." Elliot dipped his chin, grabbing the knob with one hand, the stack of papers pressed against his side with the other as he tugged the door open before closing it behind him again.

I didn't know who she was or why Adrian was carrying around a full dossier on her. But it was clear he was interested in this Emily Shaw. Which meant, suddenly, so was I.

73

MARISELA

I'd lost track of how long I'd been sitting here. But it was dark outside. Nothing but streetlamps and headlights reflecting against the windows of my office. Blinking and flashing different colors now and then. Red, blue, white, and various shades of yellow. Sometimes followed by the rumble of a sports car or street bike. The sound of loud laughter or screaming carrying past the double panes. The city was alive but the building was empty—though that wasn't unusual.

I preferred it that way. I needed the quiet. The stillness and the freedom.

I enjoyed the groaning of the copper pipes, the humming of the air vents, and the flicking of the bulbs whenever I stepped outside the door and the sensors tracked my movements to the staff kitchen. Not because I was hungry but because I knew I had to eat. Or because my legs were stiff and needed a break from sitting.

Tonight was different. Tonight I couldn't do anything

but stare. Holding my breath until my body forced me to breathe again. Hoping my eyes were playing tricks on me. But the words scrawled in bubbly handwriting wouldn't disappear.

I'M PREGNANT WITH YOUR HUSBAND'S BABY.

Another nameless girl threatening to go to the media. Another payout and another mess I had to clean up.

It wasn't the first time some random woman claimed as much. It was just the first time it came with any sort of proof.

The letter on my desk was taunting me. The open flap of the envelope fluttering each time the air circulated in its direction. Reminding me how some bastard with half a pint of Prescott blood—blood I didn't share— could take everything I'd spent years working towards. I crumbled the piece of paper into a ball, along with the sonogram that was folded up inside, and tossed it across the room.

I should have castrated the fucker when I had the chance. Kept his shriveled-up balls where I could see them. It was too late now. The last time I'd been near my husband's dick was when he'd been too drunk to pull up his own pants, and I'd been afraid of getting blamed for his unfortunate trip down the stairs.

If I were smart, I would have sucked it up and pushed him. But it was too late for that too.

I cracked my neck from side to side and rubbed at the tension in my temples. The girl could have been lying... Looking for some sort of easy handout like all the ones before her. Then again, Tate was one quick fuck away from fertilizing a houseplant if he thought it was flirting with him. And I didn't want orphaned saplings on our doorstep any more than I wanted orphaned children.

I slammed a fist down on the top of my keyboard and listened to the crunching of the plastic. Was I too old to be breaking things out of anger? Yes, I was. But it still felt nice.

At the same time, panicking wasn't good for anyone. I needed to know for sure first. I needed confirmation and then I needed a plan. But most of all, I needed discretion. The sort that wasn't easy to come by when your last name had so many zeros attached to it.

Fuck...

I swiped up my phone from my desk and dialed out, the ringtone increasing my anxiety almost as much as the sound of his voice on the other side. "Hi, Papa." I gritted my teeth, while using my sweetest tone. "I have a business opportunity I'd like to discuss." He mumbled something on the other side before I added, "Meet me at the house—oh, and bring your checkbook."

It wasn't a chill that ran up my spine. It was more like a set of claws scraping at my back. Dissecting me from the inside out so that it physically pained me to put one foot in front of the other, my heels kicking at the gravel driveway as I approached the metal sign I left in the rearview the last time I was here. The paint was new, the metal shinier, the ivy gone and the façade power-washed, but the feeling was very much the same.

Dread. And I hated it. Almost as much as I hated the reason for my impromptu visit.

I needed a favor from the only man stupid enough to help me. No, stupid wasn't the right word. Adrian wasn't stupid. But I wouldn't call him loyal either. Insane, obsessed, too egocentric to care about the repercussions? Probably that last one.

His reasoning didn't matter, though. Not nearly as much as the fact that I knew he would open the door.

I pulled the flask from my coat pocket where it sat next to my father's checkbook and took a long swig, downing enough liquor to dull my nerves and not my senses. Returning it to its placeholder before extending a finger and pressing the bell.

A second later, the heavy double doors were creaking open of their own accord and I was placing a tentative foot over the threshold. Literally walking myself into my worst nightmare.

Everything was brighter, whiter, cleaner than I remembered it being. But the eeriness hadn't changed. Neither had the antiseptic smell. It clung to the back of my throat, replacing the bourbon and triggering that part of my brain screaming at me to *run*.

I refused to run. I refused to be afraid. That was what they'd wanted. They'd wanted me broken and afraid. Pretty and compliant. I was only one of those things, though.

I'll let you guess which one.

A hand landed on my shoulder and I pivoted on a heel, my blade pressing into that familiar spot along Adrian's gut. Pressing, not puncturing. At least not yet.

He grinned. "Skipping straight to the foreplay, huh, little lamb?"

I retracted my knife before shoving it back into my pocket, next to my flask. Without letting it go completely. "I need a favor."

There was no point in pretending my intentions were honorable. *His never were.* He'd also see right through my bullshit, toy with me longer than I intended on being here, try to negotiate before finally giving me what I wanted anyway. I'd much rather cut to the chase.

"And I need to see what you look like with my cum dripping down your thighs." He shrugged. "It has been a while... Too long, Marisela."

"I'm not fucking you, Adrian."

"*Dr. Lambert.* Remember where you are, Miss Cruz." He turned around, not bothering to ask me to follow him. Because he knew he didn't have to. He had the home field advantage.

This was Briarwood. You were either doctor or patient. And right now, I was neither.

74

ADRIAN

"I have a new employee." Marisela crossed a leg over a knee, her lips pursed and her eyebrows arched high. As arrogant as she was elegant. Which made it hard to maintain my composure. "Maybe you know her?"

I leaned back in my chair, being sure to keep my posture open while hers remained closed-off. Implying she was hiding something and I was not. "Maybe I do… What's her name?"

"Emily Shaw. I heard good things. Recruited the girl right out of college."

"What is it that you want from me, little lamb?" I kept my jaw tight, feigned shock, covering it with blatantly-forced ignorance as I attempted to change the subject. "You know, from one old friend to another?"

The truth was, the girl was exactly where I wanted her to be. Under Bugs's watchful eye, within Frankie's reach, and out of Donnie's peripheral. There wasn't much I could do about Casper. But he wasn't interested in Emily anyway. Just in seeing how worked up he could get everyone else around him. It kept them all placated, or oblivious, and avoided anarchy amongst the ranks. For now. Chaos was a given with so many different personalities mixed together in one place.

That wasn't the only reason I'd tipped my hand at the club, though. I liked this color on Marisela. The jealousy matched her eyes.

"I don't want anything from you, Dr. Lambert." She paused a moment, making sure her words hit hard. *And stuck.* They didn't because it was just more lies she told herself by telling me. "I'm not here as a friend. I'm here to hire you."

I *tsked* my tongue, scooting my chair closer to the desk and bracing myself on my elbows. "You said *a favor.* Friends get favors. Clients do not."

"It's a turn of phrase, *pendejo.*"

I shrugged a shoulder. "I don't think it was. I think you need me. At the very least, I think you need my help, don't you?"

"I don't need you, Adrian." She forced out an exaggerated laugh and I leaned back again to get a good look at her.

Her hair was longer, pulled high on her head and hanging down her back, extensions after she regretted her impulsive decision to cut it all off. Her eye makeup dark and her lipstick bright. War paint for a woman who constantly felt at odds with the world around her.

I wondered how long it would take her to realize we were on the same side...

"To need something means to require it. To not be able to function without it." I pushed up from my chair and took several slow steps around my desk until I was standing in front of her. "But to want something means it would be nice to have it. Enjoyable even. Want and need are two very different things, you see. For example, I *need* you, Marisela. But it's okay for you to *want* me." I held her glare for a long moment, getting off on how it seemed to penetrate me as deeply as any pocket knife. Maybe deeper. Because the sting didn't dissipate nearly as fast.

"I think we are well past the English lessons, don't you, *Dr. Lambert?*" she hissed, but I could see the way she was squirming in her seat. Crossing and uncrossing her legs as she tried to ease the discomfort building between those plump thighs of hers. The years had been good to Marisela, made her thicker in all the right places.

I could already picture myself there, buried up to my nose in her cunt. Tasting her, smelling her, wearing her juices like my favorite cologne.

"But there's still so much I could teach you..." I grinned, dropping it as I reclaimed my desk chair and flipped open my laptop. "Go on, Miss Cruz. Tell me how I can be *of service* to you."

She sucked on her teeth before taking a long breath and replying, "I need you to run a paternity test..."

Need. I kept that thought to myself as my eyes dropped to her flat stomach and quickly flicked up again.

"Not for me, idiot," she grunted. "For Tate. *This* somehow found its way to my desk." She removed a crumbled letter from her purse and dropped it on the open space between us. "Girl claims the kid is his. I want to know if it's true, what she wants if it is, and how to make it all go away without it hitting the tabloids."

"And if it's not true?" I lifted a curious brow as I snatched up the letter and perused the contents.

"Put the fear of god in your brother, threaten his life, cut off his balls—I don't care. Just make sure something like this doesn't happen again." She reached a hand inside her jacket pocket, fumbling around before withdrawing a checkbook. Then she stood, smoothed out her skirt, and dropped a blank check in front of me. "Your retainer."

She crossed the room, her palm landing on the door handle before I called out to her and she spun back in my direction.

"Why does it matter to you? If the kid really is his, it's still a bastard. I'm sure my old man had plenty of them running around. I highly doubt I was the only one."

She tugged the door open, stepping out into the hallway as she replied over a shoulder. "We had an agreement. That's why."

Before Marisela's seat had the chance to cool in her absence, Bugs came strolling in and plopped down. He reached out an arm and swiped the blank check off my desk, flicking it twice with his thumb and index finger. "She does know this is worthless, right? Might as well write *guy I paid to kill my husband* in the memo section."

I shrugged. "Never said anything about killing him."

"But that's what you're going to do, aren't ya?"

"Dead men don't have affairs, now do they?" I countered.

"No, I suppose they don't." He laughed.

75

ADRIAN

Killing a man was easy. I didn't mean that in a deep, existential way. Remove the outside factors—morality, fear, the fact most people were programed to appreciate and protect human life— and the act of killing was relatively simple. Just like puncturing a hole in a juice box and watching the contents spill free. Or squashing a fly beneath your palm until it stopped buzzing. Until its insides popped out and dampened your skin. Until its legs detached from its little carcass and it took a bit of effort to scrape them off into the waste bin.

But I didn't want to kill Tate. I wanted my big brother to suffer. I wanted him at that brink of death, craving it, only to be ripped back again. I wanted his body to give out but his brain to remain active. To sense everything that was being done to it. To feel it. The same way I'd felt that stab to my heart every time he touched her. Every time he fucked her. Every time he humiliated her by fucking someone else.

And she'd finally given me the okay. She'd *asked* me to do it for her. Maybe not in as many words, but she did say she didn't care. Which was basically the same thing as far as I was concerned, and I wasn't about to sit around and wait for my little lamb to change her mind.

There were no take-backs.

I glanced down to where big brother was strapped to my surgical table. His chest cavity splayed open and the various devices humming in rhythm with the sound of his heartbeat. And realized how right I was. How easy it would be to puncture his pericardium. How simple it would be to squash him.

It really was a pity I didn't like things easy or simple. If I did, our little sibling rivalry would have been over as soon as I was old enough to hold a carving knife.

I maneuvered the tattoo gun Casper had fashioned out of a ballpoint pen and an electric toothbrush around Tate's rib cage, pressing the tip against the outer most layer of the heart, and slowly moved from one letter to the next until her name stared back at me from a mixture of black ink and pooling cardiac fluid.

"Who's Marisela?" Dr. Michaels grunted from the other side of the metal slab. From where he was watching me with rapt attention. The type of fascination that very few of us shared.

It was a loaded question, one I didn't have any desire to answer but couldn't avoid either. Not without showing all my cards. "Our client. Also his wife."

It was the truth as much as it was a lie. She had hired us. I just refused to take her money. And the fucker's name might be next to hers on a piece of paper but she was never free to belong to anyone else. Not when she belonged to me.

John had been right about one thing. Sometimes it was nice to watch. To get the full picture, the three-sixty view you didn't get when you were the one holding the scalpel. Though watching my half-brother flatline and be forcibly resuscitated on the operating table for the last few hours, his muscles spasming each time the paddles touched his chest, brought me a different type of satisfaction from the one Rath enjoyed. A sense of gratification that ran much deeper than a hard-on.

Bugs gestured to the screen in front of us, row after row of monitors lining the sanctum of his security room. "How long are you gonna let this shit go on?"

"As long as it takes for the fucker to pull his head out of his ass," I grunted in reply, not taking my eyes off the image of Dr. Michaels breathing life into our patient for the third time. I'd told him we weren't gonna get paid if he couldn't keep Tate alive.

Truth was *he* wasn't gonna get paid. Our newest recruit needed a little more motivation and a lot less self-pity. He didn't have an option but to use his newly-reconstructed hands. Something he'd realized the moment he'd seen the operating room door slam shut in his face. The moment I'd stared at him from the other side and gave him the ultimatum.

It wasn't cruel. It was just ripping the bandage off and giving the wound some air to breathe. In this case, we were talking about his wounded ego more than the scars on his arm and fingers.

"And what about your girl?"

I twisted in Bugs's direction and quirked an eyebrow. "What about her?"

"When you gonna tell her the kid isn't his?" he asked.

"Who says it isn't?"

"The results from the paternity test you ran, or maybe the fact we both know you had him snipped years ago."

I grinned, even as I was trying my damnedest not to. He wasn't wrong. The paternity test was conclusive. *Tate Prescott was NOT the father.* There wasn't much of a possibility he would have been anyway. Considering I'd blackmailed a plastic surgeon into convincing my brother to undergo an experimental procedure "to increase his stamina in the bedroom." All it really was, was a quick vas deferens tie-off and a handful of blue pills in place of antibiotics.

It wasn't about Tate, though. It was never about him. I didn't give a shit about how many kids he spawned over the years. It was about *her*. I refused to let him taint her with his seed. To let her carry it to term. I also knew she wouldn't like it if I intervened. So I didn't. I never touched the fucker. Not until she asked me to do it.

Call it a loophole. I called it being resourceful. Working with what I had in front of me. Nudging pieces in the right direction and letting fate do the rest for me.

And right now, fate would decide how quickly my little lamb went from dutiful wife to widow.

76

MARISELA

I crossed my arms over my chest, tapping my heeled foot as various officers and plain-clothed detectives poked and prodded around the building. Searching through files and storage cabinets. Confiscating the occasional laptop and interrogating staff members.

They weren't going to find anything. Not even the emails from Adrian. Those vanished on their own. That didn't make this any less inconvenient. Or irritating. It did, however, make it my fault. Seeing as I'd been the one who'd paid to have a well-known public figure, the face of Prescott R&D, dragged out of his bed in the middle of the night and held hostage.

The media assumed Tate was missing, being kept for ransom somewhere until the board of trustees agreed to pay up. I knew the truth. I also knew it wasn't likely he was coming back. Not if his brother had anything to do with it.

I should have known better. I *did* know better. It was just another impulsive decision I would have to get myself out of. Alone. Because I'd learned the hard way that everyone else was a complication.

I stormed out of my office and turned down the long hall that led out to a sea of cubicles, making my presence known by the loud clicking of my shoes against the tiled floor beneath me. Pausing in my steps when I saw a pair of wide gray eyes and dark lashes staring in my direction. My newest employee, watching a flurry of activity buzz by her while she stood there like a deer in headlights.

Then again, maybe a complication was exactly what I needed. Not for me but for him. Something to motivate my brother-in-law to undo the mess he'd made.

I still hadn't figured out what Adrian wanted with the girl. She was too timid to be his type, too young and naïve to be of any use to him, but she was a survivor. Had gone through hell and back, passed around the system when she wasn't at the mercy of her alcoholic mother and parade of abusive boyfriends. She was broken, and if there was one thing Dr. Lambert enjoyed, it was fixing broken things.

I might not have known everything that went on at Briarwood anymore. But I did know it was where most of our research came from. New medical devices that made it through the FDA's approval process much quicker than was normal. Or legal. Months instead of years. Palms greased and a shit-ton of cash made on both sides.

But it wasn't the money that drove my shadow man. It was the challenge. He couldn't help himself when there was a puzzle laid out in front of him. He needed to piece it all together.

Now it was just a matter of determining what about Emily piqued the doctor's interests. What he wanted to fix—or break further—and see what he was willing to do to get his hands on it. Which meant I needed to keep the girl close, closer than just working in the same building as me.

"Ms. Shaw, I'd like to see you in my office now."

Emily stared at me for a moment longer, almost as if she were in a daze.

"That wasn't a request," I urged her, not bothering to look back and see if she was following me. Like I said, the girl was naïve, but she wasn't stupid.

I dropped what was left of my cigar into my empty tumbler, the embers dying out as soon as they hit the ice, and smiled to myself. I liked smoking Adrian's Cubans almost as much as I enjoyed finishing his bottle of Michter's. They were small comforts when everything else seemed to be falling apart around me. And so was this club. The anonymity of it, the way I could be someone and no one at the same time.

I pushed my glass forward and pivoted on my stool. Glancing to the other side of the room but not staring. It had been an hour, going on two. Me sitting at the bar and him positioned at his usual booth in the corner. Each of us alone, together.

I knew where he was, and I could sense him tracking my movements. Signaling the bartender every time my drink was empty. Just a wave of a hand that had the staff all doing his bidding.

I guess I couldn't blame them. I remembered what that hand could do. What it used to be able to do. What I wished it could do again. But not much had changed over the years. I traded orgasms for work and pills for liquor. It was a way for me to lose control and maintain it at the same time. For me to loosen up without losing myself entirely.

When I looked up again, as tempted to cross the room as I was to leave it, he was gone. My cue that our little game had ended prematurely.

Pity, seeing as I was feeling generous tonight.

And not because he deserved it. He didn't. But I did. I deserved the feeling of bringing him to his knees. Of reminding him that he only got what I was willing to give him. That he might be able to take but so could I. And I had no problem adding to that box I kept on my mantle. No problem cutting lower if I had to.

I dropped a hefty tip on the bar, only to have it immediately shoved in my direction. I shoved it back, grabbed my coat, and headed for the door.

The night air barely had a chance to kiss my cheeks, my mask tucked under an arm and my hair slapping my face, before the bite of the brick wall was scraping against my exposed skin. My favorite dress bunching at the hem as Adrian's tongue pried my lips apart. Fucking my mouth like I knew it could fuck my cunt.

I pulled away enough to glare at him. "What the fuck do you think you're doing?" I hissed, my breath coming out in white puffs. Hot mixing with the cold.

"Same thing we've both been thinking about for the last two hours," he grunted, and then he was on me again.

77

ADRIAN

All it would take was a few snaps of a cellphone camera and our faces would be front-page news. The latest scandal behind the Prescott name. *Wife or Widowmaker* in bold print next to *Beloved Socialite Missing.* Because everyone was beloved when they were missing. Even more so when they were dead.

I still couldn't be fucked. Not when my cock was aching to remember what it felt like to be inside her. To feel her walls closing around me. Strangling me. Holding me there, even as the rest of her tried to push me away.

Kind of like right now. Marisela's fists were twisted in my shirt. Her nipples pebbled beneath the thin fabric of her dress—too thin for how cold it was outside—at the same time she was lifting a knee and digging it into my thigh. Struggling between tugging me closer and prying me off her, before finally settling on the latter when the heel of her stiletto drove itself against my shin.

Digging in and twisting along the thinnest part of the tibia.

I stumbled back a step. Far enough to watch her chest heave but not so far that I couldn't pull her towards me again. If I wanted to.

I did want to. She just wasn't ready for that yet. She wasn't ready to admit the fact that she wasn't angry with me. She was relieved. She was... grateful.

I was a much better husband than Tate ever was. I'd taken out the trash and she didn't even have to ask me twice.

Marisela lifted an arm, swiping over her smeared lipstick with the backside of her hand, while I adjusted my pants and watched her. Specifically, how her gaze dropped to follow my movements, no matter how much she tried to keep them focused on my face.

"If you didn't want me to fuck you..." I trailed my eyes over the length of her body, from heeled toe to pursed lips. "...then why did you follow me out here, little lamb?"

"I didn't follow you. I left."

"Same difference." I shrugged. "You came here looking to get my attention. Now you have it."

"I came here to have a drink," she threw back.

"My drink. My cigar." I reached out a hand and pressed it over her clit. Over her clothes with just enough pressure to have her squirming. Marisela might have given up on the prospect of sex, of enjoying it, but her body hadn't. "My pussy."

She steeled her spine. I could feel her clenching as she willed herself not to move. "Pretty sure it's mine, unless there's something you want to tell me?" she countered, and I grinned.

"There is so much I want to tell you, show you, do to you… but is there something you want to tell me first?"

"Nope," she replied, popping her lips. "Nothing that comes to mind."

I rested a palm on the wall beside her head, using my free hand to brush the loose strands of hair from her face. It didn't feel the same. Not nearly as soft and wavy. But much like my little lamb's affections, her natural curls would grow back soon.

"You have a new personal assistant. Pretty little thing, from what I hear…" I kept my focus on the way my fingers twirled around her hair, transfixed by the memory of dark locks sprawled out on bright-white bedsheets, until the grinding of teeth had me shifting my eyes to the right.

"Keeping tabs on me? Or is it her?" Marisela was seething.

"Her who?"

"Emily?"

"I have absolutely no interest in Emily. Or any other woman who isn't you, if that's what you're worried about, Marisela." It wasn't a lie. It wasn't even a partial truth. I wasn't interested in the girl. I was interested in Dr. Michaels's *interest* in her. In what he was willing to do for me to get to her. The same way a fisherman was interested in the worm on his hook.

I didn't care about guppies when I had a much bigger catch in mind.

Marisela slapped my arm aside, and for a moment, I

thought she was going to slap me too. Instead, she gestured for me to get on my knees. Grabbing on to the back of my head until my face was buried in her bare cunt. Nothing separating my mouth from her pussy while the hem of her dress billowed around us like a white flag signaling her surrender. Because she was the only one fighting us. She was the only thing keeping me from where I really wanted to be. Lost between her thighs.

I took a long breath and groaned.

It was normal for nostalgia to sweeten the memory of something. Increasing blood flow to certain regions of the body and simulating a time when you felt your best, altering your brain chemistry so that how it'd had been could never compare to how it actually was. The concept better than the reality.

This wasn't that. This was far more intense, more mind-altering than nostalgia. Tasting her. Smelling her. Feeling her... The fantasy couldn't compete. Neither could the images of her I saw in my head every night. The images I used to get myself off in the shower.

She wasn't sweet. More tangy and salty. But not overpowering. Not spicy but not bland either. It was the perfect balance of wet and sticky that clung to my tongue, tingling along the tip until I sank deeper and slurped down another taste. And another and another. Gorging myself like it was my first and last meal. My only meal. Except she was more than that too.

Marisela was a French dessert. Savory and decadent, yet so light and airy you couldn't stop yourself from eating the whole box.

I'd eat this one too. Suck, lap, eat. Devour. I wouldn't stop. I didn't want to stop.

Each time my neck got stiff or my jaw started to ache, I would hear her whimper or curse or sigh and that serotonin spike kept me from feeling anything but hungry. For her. For whatever her body would give me.

But too soon, she was digging her hands in my hair and tugging me back to my feet. Flipping us around and dropping to her knees. Until only one of us got what they wanted. Until my cock was empty and her mouth was full. And all I could do was watch her leave me behind again.

78

MARISELA

I tapped my nails on top of the conference table as my glare panned across the room. Each face more useless than the next. What I needed was a loophole. What they were giving me were excuses.

I owned forty-nine percent of the company; the board controlled the other fifty-one percent until a successor was named. Which meant I didn't own shit.

"I'm sorry, Mrs. Prescott. But there's nothing more we can do."

There was always more someone could do. If they were motivated enough to do it. And clearly, my legal team needed a little more motivating.

"Right. Then you're all fired. My assistant will see you out." I gestured for Emily to open the door before flipping my laptop open, keeping my attention on the screen as they all continued to stare. "Did you not understand me? I said get the fuck out."

"You can't fire us." This came from the back of the room. A young kid, probably a paralegal, with thick glasses and a pert nose. No one of consequence other than he was the only one with balls enough to argue with me.

"Can't I?"

He shook his head, tugging at the collar of his dress shirt as he tried to keep the tremor out of his voice. "No, ma'am, you can't. Large restructuring decisions cannot be made without written approval from the CEO. Terminating the entire legal department falls under restructuring."

"Very good..." I looked to Emily, waiting for her to jot the kid's name on a piece of paper and slide it in my direction. "...Aiden. You've done the bare minimum and read the company bylaws. *But*, if you kept reading, you would also know that names are not mentioned. Only titles. And since nothing has been updated since my beloved father-in-law's passing, the bylaws still state that the COO shall assume the role in instances where the CEO is temporarily unavailable. Would you agree that our CEO is *temporarily unavailable*?"

"I... um, yes... but the board—" The poor boy was trying. He really was.

"The board has no say in instances of *temporary* absences. Unless you're trying to imply my husband isn't coming back?" I arched a brow. Daring any one of them to challenge me.

There was more than one way to bring a man to his knees. Legal jargon just happened to be my weapon of choice today.

He shook his head, swallowing hard before slinking back in his chair.

"I didn't think so." I slammed my laptop closed again, if only to emphasize my point. "That, gentleman, is what I call a loophole in an *at-will* state. The kind of loophole I would hope a room full of Harvard graduates could figure out on their own. The kind of loophole I expect you all to uncover before I have no choice but to find someone who can. Understand?"

I was met by a mixture of grumbles and nods, and then silence as the room emptied much quicker than it filled this morning.

I pulled my flask out of my inner pocket and took a swig. Not caring who could see me through the glass walls. Drinking on the job was the least of my problems. Our CEO's *temporary* status was the most.

The fact Tate was "missing" might have been beneficial for today's lesson. But that was about all it was good for. Legally, I was in marital limbo. Neither wife nor widow. And without an heir, I was no better than a fucking mistress. Names didn't matter when it came to joint assets—at least according to my husband's living will they didn't.

Blood did. And the only blood between us wasn't mine either.

It had been weeks and no one had found a thing worth a damn. Not that I thought they would. I just didn't appreciate the fact the fuckers wouldn't even try. It was out of laziness, not foresight. And I didn't tolerate laziness, especially from the type of men privileged enough to have it.

"Come in or don't. But standing on the threshold just makes you seem like a pervert, Mr. Walker." I kept my eyes on the blank email in front of me, my fingers hovering over the keys without touching them. I'd sensed the kid watching me for the last five minutes, waiting for him to grow the backbone he needed to interrupt me. Something that didn't appear likely to happen anytime soon.

He cleared his throat, and I looked up to find him toying with his headset. Out of habit or anxiety, I couldn't be sure. "I think I found something..."

"Think or know?"

"Well, I know... but I'm not entirely sure it'll be something you want to hear..."

I twirled a hand in the air, gesturing for him to get on with it, and Elliot closed the distance. Approaching my desk like he was afraid it would reach out and strike him.

It wouldn't, but I might if he didn't get on with it.

"Obviously, finding Mr. Prescott alive is better than the unknowns that come with him being missing. But... proving that he is dead—or rather, proving that it's the most likely alternative—is the next best thing." Elliot lifted an arm and began rubbing at the back of his neck. "For you I mean. Not so much for Mr. Prescott, I guess."

"And how exactly do you expect me to prove he's

dead without a body, Mr. Walker?" I challenged. "Unless you know where he is or at a minimum know someone who does?"

"Um, no, of course not. But you don't necessarily need a body, not if there's enough evidence to suggest he *probably* isn't alive. We just need to follow the money. Someone like Mr. Prescott is used to a certain lifestyle. He isn't likely to just vanish into thin air without bringing a shit-ton of cash with him."

"Except all our assets are frozen until he decides to show his face. If he doesn't come looking for it, isn't that proof enough?"

"Well, yes and no. There are two things the courts require in order to declare someone legally dead. Proof is just one of them..."

I could tell by Elliot's tone I wouldn't like the answer but I asked it anyway. "And what's the other?"

"Time..."

"How much time?" I hissed.

"Seven years—"

"Are you fucking kidding me? Seven years? How the fuck do you expect me to keep this company running for seven years without proper funding!"

"Considering Mr. Prescott is a public figure, we could press for special circumstances and hopefully get it knocked down to five... Until then, I think our best bet is to look into getting some investors."

"Investors," I balked. "No one invests without wanting something in return. And usually it's a lot more than you're willing to give."

Elliot shrugged. "Then offer them something else.

Something you don't care about but they think you want. It tends to make them want it more just to take it from you."

I didn't respond. But my lips did tug at one side, fighting the urge to smirk. Kid was smarter than he looked. Which also meant he was dangerous.

"Before you leave, send Bernard in, would you?" I kept my tone neutral. Didn't want to clue anyone in to the fact I was probing the company's financials. "And tell him to bring this quarter's revenue."

Elliot nodded, clicking the door closed behind him as I watched him go. My mind shifting from the sort of ones and zeros that made up my computer screen to the kind that didn't add up on the spreadsheet Emily sent over.

79

MARISELA

Sometimes life fucked you in the ass with a cactus. And then, sometimes, it was nice enough to remember the lube. Either way, I was tired of bending over. Which was why I decided to embrace this particular cactus and see if I could force it to bloom. A *life gives you a lemon, squeeze lemon juice in someone's eye* type of situation.

Except, instead of a lemon, I had a girl on the verge of a mental breakdown. And instead of a cactus, we had a bag of evidence belonging to a dead man. I wasn't entirely sure what I could make out of either of those. At least not yet. But I sure as hell was going to make something.

I raised a hand, stopping Emily's insistent prattling before she gave us both a migraine. "I'll take care of everything. All you need to do is relax and breathe. Do you understand?" I dipped my chin, knowing that stress would have her mirroring my actions and nodding along with me.

She'd shown up on my doorstep last night, a large garbage bag in one hand and a tremble in the other. Thirty minutes later, she'd given me her life story when all I'd really wanted was a clue as to how to use it.

I had that clue now. In fact, it had been staring me in the face all along. I'd just been squinting too hard to see it. Or rather, to see *him*. And his connection to my shadow man.

As it turns out, my assistant had a stalker of her own. Someone who'd been breaking into her house and leaving her gifts. Someone clever enough to hack into our software and unintrusive enough to blend in. Someone obsessed enough to kill her date and send her the guy's belongings. Someone who I'd recently learned had more going on behind all that tech talk and fake charm.

I wasn't blind to the transgressions within my company, even if there were times I pretended to be. I noticed the way he looked at her, found every opportunity to pop up at her desk. But I'd assumed it was an innocent office fling. And honestly, I didn't care who my employees fucked—apparently neither did Tate—as long as their work got done.

After all, I would be the first one to hear if it didn't.

But then I realized Elliot Walker wasn't just some lovesick IT guy. He wasn't a random hire either. He was a mole, and my assistant was meant to be the carrot that kept him on task.

Of course, this was all conjecture. A case of having a thousand-piece puzzle dumped out in front of me while I did my best to guess the picture without the luxury of seeing the box. However, my gut told me I was right.

Dr. Lambert never wanted Emily Shaw. He said it himself. But he did want to use her. And unfortunately for my assistant, I had no choice but to do the same.

I excused myself from the parlor, telling Emily I was going to grab her some hot tea to help with her nerves. Took a sharp turn down the hall and pushed my way inside Tate's home office. Searching through all the drawers in his desk before moving on to the powder room. I quickly swung open the medicine cabinet door, and that's where I found it. The orange bottle stared back at me from the shelf, the label peeling off and the expiration date barely visible anymore.

But I knew better than anyone else that those little numbers were more of a suggestion than a steadfast rule. A way to keep health care privatized and ensure the rich got richer. And I had just as much a hand in it as the rest of them.

Prescott R&D didn't care about curing diseases, only about treating the *symptoms*. It was our business model, what kept our consumers coming back for more. The sicker they were, the more money we made. A cash grab spun to look like a humanitarian effort to prolong life. Big pharma didn't care about life, though. None of us did.

That wasn't to say we didn't want our customers *alive*. Dead men couldn't pay their premiums. But at the end of the day, the general population was talked about in numbers rather than names. And numbers were as replaceable as the EpiPens hospitals tossed out by the millions each year. Not because they didn't work but because that was what the label we'd slapped on the side told them to do. Because that was what regulators enforced, much more strictly than actual patient care. Supply and demand, demand and supply.

The truth was, you might have had to adjust the dosage to account for the decreased efficacy in these expired pills in front of me, but they'd still do the trick. Usually kicked in faster since the outer coating broke down the longer the medication was sitting there.

Was it safe? No, not entirely. But that was because there was no profit in making it safe. Not when we could focus on new and more expensive, instead of improving the viability of what already worked. Generics didn't line pockets but brand names and patented devices sure as hell did.

After Briarwood, after seeing what happened in our boardrooms, the side effects that were swept under the rug and the toxins that were fast-tracked out the door, I avoided pharmaceuticals as a whole. But none of it seemed to stop Tate. He'd pop Xannies like they were Tic Tacs and wash it all down with a fifth of whiskey.

And right now, I was thankful he did.

I swiped up the bottle. Twisted off the top and poured three of the white tabs into the palm of my hand. Using a shaving razer and the lip of the vanity to crush them into a fine powder before stirring them into Emily's tea.

I wasn't drugging the girl. I was keeping her calm so I could handle everything that needed to be done.

Including grabbing the passport I'd had doctored for her, packing our bags, and booking our flights to Spain.

Leaving the country wasn't the smartest thing to do when your husband was missing under suspicious circumstances. But I had family there. I would claim I was seeking comfort, squeeze out a few tears for the cameras. One hand wiping at my eyes at the same time the other reached into their pockets.

After all, there was nothing men loved more than a damsel in distress. It was just another mask I'd have to wear. Another part I'd have to play, another ego I'd have to stroke until everyone got what they thought they wanted.

80

More than a half dozen calls, all declined. And that was after she made it a point to hang up on me. My little lamb didn't have to answer her phone, though. Not when the tracking device on her car told me exactly where she was headed. The airport. The international departures lane. But it was her own words that clued me in to who she was *with* and why the two of them were there.

She was taking her pretty little assistant along for the ride to punish me for spying. A plan that might have been a tad more effective if she kept it to herself. But she couldn't, not when she was so fired up her mouth did all the thinking.

That was the thing about Marisela. Her rage often got the best of her. Still, I wouldn't change it, because it meant I got the best of her too. Seeing as no one made that woman more enraged than I did.

I grinned at the thought, quickly pocketing my phone

as I leaned against the doorframe of Bugs's room. Staring at him while he continued to stare at his computer screen. For a guy so fixated on watching everything that was going on in this place, he didn't seem very apt at knowing when someone was watching him instead.

"Looks like you've been made, kid."

He jolted at the sudden sound of my voice—he was getting used to his implants, not switching them off as frequently—and minimized whatever it was he was working on before meeting my glare. Which told me he was either in the middle of downloading some porn or trying to creep on his coworker again. I could only hope it was the one option out of the two that wouldn't get him killed.

Because Dr. Michaels *would* kill him. Our latest addition had already proven the lengths he was willing to go to keep other men away from his girl. Even if that girl was oblivious to the fact she was his.

I really couldn't judge, though, now could I? Killing was the least of what I would do for Marisela while dying was a given if it came down to it.

"What makes you say that?" Bugs asked. Skepticism causing the dimple on one side of his mouth to stick out. He didn't think getting caught was a possibility after he'd scrubbed his history clean and fabricated a different one for himself. But I knew it wasn't just possible. It was inevitable.

I taught my little lamb more than chemistry in those tutoring lessons of ours. I taught her the importance of critical thinking. And she was finally starting to see the bigger picture.

"Not what. *Who.* Your boss called and gave me an earful. Accused me of spying on her. Or I suppose she accused you of doing it for me." I shrugged. "Either way, Marisela knows who you are now and she's not too keen on having you around the office anymore. It's the unemployment line for you, *Mr. Walker.* Then again, I'm pretty sure I can get you an interview at Briarwood... In case you haven't heard, I know a guy."

I was being a smart-ass. Mostly because I was trying to lighten the mood and keep the kid from spiraling. I could already see the wheels turning in his head, the panic and the desperation. He'd somehow convinced himself he loved this girl, and I'd be the first to admit I didn't do much to stop it. Like I said, love was one hell of a motivator. Too bad *this* wasn't *that.*

The kid just needed to get out into the world. Spend less time on that computer of his and more time talking to real-life women. It was why the side job at Tate's company had been so good for him. I'd seen the change, the confidence and cockiness. Of course, the implants helped. But it was more about getting out of his own head, away from Donnie and their codependence. The problem was, all the doctors he'd seen told him different was bad, when really different was his superpower.

He also needed to stop jerking off so much and finally get laid. Clean out those clogged pipes and think a bit more clearly. Preferably with someone who didn't have a psycho ex hell-bent on making sure no one with a dick got within a five-mile radius of her. And that included the vibrator Dr. Michaels stole out of her nightstand.

I was judging that one. If you were jealous of a

vibrating purple dick, your insecurities ran much deeper than your scars.

Besides, Bugs didn't love Emily. He was distracted by a pretty girl with a nice rack that didn't change colors when you tried to touch it. Not that it mattered if he did, because she was never his to love. She was Dr. Michaels's—even if the fucker had an odd way of showing it. Some guys sent girls flowers. My colleague went the more gruesome route and sent his girl body parts instead. But the sentiment was there, and I could appreciate sentiment. Even if Emily couldn't.

"You have to let her go, Bugs, before this shit gets too messy. You got me."

He nodded once. Albeit reluctantly. Like a toddler who was just informed he couldn't have dessert before dinner. "Yeah, I got you."

"Good. 'Cause I've got a plane to catch and you're the only one I trust to keep the place from burning down."

Now I had his attention.

"Where you going?" He was already up on his feet and walking towards me. His abandonment issues as blatantly obvious as his deflating erection.

Guess it was porn this time.

"I'm taking a vacation." I shoved my hands into my pockets as I tried to picture it. "Think I'm gonna rent myself a nice little villa somewhere in the Spanish countryside."

"Spain? Why are you going to Spain?" he asked me.

"Because wherever she goes, I go," I replied.

81

I took another long drag from my Cuban, blowing the smoke into the air as I leaned against the wood deck at the back of my grandparents' summer home. A villa not far from the one I rented a few streets over. Voices rising and falling, laughing and conversing.

I hated these things. Big events where everyone was a version of themself that wasn't anywhere close to who they were beneath all the makeup and party-wear. I was also good at them.

Both could be true, you know. You could be good at something you hated. Sometimes it made you hate it more because it took away your excuse not to do it. It was an expectation. People *expected* you to enjoy what you were good at.

I didn't enjoy this. The noise, the crowd, the fakeness. At least not anymore, I didn't.

I'd just raised the end of the cigar to my mouth again when a warm hand glided across my back.

"Marisela." Javi hummed my name more than spoke it. A mix between a growl and purr as I spun around and he lifted my hand to his lips. Pressing a kiss to my knuckles. His eyes never leaving mine. "It's been a long time."

I nodded once. "It has."

"Sorry to hear about your mother." His brows drew together in the middle. An expression that resembled concern but not quite.

"What exactly did you hear?" I asked him.

"That she ran off a few years ago. Can't say any of us were surprised. Nora always was a free spirit." He shrugged, his mouth tipping into a crooked grin. "As are you from what I remember."

"What you remember is a girl rebelling against her father. I'm not so much a girl anymore," I countered.

"No, you aren't. Are you?" His eyes flicked down the length of my legs before slowly traveling back up. Lingering much longer than they should before landing on my face again. "Your *abuela* mentioned that you're in need of a loan? Why don't we take a little stroll and you can tell me all about your marital troubles?"

What he meant was that my grandmother told him I needed a *husband*; the loan was his polite way of turning her down. Javier Castillo wasn't interested in getting married. Just in getting his dick sucked and not by the girl he remembered biting his ankles when he told her she couldn't play toy soldiers with him.

His tastes were much softer now. Younger. More delicate than anything I could offer him. He might have been eyeing me like a piece of meat as we walk side by side, far enough away from the other partygoers that no one could hear us, but that didn't mean I was his first choice on the menu. He just wasn't the type of man who worried about going hungry. Not when opening his wallet had all the fish flopping themselves into his net without him having to do anything but stand there.

And that's what he was doing right now. Standing in the middle of the garden, his dress shirt unbuttoned and his posture relaxed as he passed me his business card.

"Let's set something up this week, discuss how this deal could be mutually beneficial for everyone." His fingers grazed my wrist as he pulled his hand back. "And bring the girl with you."

I lifted a brow, crossing my arms over my chest while pinching the card between my nails. "I didn't know you were in the market for an assistant?"

"I'm not." He grinned. "I'm not in the market for a wife either. That doesn't mean we can't... enjoy each other's company."

"Enjoy, huh?" I tilted my head, raking my glare over his dark-brown loafers and gray slacks. His matching leather belt and freshly-ironed dinner jacket. The open collar told the world he was relaxed; the designer labels told them he could afford to be. "Are you talking about me or the girl, Javi?"

He shrugged. "You know I've always thought of you like a little sister, *zorra*. Then again, I can see you're not so little anymore, hm?" It was his pet name for me when we were kids. Meant to be an insult, his way of calling me wild and untamed. I took it as a compliment.

"No, I'm not. My teeth are a hell of a lot sharper, though."

He threw his head back on a loud laugh. "I take that back. You might be taller but you haven't changed at all, have you, Mari."

"We all change, Javi," I grunted. "It's just not always for the better."

"No, not always for the better," he agreed.

"I'll be in contact." I nodded once before brushing past him. Then trudged back up the small hill and over towards the deck. Cursing his name under my breath as I swiped a bottle of wine from a nearby table and brought the whole thing to my lips.

The first swig went down easy. The second and third even easier.

82

ADRIAN

I'd thought about it. About what I was gonna do the moment I caught up to her. Considered dragging her back home and keeping her there until she realized Briarwood didn't have to be her prison, not when I had the means to make it her palace instead.

But I knew that was an impulse. The kind that had her fucking the right brother and marrying the wrong husband. The kind that came with temporary satisfaction and long-term contempt. The kind that had her running *from* me and not *to* me.

It was why I'd yet to approach her. That and because I couldn't help but be transfixed by the way the moonlight danced over her face, her eyes actually crinkling at the sides when she tipped her head back and looked up at the night sky...

She was smiling. I knew that smile. It was the one she used to give me whenever I'd climb into her room, pin her to those pretty pink sheets that seemed to sparkle against her tanned skin, and make her see stars that were so much brighter than the ones outside her window. Than the ones that flickered above me right now as I pressed myself closer to the textured wall and watched her from the adjacent balcony.

It wasn't hard to break into Marisela's rental. To slip inside the guest bedroom and slide out the glass doors so that I could get a better look at her. But it was nearly impossible to keep my hands from slinking beneath the waistband of my pants, my cock already snaking its way through my fly when she leaned forward and peered down at the sprawling landscape below us. At all the plants and flowers that couldn't compare to how flaw-less she looked with her ass cheeks peeking out of the bottom of her robe, as she bent at the waist and balanced herself on her toes.

I tried to restrain myself. But then her perfume carried with the breeze, infiltrating my nostrils and clinging to my skin until I could both smell her and taste her. Until I could practically feel her pussy gripping my cock in place of my hand. Until I could almost hear her...

I opened my eyes. I hadn't even realized I'd closed them.

I *could* hear her. I *was* hearing her. Soft whimpers and sighs and moans as Marisela's fingers worked her clit in rhythm with my palm. Her breasts exposed to the air as the robe slung lower and lower on her shoulders. Her hair a wild mess as it both clung to her skin and twisted around her.

I wanted to believe she was looking down and imagining me peering up at her. That that was the final thing that set her off when she gripped the banister for dear life, her arm shaking and her knuckles turning white, her knees buckling and her legs nearly giving out when the self-induced orgasm finally hit her.

And then it hit me too. My abdominal muscles contracting, one hand braced against the wall while the other continued to pump from base to tip. My thumb swiping over the engorged head and collecting the cum that should have been spilling down her throat and not landing on a stranger's patio furniture.

By the time I was finished, my palm tacky and the front of my boxers damp to the touch, Marisela was staring in my direction. A mix of fear and lust burning in her eyes as I tucked my cock back into my pants and began climbing over the metal railing. A few feet of open air the only thing separating my cock from her cunt or my skull from the pavement. A fact that should have given me pause but didn't.

Before she could make up her own mind, decide if she wanted to wait and see my brains splatter like an egg or chance me catching her, I'd already leaped from one balcony to the next. Snatched her wrist and held it high above her head as I forced her to look at me.

"How long, Marisela?"

"How long what, Adrian?" she hissed.

"How long have you been able to make yourself come?"

She quirked a manicured eyebrow, her free shoulder lifting just enough to be spiteful. "Depends…"

"On what?"

"On if you mean with my hands... or my vibrator..."

I tried to keep my expression neutral, sucking on the insides of my cheeks while clenching my jaw. But I knew she saw it. The shock that had my features distorting ever so slightly.

"You can't know everything, Dr. Lambert. You can't control everything. Least of all me."

"Can't I?" I took a step forward, mirroring her arrogance as I slowly guided her past the glass doors and into the bedroom. My smugness waving freely when I twisted her arm until she had two choices. Lie down or dislocate it.

My little lamb wasn't afraid of the pain, though, which was why it took her a moment longer than it would most to comply. And only because that was what some part of her really wanted to do anyway.

Marisela wanted to submit to me the way I'd always submitted to her. She just couldn't bring herself to acknowledge it.

I lowered my mouth to her throat, sucking over her carotid artery. Feeling how it pulsed in time with the pounding in her chest and the quickening of her breaths. She was still so worked up. So sensitive. Her body wasn't satisfied. It needed more. And so did my cock.

"How many times, Marisela?" I whispered into her ear, my right palm pressing her wrists against the mattress while my left cupped her breast. So that she was both focused and distracted. Defiant and obedient.

"How many times did I fuck myself or how many times did I make myself come?" she countered.

"How many times did you let him touch you? How many times did he finish inside you over the years?"

"Don't you already know?" she scoffed. "Or are you not as good at spying on me as you think you are?"

83

MARISELA

"How many times, Marisela?" he repeated, and I couldn't tell if he actually wanted an answer or not. If he was fishing for the truth or begging for a lie as his hand started to creep lower and lower. Not stopping until he found my clit like he'd had it mapped out by memory.

He pressed the pad of his thumb down, pinning me to the spot without having to do anything but keep his hand there. The slightest movement would give me the friction I was aching for. Have me squirming and grinding and seeking relief while staying still left me at his mercy. Sprawled out on the bed with nothing but a silk robe hanging off my bare shoulders.

"Give me a number, little lamb, before I come up with one of my own," Adrian grunted against my cheek. The sound not nearly as sexual as it was primitive. Like an animal with its foot caught in a trap, teetering between lashing out and asking for help.

I couldn't help him, though. I couldn't help either of us.

"Why does it matter, Adrian?" My exasperated sigh died on a moan when he shoved a knee between my thighs, spreading me wide open as he positioned himself at the edge of the mattress.

"I need to know how many bags of blood to have on hand, how many organs I need to waste to keep him alive just so I can kill him again. I need to know when we're even so I can finally put that fucker in the ground."

Adrian unfastened the button of his pants, his zipper having never made it up, and then shoved the material down his thighs with one arm until his bare ass was in full view of the open balcony doors. The tip of his cock probing my swollen pussy lips while his hold on the bed kept him from plunging forward. Just barely.

"But more importantly, I need to know how many times I need to fuck you tonight so that your cunt forgets there was ever anyone else. So tell me, Marisela, how many orgasms do I owe you? One? Five? A hundred? Give me a number and I won't stop until you get it."

I closed my eyes, throwing my head back and fisting the sheets when his resolve broke before mine did. Because it didn't matter. How many times my husband fucked me, how many times my brother-in-law planned to do the same. I knew what my body liked, knew how to balance the alcohol in my system and the chemicals in my brain, but there was no guarantee that anyone else did.

I sucked in a lungful of air, bracing myself for the pain. The stretch and the burn as Adrian slowly pulled back, only to thrust deeper somehow. In and out and in. Fast, then slow, then fast again. As if he were trying to unlock a code. His eyes glued to my face, his intense glare studying my reactions until he found one he liked. Because he could tell I liked it too.

He let go of my wrists. Dragging his fingers from my shoulder, over the peak of my breast and along each of my ribs until a heavy palm landed on my ass with an audible *thwack* of skin on skin. Adrian grinned, flexing his fingers as he grabbed a handful of thigh meat in his bruising grip and hiked my leg higher on his waist. Shifting his knee on the mattress and angling his cock to one side. And then he dropped his gaze from my face to where our bodies joined. His sole focus on the way my pussy clamped around him each time he drove forward and protested each time he drew back.

But the penetration wasn't enough. It was never enough. It didn't matter if it was made of silicone or flesh and muscle. If it vibrated or if it thrusted. If it fit in my palm or required both hands. I needed more. More than the friction, than the push and pull. More than the growing pressure in my stomach that bordered on discomfort.

I shoved at Adrian's chest, the sudden jolt causing him to stumble back a step before I grabbed him by the collar of his shirt and flipped him onto the mattress. He didn't stop me and not because he couldn't. We both already knew that if he really wanted to fuck me against my will, he would.

He was just curious. His head canted to the side and his arms spread out on the bed palm-first as I shucked off the rest of my robe and tossed it onto the floor. I didn't give him a moment to question what was gonna happen next before I climbed up his body and straddled his waist.

He smelled like me, and when I lowered my mouth onto his cock, he tasted like me too. A flavor I didn't think I would enjoy as much as I did. An odd mixture of salt and soap and a tang of something else.

Adrian groaned, his Adam's apple bobbing in his throat as he continued to watch me taste *me* on him. And then his hands were on my ass, nudging me forward. Inch by inch until his cock was popping out of my mouth and lining up with my pussy instead.

I slowly lowered myself down, pelvic bone over pelvic bone, before he guided me back up again. His palms splayed out on my thighs so that I was grinding back and forth more than bouncing up and down. It was a new sensation. A new angle that stimulated every part of me. Every nerve that wasn't enough on its own but together was everything.

"That's it, princess. Fuck yourself on my cock. Use me to get yourself off," Adrian grunted. But I wasn't even listening to him anymore. His filthy words white noise as I climbed higher and higher. And higher still. As I anchored an arm to the headboard and dug my knees into the mattress. The skin rubbing away and adding the touch of pain I needed to finally reach the ledge.

My body jerked forward, the sounds coming out of my mouth both high-pitched and guttural as muscles I didn't know I had contracted and convulsed. Ached and assuaged. My vision blurring as my blood pressure dropped like I'd just stepped out of a hot shower.

I didn't see stars or heaven or god or the devil. What I did see was the pattern of the bedsheets as Adrian tossed me onto my stomach, yanking my head back with a hand around my throat. My ass in the air and his cock shoved as far into my guts as it could go without coming out the other side.

84

ADRIAN

I'd waited ten years to fuck this woman again. A full decade to feel her coming on my cock for the first time. To hear her cursing god and crying out my name. A mix of words I didn't understand and didn't care to decipher. Because her body told me everything.

What it liked and what it liked *more.* What it wanted and how it wanted it. What had been done to it and what it had *never* experienced. Another of her firsts that was mine for the taking. Her first cock-induced orgasm.

But that wasn't all it told me. It clued me in to the fact my little lamb was keeping secrets. And I didn't mean the rows of scars that ran parallel on each side of her thighs. I knew about those. It was the extra tenderness in her breasts that had me looking for the birth control pills I found in *her* bag with *someone else's* name on them.

Which then led me to wonder...

"Why are you really here, Marisela?" I muttered,

leaning forward so that my breath warmed the shell of her ear. She was pretending to sleep, hoping I'd take the hint and leave the same way I'd come. But she knew better than that. I wasn't going anywhere without her.

"In this bed? Or in this villa?" she countered after I'd tugged the sheets aside and exposed her bare breasts to the breeze filtering in from the open window. Which was probably the worst thing for me to do when I was trying to have a somewhat coherent conversation with the woman.

"In this country."

She pushed herself upright, her arms crossed over her chest so that all I could think about now was how good it would feel to squeeze my cock between them. To mark those globes with my cum…

"Getting the fuck away from you," she replied, drawing my attention back to her face.

"Bullshit," I grunted. "If you really wanted to get away from me, you wouldn't have told me you were gonna do it. And you sure as hell wouldn't have left a paper trail so I could find you."

"Okay, then I'm here visiting family." She shrugged.

"Oh, you're visiting someone all right. But who is it really?" It wasn't just the pills that had given me pause or the realization that she'd go as far as to make sure no one knew she was taking them. It was also the messages I'd seen in her burner. The phone she didn't know I knew about because she *actually* was trying to hide that.

She narrowed her glare at me. "Javi is *practically* family. And a potential investor."

"He wants to fuck you."

"Lots of people want to fuck me, Dr. Lambert." She flicked a wrist between us. "Case in point."

"Except I did just fuck you, little lamb. Over and over and over..." I reached out a hand, brushing it across her nipple until she shoved my arm aside. "You don't need investors for a company that isn't yours," I groaned, giving myself one long, hard stroke. It didn't matter how many times I fucked her last night. It wasn't nearly enough. For me or my cock.

"But it will be mine. Won't it?" she hissed. "As soon as you make a widow out of me. Isn't that what you said? That you wanted your brother in the ground."

"You don't need anything with his name on it. You want something of your own, you can have Briarwood. I'll work for you," I told her, and I meant every word. She could have it all. *My* last name included.

Marisela blustered out a humorless laugh. "I don't want Briarwood. I've never wanted Briarwood. Besides, it doesn't have his name on it anymore. We're in the middle of rebranding, or haven't you heard?"

"You'll never get the board to agree to a full takeover as long as there's another Prescott to contest the vote."

"Good thing your ridiculous jealousy took care of that for me, then, huh?"

"He's not dead yet, Marisela," I reminded her, hating the way the threat tasted on my tongue.

"It's only a matter of time, Adrian. You won't be able to stop yourself." She leaned forward, lowering her voice as she skimmed her lips over my cheek. A gesture as tender as it was bristling. "Not when every time you look at him, you picture him touching me. Kissing me, fucking me."

The hair on my neck rose on end. I couldn't tell if she was bluffing or not. If she wanted the fucker dead or alive. Or if I'd just been another piece on her board this whole time.

I didn't like the idea of my little lamb playing me. But I didn't hate it either.

I grabbed her jaw with my thumb and forefinger, pressing down just enough to show her I was serious. "Stop with the games, Marisela. Come home or I'll drop Tate on the closest doorstep. Alive enough to keep you from rebranding anything."

She grinned. "Except you can't do that without him pointing the finger at you."

"He can't point something he doesn't have," I countered.

"We both know you won't send him back. You wouldn't do that to me."

"I won't kill him for you either."

"I don't believe you," she hissed. "I want his body, Adrian."

I lowered my face until we were nose to nose. "You'll never find all of it, Marisela."

She pulled back to glare at me. Defiance narrowing her eyes. Arrogance doing the same to mine. "Then I'll just wait five years and have my dear husband declared dead."

I nodded once. "You do that then. Just remember, whatever happens next, you asked for it." I grabbed my boxers off the floor, yanking them back up my legs before doing the same with my pants. Then I headed towards the bedroom door, my shirt slung over a shoulder when I added, "Oh, and Marisela... when you do seek out my help again—*because you will*—make sure to bring the girl. My colleague won't be nearly as patient with her as I've been with you."

85

MARISELA

The girl was a peculiar little thing. Always on edge. Her eyes unnaturally wide as though she were just waiting for some monster to jump out of the shadows, at the same time she suffered from a complete lack of self-awareness. The kind of creature that was better off on display in a zoo than left to its own devices.

It was annoying. How easy it was to creep up on Emily without her noticing.

I tapped my foot and waited for her to look up from her screen. It didn't take her more than a second to toss her e-reader aside and snatch her notepad from where she kept it within arm's reach. Her attention now hyper-focused on me and her pen held midair.

"I'll be heading into town this afternoon," I told her. This had her dropping the notepad and searching for her shoes instead. "Alone," I added, and she stopped what she was doing to peer over at me.

"Are you sure?"

"Am I ever not sure, Miss Shaw?" I wasn't expecting an answer. She knew that, so she didn't give me one. "In the meantime, I want a running list of Javier Castillo's assets. I want to know what he's really worth and not what he thinks he can offer me."

"By this afternoon?" she asked.

"*By this afternoon*," I confirmed.

"Right. Okay." She nodded once, digging her laptop out of her bag and flipping it open. And then her fingers were flying across the keys as that obnoxious clicking sound filled the silence between us.

I continued to watch her for a moment.

Emily was all I had, seeing as I couldn't rely on Elliot or whatever his real name was anymore. She was also much too quick to comply. Like a pet hamster lapping a wheel without ever questioning why it wasn't getting anywhere.

I should have been content with the fact she did what she was told. The girl wasn't my problem or my concern. Just another tool for me to discard when it was done being useful. Except she wasn't. She was bright and eager and broken enough to be managed.

I huffed, and Emily paused her typing. "Do you know why you're even doing what you're doing?" I asked her.

"Because you told me to?" she replied.

"Not literally, *nena*." I rolled my eyes towards the ceiling. "I meant, do you know why it's important to learn everything there is to know about someone before sitting across from them at the table?"

She shook her head. Emily wasn't as naïve as she

tried to appear. She *was* afraid of saying the wrong thing, though.

"Because it's better to be smart than it is to be impulsive. Interesting enough to keep your opponent engaged." I pushed off the doorframe and settled myself beside her on the bed, reaching out a hand and combing it through her hair like my mother used to do to me. Emily flinched but she didn't pull away as I separated the ends into three parts and began pleating one over the other.

"And how do you do that?" Her voice was stronger now, sounding both at ease and slightly put off.

It was a lesson in disarming someone with intimacy. Becoming the thing they were looking for more than anything else. For Emily, it was a maternal figure. It wasn't much different for Adrian. At his core, my shadow man was looking for acceptance. To be *loved* without conditions behind it.

"By making them believe you can help them, making them think you have something they want," I explained, my fingers moving faster as her hair got thinner at the end.

"Like what?"

"Could be anything really." I lifted a shoulder, out of habit since her back was still turned to me. "Your time, your attention, *your affection.*"

"And what if there's nothing they want?" she questioned, and I could tell she was genuinely curious at this point.

"Remember, life's a negotiation. Someone always wants something, Emily. And if they tell you otherwise, it's because they think they already have it. It's your job to convince them they don't."

"*Puta madre*," I hissed under my breath, as I stared up at the carved stonework of the Maria Cristina, before straightening out my dress and stomping my way inside the front entrance of the luxury hotel... that definitely wasn't an office building.

I should have recognized the address. I hadn't, which left me at a disadvantage.

A few minutes later, I was being led to an elevator and up to the royal suite where Javi was waiting for me. His arms spread over the back of the sofa and three glasses of wine set out on the table in front of him.

He glanced behind me when the door clicked closed, then back over to my face again, lifting a brow when he asked, "I don't see the girl?"

"No, you don't," I replied. "And I don't see your office."

He grinned. "You never did like to share, did you, Mari? Even as a kid."

"One of the benefits of being an only child is not having to share, *Javi*."

"I see." He stood from the sofa, reaching down to swipe up a glass of wine and tip it in my direction. I took it from his outstretched hand, my fingers brushing his just enough to keep him wondering.

"You know I don't like to mix business and pleasure, Mr. Castillo."

"And yet you work at your father-in-law's company?" he countered.

"My company," I corrected him.

"Right." He paused, eyeing me over his glass before adding, "First your mother and now your husband. Seems those around you have trouble staying in your orbit, *zorra*."

"What can I say? You fly too close to the sun and you might get burned." It was a threat. Unfortunately for Javi, he saw it as an invitation. He stepped around the coffee table until we were standing nearly tits to chest. And I shoved him back, slight pressure applied to his abdomen as I pulled away and narrowed my glare. "Business first."

"You drive a hard bargain, Marisela." He sighed, raking a hand through his coiffed hair. "It better be worth it."

I set my empty glass on the table as I lowered myself on a chair. My legs crossing in a way that had my skirt riding higher and his eyes flicking lower. "It will be life-changing. I promise."

PART FIVE

UPTICK IN MISSING PERSONS REPORTS

Public asks: missing or murdered?

Parents refuse to give up search for missing son, age 22 at the time of his disappearance.

Chicago is witnessing a troubling increase in missing persons cases, particularly amongst single white and Hispanic men. This surge has prompted community leaders, families, and advocacy groups to demand more proactive measures from law enforcement and city officials, who have been accused of allotting resources to missing women and children.

Data from the Chicago Police Department reveals that, as of late last year, 50% of the city's 32 active missing persons cases involved single men ranging between the ages of 21 and 65. This demographic is unusual compared to other cities nationwide, where most missing persons are found to be young women. Families of these missing men have expressed frustration over perceived neglect, with some cases being closed without proper investigation or family notification.

Investigative reports have uncovered systemic issues, including misclassification of cases and lack of accountability, contributing to the challenges in addressing these disappearances. This is especially true in instances where the wives or girlfriends of the missing persons have neglected to report them missing—citing long-term abuse or infidelity as the cause. One case in particular has the wife quoted as saying "good riddance" when questioned about her husband's disappearance.

To assist families of missing persons, the Cook County Medical Examiner's Office is hosting annual events to provide a platform for families to file reports, submit DNA samples, and receive emotional support. These gatherings will facilitate connections between families and resources, offering hope and closure to some.

86

ADRIAN

My little lamb paced the length of my office, her toned arms crossed over her chest. Her long, high ponytail bouncing with her steps and her ass accentuated by the tight fabric of her pencil skirt. It was no schoolgirl uniform but it might as well have been with the effect it had on me.

I didn't bother adjusting the bulge in my pants as I gave this woman my rapt attention. I'd spent years hiding who I was beneath all the nice clothes, playing a part and keeping my true nature at bay. Years moving the pieces on the board to get to this moment. And now that she was here, I wasn't about to hide what it was I wanted through it all.

It was time to capture the queen. And keep her for myself.

I reached a hand into my drawer, running my rough fingertips over the aged leather before dropping the mask onto the desk between us. The sound had Marisela glancing in my direction, her jaw ticking even as she pretended not to take notice when I lifted the mask to my face and adjusted the straps.

"You remember that night, Marisela?" I didn't wait for a response as I took a deep breath, nostalgia tipping my mouth into a grin. "It still smells like you," I hummed, leaning back in my seat and clasping my hands behind my head as I eyed her from the slits I'd cut into the front myself. "And I bet if I licked around all the little crevices, it'd still taste like you too."

I didn't have to see everything that was tucked behind her tailored suit jacket and flowy blouse to imagine what it looked like in the flesh. I didn't have to touch it to remember what it felt like either. The way she panted beneath me, my cock buried so deep in her cunt it was imprinted there... It was embedded in my mind.

"It's been fifteen years. That's disgusting, Adrian," she huffed. "And hardly hygienic.".

"*That's love*, little lamb," I corrected her.

"It's infatuation," she shot back, her glare narrowed in on me now that she'd stopped pacing.

"No, it's *obsession*. But it's also love." I shrugged, and Marisela made that little sound she made whenever she didn't like the answer you gave her but didn't have a viable retort. It wasn't a concession but it wasn't an argument either. Though I was certain that would come later. My little lamb didn't like losing.

"Take it off," she grunted, her mouth parting into a slight gasp as I started unbuttoning my dress shirt. I was two seconds away from unzipping my pants and throwing her on top of the desk when she clarified, "The mask, *pendejo*."

I lifted my fingertips from my belt buckle up to my face and slid the leather higher, letting it sit on top of my head without removing it completely. "As you wish, *princesa*."

My accent was shit, but it didn't matter when it had her smiling. I'd cut off a hand and fuck her with it if it made this woman smile.

For a moment, her hard exterior softened, her shoulders relaxing a fraction of an inch and her nails loosening their grip on her still-crossed arms. I pushed up from my chair and maneuvered around the desk, my open shirt flitting behind me as I stepped in front of her. Then I cupped the back of her head with my palm and tugged her to my chest until we were a breath apart.

"Why are you here, Marisela?" I whispered against the shell of her ear. She could pretend she was unaffected but her body had never been able to lie to me. She attempted to step back and I tugged her closer again.

"You know why I'm here, Adrian," she replied as I nipped at her neck, both of us enjoying the involuntary shiver it sent down her spine.

"I want to hear you say it."

"I need your help," she seethed.

I nodded once, stepping around her and repositioning myself behind my desk as I dropped my ass back into my chair. Set my elbows wide and steepled my hands. "It's nice that you're finally willing to admit it. Now, tell me why you're really here. In this office. With me," I clarified, in case she needed the reminder.

87

MARISELA

I hated him. *Despised* him. I wanted to aim a manicured fist at that arrogant fucking face of his. Knock out every one of his perfectly straight teeth until the only thing left for him to flash were a pair of bloodied gums.

I also wanted to shove him down on that desk and ride him until I forgot why I hated him so much.

That was the problem whenever Adrian and I were in the same room. We were like fire and ice, and I didn't know which one I was anymore. Just that when you put us together, it caused a lot of steam. The all-consuming kind that burned you up along with it. Until you didn't recognize yourself anymore. And that was exactly why I needed to stay as far away from him as was humanly possible. Something that wasn't easy to do when I needed his help. Twice over.

He was still staring at me from across his desk, leaning back in his seat. One polished shoe crossed over a knee and his unbuttoned dress shirt bunching at his sides, so that I had no choice but to stare at the sculpted abs he liked to cover up with a black-on-black suit or a set of blood-splattered scrubs. Both were equally intimidating.

I slowly lowered myself into the chair opposite him, smoothing out the hem of my skirt before pinning him with a glare. "You know why I'm here, Adrian. I paid you to do a job, and you failed to deliver. It's time for you to clean up the mess you made."

"No." He *tsked* his tongue. "You *tried* to pay me to do a job, and I refused to accept your money."

I lifted a shoulder into a half shrug. "A piss-poor business decision, if you ask me. But we both know the only opinion you care about is your own. Speaking of, do your men know they were working for free?"

I waited for the underlying threat to sink in. Instead, Adrian's mouth spread into an even wider grin. "*My men were paid. Just not by you.*"

There was that urge to punch him again.

I might have risked a nail and actually done it if I weren't so sure he'd like it too fucking much. I mean, this was the same man who nearly came in his pants when I stabbed him. The same man who saw the fact I'd drugged him, cut off a piece of his body, and returned it in a tiny cardboard box as a sign of my undying affection.

I guess it kind of was. I'd never put that level of effort into anyone else. Because no one pissed me off as much as he did.

Adrian lifted a curious brow, his smug way of telling me to get on with it. "Why now? It's been five years."

"Because you weren't supposed to kill him, *puta*."

"Who said I killed him?"

"I'm not stupid, Adrian," I grunted. "The medical examiner's office tested the bones you sent them. They came back a genetic match."

He smirked. "What can I say? My hand slipped. It happens."

"Not to you it doesn't, *Dr.* Lambert."

"All these years, and I still haven't been able to figure it out, you know?"

"Figure what out?" I huffed.

"If you actually wanted me to kill him or not... Why now, Marisela?" he repeated, as if it was going to somehow elicit another answer. An answer he liked better, seeing as what I had to say clearly wasn't what he wanted to hear.

"Because there's an issue with the will," I grumbled under my breath.

It'd taken me five years to finally get the courts to declare Tate dead instead of missing, even with the severed fingers as evidence. Just as long to raise the funds I needed to continue to run the company after most of our joint assets were frozen. Only to discover the *greatest legal minds* still couldn't find a loophole in the stipulation that stated everything went to the next living *blood* relative.

Apparently, all my arranged marriage had gotten me was a closet full of designer clothes and as much jewelry as I could shove into a suitcase. Both were useless when it came to swaying the board of directors.

It was probably why Tate was so quick to agree to my

terms. It didn't matter how many bastards were or weren't tied to his name, because I never would have gotten anything anyway. Everything was always going to go to the heir I'd never produced.

Adrian leaned forward in his seat again, dropping the arrogance in his voice as he eyed me with something that resembled concern this time. "What kind of issue?"

There was no point in trying to keep the truth from him. It wouldn't be long before the lawyers reached out. Though I had to admit it irritated me to no end that I was forced to have a front-row seat to the fucker's satisfaction.

"The kind that means I get nothing... and it all goes to you."

88

ADRIAN

I kept my expression neutral. The air so electric between us I could practically hear it crackling. It was a heady feeling, to have everything you worked so hard to get within your grasp. Or should I say just out of reach? Sitting in front of me with that sour look on her face.

You had to be careful when you were this close to the end of the board. You had to cradle the pieces in the palm of your hand or risk having them crumble beneath your fingertips. Which was why I let the moment stretch on, waited for it all to sink in before choosing my next words carefully.

"I don't want your company, Marisela. Your home, your cars, whatever other assets you amassed over the years..." I shoved my chair back and rounded my desk for the second time, closing the distance until I'd positioned myself directly in front of her.

She peered up at me, her brows creased with suspicion and her mouth still pinched like she'd been sucking on a lemon when she should be sucking on something else. Hell, she didn't even have to move. I had no problem doing all the work. *Or* returning the favor.

"I don't want anything that's rightfully yours." I grabbed her wrist and tugged her to her feet, gently drawing her closer. She didn't pull away. She didn't fight me. That didn't mean she wasn't ready to do it, though.

"What's the catch, Adrian?"

I cupped a palm under her chin, gliding a finger across the skin of her nape until all the tiny follicles were standing on end. I could see her grappling with her natural reaction to want to close her eyes. But Marisela always had more self-control than I ever did. She didn't even chance a blink as she stared back at me.

"There's no catch, little lamb. Call the lawyers and have them draw up the papers."

I reached an arm behind my back and grabbed the handset from the old black rotary phone I kept on my desk for aesthetics. It still dialed out, even if I didn't have a real use for it anymore. I tugged until the coiled cord stretched as far as it would go while little dust particles danced between us, then wrapped Marisela's clenched fist around the receiver.

She glanced at the phone in her hand before glaring up at me again. "Or you could cut the showmanship and I could just use my cell like a normal person."

"I could, but can your cell do this?" I twisted the cable around my neck and yanked once, the plastic coils embedding themselves against my Adam's apple. Marisela still had the other end clutched in her hand as I stepped far enough back to restrict my own air supply. Then I met her annoyance with a smirk.

She rolled her eyes, dropping the receiver and leaving it to dangle along my chest, and quickly added as much distance as she could between us without stepping over the threshold. "Enough of the theatrics, Adrian. I came here to discuss business, not indulge in whatever sick games you have in that head of yours." She pointed an accusatory nail at me.

Red. Her favorite color. I hadn't forgotten.

"Let's not pretend you don't like my sick games, Marisela." I unwrapped the cable from around my neck and set it back onto the desk before refastening each of the buttons of my dress shirt. If she noticed the new ink carved into my chest, she didn't mention it. "You wanna talk business? We'll talk business."

I grabbed my glasses off the shelf to my right and lowered them onto the bridge of my nose. I'd had my cornea reshaped years ago, which meant my vision was more impaired than improved when I was wearing these, but Marisela had a thing for glasses. And, well, I had a thing for *her*. Or maybe I just liked driving her crazy.

Then I pulled a pen and pad of paper from the bottom drawer, scrawled my intentions across the first clean page, and signed the bottom. Marisela's heels clicked against the floor as she approached my desk. I wave the sheet of paper in her direction and she snatched it out of my hand.

"I, Adrian Lambert, hereby relinquish my claim on everything that rightfully belongs to Marisela Cruz in exchange for everything that is rightfully mine." She read the statement aloud before landing me with another glare. "What the fuck is that supposed to mean, Adrian? *Rightfully yours?* What's rightfully yours?"

I grinned, even as I tried my damnedest not to. Because, like I said, this moment had been a long time coming. So long I was tempted to pinch myself to make sure it was real. "You, of course. You've always been rightfully mine, Marisela."

89

MARISELA

The truth was Adrian was right. He did own some part of me. A part he could manipulate like a puppet string. Twist and tug until he had me coming back and sitting in this room with him. Asking for help in exchange for giving him the rest of me. All of me. Everything I'd tried so fucking hard to preserve. Everything he'd predicted and I refused to believe.

Which left me with no choice but to cut that part out. To sever that string and leave behind whatever it was attached to. Let the remains rot until they were as lifeless as the tiny bones in the box he was currently using like a paperweight on top of a pile of folders between us.

I thought returning the toe I'd hacked off was a nice gesture. If his smugness was anything to go by, so did he. Until his smirk dropped into a frown.

Adrian saw it. Clocked what I was going to do before my brain had even registered my body was doing it—

probably because he was right when he claimed he knew me better than I knew myself. My fingers twitched, and then my hand closed around a pair of scissors he'd left sticking out of the penholder on his desk. My arm quickly rising up and just as quickly slamming down. Puncturing skin and muscle and stopping when it touched bone.

What my poor sweet shadow man didn't see coming, though, was the fact I wasn't aiming for him. The handle protruding from the meat of my thigh as blood oozed to the surface.

Usually, a sharp, shallow jab of pain was enough to ground me. Tiny slices up and down the insides of my legs where only I could see them. Right now, I needed something deeper. I needed the endorphins that came with it. And I needed the look of horror on his face. A look that told me that even after all these years, I could surprise him. Force his hand like he'd forced mine.

I reclaimed my seat, dragging it closer to the edge of the desk as I kept the scissors suspended with one leg crossed over the other. Warm fluid continuing to trickle down to my ankle and catching in the opening of my heel. My shoes were ruined and he'd have to toss the rug. But it was worth the sacrifice if you asked me.

Clearly, Dr. Lambert didn't feel the same way.

"Was that really necessary?" Adrian lifted a brow, his attempt at appearing unfazed, but I could tell I'd rattled him. His eyes jumping back and forth between my face and my lap while mine remained focused. On him. On his reaction. On the sweat beading across his forehead and how he chewed on the inside of his mouth.

"For me, it was."

"That's going to need stitches, Marisela," he chastised like a disapproving father. *I already had one of those, and we knew how things ended with him.*

"Then let's hope your hand's gotten steadier over the years." I gestured to the scar on his abdomen. The one I'd left there. And by the time I'd dropped my hand back down on the armrest, Adrian was in front of me, snatching me up by the wrist and dragging me out of his office. Along the hallway, making a left, and then swinging us inside an empty exam room.

He grabbed me at the waist, picking me up and plopping my ass on top of the table. Muttering to himself as he removed alcohol pads and gauze from various drawers and cabinets before slapping them down on a metal tray next to a sterile needle and a package of sutures. Irritation tightening the muscles of his back as he hunched over the counter.

The thing was, I could have stabbed him. It would have felt good too. At least momentarily. Seeing him so spun up was much more entertaining, though. There was a reason jilted wives keyed their husbands' cars. Men liked keeping pretty things intact. *This* was just our version of that... without having to get an insurance adjuster involved.

"And here I thought surgeons were known for being stoic," I mused, my leg throbbing in the best way even as the blood continued to pool beneath my ass.

When Adrian turned to face me again, the aggravation was gone. But so was the concern. His grip on my thigh neither rough nor gentle as he grabbed the base of the scissors and yanked them free. I knew enough to avoid the femoral artery. That didn't mean I still couldn't bleed out, especially once nothing was there to staunch the flow anymore.

But instead of putting pressure on the wound, Adrian stepped back, locking the door behind him as he aimed his glare at me. As wordless as he was judgmental.

"So what's the plan, Dr. Lambert? Teach me a lesson? Stand there and watch until I bleed out on your table."

He crossed his arms over his chest, his mouth pressed into a thin line and his pupils dilated. "No, not until you bleed out." He shrugged a single shoulder. "Just until you're too tired to fight me."

90

ADRIAN

I glanced down at my watch, then back up at Marisela's face. Twenty minutes after dislodging the scissors and she was already exhibiting significant pallor. Her lips starting to turn blue, her breaths shallow, and her eyes struggling to stay open.

My disgruntled little patient was declining fast. The blood loss affecting her much more rapidly than it should have been, even if I took into account the alcohol she chugged for breakfast. The baseline dehydration and anemia working to my advantage as cortisol and epinephrine flooded her system. Increasing her anxiety and in turn her blood flow.

Her body was doing everything it could to protect itself. Unfortunately, those same measures were only helping to expedite her quick descent into hypovolemic shock.

She had the ability to put an end to this battle of wills, if she politely asked me to stitch her up. Her pride wouldn't allow her to do it. Which was fine. One of us had all the time in the world, and it sure as hell wasn't the one with a gaping wound in their thigh.

"Fuck you…" she mumbled under her breath, her words slurring in a way that had me pushing off the wall and stepping forward to sling her over a shoulder.

I could feel the warmth of her blood seeping through my shirt as I carried her back down the hall, stopping at Bugs's door and pushing it open with the tip of my shoe.

He peered up from his computer screen, both hands *thankfully* in full view as he glanced from my face to Marisela's ass, which I just now noticed was bare, the material of her skirt bunching around her waist and exposing everything she didn't have underneath it.

"Went that well, huh?" He smirked.

I crossed an arm over my chest, using my palm to cover her. "I have some things to take care of. Keep an eye on Casper. Make sure he doesn't do anything stupid," I grunted.

"I'm not his keeper," Bugs replied, reminding me just how young he was and old I fucking felt.

"No. You're not. You'd do well to remember you're not Donnie's either," I stressed before adding, "That doesn't make it any less of a team effort, though."

He nodded once, his fingers slamming against the keyboard as I clicked the door closed again.

These kids were gonna be the death of me. If my little lamb didn't get to me first.

I flicked on the light, taking several long strides until I was standing in the middle of the room. Padded walls, no windows, a few medical devices essential for ensuring our guest's comfort, and a single metal-framed bed off to one side. A cell originally designed to quarantine well-off tuberculous patients while everyone else was lined up on thin cots along the main floor.

It was then used to confine the sanitorium's criminally insane in the 1950s after the epidemic became less widespread and expansive units were no longer needed. Briarwood offered the land and space most of the asylums didn't, and so the focused turned from overall health to full-on confinement. A dumping ground for the city's lost and unwanted souls, until Hare and Burke decided the most dangerous residents would be better off hidden away in the basement.

That was before I'd found them, of course. Before I'd helped reinvent this place from the inside out. Making it less *Bedlam* and more *Dr. Frankenstein*.

Now we used these rooms as private accommodations. These walls for research and development. The former patients having all been transferred to other facilities or lost in the shuffle of mismanaged paperwork. Patients like Donnie and Casper and Bugs and a few others who stayed behind or escaped.

I didn't care to track them down. Treating the mind

was never of interest to me. It wasn't the vision I saw for Briarwood after I took over. Not as a surgeon specializing in reconstructive medicine. In transformation. And I transformed those boys, eased what was ailing them even if it was for my own benefit.

The same way I'd transformed the figure staring back at me from across the room. I guess he really wasn't staring. He'd need eyes to do that. More like facing in my direction. Then again, he didn't have much of a face left...

But he still had ears so he could hear me, a nose so that he could smell it whenever he pissed himself from the tiny orifice I'd created at the bottom of his torso. And one arm with two fingers. He didn't need more than two to grip on to a pen. He didn't need legs either—those were sold off to a very gracious amputee for far more than they were worth. Some rich fucker who'd gotten drunk and skied himself into a tree.

Cash was cash after all. And my interests required lots of it.

I had to admit it was difficult staying anonymous. Reading article after article call me a monster. A butcher. When really I was just a businessman like anyone else. But it kept people scared; it also kept me operational. Sometimes bodies needed to be found to make a point.

Not this one though. No one would ever find this one in its entirety.

"She came back just like I told you she would." I moved closer to the mattress, despite the odor permeating from the overflowing bedpan—the dark brown color telling me his kidneys were of no use to me anymore.

He replied with a gurgle. His tongue had been the second thing to go, his cock the first, so that I could listen to him plead as I sawed it off a few centimeters at a time each day. After that, it was just too much noise. Too much whimpering and whining from someone who had more testicles than teeth.

"*How'd she look?*" I pivoted on the heel of my shoe, creating that squeaking sound of leather against tile. "I'm glad you asked. Fuckable, as always, but not properly fucked—don't you worry, she will be."

I chuckled and he gurgled again. I could only assume that meant he was chuckling along with me.

"My associate treating you well?" I glanced over to the empty IV bag. "Dr. Michaels is preoccupied at the moment, and it appears our patient care here has been lacking. That's on me. I apologize. I'll be sure to rectify that... as soon as I'm done fucking your wife, big brother."

No, the fucker wasn't dead. He was just... barely alive.

I grinned before flicking off the light, which was more for my benefit anyway, and slammed the door closed. Clanking the lock extra loud so that Tate was sure to hear the ringing in his perfectly-preserved ears long after my footsteps disappeared down the hall.

91

MARISELA

"How's that feel, little lamb?"

I could sense him hovering above me, the mattress shifting beneath my fingertips as he leaned forward. Closer and closer to that spot between my legs. His breath warm and his hands cold as he poked and prodded until goose bumps were breaking out along both sides of my inner thighs.

Unfortunately, he wasn't there to get me off but to put *something* on. A fresh bandage in place of the one I must have bled through at some point in the middle of the night.

I honestly didn't remember much of what happened between then and now. That was my own fault. I'd been angry. Impulsive. I'd goaded him because I liked the way it felt a lot more than I liked the consequences. I was also self-destructive on some deeper level.

But we both knew that.

I tried to lift my head to glare at him, and he was

already moving again, the tail of his lab coat brushing across my ankles as he stepped around the foot of the bed. A quiet buzzing sound seemed to follow him. At first, I thought it was some sort of machinery, a medical device or pump, but then I realized the cocky son of a bitch was humming to himself as he adjusted the tube currently pushing god knows what into my veins.

Not pain killers, though. The pain was still there and so was the throbbing in my temples.

I forced my eyes open, expecting to find bright lights and white walls. Surgical tools and metal trays. Instead, Dr. Adrian Lambert was smiling back at me from the confines of my own bedroom. I was home, at the estate, and not locked up in some padded room at Briarwood.

Guess he could still surprise me too.

I lifted my chin and gestured to the IV pole. "What's in the bag, Adrian?"

He tracked my movement, his glare bouncing from my face to the pump and back again. "Just fluids, Marisela. I'm not drugging you." He sighed. "You lost a lot of blood with that little stunt of yours."

"I lost a lot of blood because of *your pride*. Not *my stunt*," I countered, and he balked.

"It wasn't *my pride* that had you sitting in my office and impaling yourself with a pair of rusty scissors, Marisela. I've never been too proud to tell you exactly how I feel about you. But that was the point, wasn't it? You were testing me. Seeing how far you could push me before I snapped. Before I either fought you or fucked you. Just like you did fifteen years ago..."

I refused to answer him. Mostly because the sound of

his voice was grating on my nerves and partly because he was right. I was trying to bait him into fucking me that night—even if I hadn't realized it at the time. But not for the reason he was thinking. Not because I'd wanted to run away with him. But because I'd wanted to feel something. I'd hoped sex would somehow reset whatever was wrong with my body. And when it hadn't, I was angry. At him and at myself for being so naïve to believe he was the answer.

"Despite what you've been conditioned to think—by Tate, by your father—that's not the way love works. You can't just stop doing it because it's easier that way."

I stifled a laugh. Tried to speak before stifling another one. "That your way of telling me I have daddy issues, Dr. Lambert?" I didn't wait for him to respond. "I can't believe the orphaned bastard of a serial womanizer is lecturing me on love right now. How the fuck do you even know what love is, Adrian? How could you possibly know something you've never been given from someone else?"

Yes, I was angry again. Vulnerable and cruel. Lashing out against someone who probably didn't deserve it. At least not today. But this was who I was. Who I'd become and there was no undoing it. No going back to that girl in the window.

And soon enough, he would realize it too. He'd realize that the girl he'd been so infatuated with didn't exist anymore and he could give up on chasing after her ghost.

Adrian stepped closer to the bed, dipping his head down and pressing his lips to my ear, as his fingers trailed lower and lower on my torso. Not stopping until he reached the apex of my thighs.

"Love is kinda like sex, Marisela. Like an orgasm. You don't know what it feels like until it hits you. And then there is no denying it." He circled his thumb around my clit a few times, groaning deep in his throat, as if he enjoyed getting me off as much as *I* enjoyed *him* getting me off. Only to quickly pull his hand back and rise to his full height again. "If you aren't sure, then you didn't experience one. And if you don't know, then you aren't in love. *I know*," he grunted, bringing his hand to his mouth and sucking his digits clean before releasing them with an exaggerated pop. "Do you?"

I pushed up from the mattress, propping myself on one elbow and canting my head to the side to get a better look at him. "Is that what this is? Are you here to convince yourself that you're lovable? That *I* love you when your own parents couldn't."

"Oh, no, I already know that you love me, little lamb. I've known it since the first time I had you coming on my tongue." He shrugged. "Since I got the girl who never asks for anything to beg me not to stop."

"Then why bring me here? Why bring me home? When you had me exactly where you wanted me."

"It's simple, really. We've played teacher... doctor..." He glanced at the IV bag, flicking it once before turning back to me. "Now I think it's time we played house."

92

ADRIAN

"Play house?" Marisela laughed until the strain on her throat had her coughing. "What the fuck is that supposed to mean?" she wheezed out.

"Three days. Seventy-two hours. Just you and me. Here. Alone."

It wasn't my most original idea. I know... *Dr. Michaels did it first.* His little pet only had a few days left on her clock before he did whatever he was going to do with her in that basement. But true innovation wasn't spontaneous. It was taking a concept and improving upon it. Using what you already knew, conducting research, and controlling the variables. Except where he had given his girl a cage, I was giving mine a castle.

You see, I was nothing if I wasn't innovative.

"Three days? That's a lot of time to kill. Sure you have the stamina for all that?" She made a show of looking me over from head to toe.

"This isn't about sex, Marisela."

"So three days, alone in this house, and you have no intentions of fucking me?" She lifted a challenging brow.

"Oh, I'm going to fuck you. But that's not all I'm going to do. I'm also going to show you what it's like."

"What *what's* like?" she questioned, her curiosity as piqued as the nipples poking through her nightgown.

"What it's like to really be mine." I dropped my hand to her chin, tilted her head, and forced her to look me in the face. Not that she was avoiding eye contact, just too stubborn to give me her full attention. "What it's like to be fucked and fed until going to work is more of a chore than an escape. Until you'd rather be in bed with me than sitting in a boardroom with anyone else."

She jerked back and I let her, shoving my hands into my pockets as I watched her cheeks heat at the thought. At the images I was sure were playing in her head. At least they were playing in mine.

"Thanks for the offer, but I'm gonna have to pass." She swung her legs off the mattress and started to limp towards the door. She wouldn't get far.

"This isn't a negotiation, Marisela," I called after her.

"It's always a negotiation, Adrian," she called back, stopping when she tried to yank the door open, only to realize it wouldn't budge. She glared at me over a shoulder and I smirked.

"Did I forget to mention I had the security updated? Had the entire estate modernized while you were gone. Automatic windows and locks. *Cameras*... the whole nine yards."

"How?" One word with a million accusations behind it.

"Once you had Tate declared dead, it was easy. Seems the board prefers a mut with a DNA test over an outsider with a barren womb—*their words, not mine.*" I closed the distance until I was standing in front of her before she could get away again. Tugging her to my chest as my free hand drifted towards her lower abdomen. "I know better. I think it just hasn't been tended to properly." I dropped my lips to her neck and pressed a kiss on her pulse point. "A little effort and plenty of seed, and I think you'd be surprised at what could grow between us."

She lifted her leg, rubbing her knee against me before bringing it up. High and hard. I stumbled back a step but it did little to keep my cock from straining in my pants. She should know by now that violence was just foreplay for us.

"If you want something to *grow*, you're better off fucking the garden." She pooled a mouthful of saliva in her cheeks and quickly launched it at my face. "I don't want your bastard any more than I wanted your brother's heir. Why the fuck do you think I had the birth control pills? Don't you fucking get it? I don't want to be someone's mother, someone's wife, someone's *anything*. I just want to be me even if I don't know who that is right now."

I watched her for a moment. Her chest heaving, her pulse racing, her rage reaching its crest and then plummeting. She really thought *that* would do it.

She was wrong.

"Okay, then we won't have kids. I'd rather keep you to myself anyway."

She shook her head but she didn't move from her spot by the door. "You have got to be kidding me. Either you've gotten denser over the years, or I mistakenly gave you more credit than you deserved."

"Serious as a drug-induced heart attack, Miss Cruz." I spun around and made my way across the room, pulling back the curtains on the window until daylight was streaming in. "Besides, I think it's already working."

"Yeah, and what's that?" she asked me.

"My little experiment." I turned around to face her again, using the remote I'd concealed in my pocket to disengage the lock on the bedroom door. "We've already discussed more about our future together in the last five minutes than you and that asshole ex-husband of yours ever did."

93

MARISELA

DAY ONE

I'd tried the locks, all the doors and windows, even the hidden latches in the walls. And he'd watched me do it with that smug look on his face that told me what I already knew. I was wasting my time. He'd turned my home into my prison. A sentence compounded by the fact I had an insufferable bunkmate, who was way too happy to be standing on the same side of the bars as me.

"Where's the staff?" I questioned.

"I gave them all the week off," Adrian said from where he was leaning against the doorframe, staring in my direction. "You look tense, little lamb. How about I run you a hot bath?"

I turned to glare at him, shifting my weight onto one leg to alleviate some of the throbbing. "Sure, and why don't you toss a toaster inside while you're at it?"

"If you wanted some aftershocks, all you had to do was say the word."

He hadn't even finished speaking before he was stalking forward, pinning me to the closest surface and dropping to his knees in front of me. One hand pushing the hem of my nightgown higher on my waist while the other parted my lips. And then he was on me. Licking and sucking. Spreading his tongue wide and curling the tip. The sensations as familiar as they were foreign. Like a memory I wasn't sure was mine anymore.

I didn't know if I could come like this. But it felt good, even as my thigh ached and my muscles tensed. I grabbed on to his hair, soft and thick and just long enough to steer his face where I wanted it, and where I wanted it was everywhere. All at once. As I continued to grind myself against the bridge of his nose.

But it wasn't until he started groaning, whispering all the dirty things he wanted to do to me, vibrations traveling from somewhere deep in his chest to my clit, causing my toes to curl and my pussy to clench, that I finally relinquished control. Allowing Adrian to fuck me with his tongue and mouth and face and fingers.

He leaned forward, squeezing his arms between my thighs and bracing his palms on the wall behind me as he draped each of my legs over a shoulder until my feet were no longer touching the floor. I felt a different kind of warmth trickling across my skin and catching on my nightgown. Blood coating my fingers and the chair rail I was using for leverage after I'd reached down and realized I'd popped a stitch.

The hint of copper in the air—the extra bite of pain—

only added to the pleasure, though, as my body twisted and contorted. Thrummed and pulsed. Adrian's tongue now spearing itself inside me as his thumb stretched over my pubic bone to rub against my clit. His mouth and arm working in tandem, trembling and aching like the tension building in my lower stomach.

The sounds of him grunting and the feel of him straining were just as much of a turn-on as everything else he was doing to me. To the point I was no longer in a rush to come. Not when I could watch him lap at my pussy instead.

I looked down. Enjoying the way determination had sweat coating his hair and stress knitting his brow. And he grinned against me before biting hard enough on my clit to have me spasming and cursing at the same time. My orgasm hitting me harder than anything I'd experienced before.

"What the hell was that..." I said more to myself than to Adrian, my palms squeaking as they slowly slid back down the walls.

He answered anyway. "That was me getting on my knees and asking you to marry me, princess. It was also you screaming yes."

Then he was on his feet, my legs still too gelatinous to move and my brain too addled to argue with him, as he scooped me up into his arms and carried me out of the room.

94

ADRIAN

She was studying my profile as I tied off the replacement suture. Her eyes searing into the side of my head as I checked my work. She'd reopened her wound, leaving a trail of blood down the wall, small droplets mapping out the path I'd taken after I'd picked her up and set her down on the dining table before stitching her together again.

I glanced over at where our little crime scene had already begun to coagulate. Fingerprints and red blotches in the shape of her ass. She'd probably wanted it cleaned up and painted over. I wanted it framed.

"Gonna have to be a little more gentle next time you ride my face." I smirked as I tapped her once on the thigh. I could still smell her, feel her juices drying on my cheeks and chin. My tongue swiped across my bottom lip. Yep, I could still taste her too. "Not that I'm complaining. Everything I have is yours to ride for as long as you wanna ride it, Mrs. Lambert."

"I am not marrying you, Adrian." Her jaw ticked, my name more of a curse than an endearment. I enjoyed the sound of it anyway.

"Too late. You already said yes. Over and over again if my memory serves me right."

"Yeah, well, I'm pretty sure what people say during sex isn't legally binding. If it were, men would realize their cocks aren't as big as they think they are."

I tugged her off the table and turned her around, before bending her over the top and leaning forward so my lips were against her ear. "Happy to let you try mine on for size again. Can't have my bride regretting her decision before she even makes it down the aisle."

"Sex isn't a marriage proposal, Dr. Lambert," she moaned, the strain seeping out of her voice the moment my fingers started rubbing at her clit from behind. I loved Marisela's attitude almost as much as I loved fucking it out of her.

"Maybe not, but it is a pretty damn good example of what you can expect as my wife." I lowered my zipper, reaching into my pants and boxers and tugging my cock free before lining it up with her swollen pussy. She was still wet with a mixture of my saliva and her cum. A few more rotations of my wrist and she'd be absolutely drenched, though.

"I was married for ten years, Adrian. I have no interest in doing it ag—"

Her words died off on a groan as I shoved my way inside her, thrusting harder and faster until her face was flat against the table, her arms gripping onto the ledge to keep her body from flying too far forward.

"What you had with my brother wasn't a marriage," I grunted. "He fucked anything with a hole. I only want to fuck you."

"And yet, I don't care where either of you put your dicks."

"Except you do…" I grinned against her cheek, pulling back and driving forward again. Hard and fast, so she gasped with the added pressure in her lower abdomen. I could almost feel myself poking out the other side. Which meant I knew she could feel me too.

I didn't give her a moment to compose herself before I resumed a steady in-and-out pace. Enough to keep her quiet but not enough to get her there.

"You care very much where the fuck I put mine. You want it here." Another thrust and another gasp. The kind that had me on the edge of coming myself. "Deep inside you. Splitting you in two until all that tension melts away from your shoulders, until your legs give out from under you and the only thing keeping you upright is my arm around your waist, until you're begging me to fuck you like no one else has or can. Because I've taken the time to study you, learn you, fuck you how you like and need it. And you don't want to share that sort of dedication with anyone else, do you, little lamb?"

This time, I drew out slowly, savoring the way her body tried to pull me back inside it. Like I belonged there. Because I did.

"Be honest. Tell me what you would do to me if I even thought about another woman. Tell me how it makes you feel to imagine her coming on my cock… instead of you."

I tweaked her nipple to refocus her attention, one palm crossed over her chest, the other flat on the table in front of us as I waited for my favorite green-eyed monster to make its appearance. Her jealousy didn't just turn me on. It made me fucking feral.

"Tell me, Marisela," I prompted. "You didn't give a fuck about my brother. But I'm different. I'm yours and my filthy little princess doesn't like to share, does she?" I lowered my hand to her clit again, rubbing wide circles while keeping my cock perfectly still inside her.

She let out a low moan, mumbling to herself before hissing at me. "I'd cut it off."

"What would you cut off?" I asked, while rewarding her with another flick of my finger and thrust of my hips.

"Your cock. I'd have it stuffed and mounted on the wall so you would have to look at it every time you entered the room."

"Ah, so you wouldn't kill me?" *Now,* that *was interesting.* I lifted a curious brow, even though she couldn't see me.

"Death is a kindness, Adrian," she replied a little too calmly. "And I'm not known for being kind."

My grin widened as I continued to fuck her tight cunt with my cock and fingers, my rhythm quickening with her breaths. "No, you're not, are you."

95

MARISELA

I didn't know what his angle was. If Adrian honestly thought he could nudge me down the aisle one orgasm at a time. Like it really was that easy...

Though I had to admit I did miss it. The euphoria, the feeling of being weightless even for a few minutes. Not enough to give into his ridiculous demands but enough to enjoy his method of persuasion.

The thing was... I could be persuasive too.

I waited until I heard the water running in the other room, listening for the click of the shower stall before I slid off the bed and crept closer to the door. He hadn't bothered shutting it all the way. Which meant either he wanted me to be able to hear him or he wanted to be able to hear me. It didn't matter. I wasn't trying to escape.

Not when everything I was looking for was right in front of me. Standing bare-assed under the rainfall showerhead, his cock in his hand as he gave it several long strokes. One palm pressed flat against the glass and both eyes trained on me. As if he'd been expecting me to find him. Or maybe he hadn't. Maybe he just enjoyed the idea of being caught. Of being watched the way he used to watch me.

Dr. Lambert wasn't just a voyeur; he was an exhibitionist too. The kind of man who probably stared at himself as he jerked off in the mirror.

With each step I took, he stroked himself again, from base to tip, following my movements as I opened the stall door and closed us inside.

"Marisela, you shouldn't get your sutures wet," he groaned at the same time I dropped to my knees and he grabbed on to the back of my head to hold me there.

He tasted like soap and sweat. Like looking backward and falling forward, and I felt just as stuck between who I was when I was with him and who I was trying to be without him.

Sucking cock shouldn't have been as transcendent and self-reflective as it was. I shouldn't have liked it as much either, but here we were. Tonsil-deep and gagging on awareness.

I pulled back, looking up at him through my lashes, my mouth a breath away from the tip so he could feel it when I spoke. "If you come, it all stops now. You sign everything over to me. No more games, no more manipulations."

He quirked a brow, his thighs already trembling beneath my touch. "And if I don't? If your jaw gives out before my cock, what does that get me, little lamb?"

"My cooperation," I groaned, taking him all the way down again. Not stopping until I was half-swallowing, half-choking while he was fully seated against the muscles of my throat.

"I want more than that, Marisela," he hissed.

I released him just long enough to reply. "I don't have more to give."

Adrian slapped his palms on each side of the stall, his head tipped back as hot water pelted his face. His dark hair sticking to his forehead and droplets following the trail along his chest over to the tattoo that had been added there since the last time we were completely naked in a room together. That stupid nickname mocking me as the stream continued to cascade down the folds of his abdominal muscles before slipping along his thighs and dripping off his knees.

"You have everything to give and I want it all," he countered. And then he was lost to the sensation of my tongue flicking against his tip, my mouth clamping shut and sucking him down like the straw I dropped into my rum and Coke every day at lunch.

Instead of bubbles, though, I chugged the first beads of his precum. And he flexed his ass cheeks when I bobbed forward, releasing all the tension as I drew back. Repeating the process over and over again until he was fucking my face more than I was blowing him. Faster and faster. His grunts mixing with the sounds of the glass squeaking beneath his fingertips and the tile floor scraping against my kneecaps. His labored breaths and my quick pants.

I reached out a hand, cupping his balls while tears formed at the corners of my eyes. He was close. I recognized all the signs. The way his brows knitted, his abs clenched, the pads of his feet rocking back and forth and his cock thickening between my lips. And just when I thought it was coming, when I thought he was coming…

Nothing. The fucker was toying with me. Faking it. I didn't know that was even a thing…

He dropped his hands from the glass, grabbed onto the sides of my head and started thrusting harder. Deeper. His lips tipped up into a lopsided grin as he forced my nose closer and closer to his pelvic bone. My face pressed so tight against him I couldn't breathe from my nostrils or my mouth. And he held me there, making quick jerking motions with his hips that had him barely moving while my jaw was locked in place.

I clawed at his thighs, losing traction as my bare feet slid against the wet tiles until I was simultaneously choking and drowning beneath the shower spray. Waterboarded by the same furnishings I'd picked out and hired a contractor to install.

I didn't know if that was irony or just an odd fleeting thought as my oxygen level depleted and a sort of giddiness replaced it.

Adrian wrapped a hand around my hair and tugged me upright before twisting me around and pressing me up against the fogging glass. Entering me in one fast thrust that had me balancing myself on my toes. Except I wasn't balancing at all. He was holding me there. Supporting me and smothering me as my lungs tried to suck down the hot, thick air.

"Don't ever underestimate how much I want you, Marisela. All of you," he mumbled next to my ear, closing his teeth around the lobe and biting down hard enough to mark me. "Not just a part of you. Not just what you want to show the world. All the broken shards. All the ugliness you keep to yourself. I want every depraved piece of you. I want to taste it, savor it and worship it until you have no choice but to do the same."

96

ADRIAN

DAY TWO

She slept differently whenever she was curled up in bed beside me. She didn't notice it but I did. I noticed everything. From the way her breaths seemed slower. Softer. To how her expression relaxed. Her lips more parted than pursed. The effects of multiple orgasms increasing her prolactin levels and making it easier for her to sleep.

Sex was different for me, though. At least with Marisela, it always was. Couldn't really remember what it was like before her.

But watching her gag on my cock? Pressing her up against that glass and fucking her? It heightened my awareness.

Sure, I was calm too. Enjoyed the serotonin and dopamine spikes. But I couldn't close my eyes and sleep. I didn't want to. Almost as if my subconscious knew this feeling was temporary. At least it had been. It wouldn't be anymore.

It was time to keep a tight leash on my little lamb—whether the collar was around my neck or hers was dealer's choice. Either way, it was there. Strangling one until the other decided it was much easier to breathe when you stopped tugging so damn hard.

I pushed up from the bed, careful not to disturb her as I closed myself inside the bathroom. Splashing some cold water on my face to rinse away the dried blood collecting on my cheek. Didn't know if it was hers or mine anymore, just that it came from under her nails when she tried to claw at my eye.

I'd wear her marks with pride, though. Same as she would wear my ring when we were done here. It was only a matter of time before Marisela accepted that we belonged to each other. We always had, which was why she and Tate were doomed from the beginning.

Fate doesn't care how much money you have. You can't fight it. And Marisela and I were written in the stars since the first time I'd seen them blinking back at me after she came.

My glare dropped to where I'd had a part of her carved into my skin. Bold, black letters staring back at me in reverse. Little Lamb. So that every time she looked at me she was reminded that I gave her my name first and forever.

I wiped my face and tossed the damp washcloth into the laundry basket before turning around and heading down the stairs of my childhood home. A world I was never allowed to be a part of and now owned.

It wasn't just ironic. It was vindicating. That didn't mean I liked being here. This house—these walls—haunted me just as readily as the woman in the well. My future mother-in-law, now that I thought about it...

I should have burned it all to the ground, forced Marisela to come live with me at Briarwood. But I wasn't looking to trap her. I didn't *want* to trap her. I was conserving her energy. Containing her. Until she accepted she couldn't fight fate either.

By the time I had breakfast set out on the table, I could hear Marisela's bare feet padding down the hall. Tentative, like she was afraid of what she might find when she turned the corner. Or maybe she was still looking for a quick escape.

She was out of luck if she was. Bugs had all the exterior locks set on a timer. I couldn't even leave if I wanted to. Good thing there was nowhere else I'd rather be.

"Morning, princess. Sleep well?" I hummed as I poured her a large cup of black coffee. Dark and bitter, just like my girl.

I preferred cream in mine... *just like my girl.*

"What's all this?" Marisela waved a hand around the table. She'd been too disgruntled to sit down and enjoy a meal with me last night. But I considered today a fresh start. For both of us.

"That's breakfast, lamb." I grinned. "I'm assuming you have heard of it?"

"It's very... *domestic*," she spit out the word as if it was painful to say.

"You should know I take my roles seriously by now." I shrugged. "Doctor, teacher, husband... I don't do anything in halves."

"No, you don't, do you... seeing as you are still one hundred percent delusional," she muttered under her breath before dragging the dining chair forward and claiming a seat as far across the table as she could possibly get from me.

I set her usual sliced grapefruit in front of her, along with the sugar dish. Then turned on a heel and grabbed my own plate of bacon, eggs, and toast. Shifting everything over until I was seated next to her.

Her eyes flicked from the pile of bacon, to the piece of fruit. I would never deprive my girl. What I would do was show her that sometimes I knew what she wanted better than she did. And I would give it to her. All she had to do was sit back and let me.

She played with her spoon, watching me out of the corner of her eye as I plucked the crispiest piece of bacon from the top, twisting it between my fingers before lifting it to my face to give it a long sniff. It wasn't thick or greasy. I'd taken the time to thinly slice it and set it out to drip dry. I opened my mouth, prepared to pop the entire thing inside, only to stop and offer it to her instead. My hand outstretched and the bacon hovering just out of reach of her mouth.

Marisela leaned forward and wrapped her lips

around my fingers. Taking my breakfast with her before leaning back in her seat with a satisfied smirk on her face. Like she'd accomplished something when all she'd done was eat out of my hand.

"I meant it when I said I take marriage seriously, lamb. Whatever's mine is yours. Always." I grinned, but she wasn't anymore.

97

MARISELA

"It looks like it's getting infected." I poked at the pustule bubbling up on my thigh until it popped open and started leaking onto the sofa cushion, then glared over at Adrian, who was fussing with the old record player in the corner of the sitting room. Trying to dust it off and get it to work.

While I had to admit the silence was stifling, I wasn't sure a bunch of antiquated music coming out of a machine that was older than I was would be any better.

But he appeared more than content to try.

I shook my head and let out an annoyed huff. Clearly, his version of *playing house* was different from mine. I pictured sharing a few lackluster meals over forced dinner conversations, fucking whenever we felt the urge, and then going on about our business as usual—albeit under more confined circumstances.

He *meant* full-on lockdown. No television or internet. Outside contacts or devices. Fucker even went as far as to have someone block the Wi-Fi signal—pretty sure I knew who *that someone* was—so I couldn't connect to my email if I tried.

I had tried. Because missing this much work might actually kill me before this infection had a chance to set in. My devices were like an extension of a limb, and yet no one seemed to notice I hadn't answered them in days. Which told me all I needed to know about even my most loyal employees.

They didn't give a fuck about who was behind the desk. Everyone was replaceable.

I felt a twinge of guilt, as my mind wandered to Emily, and quickly shoved it back down again. If my father taught me anything, it was that relationships were a liability. It was smarter to sever them before they could be used against you. The way he'd used me to keep my mother in line, then used her to do the same to me. I didn't engage with people I wasn't willing to lose. The occupants of this room included.

"I told you not to get it wet," Adrian replied, his tone dry and obviously unamused.

"Probably should go to the hospital and see a proper doctor. Wouldn't want to have to amputate a leg in such an unsterile environment, now would you, Dr. Lambert?"

He glanced at me from over a shoulder, not bothering to turn all the way around as he reached into a pocket, pulled out a bottle of pills and tossed them in my direction. "Take one, twice a day. It's better if you put something in your stomach first."

I twisted the top off and peered at the large white capsules covering the bottom. "These are horse pills."

"I've seen you swallow a hell of a lot bigger." Adrian chuckled to himself, and I rolled my eyes. Nearly forty years old, and the man still had the sense of humor of a horned-up teenager.

I swung my feet off the sofa and hobbled over to the bar cart, grabbing myself a tumbler and a heavy serving of whiskey. Adrian turned and watched me cross the room with a cocked brow.

"Something." I lifted the glass in his direction before tossing back the contents. Popping a pill into my mouth and then chasing it down with a few more gulps of whiskey.

"I meant food, Marisela," he grunted. It only took three long strides and he was standing in front of me, prying the liquor from my hands and dumping what was left on the carpet between us.

"Should have been more specific."

"You're being difficult on purpose," he said.

"I'm being myself. If you find that difficult, you can leave," I countered.

"I'm prepared to give you a lifetime. You can give me three days, Marisela." He lifted a hand, brushing his fingers over my lips before shoving his thumb inside my mouth. "I am not asking for much."

I sucked on the tip long enough to get him comfortable, just like I had during breakfast, then clamped down hard. I knew it was better *not to bite the hand that feeds you.* I also didn't care.

He pulled his thumb back, dropped his arm, and shook his head. "What happened to the cooperation you promised me, lamb?"

I shrugged a single shoulder. "What can I say? I lied."

Adrian *tsked* his tongue. "We don't lie to each other, dear."

"*We* don't?" I questioned, and he shook his head.

"No, we don't."

"But we don't tell the whole truth either, now do we?" We both had secrets. Some worse than others. We also kept the darkest of them to ourselves because despite what Adrian liked to tell me, no one truly knew anyone else.

Sure, we knew pieces. We got glimpses. But everything else was filled in until the full picture became more what we wanted to see than what was actually there.

"Depends on the situation, lamb." Adrian took a step back, shoving his hands into his pockets as he eyed me for a moment. "What else aren't you telling me?"

"There's plenty I'm not telling you, Dr. Lambert. Question is... do you really want to know?"

"I want to know everything, Marisela."

I grinned at his confidence, and perhaps at my own naiveté because the last thing I should have been doing was giving this man something he could use against me. But I just couldn't help myself. Just like with the scissors, I wanted to see the look on his face...

98

ADRIAN

"Everyone has skeletons in their closets, Adrian. These are mine." Marisela lifted a nonchalant shoulder as my eyes bounced from the pile of mummified bodies stuffed behind a faux wall in the basement back to the smug expression on her face.

Didn't know how we'd missed them in the initial sweep of the house; then again, I'd lived here my entire life without knowing about the tunnels.

"Yours are a lot..." I muttered under my breath, struggling to find the right word as the odor of decomposition burned my nostrils and stung the corners of my eyes. "...fresher."

Or less fresh? Wasn't sure if we were referencing skeletons or patients at the moment.

"Don't have the stomach for it, Doc?" she challenged. "And here I thought you'd be used to the smell by now."

"Wouldn't be very good at what I do if the bodies on my table ended up like... that, now would I?" I fired back, throwing out an arm towards a face I couldn't recognize beneath the liquified organs and leathering skin.

Marisela crossed her arms over her chest, her manicured fingertips tapping against an elbow. "You said you wanted to know everything. Meet everything."

"Does *everything* have a name?" I grunted in reply.

"Several." She nodded, swinging a hand out to point at each lump of bone and flesh as she listed them off one by one. "Bernard Stevens, my assistant found out he was skimming off the top. It's funny how men think you're willing to fuck them even after they've admitted to stealing from you. Didn't even question why I was leading him into the basement. And that pile there? That's Javier Castillo—what's left of him anyway. Unfortunately, you were right. Javi got a little handsy after writing me that check. But don't you worry. I made sure it cleared first."

"Do I even want to know how you got those through customs?" I dipped my chin towards the humerus bones I now knew were imported from Spain.

"I know a guy."

"Of course you do," I muttered, as she stepped closer to the corpse tucked all the way in the back of the alcove and I flicked a flashlight at its head.

"Oh, and you should remember *him*. Adrian Lambert, I'd like to reacquaint you with my father, Hernando Alonzo Cruz." She reached over, grabbing the skull by a tuft of hair, and lifted it off the ground. "Don't be rude, Papa. Say hello to Adrian." She released him with a thud against the concrete, and I watched another layer of decayed epidermis tissue slip free and slide off his zygomatic bone. "Papa was a little harder to convince, but a quick shove down the stairs and he didn't even know what hit him—it was the concrete." She grinned. Following it up with a huff. "I didn't get anything for that one. Fucker didn't name me in the will. Felt good anyway..."

"You can't leave a bunch of bodies to sit here and rot under your house, Marisela." I lifted the heel of my palm to my right eye to trigger my oculocardiac reflex and hopefully reduce some of the stress building at the bridge of my nose.

"Wasn't my plan." She shrugged. "But my plans changed, as you can see."

"Can't have your name tied to a bunch of missing people either." I shook my head. I wasn't judging her actions. I didn't care who met the other side of her blade —I could just make out the multiple knife-sized puncture wounds. It was her methods that gave me pause.

"Hundreds of people are reported missing in this city every year," she replied while eyeing her nails.

"Yeah, and how many of those reports are connected to you?"

Another shrug. "At least three."

"Fucking hell." I could feel my eye twitching. That was what this woman did to me. She made my eye twitch. "I'll send my guys to take care of it."

"I don't recall asking for your help." She turned on a heel, limping towards the stairs. "Or your services," she called out over a shoulder, and I grabbed her wrist to stop her.

"Too bad. You're getting it anyway." I tugged her to

my chest until my chin was resting on the top of her head and quickly inhaled the scent of her shampoo in place of the decay. I much preferred one over the other.

I didn't have a sensitive stomach. What I did have was an appreciation for a sterile work environment. Which meant I was crawling out of my skin as I peeled my shirt off my back and stepped into the shower for the second time in a few hours.

Death could literally seep into your pores. The enzymatic degradation infiltrating the mucous membrane of your nasal cavity so that decay clung to the tiny hairs inside your nose for days. Like a phantom odor you couldn't stop smelling. And I didn't need another reminder of what I'd seen in that basement.

Fresh bodies, *blood* never bothered me. There was plenty I could do with them. So much I could use. Alter and create. Those rotten piles of meat were far beyond that.

Now they were just another problem.

I finished rinsing off. Stepped out of the shower and wrapped a large white towel around my waist before returning to the bedroom, where my girl was spread out on the covers with a book in her hand and nothing but a robe covering her.

I walked to the footboard, dropped the towel, and climbed onto the mattress so that I was positioned between her thighs. Hooking my arms under her legs and tugging her bare pussy closer to my face. That first lap of my tongue had me forgetting all about the basement, all about whatever forces had tried their damnedest to keep us apart over the years. It also had Marisela dropping her book.

I pulled back to look at her. "Don't let me interrupt you." I grinned while dipping my chin towards the title on the spine that told me my girl was reading smut. "I don't mind a little friendly competition, princess. In fact, let's see who can keep you more entertained. Me or whatever six-foot werewolf mafia Don had you so engrossed you forgot to join me in the shower."

Marisela glanced in my direction before swiping up her book and returning her focus to the pages. "You told me not to get it wet."

"You're right. I did." I lowered my mouth to her cunt again while breathing in my favorite scent. "Because that's my job."

And then my face was back where it belonged as I gorged myself on pussy juice and precum. *My precum.* The trail I'd left on her skin after I'd finished fucking her a few hours ago.

ADRIAN

DAY THREE

I glanced at the orange bottle of pills on the nightstand before looking up at Marisela again. Watching as she bounced back and forth on my cock, her tits cupped in each one of my hands. She dropped her palms onto my chest and started grinding against me harder, her hair blocking her face from view.

But I didn't need to see it to know what it looked like. Her top teeth dragging over her plump bottom lip and her eyes squeezed shut in concentration.

I thought she might have caught on by now. Tried to push me off her the first time I didn't pull out. Instead, she clung to me tighter until my cock stopped twitching inside her. Then shoved me down onto the mattress and rode my face.

I didn't mind tasting myself when I was tasting her too. I also didn't mind if the heavy dose of antibiotics I was feeding her just happened to interfere with her progesterone levels.

Knocking her up wasn't my goal but keeping her was. And I didn't care how low I had to steep to do it. My little lamb should have understood better than anyone else. It wasn't much different from what she was willing to do to keep her company.

"Fuuuuuck," I grunted when she did that thing where she rolled her hips, reaching a hand behind her back and latching on to my balls so that I was coming before I could stop myself.

She was getting better at it. Using my body against me the way I'd learned to use hers. Not that I did much to interfere. Fucking my cum deep into her pussy wasn't just my favorite hobby. It was also something I had no problem doing over and over again. My recovery time as quick as my hand with a fifteen blade and a pile of absorbable sutures.

I flipped Marisela onto her back, draping her legs over my shoulders as I peered down at how pretty my cum looked spilling out of her pussy. Like an over-ripened peach with the juices pooling at the top. Except my lamb was so much sweeter. Salty too. Just the way I liked it.

I reached out a finger and scooped up enough to have her writhing beneath my touch as I slowly circled my thumb around her clit. And she grabbed onto the headboard for leverage, her elbows in the air and her chin lifted towards the ceiling.

I wanted her eyes on me, watching what I did to her. But more than that, I wanted her to feel it. Feel my mouth sweeping across her puffy pussy lips, moving higher to nudge against her clit before coming full circle as my tongue penetrated her the way my cock was aching to do all over again. I wanted her to feel my cool breath bristling over her heated flesh. The bridge of my nose nudging at just the right spot each time I rocked my face closer to her cunt. And I wanted her crying out in ecstasy, aching to be filled and fucked and frothy. Dripping until the sheets were staining the mattress and her lips were screaming my name.

Not god's. Not *his*. Mine.

She dug her nails into my shoulders, rotating her hips at the same time my tongue glided in and out of her and my nose stimulated her clit. Getting the dual sensation she needed before the spasms took over and had her squirming in my hands. Her voice hoarse and her skin tacky with sweat.

I grinned against her thighs, working my way up her torso until my mouth was claiming hers. A mix of her cum and mine creating a translucent film between us as I pulled back to look at her flushed face.

She pushed me aside and slid off the bed, grabbing the bottle of antibiotics before making her way towards the bathroom. The sway of her wide hips compensating for the injury to her thigh. Didn't make her any less sexy, though. If anything, it added to it. Her attitude and resilience more of a turn-on than that round, heart-shaped ass of hers.

I listened to the tap running in the sink, Marisela forcing down another dose before walking out the door and turning to face me. "These won't affect my birth control pills, will they?"

I sat up on the bed and scanned her expression, searching for... I wasn't even sure what. But it wasn't there, whatever I thought I might find. Instead, stoicism stared back at me.

It would be so easy to lie to her... But I couldn't bring myself to do it.

This experiment wasn't just about Marisela. It was about me too. About what kind of man I wanted to be *to* her and *for* her.

"They could."

"And you knew that?"

I nodded once.

"And you didn't warn me." She leaned against the doorframe, watching me expectantly. "Why?"

"Insurance," I repeated the same thing Bugs told me the day he dug up that dirt on Rath.

She kept her glare locked on my face. "I'd just kill it, you know. You can't force me to carry your bastard, Adrian."

"Wouldn't be a bastard if I married you first," I reminded her. "Besides, I wouldn't let you. I'd confine you to a room at Briarwood if I had to."

"Your logic is insane."

I lifted a shoulder. "Brilliance usually is."

Marisela threw her head back on a laugh. The sound more skeptical than amused. And then she was stalking in my direction, stopping when she was at the edge of the mattress and standing between my legs. She lowered her lips to my ear while grabbing the tip of my finger and rubbing it along the inner lining of her belly button, across the slight umbilical scarring I could feel there.

"I already told you I don't want kids, Adrian," she whispered. "Which is exactly why I had Dr. Espósito ensure I couldn't." She tapped a palm against my cheek twice before pivoting on a heel and sauntering back towards the bathroom again. "But I do appreciate the honesty," she yelled out as she slammed the door behind her.

100

MARISELA

I sighed, pacing the length of the bedroom, my short black robe billowing behind me when I pivoted and started walking in the opposite direction.

This man was infuriating. Neurotic and egotistical. The kind of man who loved me as much as he loved the sound of his own voice. In his *own* way. And I guess I loved him in my *own* way too. At the very least I loved how he made me feel...

Good sex was the one thing I *was* willing to negotiate on while marriage was the one thing he wouldn't let go. Dr. Lambert wanted a wife, a mother for his children, a partner for his madhouse. And I wanted...

Well, I wanted none of that.

Three days, three months, three years... it didn't matter. Time wasn't going to change my mind and it sure as hell had done nothing to change his. We were at a stalemate.

Which was exactly why I'd taken matters in to my

own hands. Birth control pills could fail but a tubal ligation couldn't—at the very least it wasn't likely.

I ran a fingertip over the little scar and grinned to myself. The single-incision site ensured the surgery I underwent last year was barely perceptible, even to the trained eye. It also ensured my shadow man was shit out of luck if he thought he could trap me with his brat.

Fucker assumed he'd gotten me with the antibiotics. As if my knowledge of pharmacology wasn't better than his. Yes, he had his prescription pad and his chemistry lab but I studied the compounds and mechanisms. I accumulated the raw data and I manipulated it to my advantage. Just like I needed to manipulate him.

And if I couldn't do that, well, then both of us were fucked...

"I am not handing it over, Adrian. I don't care if I have to hold a knife to each of their throats and force the vote. It's my company."

It shouldn't have meant as much to me as it did. It was just a building full of compounds and devices. Office space occupied by people who came and went and employees whose names I didn't care to know. Still, each one of those contracts, every deal made in the last ten or so years had been my doing.

I might not have been there for its conception but Cruz Research & Development wasn't any less the fruit of my labor. It wasn't any less mine.

"I never said you had to, Marisela," Adrian huffed from where he was standing and watching me make a pattern in the carpet. "I never asked you to stop working. I said I wanted you to *prefer being with me.* Just because you prefer to stay in bed doesn't mean you don't get up and go to work in the morning. Life is about doing the things you don't want to do sometimes. But it's also about enjoying what you can. I want to be that thing you enjoy, Marisela. The thing you want to do more than anything else. It's as simple as that."

"Nothing is simple," I was quick to remind him.

"You're taking what you know to be true in one situation and applying it to others. It's called cognitive distortion," he said in that condescending tone he liked to use whenever he was trying to convey that he was smarter than everyone else. "Instead of listening to what I am telling you, you are twisting it into what you think it means."

"Tate—" I started to say, only to be cut off.

"I am not *him* any more than you are her."

"Her?" I pivoted around to glare at him, noting the way his eyes softened. His voice less clinical and more... placating. It irritated me just as much. I didn't want to be placated. I wanted to be fucking heard.

"The woman you think you need to be to survive," he clarified, and I resumed my pacing.

"I hate you."

"I know. And I love you too," he replied. I flicked my glare up to meet his smirk. "See? That's exactly what you sound like."

"Yeah, except you're serious."

"I am." He nodded. "But I'm also self-aware enough to recognize it."

"Self-aware or delusional, Dr. Lambert? Because

there really is a difference and plenty of medication if you need a referral."

He shrugged a shoulder, his arms still crossed and his head cocked to the side. "I enjoy my delusion, Marisela. I enjoy the idea of someone loving someone else so much there is no world where they aren't together—it's not a possibility. Do you enjoy yours? Do you enjoy believing that being alone is so much better than being with a man who would get on his knees for you?" As he said the words, he lowered himself onto the ground. His elbow propped on one thigh and a velvet box in his hand. "Because it sure as hell doesn't seem like it."

I looked from his face to the ring staring back at me. "So you're saying you'd rather be crazy together than alone and sane."

"That's exactly what I'm saying. Good to know you're finally listening, lamb."

101

ADRIAN

DAY FOUR

I stared at Marisela from across the boardroom table. I shouldn't be surprised that this was how we were doing things. Wasn't exactly how I pictured it over the years. Wasn't all that romantic either. But fuck if seeing her like this, all primed and ready for an argument, wasn't a turn-on.

I adjusted myself in my chair and shot my little lamb a grin as I imagined what she would look like spread out on this table, her skirt pushed up around her waist and her hair falling free from her tight ponytail.

Marisela cleared her throat, drawing my attention back to her face. "You claimed marriage wasn't a negotiation. I argue otherwise. What is it if not a deal of some sort? One party wanting something from the other party in exchange for something else. So here's my starting offer." She paused, shuffling the documents in front of her like I didn't know they were blank and that this was all for show. "One year, trial basis and a prenup that says I get all the Prescott assets in a divorce."

I shrugged a single shoulder. "Forever, no trial about it. You get everything without a divorce because I'm not giving you one."

She shook her head. Another pause and a sip of her mug, which I knew was more whiskey than coffee by this point. "Five years, trial-basis, prenup, and fifty percent of Briarwood's profits." She lifted a challenging brow.

"No trial basis, no divorce," I repeated. "And seventy-five percent of *my* profits after you agree to work by my side."

My boys still had to eat. Even if most of their shares went up their noses or out their cocks somehow.

"Ten years, trial basis, prenup, seventy-five percent of *your* profits. But I stay at CR&D and you hire my assistant in my place."

"You mean Emily?" I barked out a laugh before I could stop myself. "The only *place* that girl is going is in the ground. He plans on killing her."

Marisela's head jerked up in my direction. Her expression a mix of skepticism and something else... "I don't think so," she balked, her lips tipping up into a smirk she hadn't earned. "Elliot hardly seems the type."

"He's not. But Dr. Michaels is. So let's keep that boy's crush between you and me, eh?" I replied, earning my own smirk, seeing as only one of us was in the know right now. "I'm sure she told you what happened to the last guy who got a little too close for the fucker's comfort."

"Doesn't matter. He's not going to hurt her." Marisela nodded, and it was obvious she was trying to convince herself. Because she didn't know the man like I did.

"Mm, no guarantees. My colleague has his heart set on making that girl suffer." I watched her face contort, her lips twist. But it wasn't disgust this time. "Is that concern I see? You've gotten soft, princess."

"Not concern," she was quick to insist. "I just hate wasting talent. Emily's smart. Taught her everything I know. She will talk her way out of it."

"I don't think Dr. Michaels is the listening type. At least not from what I've seen. Violence is more his go-to."

"But he is the obsessed type, isn't he?" she shot back. "Which means the last thing he'll do is give up the object of his obsession. Even if he knows he should. Now what's your counteroffer, Adrian?"

"No divorce. The only way out of this is with one of us dead—" I started to say, and Marisela cut me off before I could finish.

"I can agree to that."

"I'm not done," I snapped, my voice harsher than usual. But she liked it. She liked the shift in power. She liked pushing me to my limits. And she liked violence too. I could see her squirming all the way from here. "No divorce, fifty percent of my profits—I'm assuming I'll have to give the girl a salary *if* she survives. You stay at CR&D, with my blessing, but you live at Briarwood with me. Nonnegotiable, Marisela." I tapped the top of the table for emphasis. "In my bed, every night. If I have to pick you up and carry you there myself, I will."

She pursed her lips together for a long moment while appearing to chew on her response. "Fine. Deal," she agreed with a quick dip of her chin. "But what are we going to do about the body in the well?"

"What body?" I asked, even though I knew the answer.

"My mother. Isn't that where you put her?"

"It is. But how do you know that?"

Marisela shrugged. "The staff likes to talk. And I like to listen."

"Yeah, and what did they say?" I was more curious than anything else, seeing as the only person who knew about the dumpsite was in this room. And it wasn't the girl sitting in front of me.

"Just mentioned the woman who haunts the well. The rest wasn't hard to figure out."

"Right." I nodded once, not bothering to mention that that story had been circulating since I was old enough to hear the whispers. It *was* about someone's mother. It just wasn't Marisela's. "I'll have the boys take care of that one too. We can discuss any arrangements you want to make afterwards."

She glanced down at her hands before peering back up at me again. There were no tears, though. Just a deeper understanding of the woman who refused to ever let anyone see her cry. "Thank you," she whispered.

"Of course," I replied. Because if anyone knew what it was like to lose their mother, it was me.

102

I couldn't hear anything past the buzzing and sawing and occasional cursing that traveled up through the vents and rattled the vintage registers in the walls. Adrian's men were here taking care of my mess in the basement. Chopping up bodies and making it easier to dispose of them before they moved on to the well. Until they moved on to my mother.

I hadn't thought about her in years, if I were being honest. I should have been horrified. I wasn't. Knowing she was so close was a comfort in a weird way. The guilt waning like the water that was seeping into the earth instead of keeping her afloat.

I hadn't left her behind. Not if she was out there.

Before I realized what I was doing, I was crossing the foyer and headed to the front door. Swiping the keys to their van from the table in search of a flashlight and maybe some rope.

I couldn't explain why today was the day I needed to

find out for myself. But I did. I needed to know as much as I didn't want to know.

It was like that Austrian guy and his experiment with the cat. Until I saw it with my own eyes, my mother was both in the well and she wasn't. And the moment the guys went looking for her would be the same moment I'd know for sure. The same moment I'd be forced to face the reality of what we'd done to her. What I'd asked someone to do to her because I was too much of a coward to do it myself.

It wasn't a moment that needed an audience.

My heels kicked at the gravel driveway, the sun beating down on my bare shoulders as I made my way towards the gray panel van. Unlocked the back door and swung it open. Illuminating the dark interior as a stream of light reflected off a set of metal cuffs, and my eyes tried to focus on the arm they were attached to. Following the glint up to the hook in the ceiling that kept her body suspended on her tiptoes and her sundress flickering in the wind.

The girl didn't move. She didn't speak either. Whether or not she could sense my presence was as much a guess to me as was what had been done to her over the last week or so. Her face was covered several times around but I didn't need to see it to recognize her.

Emily Shaw. My former assistant and their current prisoner.

I didn't care what became of her. Why she was hand-cuffed inside this van or what those men planned to do with her. At least I shouldn't have cared. Caring and trusting were what had gotten her into this situation to begin with. Still, I found myself fiddling with the lock and freeing her arm.

After this, Emily was on her own. She could run or she could stay. What she couldn't do was say she didn't have a choice anymore. I'd done my part. In both putting her here and letting her out.

The rest was up to fate. And how quickly her feet could move across my front lawn.

I swiped up a coil of rope from one of the shelves in the van, before tucking a flashlight under my arm, and then walked off without a backward glance.

I couldn't hear the power tools buzzing anymore. Which meant my former assistant didn't have much time to decide if she was going to keep standing there with a blindfold on her face or rip it off and run.

"What exactly were you planning on doing with that rope?" Adrian asked, the crunching of sticks and leaves alerting me to his presence long before his voice did. "Gonna climb down and have a look yourself?"

"I don't know, honestly." I didn't bother turning around, my elbows resting on the edge of the well as I peered into the hole like if I kept staring I could see her. I couldn't. "Is she really down there?"

"Yes." He came up behind me, closing his arms around my waist and tugging me closer to his chest while resting his chin on my shoulder.

"How far does it go?"

Adrian sighed. "I'm not sure."

"Maybe we should just leave her there, then. I doubt anyone will think to go looking."

"They never did for my mother. So you're probably right."

I spun around in his hold, linking my arms around his neck as I peered up into his eyes. I couldn't tell you what I was hoping to find. Empathy? Disapproval? What I could tell you was that I saw a hint of sadness instead. Sadness and acceptance. Adrian saw something in me I couldn't see in myself. And I had to admit I enjoyed his version much better. Even if it was still a little rose-tinted at times.

"She's down there too?" I asked him.

"That's what they say." He lifted a nonchalant shoulder before adding, "But who really knows?"

"Aren't you curious?"

He nodded once. "I am."

"But not enough to check?"

"Nope." He shook his head. "Not enough to check."

"Maybe you should."

"Yeah, maybe I should," he agreed, lowering his face and capturing my mouth in a kiss that was as possessive as it was comforting.

I didn't know what it meant to feel... *that* before now. Sure, I remembered what it was like to have my mother hold me close when I was little. What it was like to look to her for comfort as a kid. But that was different. *This* was different.

This was understanding. It wasn't loving someone

because it was something you should do. Like a parent *should* love a child. It was loving them despite everyone telling you that you shouldn't. It was choosing them despite the horrors that surrounded each of you.

Or maybe it was because of them. Maybe those horrors were more of a comfort than anything else. Because they helped us feel less alone in the darkness we found ourselves trapped inside without any hope of climbing out.

EPILOGUE
MARISELA

ONE YEAR LATER

I looked over at my husband, the sound of his slightly-heavier steps drawing my attention from my computer screen up to him, before my eyes dropped to the *thing* he was holding in his arms.

"What is *that*?" I pointed a red-tipped nail across the desk, and Adrian's grin just stretched wider over his face. A sign I wasn't going to like whatever it was he was planning to tell me.

"This…" He shrugged his shoulders outward, pushing *it* closer in my direction. "…is a small human, Marisela. Some might even go as far as to call *it* a baby."

"Right… And who does the small human belong to?" I couldn't stop myself from scrunching up my nose. It wasn't that I didn't like children. It was just that…

Okay, fine, I didn't like children. Then again, I really didn't like anyone.

"Us. He belongs to us, little lamb. At least he does now."

"What do you mean he belongs to us, Adrian?" I pushed up from my seat. Doing my best to hide the way my voice trembled. I wasn't stupid. I saw the resemblance. The dark eyes, the darker hair. I'd done the math in my head as soon as he walked in. This kid sure as hell wasn't mine but that didn't mean he wasn't *his*. The man who'd promised to be loyal to me even though his brother never could be. "Where did you get it?"

My husband watched my face for a moment, shifting the kid higher on a shoulder and tapping a hand against its backside as if it were the most natural thing for him to do. "I didn't fuck someone else, Marisela."

I crossed my arms over my chest and pinned him with a glare as lethal as the knife I kept in my top drawer. "I know you didn't. You wouldn't be breathing if you did," I countered.

"It is nice to know that you still care, though."

"Enough with the games, Dr. Lambert. Whose kid is that and where did you get it from?"

"I'm not playing games, Mrs. Lambert. I already told you. Little AJ is ours."

I quirked an eyebrow. I didn't need to ask him what *AJ* stood for. Knowing this man's ego, I could already hazard a guess. "Right, and where is AJ's mother?"

He smirked. "I'm looking at her."

I lifted a hand to stop him. "Nope. Nuh-uh. Not happening, Adrian. Are you insane?"

"I know the perfect place for us if I were…" He started

to smile again, before his mouth dropped into a thin line. "His mother was part of a job. He wasn't. I couldn't just leave him there."

"And why not?" *I would have.* If the kid survived, he'd be stronger for it. If he didn't, well then, that would have been nature taking its course, wouldn't it?

"I might be a murderer but I'm not a monster, Marisela. I'm not gonna leave a kid to starve to death. Would have been weeks before someone came looking for 'em."

I shook my head, lowering myself back into my office chair and tucking my legs under the desk. "We are not a daycare. Drop it off at a fire department or something." I waved a dismissive hand.

"And have them ask questions? I don't think so. That's a novice move and we both know it."

"A novice move is strolling in here with an armful of evidence," I mumbled under my breath. I loved this man. I really did. As much as I could love anyone. But that didn't mean there weren't times when I wanted to kill him. Times like now.

My husband collected people as if they were stray dogs. And I wasn't a dog person either.

I could feel Adrian watching me. I didn't bother looking up to confirm it. "He needs a mother, Marisela..."

"And I need you to both get the fuck out of my office. I have work to do."

Instead of bothering to listen to me, Adrian maneuvered himself around my desk. Leaning against the stack of drawers as a pile of paperwork tumbled to the side. He reached out a hand, brushing it over my cheek while forcing me to look up at him. "Don't you want to raise a baby with me, little lamb?"

"Not particularly."

He lowered his face, keeping the kid pressed to his chest, as he skimmed his lips over mine. "Please…"

It was the way he said it. The way he begged that always had me giving in to his ridiculous demands. I couldn't explain it. *Believe me, I wish I could.* There was just something about the thrill it gave me. The fact that I knew he would literally get down on his hands and knees for me and only me…

It was a manipulation tactic, I had no doubt. But that didn't stop it from feeling any less good. And I'd always been weak when it came to indulging in what felt good.

"Fine," I huffed. "But you're feeding it, changing it, and all that nonsense. If you want a pet, you're the one taking care of it."

"He's not a pet, Marisela. He's our child. A little piece of you and me. At least he will be when we're done with him." Adrian brushed his mouth across my forehead before rising to his full height. "I'm going to go home and put 'em to bed. Then, if you're a good girl and eat all your dinner, we can work on making little AJ a sibling."

"Never going to happen—one of us is fixed, remember?" I grunted, watching as he made his way towards the door before I called out, "Oh, and, Adrian?"

He glanced back at me over a shoulder.

"If you're a good boy and stop taking in strays, I'll keep the tip of my knife from having to dip below the waist."

"I already told you, little lamb. Whatever piece of me you want, it's already yours. It's always been yours."

THE END

C_ONTINUE_ READING FOR A BONUS CHAPTER YOU DON'T WANT TO MISS!

BONUS CHAPTER:
CASPER

"Y**ou're** digging into my skin, asshole." Bossman said it like it was a bad thing but we all knew it was as close to a pet name as any of us were gonna get. Besides, I was his favorite. Least I was before he brought that brat home.

"Turnabout's fair play, Doc." I grinned while touching up the letters on his chest for what had to be the millionth time. He and the wifey went at it like street dogs fightin' over the last piece of *moskovskaya*. Were just as vicious too. "So, what's with the kid? Marriage life that boring you gotta bring in a third?"

"Aw, someone upset they ain't the youngest anymore, huh?" a familiar voice replied, and my glare shot over to the doorway. Following the black riding boots up a pair of thick jean-clad thighs, a pierced naval, and my favorite pair of tits sticking out of a cropped leather vest.

"Don't gotta be the youngest when I'm the cutest, sweetheart." I winked.

Danica Rossi was the only mouse to ever make it outta my trap. Not that I had any intentions of fucking her a few years ago. Just that I didn't have any intentions of *not fucking* her.

"Here to finally let me stick ya?" I turned in my swivel seat, widening my legs and twitching my dick while buzzing the needle.

Myshka could have it any way she wanted. A jab was a jab in my book. And I fucking loved jabbing shit.

She dropped her eyes to my lap, then moved 'em up to the tattoo gun in my hand. "Yeah, no thanks to both."

"Speaking of pricks..." I twitched my cock again. "Where's yours?"

"Right here." The Irish fucker with a dick much smaller than mine—trust me, I measured—popped up behind her quicker than the leprechaun at the end of the rainbow. Nixing my plans of having a taste of that golden pussy he didn't seem keen to share. At least for now.

It was only a matter of time before our friendly neighborhood bounty hunter got bored of the same old shamrock-flavored cock. *Everyone knew vodka was better. Lasted longer too.*

I wiped the blood off Lambo's chest as he stood from his chair and extended a hand. "Good to see you, Danica."

"Not like you gave me much of a choice, now did ya, Surge," she grunted.

"Deal's a deal." He shrugged, and I sat back to watch the chaos unfold. Maybe even create a little of my own to keep things interesting.

Boredom was the real killer at Briarwood. *Don't let anyone else tell ya different.*

"Just cut to the chase, Doc. What do you want and how much is it gonna cost me?"

"Won't cost you anything, Rossi." Bossman grinned or at least I thought he was grinning. His back was to me. He reached into his pocket and pulled out a photo, and I leaned over his shoulder to get myself a peek. "I want you to find these women for me."

"And do what?" Danica lifted a challenging brow, at the same time I raised a hand and yelled out, "I call dibs on the brunette! She looks feisty."

He ignored me. Papa Bear was annoyed. "Hire 'em to put out a hit," he told her.

"On who?" Danica pressed.

"Me," Bossman replied, and I laughed so loud I had everyone turning my way.

He didn't say anything else, just shot me that glare that suggested I make myself scarce if I didn't wanna end up strapped to a metal bed with a needle in my arm.

Don't get me wrong. I liked my drugs. I just liked 'em more when I was the one putting them there.

I pushed off the counter, leaving the adults to talk business as I went in search of someone else to fuck with. Didn't take me long to find that someone either.

A groaning sound had me slipping past the caution tape and down the hall of private cells. The noise was nothing new. *Bugs was a groaner.* Especially when he was going at it a little too hard on his dick. But where it was coming from sure as fuck was. I paused next to the third door, my focus stuck on the giant-ass padlock keeping me from whatever was on the other side. For a few seconds anyway.

A quick pick later, and I was tugging it open and peering into the room. Grinning as soon as my eyes adjusted to the darkness and spotted the human-sized Fleshlight in the corner. No teeth and plenty of holes to choose from.

I tilted my head, the wheels turning faster as I swiped up my walkie-talkie and called over the line. "Hey, Don-Don. Guess who found a new toy for you to play with..."

Have you met Danica Rossi? Read her story here:
Half Cocked by Sybil Knight

COMING SOON

CURIOUS AS TO WHICH ONE OF THE RENEGADES WILL BE THE NEXT TO FALL?

PREORDER BELLS NOW AND DISCOVER WHO THE RUSSIAN GHOST IS HAUNTING.

OBSESSION. NAH, I WOULDN'T CALL IT THAT.

OBSESSION WOULD IMPLY I GAVE A DAMN ABOUT THE LITTLE RODENT I WAS SWIPING BETWEEN MY PAWS RIGHT NOW. AND THE ONLY THING I GAVE A DAMN ABOUT WAS WHATEVER COULD GIVE ME THE QUICKEST HIGH.

THIS WAS MORE OF A CURIOSITY... A CAT KICKING AROUND A DEAD MOUSE RIGHT BEFORE HE DROPPED IT OFF ON SOMEONE'S DOORSTEP.

WHICH WAS EXACTLY WHAT I WAS INSTRUCTED TO DO.

YOU FIND A RAT, YOU CALL AN EXTERMINATOR. IT WAS SIMPLE MATH. IT WAS ALSO A REAL MR. AND MRS. *KUZNETSOV* SITUA-

TION WE HAD GOING ON, SEEING AS MY *KOTYONOK* THOUGHT SHE HAD CLAWS.

LITTLE DID SHE KNOW, THE ONLY DIFFERENCE BETWEEN A DEATH TOLL AND A DINNER BELL WAS WHOEVER WAS HOLDING THE FORK. AND THIS FELINE COULDN'T WAIT TO DIG IN.

DING-DING, BABY. DING-MOTHERFUCKING-DING.

BELLS IS A DARK SPIN ON THE FABLE "BELLING THE CAT" AND BOOK THREE IN THE RENEGADES SERIES. EACH TITLE IS A STANDALONE IN AN INTERCONNECTED WORLD WHILE EACH STORY IS A RETELLING OF A FAIRY TALE, NURSERY RHYME, FABLE, ETC. THE FOCUS IS DARK ROMANCE SO PLEASE HEED THE TRIGGER WARNINGS AT THE BEGINNING OF EVERY BOOK.

THE RENEGADES SERIES:
BOOK 1: SKIN (FRANKIE'S STORY)
BOOK 2: LAMB (THE SURGEON'S STORY)
BOOK 3: BELLS (CASPER'S STORY)

COMING SOON

While you wait for Book 3, indulge in some of the off-screen chaos:

Preorder I'll Be Seeing You and discover how easily the lines blur between doctor and patient, crazy and sane… when you're locked inside the walls of Briarwood.

Even serial killers have a type. Unfortunately, tonight, that type is you.

You can feel it, can't you? The way I've been watching you night after night. Patiently waiting for you to turn around and give me a glimpse of those eyes.

Don't be shy. I know you want this as much as I do.

Atta girl. Look at you! You're perfect. Just fucking perfect. Like I knew you would be.

The more that I think about it, you could be her twin.

You know what that means, right? You're the one. At the very least, the *next* one. Maybe the *last* one if you don't fuck this up like all the others.

We can figure that out later, though. When I move on from watching to doing.

Because you might not see me, sweetheart. But I'll be seeing you. Real soon.

I'll Be Seeing You is a dark standalone novella and a spin-off of The Renegades Series. The focus is dark romance so please heed the trigger warnings at the beginning of every book.

ACKNOWLEDGMENTS

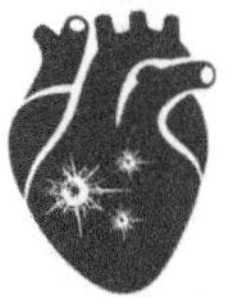

Thanks to everyone who has been a part of this long-ass process. To everyone who has shared, liked, commented, and preordered. To those of you who took a chance on me and my fucked-up brain. And to those who love the fictional characters that live rent free in my head. I could not have done it without you, and I am so very humbled.

I also wanted to say thank you to my ARC readers, who are taking time out of their busy schedules to read and review my book. And thank you to those of you who went as far as to read and review my prior publications too—I see you and I am so grateful for you.

A special thanks to Dahlia Reign (as always) for beta reading. Without her, this book would have been at least two chapters shorter. And to Author Kat Jackson for the QR code idea. IYKYK.

ALSO BY SYBIL KNIGHT

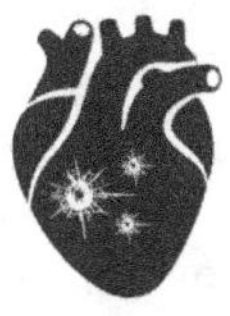

THE TRUTH AND LIES DUET:

The Harsher the Truth

The Sweeter the Lies

THE RENEGADES SERIES:

Skin

Lamb

Bells

STANDALONE NOVELS:

Half Cocked

Kill Joy

STANDALONE NOVELLAS:

The Sins of Our Fathers

V Card

I'll BE Seeing You

The More the Merrier

Eat Your Heart Out

More titles to come...

ABOUT THE AUTHOR

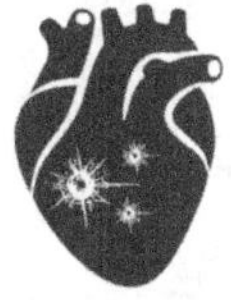

Sybil is a true east coaster with a love for true crime and caffeine. When she isn't working or writing, she is talking about working or writing.

Her stories range from gray to black, with darker themes throughout. She prefers heroines with a kick-ass mentality and the heroes who know how to rein them in. The mental and medical aspects of her books are well-researched, though they are given a humanistic approach and diagnoses aren't the focal points. She believes her characters don't need to wear labels in order to get their messages across.

Her books are mostly standalones, though her characters may interact and intersect worlds. Additionally, she works closely with and writes alongside author Dahlia Reign and some characters will appear in cameos in each of their publications.

Sybil welcomes emails from readers if there are concerns or questions regarding any of her publications.

Email: authorsybilknight@gmail.com

www.ingramcontent.com/pod-product-compliance
Lightning Source LLC
Chambersburg PA
CBHW060602300726

48975CB00005B/1412